SPUR DOUBLE EDITION!
TWICE THE FILLIES! TWICE THE FIGHTIN'!
A $9.98 VALUE FOR ONLY $5.99!

NEVADA HUSSY

"How do I know you're telling the truth?" Spur asked.

"Why would I lie about something that could get me killed?" said Stella. "Hell, by now there are too many wives in town for fancy women like me to count much. Was a time when we was top drawer around here. When women was scarce, all the men treated us girls like queens of the court. Then too, that kind of theft would hurt this town, put some small outfits into bankruptcy and cut down on my own business income. That's two good reasons why you should believe me."

Stella slid off the bed and began to dress.

"I got to get back for the early evening trade," she said. "What I told you, every word is gospel true. You can come see Stella anytime. But don't even try to talk to me except upstairs. I don't want that damn Sommers cutting me up!"

WYOMING WILDCAT

"Don't shoot, Pa!" the girl screamed. Before McCoy could do more than start to turn toward the naked girl she was on him, her strong right arm around his neck from behind, choking him. She knew what she was doing. He rammed one elbow backward to try to hit the girl's stomach. She avoided his repeated thrusts with his elbows and tightened her choke hold.

McCoy had time only to hear the ring of laughter from the girl's father and the roar of the shotgun as he faded toward total blackness. Just as the darkness closed around him he wondered if the damn rawhider had blown him in half....

SPUR

NEVADA HUSSY

WYOMING WILDCAT
Dirk Fletcher

LEISURE BOOKS　　　**NEW YORK CITY**

A LEISURE BOOK®

December 1995

Published by

Dorchester Publishing Co., Inc.
276 Fifth Avenue
New York, NY 10001

NEVADA HUSSY Copyright © 1985 by Dirk Fletcher

WYOMING WILDCAT Copyright © 1992 by Chet Cunningham/BookCrafters

Printed in the United States of America.

SPUR

NEVADA
HUSSY

ONE

October 1874

(Virginia City, Nevada found her place in history one day in 1859 when placer miners began throwing aside heavy bluish sand and blue-gray quartz they called the "blasted blue stuff." They were hunting gold in one of several placer mines on the slopes of Sun Peak, later named Mt. Davidson, where it lifted thirty-six hundred feet above the valley of the Carson river.

In June one miner gathered up a sack of the blue stuff and sent it over the hill to Grass Valley in California for assay. The reports that the "blue stuff" was rich silver ore caused a virtual exodus from several small California towns. When news of the rich strike of heavy gold ore leaked out, a thousand men hurried the hundred miles to Washoe and Mt. Davidson where a staggering settlement of tents and shanties sprang up overnight at Gold Hill and another at the site of the first "blue stuff" discovery which soon became known as Virginia City.

The fabulous and brief life of the Comstock Lode had begun. It would last as a large factor in Western U.S. mining from 1860 only to 1880, and thereafter become the site of the two ghost towns. But the hardy souls who

5

battled the shafts, tunnels and drifts to say nothing of
the hundred and ten degree underground heat and the
surging floods of subterranean water knew nothing of
the quick, tempestuous life Virginia City would have as
a burgeoning mistress to over a hundred thousand
miners who came, worked there and left.

The fortunes flamed in the 1860's, then faded and
resurged with the famous Consolidated Virginia mine
in 1874 and 1875. Spur McCoy arrived in the hurdy-
gurdy village on the side of the mountain in 1874. The
population that year was 18,304 and there was a
saloon, bordello and gambling hall on every other
corner.)

MARY BETH FRANKLIN stood in the sloping
street of Virginia City watching the miners coming
out of the holes in the ground. She hated those
tunnels and shafts and drifts! She hated them more
than anything she had ever known in her entire
eighteen years. She blinked and then slashed with
her hand to wipe away the surging tears. Her
father had gone into those same holes.

One day less than a year ago they had brought
out what was left of him, his body mangled and
crushed by heavy machinery. She hated that
machinery!

Mary Beth stood on this corner each day when
the men went home. She handed out leaflets to
everyone who would take them. Each week she
had a new one which she wrote and which the
printer, Mr. Jacobs, provided for her without
charge. He had been a good friend of her father.
The message today was shorter than most:

"Men of the mines. You must demand that the owners guarantee better working conditions and provide more safety equipment. Every day men die in the mines. My father died a year ago in Hale and Norcross Number Three, and nothing has been done to make safer the area where he worked.

You are men, not work animals! Demand from the union and the owners that you be given a fair chance to work and to live, so your wives and families will not be begging in the streets.

Talk to the mine owners, the foremen and the shift bosses. Make them understand that a work stoppage is the only way management will listen. The owners must be made to feel the pinch of no production, which will slow down their rush to become millionaires a hundred times over!

Please talk to the other men, urge your union to make demands, speak with one voice! You are the only ones who can keep yourselves alive while you work like animals deep under the ground!"

Mary Beth handed a paper to a passing miner, who looked at it and dropped it.

"Can't read," he said over his shoulder.

Mary Beth was not a beautiful girl, being short and a little broad in the hips, but her face was attractive and lately she had more than a dozen men courting her. She knew that was because there were two men in Virginia City for every woman. The eligible women to marry were few and most already taken.

But she would not marry yet. She had promised her dead father that she would crusade for a year for better working conditions and to plead for more safety equipment in the mines. She would hold to her promise. She turned, stepped up from the dust

7

of the street to the boardwalk in front of the Virginia City Tin Goods Store.

She looked in defiance at the store owners. Most had warned her not to stand in front of their stores to hand out her papers. The merchants were safe, they were making more money than ever before in their lives, and she felt sorry for them. Because they, too, were feeding off the dead men who lay in the cemetery at the edge of town.

At least no one had tried to keep her from handing out her message. Once an itinerant preacher had prayed with her, but when he walked away he did not take one of her handbills.

She looked up as a man stopped in front of her. She did not know his name, but she had seen him several times before. Usually he was with Mike O'Grady in his fancy four-horse carriage. It took four horses to pull the rig because it was so big, so expensive and so heavily built.

"We can't have you doing this anymore, Mary Beth," the man said.

He was taller than she, wore a dark blue suit and vest, a gold chain linked his vest pockets, and he wore an expensive low crowned beaver hat.

"What?" she said both in surprise and to give her time to think.

"I said we simply can't have you trying to stir up the men this way. The mines are as safe as any can be. You must go home and stop this public display. It is very unladylike."

"Let me go and talk to Mr. O'Grady. He owes my mother and me at least that courtesy."

"Little girl! He owes you nothing. You were paid

8

a two hundred dollar death benefit because of your father's loyal service. That was not required."

"The money has been spent on food and clothing. How long do you think that much money will last?"

"Then you will have to marry and settle down. Let your husband worry about the finances. That is no affair of mine or Mr. O'Grady. But when you insist on spreading gossip and seditious slander such as that garbage, it is our concern. And we shall stop you each time you try."

The man snatched the sheaf of papers from her hand, then bent and picked up the bundle of the rest of the five hundred handbills and walked quickly down the boardwalk.

"Stop! Thief!" Mary Beth shouted and ran after the man, pounding with her small fists on the man's back and arms.

He stopped, turned and pushed her shoulder, sending her reeling against the dry goods store.

"No!" a strong voice thundered.

Mary Beth saw only a flash of color as a tall man in a soft brown hat with Mexican silver pesos around the headband, swept past her and stopped the man who had her handbills.

"I believe you have something that belongs to the lady," Spur McCoy told the man in the blue suit.

The mine owner's flunky bristled, his eyes narrowed and his breath came in short gasps.

"It's no business of yours. On your way, or I'll have you arrested."

"The papers," Spur McCoy demanded, holding

9

out his hand.

The slightly shorter man in the town suit spun and started to take a step away.

Spur grabbed his shoulder, turned him around and slammed his fist into the soft belly. When the man bent down in agony, Spur's right uppercut hit the point of his jaw, lifted him off his feet and dumped him unconscious on the uneven boardwalk. He dropped the papers, and Spur picked them up, straightened them, then handed them back to the girl who stood with her hand over her mouth in surprise.

"I believe these were yours, Miss."

"Oh. Yes. Thank you." She looked away.

"Are you all right?" Spur asked.

"Yes. He didn't want me to hand out my leaflets. He's from one of the big mines."

"And this is a mining town. Could I have one of the papers?"

She handed him one. "My father died in a mine. I'm just trying to save some of the other men who will die. Are you a miner?"

"No, I'm reading for the law."

"Oh, then perhaps . . ." Her gray eyes came up and stared at Spur for a moment, then she shrugged. "No. It's no use. Thank you for helping me. I must hand these out." She moved down the street giving the papers to everyone who would take them. As she returned she scooped the handbills from the boardwalk where people had thrown them down.

Spur watched for a moment, then looked for his suitcase with the double straps around it. He found

10

it where he had put it down when he saw the man snatch the handbills from the girl. He didn't even know her name. He probably never would.

Spur McCoy checked the signs on the buildings along the nearly level street carved into the side of the mountain and ahead of him he saw the New Frontier Hotel. There should be a reservation for him there, one of the hotel's two-room suites with a bath on the same floor.

Ten minutes later he had checked in at the desk, settled in the second floor room 202, and looked over the long telegram he had received at Denver.

He knew it by heart. He was to proceed by rail to Reno, Nevada, where he would take a branch rail line to the mining town of Virginia City. Once there he would be a lawyer checking out the possibilities of opening a practice.

"Your assignment is to determine the accuracy of rumors we have heard that a robbery attempt will be made when gold and silver bullion is transported from Virginia City to the San Francisco mint. Such transport will be by rail. There is supposedly a well organized plot brewing to steal the whole trainload of gold and silver. If such a plot exists, it is your job to defuse it. If that is impossible the plot must be foiled before it can be put into use when the train leaves for San Francisco sometime during the week of October 15, 1874."

Easy, Spur thought. Just waltz up to everyone in town and ask if they were going to rob the gold train. Simple.

Spur McCoy was one of the handful of United States Secret Service Agents in the nation charged

11

with upholding the laws of the federal government across every state and territory. His boss in Washington D.C. was Gen. Wilton D. Halleck, the number two man in the agency who gave orders, and listed their priority. William Wood, the director of the agency, had been appointed by President Lincoln and each of the succeeding presidents.

Spur's permanent Secret Service office was in St. Louis, where his responsibility included the entire western half of the U.S. His operational cover story was that he headed the St. Louis branch of Capital Investigations, with main offices in Washington D.C. and New York City. In St. Louis Fleurette Leon was in charge of the operation when Spur was away, which was most of the time.

He had only one contact to find in Virginia City who might be able to give him some leads. She was the woman who had sent letters to the government every day for a month about the problem. Her name was Stella. She worked at the Golden Nugget Saloon. The lady was a bar girl, dealt poker, blackjack and faro when needed and could be sweet-talked into bed after closing time if the cash was right.

Spur took off his shirt and vest, washed as well as he could in the heavy porcelain bowl and put on clean clothes. He brushed back his reddish brown hair, and buttoned a new, brown, soft leather vest he bought in Denver. It was a little after three in the afternoon. The sun was low in the sky and the October air had a nip in it at the elevation of 6,205 feet.

The big Secret Service man walked down Main Street, then turned into Fifth where most of the saloons, bordellos and gambling halls clustered. He found the Golden Nugget halfway down the block. It was not the biggest, had glass windows, a large mirror behind the bar and twin stairs that led to a second story that vanished down a hallway he expected led to about twenty extremely small bedrooms.

No sawdust on this floor. He pushed his low crowned brown hat back and shouldered through swinging doors. Spur looked much the same now as when he came off the train, with one exception, he wore a big army issue 1873 Colt .45 low on his right hip. The bottom of the holster was tied down to his leg so the weapon and the way he wore it gave a subtle message to half the drinkers along the bar. This man can use his six-gun.

Spur bought a cold beer and turned, watching the action. There wasn't much yet. The shift at the mines would change soon. Some now worked two shifts, since it didn't make any difference what time it was a thousand feet down into the mountain. Spur was not claustrophobic, but he did not enjoy wandering around in deep mines. Those thousands of tons of dirt and rock over his head were a constant worry. He hoped that this assignment would not put him down in a mine.

The Golden Nugget had a long bar complete with brass rail and glistening varnished top. On the other side of the room there were a dozen tables for drinking, and another dozen next to the far wall for serious gambling. Monte, poker, and craps were the biggest demand games. Only two poker tables were in use.

The spot beside him at the bar was open and a girl in a low cut dance hall dress slid in next to him. The dress was bright red, with a tightly cinched waist and a flare below that reached just short of her ankles. This was shockingly short since it showed two inches of leg over her high topped shoes. A small brown mole marred the inside of her right breast where it had been pushed up to form three inches of cleavage.

Her mouth was painted red, her eyes shadowed and a touch of rouge brightened her cheeks. Even with all the paint, she still looked like a farm girl from Kansas, which was what she was.

"Buy a girl a drink?" she asked and smiled. Her fingers stroked his arm and curled around his neck.

"Only if your name is Stella. Friend of mine said I had to see Stella next time I got to town."

"Damn."

"Is she here? Which one is she?"

"I must be in the wrong business," the girl said. She snorted and shook her head. "The one in the blue dress, that's Stella. We call her old Prune Face with the Big Tits."

"Oh, that one," Spur said. He left the rest of his glass of beer on the bar and wandered toward Stella. She had been talking to two miners at a table, and when he came up she turned to him.

"Buy a girl a drink?"

"Sure. Bring me a beer and whatever kind of watered down tea I'm paying whisky-price for, for you. I don't mind." He gave her a silver dollar. She grinned and headed for the bar. Spur chose a table far away from the others. Stella was no knockout beauty, but the other girl had been right. In the tits department Stella was a winner. She came back quickly, found him at the table and set down his beer and a tea-colored drink in a whiskey glass for herself.

"I hear your name is Stella."

"Right, who told you?"

"Friend of mine from back east."

"Fame, it really travels now with the train."

"This friend is in Washington D.C. His name is General Halleck."

Stella almost dropped her drink.

"The letters finally got through." She looked around. "You didn't tell nobody you was coming to see me, I mean here in town, did you? I seen girls chopped up in small parts for less. You got a hotel room?"

He told her.

"I'm going to be sick. I feel it coming on. I'll be at your hotel room in half an hour." She stared at him. "Damn, but you are pretty."

"Are you in any danger?"

"Not as long as they don't find out. Hey, don't they have real bath tubs at that hotel, where you can sit down and stretch out, almost lay down in the water?"

"I'll have a hot bath waiting for you. Now we better talk a little so everything looks normal. You go get me another beer and than a half hour later

15

you come to my room, 202 in the New Frontier."

"Yeah, I know. And I'll use the back stairs. Hey, I been around this town for three years." She smiled, then leaned in and kissed him on the cheek. "Damn, I better get another beer for you. You drink it, then slap me on the bottom and pinch a tit and I yell at you and drift on to somebody else. You got it?"

Spur nodded.

A half hour later he had a bathroom on the New Frontier Hotel's second floor reserved, saw that there were three buckets of steaming hot water there and one of cold, then he waited for Stella.

She came to his room precisely on time, saw he had taken off his vest and hat but still had the six-gun on.

"Figure you'll need that pistol?" she asked, closing the door and leaning against it. She had changed to a simple print dress that buttoned high around her throat. Stella laughed. "Hey, relax. First I have a real bath, then we talk." She paused. "What's your name?"

"Spur McCoy."

"Good, I like that. Spur, you going to take a bath with me?"

"Too much bathing ruins the skin."

"Chicken, huh? Well, at least you can scrub my back." She looked at the bed. "There's an extra blanket in the closet. Bring it along. But not when anyone else is in the hall. No sense getting both of us thrown out of here, is there?" She winked, opened the door and went across the hall to the bathroom. She knew where it was. McCoy

16

grinned, took the extra, soft blanket from the closet and when no one was in the hallway, stepped into the bathroom and locked the door.

TWO

STELLA HAD EMPTIED one of the buckets of water into the six foot long, roll rim, white enameled tub and Spur saw that it was one of the best ones. It was a real luxury item. The woman had taken off her clothes and now when she turned to look at him her full breasts hung down and Spur couldn't help but gasp in surprise.

"I'm speechless," Spur said as she stood up. For a moment he was fearful that the massive breasts might prevent her from coming upright. She turned toward him and he laughed softly.

"You have the most beautiful figure I've ever seen," Spur said.

She shrugged. "Yeah, good tits, but them and a quarter will get you lunch at the little eatery up the street." She nodded. "Course it is nice to be noticed." She poured the next two buckets of hot water into the bath tub and then half the cold and tested it.

"Sure you don't want a bath?" she asked.

"Just had one," Spur lied, and watched her step into the tub.

"When I get rich, I'm going to have one of these, and all the hot water I want . . . and two little boys

18

to heat water and fetch and carry it. I'll have it all piped down to the tub with a tank upstairs for the hot water and let it come down through the pipes . . ." She shrugged. "I do carry on sometimes." Stella sat down in the water and pushed her legs out, then slid down until only her face was out of the water.

"Oh, lord, I can die happy now." She lifted out of the water and sat up straight. "You know those letters I sent?"

"I heard about them by telegraph."

"I know lots more than what they said. I can tell you two of the men who are setting up the plot." She hesitated. "They are . . . customers of mine, and they both talk in their sleep'. I could be a rich woman now if I used everything I hear." She paused and twisted her face. "I'd either be rich or dead, probably dead, 'cause the kind of men I work with are not the most kind, forgiving or understanding. That's why I don't ever want to be seen with you. They find out I talked, and I'll wind up as gear grease for some mine machinery about three thousand feet underground."

Spur had sat on the only chair in the small room. She waved.

"Hey, come on over here and scrub my back. I'm not giving up this chance."

Spur had felt the pressure building up ever since he came into the room crowded full by the woman and her beautiful breasts.

"Stella, I can't possibly wash your back . . . unless I get to wash your front too!"

"Oh, yeah, and I get to play with your balls! Get

over here and help me enjoy my bath. It's been almost a year since I got to use one of these fancy damn bathtubs."

Spur washed her back with soap and the provided cloth, then she turned and he delicately scrubbed her breasts. He had only finished one when she caught his hands.

"Spur, you sweetheart! Are you getting in the tub with me or am I getting out on that blanket?"

He stood, slid out of his clothes and pointed to the blanket. She squealed in anticipation and stepped from the tub, dried herself quickly and helped Spur pull his boots off. When he was as bare as she was, she sat on the blanket she had spread out on the floor.

Spur took the straight backed chair and pushed the back of it under the door handle so that it rested on two of the four legs. Now no one could get in the bathroom even with the key.

McCoy knelt down beside her and she grabbed his swinging penis which had only started to fill with hot, eager blood.

"You a slow starter?" she asked.

"The only thing I do slow is stop," Spur said. He caught one of her breasts and massaged the big nipple until it grew even more and throbbed.

"Chew on them," Stella said, her eyes closed. She bent over farther until her breasts hung straight down, and Spur slid under one and gulped it into his mouth. For a moment he thought he was going to be smothered, then he chewed and licked the pulsating nipple. As he did he felt her hands at

20

his crotch, and quickly he responded to her urgings.

"Spur, you know I was only twelve when I got banged the first time. Course by the time I was ten I had more tits than my mother did, and when I was twelve I had boobs about like I have now. It was the damn ice man! He brought ice every day. We lived in New Jersey then. He came and put the ice in the ice box, and every day he asked me if my mother was home. She usually was. Then this day she wasn't and I told him. I didn't know no better.

"He grinned and said he had some special eating ice. He brought it in, pushed some down my blouse and then said he had to go get it, and his hands were all over me. I'd never felt anything like that. I was just sexed earlier than other girls I guess. He had my blouse and everything off me and his big dick out and I didn't have any idea what he was going to do with it.

"Then he spread my legs and I yelled and he put his hand over my mouth and pushed. I felt it go in and couldn't believe it. I mean I was only twelve and didn't know nothing about sex or fucking. That damn iceman taught me a lot in two hours that afternoon!"

Spur came out from under her breasts and pushed her down on the blanket. Her slender legs spread and he moved between them. He could feel the heat of her thighs, her eyes glistened in anticipation.

"Do it!" she said softly. "Push him inside of me before I explode!"

21

He lowered and pressed forward and they were mated. Her legs came over his back and locked together and she began a slow motion with her hips as she lifted part way off the floor. It set Spur on fire and he thrust forward in a slow rhythm, then stopped and kissed her breasts. When she looked at him he had an answer.

"Stella, I want to make this first one last as long as I can."

"Good, then we'll both take a bath. I saved one bucket of hot water. No I didn't. By that time it won't matter."

A few minutes later they turned over without coming apart so she was on top and she showed Spur a fancy little hip movement that he had never experienced before.

"Easy," Spur said.

Stella shook her head. "Now is the time," she said and increased the side to side motion and then round and round and Spur felt her whole body go into a spasm that shook her and rattled her until she screamed, and then moaned in the joy of the climax that came again and again. Her face twisted and she drove at him harder with her hips until she burst again in an intense physical rapture that Spur had never seen a woman experience before.

A third time she thrust against him and this time when the tremendous surge of powerful emotion had washed through her again and again, and at last moved on, she fell against him totally spent. A moment later she roused and leaned back and grinned at him.

"That's what I call a girl's night out. Not often I

get to really let go with a customer. Not unless I know him well, or like this I'm with a man I go bonkers over." She laughed. "Is this one lasting long enough for you?"

At once she used her practiced art of bringing him to his own fulfillment. Spur shouted and drove upward against her again and again until he thought he would explode, and then he did and she kept working at him until he had drained the last of his juices and fell back washed out and exhausted.

She moved gently off him and they lay side by side on the doubled blanket on the floor.

Ten minutes later she sat up.

"Now, how about that bath fit for two? I never did get all of my fill of that hot water in the glorious tub."

A half hour later Spur brought dinner to his room from the small dining room below and Stella and he ate. As she picked at the roast chicken she told him about the town, and what she knew of the plot.

"Spur McCoy, you've got to remember that this is a rambunctious town. It was nothing more than two shacks back in 1859 when them old scallywags was placer mining up the creeks from the Carson river. Then overnight we had two thousand men here scratching and clawing, cheating, claim jumping and murdering each other.

"Now here we are fifteen years later and things ain't much better. Yeah, we got government and a mayor and policemen and a sheriff, but still men are scratching and clawing, cheating and claim jumping. They just do it different now."

"Big mine owners call the shots?"

"Damn right! Nothing gets done unless they want it done. And what they don't want done stays undone. Three of the really big mine owners run this town. The other smaller owners try to get inside, but they don't have much chance. And, damnit, they are right. There is no reason on this desert mountain why there should be a town here, except for the gold and silver. When they run out, this town is gonna shrink up like a just cum prick. Right down to about two hundred people, if that many. Might be a ghost town with nothing but memories living here."

"Now, Stella. Who is trying to steal the gold shipment?"

"I only know two names. One of them is Guy Pritchard. He's maybe thirty-three or four, likes me to tie him up beforehand. Anyway he's one of two engineers on the little steamer that comes in from Reno on the branch railroad. He's scared shit-less, but he's going through with it because they promised him a million dollars if the whole thing works right."

"The engineer, that makes sense. But he isn't planning it."

"No, you're right. He's a flunky, and they probably will kill him when it's over to shut him up for good. The other gent could be the mainspring. Once in a while I get a message to come to somebody's house. Boss lady says fine, as long as I split fifty-fifty with her. Three times now I been to this one big house.

"Gent's name is Rush Sommers. The Rush

24

Sommers. Used to own the old Crown Point Mine. Now he's into something big again with what they're calling Consolidated California. He sent a hack for me, told me to bundle all up with a hat and veil so nobody could tell who I was. His wife was in San Francisco. He told me she knew he fucked around."

"Did he talk in his sleep, too?"

"Oh, yeah. But he bragged before he went to sleep, then bit his tongue and told me if I didn't forget what I just heard he'd cut my tits off. I swore up and down I hadn't even heard what he'd been talking about. Convinced him I was concentrating on his big cock and I couldn't think about anything else. He believed me."

"What was the big secret?" McCoy asked.

"He said he just put his team together and was celebrating. He said he had the engineer tied up, and a key man in the sheriff's office, as well as an ex-banker from the east now running a saloon who could help him dispose of the gold."

"That was it?"

"He figured it was too much, he shut up his trap like a barn door in a big windstorm. Then I figured I better earn my money and I gave him more than he wanted, and he passed out about ten o'clock. The rest of the night he slept and talked and I remembered every word.

"The gist of it was that he was running into cost problems with the Consolidated Mine and needed some fast money to get to the really big veins he's sure are down there around the sixteen-fifty to the two thousand foot level. How better to get the cash than to steal the gold shipment? He would have little of his own bullion on the train because he was still developing Consolidated. A perfect set up. He would know when the train was starting out on the trip to Reno.''

Spur pushed his dishes away and stared at the woman. She hadn't bothered to dress yet, and Spur marveled at the perfectly formed yet big breasts that sagged a little from their own size and weight. He reached over and played with one as he talked.

''So we've got a railroad engineer, a deputy sheriff, a saloon owner and one of the biggest mine owners in town. That's quite a cast. How do I know you're telling the truth?''

''Why would I lie about something that could get me killed? Hell, by now there are getting to be too many wives in town for fancy women like me to count much. Was a time when we was top drawer around here. Even three years ago when women was scarce, all the men treated us girls like queens of the court. We was special, since we was females, and some of them placer miners hadn't seen a woman for two years. They would walk ten miles just to watch us walk down the street. And we got respect back then.

''Then too, that kind of a theft would hurt this town, put some small outfits into bankruptcy and cut down on my own business income. That's two fucking good reasons why you should believe me.''

''Okay, I do. We heard a rumor from another source too. I've got two names but we don't know the other two.''

She nodded. He bent and kissed her nipple, then

26

licked it and sucked on it until it filled with rushing hot blood and enlarged until it was as thick as his thumb.

"Spur, you tit-sucker! You know how to make a woman feel wanted."

"Part of my strategy. Which saloon owner could it be? You said he was from the East. Would he have an accent? Which one do you figure he is who is in on the robbery?"

"There's two of them are possible and I'll tell you right after you ream me out once more with that wonderful big fence post you keep hidden between your legs!"

Spur chuckled. "Fence post! Now that is a new description. Shall we try the bed this time?"

It was better than before. Spur delighted in her large hanging breasts and the different ways she used to entice him into climaxing. This time she kept lifting her legs higher and higher until she rested them on his shoulders, bending herself in half and Spur yelped and drummed her with a dozen hard thrusts in a climax that left him panting.

She let him recover, then slid off the bed and began to dress.

"I got to get back for the early evening trade," she said. He watched her putting on her dress. "What I told you, every word is gospel true. I can't tell you no more unless I get something direct from the parties involved. But I don't think they'll risk an all night with me again this close to the time it's supposed to happen.

"Oh, the two saloon owners. My best bet is Haywood Lockland, who runs the Wide Vein gambling hall. The other is Max Giardello, the guy who owns the Golden Nugget.''

"So you better be double extra careful,'' Spur said.

Stella reached up and kissed his lips softly. "I'll be careful, damn touchy about this subject. Hey now, you can come see Stella anytime. I'll always make room for a free pop for you! But don't even try to talk to me except upstairs. I don't want that damn Sommers cutting me up!''

He rubbed her tits and walked her to the door. "Stella, there could be a reward in this if we catch everyone and prevent the robbery. It would be enough cash for you to set up your own house somewhere, or even move to San Francisco and live like a gussied up lady for the rest of your life.''

"Or even hook some rich dick in San Francisco and marry him?''

"Even that good. So keep your ears open.''

She reached down and rubbed his crotch, kissed him again and slipped out the door when no one was in the hall.

But someone had seen her. Lottie, the madam of the Golden Nugget Saloon, had watched Spur when he talked to Stella, and then had him followed when he left. Something about him she didn't like, or maybe she did like, she wasn't sure. Then when Stella got "sick," Lottie followed Stalla and saw her slip into the bathroom with Spur close behind.

This was more than a bath and a private romp on the bed. Whatever it was, Stella would find out. If nothing else she would satisfy her curiosity about the big hunk of man. She learned from the hotel clerk that he was registered as Spur McCoy. She would find out what he was doing in Virginia City, and she would find out if his slim powerful looking hips could hump her as well as she imagined.

THREE

THE TALL, SLENDER man sat there in his hotel room staring at a corpse. He should be moving, running again, getting away. Perhaps this was the final curtain for him.

He stood and looked at his reflection in the wavy glass of the primitive Western hotel mirror. Aging lines showed plainly. There was no way to deny them. If he were still on the stage he would be slipping into the character roles he had detested in his salad days. Now it was so much different.

Mark Wilkes stepped over the body on the floor and slowly began packing his one carpet bag. It could be stowed easily, sat upon in a pinch and if he lost it there was little of value in it. It had not always been this way.

The pool of blood on the floor had stopped growing. That meant the knife wound had at last killed the man. When his heart stopped beating, pumping actually, the blood flow ceased. Just as well. There would be less for the maid to clean up. He snorted at his sudden concern for the unknown maid, while a man he had known for ten years, indeed had toured with for five, lay at his feet dead and half way to heaven, yet Mark could not summon a whit of sympathy, remorse or compassion for him.

Since April 15, 1865 he knew that he would be living in a shadow for the rest of his life. He never dreamed how deep and dark and long lasting that shadow would be. Perhaps John had been the lucky one, dying so quickly and undoubtedly by his own hand. John was not the kind to play that kind of a scene, not the trial production and the court and sentence and then a public execution. Not John, he would take the option of a quick, dramatic spectacle kind of a curtain.

At first there had been no guilt associated with Mark. He was the loyal Northern sympathetic brother along with the rest of the family. True, he had continued to work with Edwin in some of his plays, when the part was right, but there was never any official suggestion of collusion between the two brothers and the assassin.

But some of the fraternity of thespians knew. Mark could never figure out how they discovered it, but they knew. That first few months there had been sympathy, then when that wore thin the hints began and it was in New York City when the first one of the old crowd had come forward and complained of being a bit short of cash, and asked Mark for a five hundred dollar loan.

It had been blackmail pure and simple, and when the actor freely admitted that he had no intention of paying back the money, Mark had struck out at him blindly, knocking him down. As he fell he hit his head on a brick fireplace hearth, and by the time Mark knelt beside his friend, full of apologies, the man was dead.

Mark Wilkes dropped out of the profession then, took odd jobs, moved around, but in almost every large city, someone knew him, and if they chanced to spot him on the sidewalk or in a shop, the eventual contact would be made.

The next two blackmailers he simply beat into a bloody mess and let them go, but the fourth one he killed with a shot from a pistol. He had no remorse, no bitterness, no recriminations. Such was the role that the casting director had given him to play, and he would play it out as long as there were lines for him to give.

Now, he was wondering if the lines indeed were about to run out. He was in Denver, and had made the mistake of slipping into a presentation of *Hamlet* being performed by a traveling troupe, only to find that the theatre was a small hall with bad lighting on stage. One of the actors recognized him from the back row, and the all too familiar scene took place.

Mark Wilkes looked at the body now and hardly remembered his name, Phil something. A man in his forties who should have known better. He bent and found the light purse and change in the man's pockets, then tipped him out the window into the alley, and covered the bloodstains on the floor with a small rug. Mark checked out and headed west again.

The farther the better. He bought a ticket to

Reno, Nevada. Surely no one would know him there. Yes, Reno would be his haven.

In those first few years he had taken a variety of names, anything that was different enough from that of the assassin of President Lincoln, the infamous John Wilkes Booth. For ten years Mark Wilkes Booth had used the stage name of Mark Wilkes, as his brother had used John Booth. Now he shunned even his middle name and adopted a variety of names, each picked to fit the part he had selected in the community where he attempted to blend into the background.

Somehow it never worked.

Mark Wilkes Booth picked up his carpetbag and walked to the desk where he checked out and hurried to the train station. There was a train heading west in half an hour. He took it. He was well out of town before the maid discovered the blood. Then they found the body dumped in some weeds in the alley. They telegraphed ahead to the next station, but there was no one on the train by the name of Mark Masterson.

A deputy sheriff stared at each of the male passengers critically, but found none that even remotely matched the description given him on the telegram. He let the train continue.

A rather large woman with horn-rimmed glasses harumphed at the delay. When the train continued, she retired to the woman's room where she quickly removed makeup and changed herself back into a man, only this time with a full beard, moustache and black hair. Mark Wilkes grinned at his new reflection. He was sure no one would be checking the train again and if they did he would still fool them. He hadn't been an actor and a wizard at makeup for fifteen years for nothing.

Reno was a small town but still it looked too big to Wilkes when he landed there. He took the small branch line train with one coach heading for Virginia City. It was a mining town, people said. He could work at his second profession, gambling, which was half acting. Yes, he would be safe and secure in Virginia City. In time he would grow a moustache and beard of his own. Now what should he do for a name? He needed a new one, a Western name with some dash to it. A gambler's name!

By the time the little train rattled nearly thirty miles up the tracks and then north to Virginia City, he had his new name. He would be Monty Jackson. It had a nice western ring. And the game of three card monte was a favorite out here in no man's land. It would be a good alias for him.

Monty Jackson wasted no time in settling in once the train arrived at the rough, unkempt, bawdy and roughhouse village of Virginia City that he was told boasted over eighteen thousand residents. He had worked the new town routine many times before. He checked in at the first hotel he came to, paid for a week's room in advance and asked where the best gambling house in town was located. He checked in at 12:15 p.m. on that second day of October in 1874. By 1:30 he had obtained a table at the Westward Ho Gambling Emporium, and dealt his first hand of five card draw poker to three miners who insisted the game have a dime limit per bet.

Monty Jackson sighed. He would move up in the gambling world as soon as he could.

He did. By suppertime he had a game going with one merchant, a foreman of a mine and a mining stock salesman. There was no limit on the betting. He had just won an honest hand with over fifty dollars in it. He watched critically and saw the stock salesman dealing off the bottom of the deck.

Monty looked at his cards, threw them in and stood up. "I'm out of the game," Monty said.

"You got a lot of my money," the dealer said.

"And you're dealing off the bottom."

The other two men at the table stopped talking.

The dealer stood up, his hands limp at his side. "You say I'm cheating?"

"I sure as hell am."

The other two men at the table backed away. Men at tables and at the bar behind both men moved quickly to each side.

Both men looked hard at each other. "Might as well draw on me right now, cheater," Monty said. "That way I won't have to watch my back all day and all night."

The mining stock salesman snarled and darted his hand into his jacket for the derringer that rested there.

Monty had spent three weeks selecting and learning how to shoot a pistol before he started west on his gambling run five years ago. He had kept in practice. He smoothly drew a five shot .32

caliber revolver from his belt holster under his jacket. The Adams pocket revolver was only eight and a half inches long. He had it out and trained on the other man before the other man found the butt of his derringer.

"Apologize and live," Monty said.

"Damned if I will!" the man shouted and tried to draw the weapon.

Monty shot him in the heart and he died as he staggered backwards a step, crashed over a chair and tumbled to the floor.

Monty sat down and put his pistol away. "Gentlemen, I think the game is over for today. I'll be involved for several minutes with the police who I'm sure will have some questions. I would appreciate it if both of you would stay and swear that this was self defense."

"I saw him cheating, too," the shorter of the two men said.

"So good of you to call him on it," Monty said with a good deal of scorn and turned as a sheriff's deputy came in wearing his strange uniform of blue and his little billed cap.

The police asked questions, took statements from witnesses and had Monty swear on paper that it was self defense. He didn't even have to go to the sheriff's station.

Monty went to the bar and had two quick shots of whisky, and started to carry a third one to a table when he saw a man stride into the gambling hall and start a quick scan of each person in the room.

The back of his scalp tingled and he turned, went past the bar and out the back door into the alley.

36

Monty Jackson, also known as Mark Wilkes, leaned against the back of the gambling hall and shivered. He had not seen the man for nine years. But there he was, his hard eyes searching, just as they had been searching in Virginia so long ago.

The man was Spur McCoy, of the United States Secret Service, one of the men assigned to try to piece together the whole plot behind the assassination of President Lincoln. Four times McCoy had talked with John Wilkes Booth's brother, Mark. Four times they had agreed that Mark knew nothing that would help in the investigation. Mark had demonstrated his loyalty many times to the nation. He had been loyal to the North, and said he was not aware that his brother had such strong ties with the South.

Four times, Mark Wilkes Booth had played the part of an unjustly accused man, and four times he had convinced the young investigator. His acting skills at least had not forsaken him. Then there was to be a fifth meeting. A friend had warned Booth that he had been compromised, one of the plotters had given evidence to the government with the promise that he would be set free.

Mark Wilkes Booth had taken the next train south, then west, and he had used three disguises to outwit those who had followed him. For a year various government agencies had tried to trace him. Then they had given up.

Now Spur McCoy was back on his trail.

He must kill the government agent.

He must have a different disguise for the role of the killer.

Quickly Monty Jackson walked back to his hotel, going in the side door and up to his room. From the special case in his carpetbag he took out his makeup materials and went to work. In a half hour he became an old man, with gray beard, a balding head, thick eyebrows and puffy cheeks achieved with cotton balls.

Downstairs he found a young lad and gave him a job. He tore a five dollar greenback in half and gave one part to the boy of sixteen.

"Son, if you can find out where Spur McCoy is staying, and his room number, I'll give you the other half of this five dollar bill. Men work all day in the mines for four dollars. He'll be at one of the better hotels. Can you do it?"

The youth nodded vigorously and hurried away. There were only five hotels where strangers stayed. He could go over their registration books in a half hour.

As it turned out the young boy found Spur McCoy's name and room number on the second try, and rushed back with the information to where the old man sat outside the hardware store in a wooden chair tilted back against the building.

"You sure, son?"

"Absolutely. I asked the clerk. He came in yesterday, and is looking all around town. Claims he's looking for somewhere to set up a law practice."

"Sounds right." Monty gave the boy the other hand of the five dollar bill. "Look sharp at that bill, son. It's not real. Stage money somebody passed on me. But I do have a genuine greenback."

"I'd rather have a silver dollar, sir," the youth said.

Monty laughed, tossed a silver dollar in the air and the youth caught it and ran off toward his home. It was the most real money he had ever earned in his whole life! He had no idea it was blood money.

Monty moved slowly toward the New Frontier Hotel. He touched the pistol under his coat. Nobody would notice an old man going into a hotel, or wandering around looking for his room. Old men were tolerated, because every man knew that someday he would be in the same situation.

He walked into the hotel and up to the second floor. At room 202 he listened carefully. No one was moving around inside. It was early. McCoy might be out testing the fancy ladies of the town. Monty could wait. He would kill McCoy and the old man would vanish. Tomorrow afternoon Monty Jackson would be back at his table in the gambling hall, and once more his life would be secure, even if for only a few weeks or months.

He sighed as he waited. Perhaps his brother, John Wilkes Booth, had known what it would be like; perhaps he had made the better choice when he killed himself with his own pistol nine long years ago.

Perhaps.

Then Monty scowled and gripped the pistol. Someone had started up the wooden steps. At first he saw nothing. He had slumped against the corner of the hall next to the stairs. Slowly the man came higher and Monty could see a low crowned brown

39

hat and then the penetrating eyes. The man was
Spur McCoy.

The Secret Service man was about to die!

FOUR

BIG GAME HUNTERS, Indians, some farmers attuned closely to the ground, and certainly men constantly on the run from lawmen and bounty hunters, all have one trait in common: they can smell danger and threat as if it were an angry skunk with its tail up ejecting its protective fluid.

Spur McCoy had learned the art of self preservation through several years of hunting men, and being stalked himself, and now as he came up the stairway to the second floor of the New Frontier Hotel the vibrations pounded at his consciousness and he ducked down below the floor level of the second landing.

At precisely the same time he dropped, the disguised old man waiting for Spur on the second floor, pulled the trigger of his Adams pocket revolver, sending two rounds through the dimly lit rectangle of space where his enemy had so recently stood.

Monty Jackson knew he had missed. He eased backward into the vacant room behind him. Closed the door quietly and walked to the window. His escape route had been carefully scouted. Even before he heard movement in the hall, he had raised the window and stepped out on the narrow band of roof around the second floor. This led to the first floor slanted roof near the back of the hotel on the alley side and a short drop to the ground.

Long ago he had made it a rule never to jump more than four feet. He knew all too well what a broken ankle could do to a man on the run. He completed the drop and was out of sight before he heard cursing at the open window above. He figured it was the window he had just escaped through, and the Secret Service man was making all the noise.

Inside the hotel stairway, Spur McCoy had his .45 cocked and ready as he edged up to the top of the stairs and looked down the second floor hallway.

No one was in sight.

He saw several doors on both sides of the familiar passage. The bushwhacker could be behind any of them waiting for him to come down the hall. There was no chance that Spur could watch six doors at the same time. He waited, his eyes barely over the hallway's floor level, hoping the attacker would make one more try.

He listened. Footsteps? Where? A moment later he heard what could only be a window sliding upward, but from what room? To his right were the alley windows. Those on his left opened on the street. It would be the alley side for an easy and unobserved escape. Which room? The second one for the best shot. He ran to the room, tried the door. Locked. Maybe the first door. He tried it.

Unlocked.

He thrust it open and dodged against the hall wall. There were no shots. He looked inside the room. Unoccupied. Thin curtains blew out an open window. Spur rushed to the window in time to see a man lowering himself in the shadows of the first floor to a hanging position, then drop to the ground. There was no chance for a shot. No way to know who he was.

Spur went to his room, packed his bag and moved two doors down to an empty room. He pocketed the key and went downstairs. At the clerk's desk he spoke softly.

"Somebody just bushwhacked me but missed. I've moved down the hall two rooms. Leave me registered on your books in the same room. I'll pay for the other room when I move out. If anybody finds out from you what room I'm in, I'll rearrange your face."

The clerk nodded. "Yes, sir. I've still got you on my books in that room and I'll mark the other one held for repairs."

Spur nodded and continued into the dining room. He had just sat down when one of the young waiters came up to him with a note. Spur opened it and read:

"Sir. I hate to eat alone. Would you do me the honor of being my guest at dinner? I have the small, private dining room at the rear."

He looked at the waiter. "Who sent the note?"

"I'm not supposed to say."

Spur handed him a silver dollar. The young man, who was not over sixteen, grinned.

"The lady's name is Tracy Belcher, Mrs. Tracy

Belcher, widow of one of the big mine owners. She still helps run the company with the original three other partners. She is quite a lady. Eats here three nights a week because the hotel hired away her chef. Antonio likes to cook for everyone, not just her. She usually asks someone to eat with her.''

Spur did not hesitate. A mine owner. It would be a good contact if nothing else. He nodded to the boy who led him through the dining room to the slatted door at the end. The waiter knocked, then opened the door and stepped aside so Spur could go in.

The room was about fifteen feet square, with a table for twelve in the center. Two places were set at one end. The chairs were upholstered and of fine design and workmanship. Around the sides of the room sat more overstuffed furniture. The walls had delicate oil paintings, and the ceiling was covered with an intricate pattern of varnished wood paneling.

At the side of the table sat a woman of about thirty-five, who had been carefully made up, and her soft blonde hair combed precisely. He guessed that she was not slender from the generous size of her arms and shoulders. The dress she wore was low cut politely showing a touch of cleavage, but not enough to be vulgar.

She held out a delicate hand with nails covered with some clear kind of decoration.

''Good evening. My name is Tracy Belcher. I'd be pleased if you would have dinner with me tonight. I am a widow and an extremely forward person, my partners tell me. They say I act more like a man than most men. Does that frighten you?"

"Certainly not. I'm Spur McCoy, some people think that I am a bit too aggressive myself, but I don't listen to such talk. I would be delighted to have dinner with you. Someone said you know the chef."

She waved him to the chair opposite her and stared into his eyes.

"Yes, dear Antonio, money means nothing to him. But we can talk about him later. Let's talk about you. I'd say you're about six feet two, and right at a solid two hundred pounds. Reddish brown hair that usually won't stay combed, and a big moustache to match. I adore moustaches! The mutton chops aren't bad, but could stand a trimming. Bright green eyes and a sun-browned face. You spend some time out of doors."

"Some," Spur said.

"Don't worry about ordering. I always order a day in advance. Our dinner will be along presently. Tell me about yourself."

"Not much to tell, ma'am. I'm reading the law and looking for a place to set up a practice. I was Harvard class of fifty-eight."

"A Harvard man! Well, our little town is at last getting some class. And call me Tracy. Do you know what I do in town?"

"Yes, ma'am, Tracy. You and your partners run the Belcher Number One and two silver and gold mines. And I hear that you do most of the running."

She smiled, her blue eyes sparkled. He saw that

her skin was unusually soft and clear. "And you disapprove of a woman doing that?" her brows went up and he saw she was ready to defend her stand.

"Not at all. I figure a woman's got the right to do anything she wants to, dig ditches, run a steam locomotive, work in a mine, even raise a family."

"Don't be impertinent, young man. I'm older than you are."

"Not one hell of a lot. You're thirty-five."

She laughed. Two young men came in just then with covered trays and Spur soon found himself delighted to be working his way through a seven course dinner. Pheasant and fileted trout were featured with six kinds of vegetables, soups, salads, and three delicious desserts. Rich, dark coffee finished the meal.

They talked about Boston and New York. Tracy had never been east of Denver and she was yearning to go. Spur goon got the conversation back to his problem.

"I'm looking for a place to practice, maybe pick up a big client. What about this Mike O'Grady I hear about? Would he be a good one to approach about being his lawyer?"

She laughed. "O'Grady is lawyer-poor. He's got two big firms in San Francisco and one in Reno. No luck there."

"Maybe I could work for you?"

Tracy nodded. "Maybe. You any good on labor relations? We have over four hundred men working at the mine. They still get four dollars a day, a contract we signed when things were rich and plush in this town. Things haven't been so good lately.''

''Sorry, that's not exactly my field.''

''What is your field?''

''More into investigatiion law. Helping solve problems in legal tangles, rights of way. I've done a lot of reading about vein rights. In most mining communities the claim rights extend at ninety degrees straight down into the ground. But here in Nevada the new principle has been established that once a hard rock vein has been claimed within the surface claim area, the owner of that vein has the right to pursue it even if it extends beyond the vertical limits of his claim.

''As the owner of that vein I can follow it under four other surface claims and still have rights to it. The big problem comes when a vein pinches out and then continues perhaps a half mile away. Some argue that it is undoubtedly the same vein, since it is in the same horizontal strata of rock where the rest of the vein had been. Others say in this instance finders-keepers. Whoever runs into that pinched off vein is the new owner.''

''That's the latest, is it?'' Tracy asked. She showed more respect now as she glanced at him. ''You just might be some good to us at that. Why don't you come around to the office tomorrow and we'll see what we can set up?''

She smiled and stood. Spur knew that she was a little heavy, but he was surprised. She was more solid and stocky than fat. The way she moved caught Spur's attention, as if she were dancing, or on the stage.

"You are going to escort me home, aren't you?"

The tall man smiled at her and she smiled back, then he shook his head. "I would love to, but I have an appointment in ten minutes I need to get ready for. Any other time. I'm sure you have a carriage waiting. I'd be honored to see you into your rig."

"If that's the best I can do. Where are you staying? I'd like to have you over for tea, or supper or something?"

He told her.

"It's been a delightful evening. I almost never get to talk to a Harvard man." She smiled, stuck her tongue out at him and laughed, then led the way to the lobby and the front door. He took her hand and kissed it solemnly the way he had seen so many foreign diplomats do at parties and gatherings in Washington D.C. He watched her go with curious amusement. She had asked him to see her home for more than a goodnight kiss on the hand.

Spur shrugged and went up to his new room. She was not one of his primary figures in his current case, so for now he would shunt her aside. But perhaps sometime later.

McCoy had spent little time worrying about who had tried to gun him down in the hallway. As a Secret Service agent with several years of duty, he knew he had made scores of enemies. He might run into one in almost any town in the west.

He thought about the two leads he had on the gold train takeover, Rush Sommers, and Guy Pritchard. He would see the mine owner tomorrow about some kind of legal work. He would have to find out when Pritchard, the engineer, made his runs. The saloon owner was a possible lead. He would be more approachable tonight. Spur checked his face in the wavy mirror, dug out his straight razor and gave himself a quick, close shave, splashed on some witch hazel and bay rum after shave lotion he had made up at the druggist, and headed for the Golden Nugget. He would not even smile at Stella.

The Golden Nugget was booming. Every card table was filled. Eight girls in low-cut dance hall dresses flounced around the big room. He let his glance slide past Stella who looked at him briefly then kissed the miner she was with at a table. True love.

Spur ordered a beer at the bar and when it was nearly gone he asked how he could talk to the owner.

The apron behind the bar laughed with a voice damaged by an accident. He talked with a hoarse whisper that was distinct but took concentration to understand.

"Boss is upstairs. You got business?"

"Yes, I'm a lawyer, new in town. Frankly I'm looking for clients who might need a lawyer on a retainer basis."

"Damn lawyer talk. I'll see if he wants to meet you."

The barkeep looked at Spur again, noting the clean tan shirt, and leather vest. He shrugged and whispered something to another man behind the bar who left at once.

As he waited, McCoy watched the women. The

dance hall "girls" were always the first females to brave the primitive conditions and come to a mining camp, or a railhead town or a prairie settlement. They hurried in knowing they would be used and abused, and put their bodies up for sale. But they also soon found out that the first few women in any settlement were treated like the grandest ladies ever. They were the belles of the ball, queen for a year, the secret sweetheart and the girl back home for every male in the camp.

Men were so starved for women that most simply sat and watched them when they walked down the street. He had seen unshaven, uncouth, violent and outrageous miners and cowboys revert to stumbling and mumbling goons totally embarrassed when a dance hall girl sat down beside one of them in a bar.

Since there were so few women, most of the men did not have the slightest hope of even talking to one of the three or four in town, let alone touching her or wonder of wonders, taking her to bed. That shyness soon wore off, but still the women, any women in a mining camp, which grew to be a small town, remained ladies of stature to the first men in the place.

As families came, and wives joined husbands, the "good" women of the town launched a subtle and always successful campaign to establish the "upstanding" side of town and womenfolk, from the "easy women" and the "prostitutes" they collectively identified as "those terrible dance hall girls."

Virginia City with its churches and civic organizations and almost twenty thousand people had long since passed into the time when the dance hall girls had been put in their proper place.

The girls in the Golden Nugget came in several shapes and sizes, but all female, all willing and ready to sell you drinks, give you a kiss and jump into bed upstairs in the tiny rooms, if you had the going rate of one dollar, two dollars or three dollars depending on the number of girls in town and the number of men.

Someone stepped to the bar beside Spur and cleared his throat.

"You've been watching our ladies," a voice said with a touch of an eastern accent.

Spur turned saw a black haired man a head shorter than himself, with a slightly dusky complexion and the smell of garlic on his breath. The agent dropped into his Boston accent with ease.

"Yes, I am, a hobby of mine. Are you Mr. Giardello?"

"Yes. And you've got to be from Boston. You the lawyer fella?"

"That's right. Just got into town. Do you have a few minutes to talk?"

"All the time in the world, but I don't need to be paying you twenty dollars a month on retainer. That's the going rate. I don't have much trouble. If I need a lawyer I go see one."

"That makes it tough on young lawyers."

"True, but easier on saloon owners." He

51

motioned to one of the girls walking by. "I'll keep you in mind. Now, enjoy yourself. How about a free beer on the house and talk to June, here. She's one hell of a good time under the covers."

Giardello winked and walked away.

June moved up to the bar beside him, came closer than was needed and her breasts brushed his shirt.

"Have the free beer, Tony never gives nothing away," June said.

Spur grinned at the short girl. She had lots of breast, a thick waist and generous hips. But to the miners she was female and that was all that mattered. She nodded at him.

"Yeah, I know, what's a girl like me doing in a dump like this? You don't want to find out." She called the barkeep for the free beer, set it up for him and reached up and kissed his cheek. "Remember what Tony said. You interested later on, I'm a damn good fuck."

Spur reacted to the word and she laughed, then moved on. Spur sipped at the beer, watched Stella at a back table, then wandered out of the bar.

He evaluated Tony Giardello. The man might be capable of working as part of a huge conspiracy plot and robbery on the scale this was supposed to be. But Spur doubted that the man could plan it. The suspect he had to see was Rush Sommers, the owner of the Consolidated California Mine Company.

Spur went out the bat doors and at once stepped to one side away from the backlighting. He stood for a moment in the gloom of the unlighted boardwalk, remembering that there was at least one man in town interested in putting bullet holes in Spur McCoy's hide.

Then from the shadows came a voice, low but insistent.

"Spur McCoy, don't turn around. Just stand there. I need to talk to you. It's urgent. I'm not trying to hurt you. I have something of vital importance to tell you."

FIVE

SPUR McCOY SNAPPED around in a tenth of a
second, his .45 Colt six-gun out of its holster and
aimed at the shadows.

"Easy, pardner, take it easy. I got no gun on you.
I don't even own a gun."

"Come out of there slow, with both hands on
your shoulders. You have a gun in your hand and
you're one dead coyote."

"I'm coming out. See, no gun. Told you, I don't
own a shooting iron."

Spur watched the small man emerge from the
shadows. He was in his twenties, shorter than most
men, maybe five-five.

"See, no gun. Now please come back here out of
sight so I can deliver my message."

Spur eased his weapon back in leather. "You can
talk easy enough right there."

"Okay. I work in the Storey County Sheriff's
office as a clerk, and today we got a telegram from
back east. Sheriff read it and read it again, showed
it to one of his deputies and they talked about it for
ten minutes nonstop. Then he called me in and told
me to find you, but not to let anybody see me

talking to you. Sheriff wants to see you right away over at the courthouse.''

"How did you find me?''

"Not so hard. Talked to the desk clerk at your hotel, he give me a description, then I just walked around until I found you. Course I thought two other guys was you, but they said they wasn't.''

"Meaning if you can find me, almost anyone can. Let's go, where is the courthouse? I'll talk to the sheriff, but only outside and in the dark. How many deputies does the county have?''

"Twenty-seven.''

"Dandy,'' Spur said wondering how he would flush out one bad deputy from twenty-seven.

They walked three blocks, then half another one and turned in at the lower floor of a large building. They went down steps to the half basement where the sheriff's office was.

Spur stepped into the shadows outside the main entrance.

"Ask the sheriff to come out here. He should know why I'm asking him to do this.''

"I've never done that before,'' the small man said.

"Live a little. Try it. Tell him I said it's the only way I'll talk with him.''

The clerk frowned but went into the sheriff's office. Less than a minute later a tall, slender man wearing two pearl handled six-guns slung so low he could never draw them, and a white high crowned Stetson came through the door and stopped.

"McCoy, you out here?''

"Thanks for the public announcement, Sheriff. If you want to talk come over here and lower your voice."

"Uh, yeah. Will was chattering something about you not wanting to come inside." He walked into the shadows, saw Spur and held out his hand.

"Evening. I'm Sheriff Clete Gilpin."

"You must know who I am. What I want to know is what that telegram said and who else knows about it?"

"Well, Mr. McCoy, it said you were a federal lawman and you had certain business in Virginia City, and my office was to render to you any and all assistance possible."

"That's all it says?"

"Yep, got it right here." He passed the yellow paper to Spur who walked to the edge of a window and read the message. It came from the "Justice Department" and was signed by Gen. William Halleck.

"Is it an authentic message?"

"Yep, Sheriff, it sure is. Now I want you to forget all about it. If I need any assistance, I'll get in touch with you. No mention of this is to be made to any more of your deputies than already know."

"Yes sir. One thing I'm good at is following orders."

"Not orders exactly, Sheriff. This is your county. I'm only making a suggestion. Of course if you don't follow my suggestion I stand a fifty-fifty chance of getting my head blown off. I simply wouldn't appreciate that."

"No sir, Mr. Mc . . . No sir. I can understand that. Yes, sir, I sure as shootin' can. So as to speak."

"Sheriff, who else knows about this message?"

"Only two of my deputies. Captain Wilson, and Sergeant Anders. Both top men."

"Fine, tell them what I told you. They are to tell no one I'm in town, and certainly not that I have any federal connection. Less than two hours ago somebody tried to blow my head off in the hotel. He got away before I saw him. I hope you'll take my cautions seriously."

"Yes sir. We will. We don't even know your name."

Spur took out a packet of stinker matches, tore off one and scratched it on the base of the stuck together bundle and when it flamed into life, burned the telegram.

"Thank you, Sheriff," Spur said and faded along the front of the building and out of sight.

As Spur walked back toward his hotel he decided the bushwhacking had been entirely separate from the robbery plot. It had come too fast. Therefore, the two quick shots had been from an old enemy, or someone who hated Spur from another day, another place. It was a bad luck for McCoy. But it could have nothing to do with the Virginia City train robbery.

There was little he could do to protect himself from the unknown foe. But he would do what he could. He registered at the International Hotel, the most elaborate in town, an imposing five story brick building that was said to have the best food between Denver and San Francisco. Spur used the name Greg Scott. He paid for a room for three nights and the clerk never looked at him twice.

In the barren room he stared down at the two main streets he could see from the third floor front window. He did not worry about the assassin on the prowl. Spur had lived with this kind of danger every day since his first year of duty when a crazed woman came at him with a butcher knife because he had helped send her husband to prison for counterfeiting. The danger was always there, this time it was evident and deadly so he would take special care, but he would also get on with the assignment.

As Spur lay on the lumpy mattress he thought back over his life and was surprised that he was now in Virginia City trying to prevent the looting of a gold train of an estimated thirty million dollars.

In his undergraduate days in Harvard he had no fantasies that would match the adventures he had experienced in the last few years.

He had graduated from Harvard in fifty-eight, with warnings from one of his professors that the nation was tearing itself apart over the slavery issue, and eventually brother would battle brother over it as the North and South fought a great war. Spur had scoffed at the strange and unconventional ideas, and hurried back to New York City where he worked for two years in his father's import and retail firms.

When the war broke out in 1861, Spur applied for a commission in the Infantry and was accepted at once as a second lieutenant. He fought for two years in some of the bloodiest battles of the war, was slightly wounded only once, and then was sent to Washington on special duty.

He had been requested by Senator Arthur B. Walton of New York, a long time family friend. Spur McCoy became an assistant to the senator.

In 1865 soon after the enabling legislation was passed by Congress, Charles Spur McCoy was appointed as one of the first U.S. Secret Service Agents. Since the Secret Service was the only federal law enforcement agency at that time, it handled a wide range of law-breaking problems, most of them far removed from its first task of preventing currency counterfeiting.

Spur remained in Washington for six months, then transferred to head the new office in St. Louis, which would handle all complaints west of the Mississippi. He was chosen from ten applicants for the job because he could ride a horse better than the others and he had won the service marksmanship contest. His superiors figured both talents would be needed in the Wild West.

In the Golden Nugget saloon, business had tapered off. Four of the girls were upstairs flat on their backs humping up a storm with paying customers. A drunk slept on the end of the bar. Tony Giardello, the displaced easterner who owned the establishment, motioned for his barkeep to throw the soused man into the street. He waved at three of the girls not with customers and motioned them to the side of the bar and glared at them. One of the three was Stella.

59

"Ladies, I got me a bad feeling. Tonight some jasper came in here and tried to get me to take him on as my lawyer. Ain't never been anybody try to do that in my five years in Virginia City. Gives me a bad feeling like I said. Then I got thinking about this laywer-guy and I remember seeing him in here before. He's big, couple inches over six feet with sandy reddish brown hair, mutton chops and a full moustache. Any you girls remember him?"

One of the women nodded. She was Katie. "Yeah, I saw him. He asked me if I was Stella."

Tony turned to Stella. She shrugged.

"Can I help it if one man tells another about how good I swish my little ass around upstairs? He was looking for a good time. That still is part of our job around this place, ain't it, Tony?"

Giardello growled in reply. "Yeah. Sure as hell is. But it wasn't your ass he came to see, it was your big tits." He scowled at her. "I still don't like it. Got the idea he was snooping. Just watch out for him. He come in here again, you tell me, pronto!"

The girls nodded. He caught two more who were not busy and talked with them.

Katie walked away with Stella.

"Didn't mean to get you in trouble, Stella. But he did ask me and then I saw you talking to him."

"Yeah, we spoke, business. He was short of cash. Said he'd be back, but I guess he stopped in somewhere else."

"Don't let Tony ride herd on you girl," Katie said.

Stella shrugged. "Don't worry about me. Tony Giardello ain't man enough to give me trouble."

Stella said it bravely, but when she turned away, smiling at a man with a bottle of whisky heading for a table, she shivered.

Tony talked with the rest of the girls when he found them not busy. Nobody knew anything else about the big lawyer man. Tony went out the alley door and walked to the courthouse. When no one was looking he ducked in the side door and went around to the Sheriff's office.

Sgt. Anders held down the duty desk tonight as Tony knew he would. They went into the deep shadows outside just in front of the office, looking out on the dark street.

"Heard you wanted to talk to me, Anders."

"Yep. We might have a problem."

"He about six-two with sandy brown hair?"

"True. Sheriff got in a special telegram about this bird, from Washington D.C."

"Thought he was off kilter somewhere."

"Telegram said his name was Spur McCoy and he's a federal lawman of some kind with 'certain business' in Virginia City. The sheriff's office is to render to him 'any and all assistance possible.' It was signed by somebody from the Justice Department, some general."

"Yeah, could be trouble. Then again, he could be here on any of a hundred other problems. The others know about this?"

"You was the only one I could find. You better tell Sommers and let him handle it."

"I see this McCoy again, I'll take care of him myself, permanently."

"No! Sommers said no killing until we get the

actual operation underway. We've been planning this for six months, we can't let the roof cave in on us now because we make a stupid killing. You better go up and tell Sommers. The sooner the better. I can't get away from here until morning."

Tony Giardello nodded, grudgingly. "Yeah, you're right. I'll get up to his big house right now. You know anything else this jasper from Washington might be sniffing around here about?"

"Nothing the sheriff's office is working on or knows anything about. Course, maybe they wouldn't tell us."

Somebody walked toward the sheriff's office. Sgt. Anders hurried back to his desk and Tony slid away in the darkness, headed for the big brick house at the end of the street with the large gold plated rooster that served as an expensive weathervane on the very peak of the three story mansion.

Damn, he hated telling Sommers bad news. But somebody had to. Ever since they started putting this together after an all night poker game, the project had excited Giardello. There was nothing like doing something illegal, just for the hell of it! And if a guy could grab off six or eight or ten million at the same time . . . !

Yeah, he'd wake up Sommers and tell him. He had a feeling the big man with the big mine was going to be mad as hell.

SIX

THE YOUNG BLACK man who answered the door at the Sommers' mansion up on the side of the hill in the "owners-managers" section of Virginia City, stared at Tony Giardello for several seconds through an iron grillwork, then he nodded. He asked for a name, then turned.

"I go tell Mistah Sommers you here. You wait right there."

Tony did not like to be told what to do by a black man, but there was nothing else he could do but wait.

A short time later the black youth hurried back to the door, unbolted it and nodded.

"Mistah Sommers say you should come right up. I'll show you the way." He locked the outside door, then walked ahead through a long corridor, up a flight of curving, open stairs and down another hallway to an ornate door.

The young man knocked, unlatched the door and motioned for Tony to go into the room.

Past the door, Tony found himself in an ornate bedroom. It was more of a den than bedroom. A moose head glared at him from the far wall, a bighorn sheepshead stared glassy-eyed straight ahead. On the wall across from the door sat a four poster bed. The posts were carved figures of naked girls, but held up no canopy.

"Hey, sorry, I can come back," Tony said.

Rush Sommers sat astride a naked girl, and another stood in front of him with her crotch covering his face. The man leaned back from the girl and glanced at his visitor.

"Giardello. Hear we got problems. Don't mind the girls, both are Chinese whores who can't speak or understand a word of English. But they are damn good when it comes to cunt and tits." He lunged ahead a dozen times and Giardello realized Sommers was having intercourse with the girl lying on her back underneath him.

"Well, what kind of problems we have?" Sommers said, not stopping his sexual encounter.

Sommers gave a shout and climaxed. At once he rolled away from the girl and sat on the side of the specially made large bed and gasped for breath.

Sommers was a big man, a little over six feet tall, with carrot-red hair, the residue of freckles on his face, arms and shoulders, and a body that had expanded with his income until it now weighed a little over two hundred and sixty pounds. He mopped his face with a towel and stared at Tony.

"What's the matter, you never seen a man fuck a Chinese whore before?"

The saloon keeper laughed. "Afraid not, but it looks interesting."

"You can have them both for the rest of the night right after we settle our business."

Giardello sobered. "Got word from Sgt. Anders

down at the sheriff's office that the Federal government has sent a man into town. The Justice Department telegraphed the sheriff to give this guy all the cooperation he asks for. Guy's name is Spur McCoy. And Anders said the guy was mad as hell that the telegram came at all. He wants it all kept hush hush."

"McCoy?" Sommers said in surprise. "Yeah, I've heard of him. A mean, talented sonofabitch. He's with the U.S. Secret Service. I was in Denver once when he took on three guys. Damn good with that six-gun and a rifle. Question is, is he here about our little play, or is it some other Federal problem?"

"I can't help there. Anders said the telegram didn't say why this McCoy was in town."

"So find out."

"How, walk up to him and ask him? I'd rather see him have an accident in one of the back alleys."

"No. Too damn risky now that we're so close. The day we take over that train we can blast anybody we want to, but not until then."

"We, hell! You'll be sitting in your office talking with the sheriff about some problem at the mine, or another public welfare project so you can establish an ironclad alibi. The rest of us will be taking all the risks."

"My money is financing the whole thing, Giardello. You want out you just say so and we'll replace you."

"Hell no! I'm just worried about this McCoy."

Sommers stood, his naked belly folding over his waist in a huge bulge. He motioned to Tony.

"Come on, try out some good pussy, born in China. Haven't been inside this country more than a month. Just as wild as hell. You ever fuck Chinese style?"

"Our business done?"

"Damn near. You find out what McCoy is here for. If it's us, we'll decide what to do about him." Sommers motioned to the two naked Chinese girls who had been sitting on the bed. They giggled, hurried to Tony and pulled him down on the bed, then began undressing him. One lowered a small round breast into his mouth and he mumbled something as he began chewing on the morsel.

"You don't mind if I watch, do you?" He went on without waiting for or expecting a reply. "Then too I want to talk over a couple of details with you. We're down to the last week the way it looks. The actual day of the shipment is never known until the last day. Somebody in San Francisco decides and sends a coded message. The same kind of coded telegrams have been coming for three days now.

"We get the word about eight o'clock in the morning, and by midnight of that same day, the bullion has to be all loaded from the vaults of each individual mine, put on the train on the siding and the guards all set in place.

"I'll know about the timing, since we have a small shipment of silver going out on the train." Sommers was sitting on the edge of the big bed. He slapped his thigh. "Damn! Stealing my own silver. How about that!"

Giardello was naked by this time. The sight of the two nude Chinese girls had given him a solid hardon, and one of the girls played with it. The stroking made Tony quiver with anticipation.

"What about the damn army?" Giardello asked. "They going to have a bunch of armed troopers on the train this time?"

"Ten armed soldiers have been riding each train in and out of Virginia City for a week. It will be the same on the real run."

"Ten, that's not so bad," Tony said. "We can handle that many."

"Do it easy if you use those special dynamite bombs we made," Sommers said.

Tony had made the bombs himself. He had learned the trick back east from a friend of his who turned to bank robbing. It was the simplest kind of bomb. Take three sticks of dynamite and tape them together. Then tape on the outside of the dynamite two hundred four-penny nails. When the dynamite goes off, the nails are blasted outward like grapeshot, tearing a man in half if he's up close to it. He'd seen men killed up to a city block away by flying nails from that kind of a bomb. They would use the dynamite shrapnel bombs on the soldiers and anyone else who tried to stop them.

The bombs all had fifteen second fuses, so they had to be careful that they got fuse that burned at a foot a minute. Anything faster and a bomb might go off before it could be thrown.

Tony stared in delight as the two girls played with him. One was lying on top of him, and the other lowering her delightful little bottom over his face.

"How do we know we can get our engineer on this run?" Giardello asked.

"Easy. I find out when the train goes early in the morning. I tell him and we knock the other engineer in the head, or get him drunk or take him on a long ride in the desert. Pritchard has a reputation for wanting to work all the time. He'll accidentally be down at the station house when they discover they need an engineer."

"And he stops it right where we tell him to?"

"He will. He wants the money. I gave him two hundred dollars last week just to keep him interested." Sommers laughed.

"He still thinks he's getting a half million?"

"Indeed he does."

"And I'm the man who takes charge of the bullion and gets it remelted and cast and stamped and sold in some other part of the country."

"That's your job. And you know the first ten million comes to me to get my Consolidated back in operational condition."

"And I get the next ten million, and we split the rest," Giardello said. He looked down and moaned. "Oh, damn! Not yet!" One of the girls had his erection jammed in her mouth and was sucking and pumping up and down on it. She had two fingers pushed as far up his rectum as possible searching for his prostate trigger. The other girl spread her legs and lowered her pink nether lips within an inch of his face, and his tongue reached out just as she lowered more.

Sommers sat there with his big fist gripped

tightly around his penis as he slowly masturbated.

"Welcome to the two for one club, Giardello. Doctor said my heart will probably give out one of these nights when I have these two and a cute little black girl in my bed all at once, and all bare assed and bare tit naked, but damn . . . what a great way to go out!"

Tony Giardello worked over his own fancy ladies whenever he had the urge, but he could not remember such an uninhibited display of sexual pleasures as the two Orientals gave him. He couldn't concentrate on what Sommers was saying for a few minutes as he achieved one climax and then another almost on top of it. He could never remember such intensity, such a release, and as he lay on the bed totally exhausted, the small, slender Chinese girls rolled him over on his stomach and gave him a relaxing massage.

Tony woke with a start.

The two girls were gone.

Rush Sommers sat in a big chair, a whisky bottle in one hand and a huge piece of chocolate cake in the other.

"Woke up at last," the rich mine owner said. "Thought my girls might have given you a fatal fuck, but I think you'll make it."

Giardello shook his head and sat up. He blinked and yawned and then pointed at the whisky bottle. Sommers passed it over and the saloon owner took a long drag.

"Now, you should be ready to talk business. Have you seen this McCoy guy?"

"Fact is he came into my place wanting me to hire him as a lawyer. Don't know why he picked me, unless he is trying all the saloon owners. I'll find out tomorrow."

"That don't matter. Get in touch with him and hire him. Tell him you have somebody suing you for something . . . maybe he got shot in a shoot-out in your place. He was an innocent bystander. Tell McCoy any kind of story. Then start finding out about him. He might slip up and say the wrong thing."

"Yeah, he might. I'll try it." He shook his head. "Damn but them little Chinese girls are great! Like to get a couple for my place. Who cares if they can speak English or not when they fuck good?"

"Expensive. You have to buy them from some old Chinaman in San Francisco. He steals them in China and brings them over."

"Maybe. I'm still not sure just how the last part of this stickup is going to work. We get the train stopped and unload the gold and silver. Then what do we do with it until I start melting it down and selling it?"

"You let me worry about that, Giardello."

"You've been saying that. But I think I am entitled to know. I'm putting a lot into this, it's a big gamble. And remember I can lose twice, both here and back in New Jersey."

Sommers had not dressed. He took the whisky bottle back and washed down a big chunk of chocolate cake with chocolate frosting.

"All right, Giardello. I'll tell you. We stop the train less than three miles outside of town. We have twenty pack mules out there and five drivers, and we load that gold on the pack mules as much as they can each carry, and we bring it all back here to Consolidated's vault at the mine. That will be about two a.m. to five a.m. with nobody awake to see it. We make as many trips as needed. Who would think to look for stolen gold in the vault of one of the men stolen from?"

Giardello looked shocked at first, then a smile slipped around his face and he guffawed in delight.

"Yes! Perfect. Sommers, you are a goddamned genius. Not even I could think up that kind of hoodwinker. That's great!"

"Glad you like it."

Giardello stretched, rubbed his genitals. "Where the hell are them little slant-eyed whores? I'm ready for another go-round with them. You did say all night, didn't you, Sommers?"

The big man laughed whistled through his teeth and the two girls burst into the room, both wearing white nightgowns.

Sommers pointed to the two girls, then to Giardello, and at the door.

"Try a new bed this time. In the next room. They are yours until tomorrow noon if you think you can hold out that long."

"All of this and fifteen million dollars," Giardello said. "I think I can hold out for both!"

The girls had slid out of their loose nightshirts and pulled Tony toward the next room.

As soon as they left, a Mexican girl came into the room and changed the sheets on the bed. She was young and slender with big breasts. She opened the buttons of her blouse letting her big, brown, black tipped breasts surge out.

Sommers patted her bottom, shook his head and fell on the bed. A man needed a little sleep.

He thought about Giardello. The man could be useful. He would be in command on the train, and of the transfer. But there was no chance that Tony was going to get his hands on half the gold and silver. No chance at all. He would be a witness. On this one there could be no witnesses. None whatsoever. That's why it had to be held to such a small group of participants. There would be fewer to kill. He smiled. With the thirty million from the gold and silver, he would be able to complete the deep tunnels on the Consolidated, and open up another fifty to one hundred million in high grade silver and gold ore.

Yes, this whole operation was looking better all the time.

But what about Spur McCoy? Was he in town to try to stop the great train robbery?

Rush Sommers thought about it for half an hour. He was not a stupid man. He had taken a mining degree in the east before he moved west. His father had been a small manufacturer who had never made—nor lost—the fortunes that his son had. The present was simply a low point in his career. He would rise again, and damn soon!

The more he thought about Spur McCoy, the more he decided that he must check the man out. He must be certain within two days one way or the other.

There was a private detective in Virginia City he

had used before. The man was reliable, close mouthed and could be silenced if the need came up.

Sommers sighed and settled down in his huge bed and blew out the kerosene lamp.

Yes, if Spur McCoy was in town to stop the train robbery, then Spur McCoy would be quietly and unobtrusively killed and buried, leaving no trace that he had never been in Virginia City!

SEVEN

McCOY HAD BEEN up since dawn. He walked around the southern part of Virginia City were the Virginia and Truckee railroad came into the Julia mine. Somewhere along here was the point they would load the gold and silver bullion on board the special train to take it on the first leg of its rail trip to San Francisco.

Great heaps of tailings showed in back of the Julia mine buildings. Smoke trailed from four smaller stacks on the right side of the three story building. The Cholla Potosi works stood behind him, up the hill a long New York city block. Another six blocks up the hill right at the face of the mountain stood the Fulton Foundry.

Down near the tracks there were only a few scattered, one story houses. A half block up the street from the Julia mine stood a three floor boarding house. Security around here would not be hard, and he was sure the mine guards and the sheriff had planned how the gold and silver bars would be loaded. Most of the raw metal would be in standard ten pound bars.

He watched the men coming to work in the mines. The temperature on the surface was around sixty degrees this brisk October morning. The elevation of 6,025 feet put an added nip in the air. But Spur knew that the deeper the men went into the ground, the hotter it would become. Soon they would be in steaming tunnels and drifts where the temperature would reach as high as a hundred and eight degrees. Most of the men threw off their clothes and worked in the briefest of loincloths.

Many could labor at the tunnel face only fifteen minutes before they staggered out to pipes of fresh air and barrels of ice water and to douse their heads in cold running water.

Spur wondered why men put themselves through such torture, but he knew why: to make a wage that was barely livable.

An hour later he had breakfast. He then walked to the Little Gold Hill Mine, the first major discovery made in the area back in 1859. He asked to see the president of the company and was shunted to a vice president who quickly told Spur that they had three lawyers in town and two firms in San Francisco that took care of their legal needs.

Spur thanked him and left.

A half hour later he sat in the office of the president of the Crown Point Mine. The man said the site had been worked out and they were in the process of refinancing so they could do some more exploration at deeper levels. They really had no use for a lawyer.

Spur left at once. He did not care what each of the owners said, he was simply setting up a pattern so he could call on his main target for the morning, Rush Sommers out at the Consolidated California

Mine. He knew the mine had been worked out once, but then new money had driven shafts and drifts down into the sixteen-fifty foot level where a huge pocket of ore had been opened last year.

When he gave his name to the young man in the outer office, he was ushered in at once to an ornate room that looked more living room than business center: thick rugs on the floor, fine, overstuffed furniture, oil paintings on the wall, and fine china set for a midday dinner at one side.

"Mr. Sommers?" Spur said, holding out his hand.

The large man rose slowly from his chair and nodded. "Yes, and you must be this Spur McCoy I've been hearing about trying to find himself a job here in town. Enough people going bankrupt that there should be lots of business for a lawyer."

"The fact is, Mr. Sommers, I'm not having much luck. Since your company seems to be in the middle of a big vein, I thought you might want to tidy up any of the business items that have been overlooked in the rush to produce."

"Alstairs and Johnson, best law firm in town, handles all of our work. They are right on top of everything." Sommers said it as he quickly evaluated the big man facing him. He was disgustingly slender, and muscled. His eyes were hard and he wore a six-gun on his thigh.

"I've never seen a lawyer with a gun tied so low before. Why is that, Mr. McCoy?"

"Old habit. Put some time in as a sheriff in a little town as I read for the law. Just kind of feels comfortable there."

"Yes, I imagine it would. I've always admired men who weren't afraid to wear a gun like that. Kind of an open challenge for any fast gun to call you out and draw down."

"Not sure about other men, but I never have that kind of problem."

"Mmmmmm. Never can tell when we might need a new hand on our legal work. From a general standpoint, just where do you stand on the principal of lateral support when applied underground?"

Spur chuckled. "You trying to trap me, Mr. Sommers? Plain to see that there isn't any need for lateral support underground. Say your claim is following a vein and works in an area that is vertically under the claim stakes of another mine. You are legally correct in following your claim into any section, as long as it is contiguous. This is true even though you have penetrated under the claim of someone else. Your claim, your ore no matter where it wanders.

"However, the problem comes in your failure to shore up under the large room or cavern or pocket of ore, say forty to fifty feet tall, and the surface claimant sustains a loss when his tunnels above your working area cave into your digs."

Sommers nodded.

"Just checking. Surprised how many people claim they are one thing these days, when they don't know their ass from a mineshaft."

"That's always been a big problem in my profession, Mr. Sommers. Men claiming to be lawyers who don't know a tort from a brief. One of these days we'll have rigid standards of education and special tests to pass and a whole system of ethics set up controlling the legal profession.''

Sommers stood. "It's been interesting talking to you, Mr. McCoy. Perhaps we'll meet again. This is a small town.''

Spur thanked him for a time, and walked out of the office. He had absolutely neutral feelings about Rush Sommers. The man was fifty, maybe fifty-five. He seemed to know what he was doing, ran a big and successful mine. Why would a man like him even think about stealing thirty million worth of gold and silver?

Outside Spur changed his mind. Nobody needed a reason to steal thirty million dollars. The money itself was the reason.

He continued down the street, then up several more until he came to the Belcher Mine. Inside a friendly face grinned at him.

"About time you got here. What's the idea of job hunting at half the mines in town before you come here? I told you to see me this morning." The speaker was Tracy Belcher, her smile an ore car wide and her arm soon linked through his as she steered him toward an adjoining room.

She ignored the others in the large outer office next to the mine, closed the door and poured whisky mixed with branch water without asking him and gave him one.

"Here's to friendship," she said. "May it grow stronger and stronger each day."

Spur lifted his glass and drank. It was good whisky.

78

"Now what's this about your looking for work?"

"Looking over the field."

"Stop looking, you're hired. We paid our last lawyer two hundred a month, is that enough?"

"Plenty, but I can't go to work for a week."

"Fine, no rush." She took another long pull at the stiff drink and laughed. "I have one rule, no hanky-panky in the office. At home, in a restaurant, hell, out in the desert, but not in the office. Not after you're working here." She went to the door and silently slid a bolt into place, then began unbuttoning her dress top as she walked toward Spur.

"You've been staring at my titties. Want to see them all uncovered?" She said the words softly and stopped in front of him and opened her dress and lifted the white silk chemise. Her pink-white half orbs jiggled invitingly. Large reddish areolas circled brown nipples that seemed to quiver with excitement.

Spur didn't move.

She pushed hard against Spur's chest and reached up to kiss him, pulling his head down with one hand. The long, hot kiss caused her to growl deep in her throat.

"Go ahead, Spur. You can play with my titties. They won't break. They do like to get kissed, too."

Spur bent and kissed each thoroughly, biting the pulsating nipples. When he straightened her eyes were closed. He kissed her nose and her lids flew open.

"First some business. What do you know about Rush Sommers?"

"He's a sonofabitch I wouldn't trust from one of my tits to the other. He's a grasping bastard who kills more men in his mines than the rest of the owners combined. He's out for the most money he can make in the fewest years. He's not one of my favorite slobs. I stay away from him whenever possible."

"If he had a chance to cheat or to steal a few million dollars, would he do it?"

"Damn right. That bastard would steal his grandmother's fase teeth if he could make a dollar doing it!"

She rubbed her breasts with one hand, her eyes glittered. "We through with business yet?"

Spur grinned. "You're japing me about this, right?"

"I'm serious. I want you right here, right now, without taking our clothes off. Right down on the fucking rug!"

She lay down on the carpet, spread her legs, and then hoisted her skirt up and pulled down knee length drawers kicking them off one leg. He saw a V of black hair at her crotch and a flash of pink, wet flesh.

"Fucker! Get your big cock down here and push it into me," she whispered.

Spur shook his head in amazement, knelt between her spread knees and opened his fly.

"Faster! I want you inside me right now!"

Spur pulled out his hot pole and bent down. Her hand caught his penis and guided it, pulling him forward and lunging up at him, then she purred contentedly as Spur felt his tool slide inside her. At once she began gripping him with her vaginal muscles and relaxing until it set Spur on fire and he began pumping hard and fast. She grinned.

"Damn, the old pussy lips still got the technique! I knew I could get you so hot you'd pop in about twenty seconds!"

She began pounding upward at him now and in less than a minute they both climaxed in a gushing of hot breath as they tried to hold the sound down.

Tracy grinned at him, squeezed a tear out and brushed it away. When they stopped humping Spur lifted off her and she sat up and dressed again quickly, brushed back her hair while Spur buttoned up. She led him to the door, unbolted it softly and stared at him seriously as she opened the barrier into the outer office.

"That's a good suggestion, Mr. McCoy. You bring the whole thing written out to my house tonight, and I'll have my other lawyers look it over. I can't promise you anything. Fair enough?"

Spur wanted to laugh but he couldn't. A thin line of sweat beaded her forehead.

He said that would be fine. He would be there at eight o'clock as they had agreed. She winked at him and he went out the door and into the street laughing softly to himself. That was the quickest lovemaking he could remember! She had been so ready, so needing that she barely had time to get the door closed. Tonight. He would go to her place tonight and see what else he could learn about Rush Sommers. Stella had said he was the man behind the conspiracy, and Spur believed the tip more and more. Tracy's confirmation of his basic character counted a lot. Spur guessed that the lady had at some time been spurned by the big miner. But that was none of Spur's affair. He turned to other matters.

He had his eyes down thinking about his next move and failed to see the buggy charging straight at him as he started across the street. Had he been watching there would have been no problem. Now he had to dive to the left into the dirt of the street to avoid the deadly horse hooves as they pounded into the ground where Spur had stood only seconds before.

With fury in his eyes Spur jumped up.

EIGHT

SPUR McCOY JUMPED out of the dirt and did not bother to dust himself off. Instead he raced after the buggy and horse that had almost killed him. There was a lot of traffic that morning on the narrow D Street and the buggy had to slow down. Spur charged up to it and grabbed the side of the rig to swing inside as it kept moving.

The driver, a gray haired man with a full beard and derby hat, saw the figure lunging into the small buggy, and he jumped out the far side, giving the horse free rein.

The horse, surprised and startled by the unusual happenings behind her, lunged ahead, dodged an oncoming freight wagon and smashed the side of the buggy on the corner post of a small restaurant. The jolt stopped the buggy so suddenly that the horse was thrown to her knees. She scrambled up, screaming in sudden pain.

Spur had left the buggy almost as soon as the old man had, and darted after the surprisingly elusive figure. The man obviously was not as old as he appeared.

The driver ran into the Ho Fat Chinese laundry. Spur dashed in behind him. The man had vanished. A short, rough lumber counter in front of the store barred the way. An old Chinese man with a stringy beard, eyeglasses and the ever-present braid down his back sat on a stool behind the counter smoking a water pipe. He looked at Spur with glazed eyes.

Behind him were three rows of women scrubbing clothes on wooden and metal wash boards propped in round metal tubs. On the other side a row of women worked with sadirons. A pistol shot cracked in the narrow building. Women screamed and fell to the floor. Spur dropped behind the protection of the counter hoping it was substantially built. Another shot boomed in the confines of the laundry.

McCoy peered over the top of the counter and saw the man, now without the gray hair or gray beard, dash through the back door and into the alley.

By the time Spur got to the alley door, he could not spot the bushwhacker. The man was about the same size as the figure he had seen dropping off the roof when he had been shot at in the hotel. Who was this guy?

He watched the alley both ways. There were stacks of pasteboard boxes on each side. The back doors of small businesses lined the sides of the narrow track. Movement showed halfway down the alley to the right. Spur lifted his six-gun ready to fire, but a small boy came from behind a stack of crates with a foot square box and went down the other way.

From the other direction a door slammed, a man

came from a business and walked away from Spur.

"Just a minute!" Spur called and ran toward the man, who turned and fired, then rushed back into the building.

When Spur got to the door he saw it was a hardware store. He went through the door into the darkness beyond low in a crouch. When the door opened two shots blasted from inside, but both were over Spur's low bending form. Spur fired one shot at the flashes in the dark, then a door opened and someone darted through it.

The big Secret Service agent bumped into several things on his way to the door, and by the time he got to it and opened it, he saw he was in another back room, and a man was holding a six-gun to the head of a middle-aged woman.

The man was medium height with a receding hairline and glistening eyes, a little wild now.

"Throw down your gun, McCoy, or this woman gets her head blown off!" the man shrieked.

Spur lifted his six-gun and aimed it at the man who was hidden only partly by the bulk of the woman.

"No chance. You shoot her and you're both dead, because I can't miss at this range and you can't kill her and me too. Give it up. Why are you trying to kill me? Who the hell are you?"

The man's expression changed completely. He became cunning and sly, pulled the woman up so that she covered all his body and started to drag her toward the open door leading into the main part of the store.

"I know you, McCoy. You'll never let this

woman die. You're soft in the heart. Make you a deal. You stay inside and let me get out the front door, and I won't kill this old biddy."

Spur edged closer. He had a good look at the man. This eyebrows over blue eyes, a straight, almost sharp nose, small mouth with a firm chin, and ears that clung closely to his head. He was about fifty to fifty-five. He moved with the fluidity of a dancer. It puzzled Spur.

"No closer or she dies!" the man said. His voice came like a studied command, sharp, forceful. For a moment it seemed to McCoy that the bush-whacker was playing a part, giving a performance. Then he glanced behind him, and pulled the woman with him, giving Spur almost no chance for a killing shot. If he did get in a lucky head shot at this distance, it would still give the desperado time to kill the woman with a reflexive jerk of his trigger finger.

"I'll let you go outside," Spur said, moving forward himself whenever the gunman looked away. "When you get outside let her go, and defend yourself."

"Against you? I'd have no chance."

"So you'd rather shoot me in the back?"

"Given the chance, yes."

Then the man and woman were out the door. Spur sprinted through the kegs of nails, axes and shovels and other hardware items to the front door. The woman lay on the boardwalk, the man ran down the street dodging wagons and horses. Spur charged after him. A sudden runaway horse angled

86

across his path and McCoy was momentarily slowed. He caught sight of the bushwhacker cutting downhill and heading for one of the mines.

It was shift change time. Hundreds of miners milled around the entrance to the mine, waiting to get in the cage that would drop them down the shaft to their assigned tunnel and drift for the day's work. The men were all dressed much the same: round, shapeless hats, brown or black workshirts and pants of the same type. He looked sharply but could not see his target who was without hat, but was wearing a white shirt and vest under a blue coat.

He found the coat abandoned. Just as the second cage in the stack of three dropped down a level so more men could crowd into the cage above, Spur spotted the man looking out from a descending lift. Spur ran through the miners, got to the cage and spoke sharply to the man assigning workers to the various levels.

"That man with the vest who just got on the cage. What level did he go to?"

"He's dropping to eight hundred foot. Said he's doing some survey work for the owner. Don't matter to me. I just work for pay."

"Get me on the same level. The man's a killer. I'm a United States law officer."

The man nodded, pointed to the cage and promised him the same eight hundred foot level tunnel. Spur jumped on board the metal cage. It was really an open platform with a "V" shield of a roof over it to prevent rock fall on the passengers.

Each man had to hang on to cables that supported the floor to the bars across the top. Over that hung a metal frame to which was attached a newly developed woven wire flat cable eight inches wide and nearly a half inch thick.

Ten men crowded on the narrow platform, a bell sounded and the three cages dropped away into the inky blackness of the tunnel at the Consolidated California mine, just down the hill from the International Hotel.

The braided cable sang a sickening sound as it let the three cages go sliding down into the heart of the Washoe, into the fabulous Comstock Lode, into the guts of Mt. Davidson.

As they dropped down, and down, and down, Spur thought surely they were blasting straight into hell. The speed of the cages increased, and then seemed to level off as level after level flashed by, faster than the woods outside a train window.

Some of the levels showed only a flickering candle, some a dozen miner's lamps held by men moving off to work. Gradually the speed reduced and they could see more at each level, until the cages below them came to a stop at the eight hundred foot level tunnel. The cages under them emptied out into the tunnel, and at last Spur's cage lowered to the tunnel mouth and he moved off the platform with the others.

He had never been in a deep mine before. This hard rock mining was new and strange to him. The tunnel mouth was like a "main street" with several other tunnels branching off it. Some had rails on them where the large hand-pushed ore carts sat.

At once he looked for the bushwhacker, and saw him being ordered down the main tunnel with a crew of men carrying picks and shovels. Spur pushed past a burly foreman who swore at him, and hurried after the clot of men with his quarry at the lead.

The roof of the tunnel was nearly eight feet high. It was shored up with "square sets" of sturdy wooden timbers. These timbers, twelve to fourteen inches square, were built in rectangular frames four to six feet long, and six to seven feet high. They were square box frames with the top of one "box" forming the bottom of the next "box" that was built on top of it.

Such a framework with each timber fit snugly together with mortice and tendon joint was tremendously strong, and could hold up the ceiling of some of the largest "rooms" of ore extending sixty to eighty feet high.

Spur saw that at some points along the way the hollow cores of these square sets were filled with rubble and worthless rock, to make them even stronger.

Ahead he saw the bushwhacker turn into a side tunnel or "drift" as the miners called it. The rest of the workers continued ahead down the tunnel with the tracks toward what he guessed was the end of the tunnel where they would pick out the ore.

For the first time Spur realized the tunnel was getting hotter. He touched the walls and found them moist and warm. He unbuttoned his vest and then his shirt.

There was no light in this part of the tunnel, and

Spur had only a candle he had been given by a foreman at the start of the tunnel. Ahead he saw the wavering light of the other man's candle. If the thin, small light went out, the tunnel would be the blackest place that Spur could imagine.

He wiped sweat from his forehead. There was a good chance the other man could hide his light, or put it out and wait for Spur to walk up to him, making a perfect target with his own candle.

The Secret Service man shielded his candle from the front, and stared ahead until he was sure he saw another candle, then he continued.

He splashed through puddles of water, and at times small flows of water rippled near the tracks. He avoided them when he could. Ahead he noted that the light had ceased to waver, as if the man holding it had stopped walking. Spur held his candle behind a square set beam at the side of the tunnel and watched. The light moved. He figured the other man was no more than a hundred feet away. Here the tunnel was straight.

Then the light moved again, faster now, up and down as if the man were running. Spur tried to keep up. The tunnel curved and he lost the other light for a moment, then it came back.

Suddenly the other light was gone.

Had the bushwhacker fallen down and snuffed the candle?

Had he put it out and waited in a trap baited and ready for Spur?

The Secret Service agent moved ahead slowly, shielding the light, staying out of its glow, holding it as far from his body as he could.

After ten minutes of slow progress he found that the tunnel had reached a "room," a pocket of ore which had been worked out. It was over forty feet tall, and the square sets held up the "roof" rock. Somewhere in there the bushwhacker crouched waiting.

Spur squatted by the side of the tunnel just back from the pocket and studied what he could see of the square sets. Far to the back he spotted the glow of the candle.

A pistol roared less than ten feet away, and Spur felt the hot lead slug tear across his left arm, burn away part of his shirt and bloody a crease in his flesh.

He jolted backward, nearly lost the candle, and knew the man had set his candle far to the rear, and come back for a sure shot. If the desperado had been a better marksman, Spur knew he would be dead. The explosive sound of the shot in the enclosed tunnel echoed and re-echoed up and down the length of the tube. A few rocks fell from the sides of the room.

Spur quickly put his candle on a rock shelf on the edge of the tunnel and hurried in the darkness fifteen feet back down the cavern away from the light from his own candle.

He waited.

For several minutes there was no sound. Then Spur heard boots scraping along the rocks and rails. They went slowly at first. He sensed rather than knew that someone was running toward him. The gunman came into the light with his six-gun out and he fired twice at the candle, although it must have been obvious that no one was holding it.

Spur had drawn his Colt and aimed with precision as the man came to a stop near the candle in the glow of its one candle power. Just as Spur fired, the bushwhacker screamed and turned. The heavy slug hit the killer's gun hand, broke his thumb, nearly blasted off his smallest finger, and sent the small revolver spinning away in the darkness.

The bushwhacker screamed again and again and ran blindly down the tunnel, his own candle forgotten in the pocket, his hand bleeding, and paining him. He ran out of stark, uncontrollable terror. The walls had been closing in on him. As soon as he got on board the cage he knew he had made a mistake. But it was too late. When McCoy saw him in the cage even at the surface, he was sure he was deep in trouble.

Mark Wilkes Booth ran ahead, his hands out. The rock wall slammed against him, his arms scraped across rock and rough timbers and he fell to the rock floor again. He sat there panting. Booth trembled with fear and agony. Never had he been so frightened! It was a deadly, all-encompassing terror that shriveled his mind into a raisin and left him functioning on gut level reflexes.

Run! He had to run! His hand throbbed. He knew he had lost too much blood, but he lacked even a handkerchief to wrap up his thumb and finger.

He ran again, hit the wall as the tunnel turned. Then he felt ahead and found only rough rock. Wilkes stumbled on something and fell on the ground. He touched a pick and two shovels. He was at the end of the tunnel. There was nowhere to go.

Something made a noise in front of him. He wasn't sure what the noise was.

Something alive touched his foot, then moved away. A rat?

Mark Wilkes Booth shuddered. He heard the new sound, and this time it was clear—the agitated, unmistakable sound of a rattlesnake warning an enemy to stay away.

Booth looked behind him and saw the light moving toward him.

The shovel! He could slam it against McCoy's head, take his candle and walk back to the cage where he would demand to be taken to the surface!

Sweat streamed down his shirt. His trousers were half soaked with his perspiration. He started to reach down for the shovel, but something touched his shoe, then worked its way across it.

The rattler was on his shoe!

Booth screamed, a wailing cry of frustration and anger at the world for treating him so badly.

The chilling sound of a dozen rattlers chattered in the tunnel and all around him.

Booth screamed again and stepped to one side. His foot came down on a squirming, living animal. He jumped away and at the same time felt something hit his shoe. Another object hit his leg.

A cry of desperation, pain and agony shattered the quiet tunnel, as the rattler's fangs sank into his soft flesh, deposited their vemon in a fraction of a second and withdrew.

Booth leaned against the tunnel face. He felt

93

something slither over his hand and jumped back.

He knew he had been rattlesnake bitten. One wasn't so bad if he could get to the light and cut open the fang marks.

Before he could move, the second snake struck, then a third and a fourth set of fangs dug into his legs.

Mark Wilkes Booth screamed. His voice penetrated the farthest stretches of the tunnel, bouncing back and forth like a continuing cry of dread and anguish.

Spur McCoy moved up slowly. He was still fifty feet away when he heard the rattles of the snakes. The agent stopped and held the candle lower. A three foot rattlesnake slithered toward the light. He kicked the reptile back the way it had come before it could strike.

"For God's sake help me, McCoy!" The voice was deep yet laced with terror and agony. "Rattlers, McCoy! Don't know how they got in here. Must be hundreds of them! I've been bitten, need a doctor. Get me out of this nest, McCoy!"

"What's your name?"

"Booth, Mark Wilkes Booth. Yes, the infamous John was my brother."

"Booth? Then we've met before."

"Yes, in Virginia nine years ago. Now get me away from here!"

"You did help your brother that night at Ford Theatre in Washington, didn't you?"

"Yes! I helped him plan how to do it, got him to the balcony and helped him get away after he shot

Abraham Lincoln. Now get me the hell away from these damned snakes!"

"How many times have you been bitten?"

His voice came softer now, but intense. "I'm not sure. Ten or twelve times. Everytime I move. Help me, Spur!"

Spur checked the floor of the tunnel, found some splinters where an errant ore car had jumped the track and shattered a bracing timber. He lit a sliver, then a thicker piece of wood until he had a torch and held it low as he walked forward. There were only three or four snakes on the tracks. Spur chased them ahead of him with the fire.

". . . for God's sakes . . ." He heard another soft plea from the doomed man.

Spur knew that one or two bites from rattlers could be treated with success if done quickly enough. But a dozen bites, pouring that much venom into a man's blood stream made it almost impossible to save his life, even if a doctor was right there.

McCoy moved ahead slowly, deliberately, flushing the snakes in front of him with the fiercely burning torch.

"God, have mercy on my soul," Booth said softly in a clear, perfectly enunciated voice, the work of a consummate actor. "I have sinned. God in heaven I have sinned, have mercy on me, a sinner!"

The words stopped. In the glow from his torch, Spur saw the man a dozen feet ahead. He sat on the tunnel floor between the tracks. More than a hundred three and four foot, fully grown rattlesnakes crawled over him, sensing his body warmth. Everytime he moved another snake struck him in his side, his arm, his leg.

Slowly his head drooped forward. When Booth opened his eyes he saw the flashing, deadly black eyes of a rattler a foot in front of his face. In a lightning thrust the triangular head of the snake slashed forward, its fangs piercing Booth's cheek, gushing the deadly fluid into his mouth.

Booth shook the reptile free and screamed. A dozen snakes coiled and struck him again and again. He writhed on the tunnel floor in the semi-darkness of the flickering torch and each time he moved another group of rattlers struck.

He bellowed in anger and fear once more, then gave a long sigh as he died and the last breath whistled from his mouth.

Spur turned. John Wilkes Booth's brother! He hadn't thought about him for many years. He had died of shock more than the poison. The accomplished actor had been killed by the emotions he had lived by. Shock and fear and simply knowing that he was going to die had killed him. The rattlesnake poison would not have done its evil work for three or four more hours.

Spur McCoy kicked one slithering snake away, walked slowly back toward the big pocket room with its multiple square sets. He found Booth's candle and took it with him. A single candle like that set against a timber had been responsible for one of biggest and costliest mine fires in the Comstock.

The heat hit him again as he trudged out. He took

off his shirt and vest and carried them, grateful that he did not have to work in this hole in the ground. It had to be one of the worst jobs in the world.

He had to stay at the end of the tunnel for two hours before the cage was sent up with an injured miner. His legs had been broken by a rock fall. Spur held him on the floor of the platform as it rocketed to the surface almost as fast as he had ridden it down.

Eager hands helped the injured man at the surface.

Slowly Spur put on his shirt and trudged up the hill toward the International Hotel. He would go in the back door and take a bath. He snorted in continuing surprise. So Mark Booth had helped his brother, and four times he had fooled Spur. The man was an actor, he deserved the title. But somehow Spur was disappointed in the scene the master thespian had played when his private final curtain came down.

NINE

TWO HOURS AFTER Spur came up from the eight hundred foot level of the Consolidated California mine, he lay on his bed in the Continental Hotel catching his breath from his hot bath. He had pulled on underwear and pants and lay with his hands behind his head.

A key turned in his door lock and before he could grab his gun from the dresser, a woman stepped into the room. He had seen her before at the Golden Nugget. Spur had sat up when he heard the key turn, now he lay back down and put his hands behind his head.

"If I'd been a bushwhacker, Spur McCoy, you'd be dead by now."

Spur just looked at her. She was older than most of the girls at the Golden Nugget, perhaps the first lady, the company madam.

"You're not much of a gentleman, not even standing when a lady comes into a room. I'm Lottie."

"Yeah. You swing your tits around at the Golden Nugget. And I'm an impolite sonofabitch."

She laughed. "That ain't what Stella tells me."

"Stella who?"

"The Stella you were humping in the bathroom at the New Frontier Hotel a couple of days ago. On a blanket on the floor. No she didn't tell me. I followed her and saw you both go inside and I knew how Stella sounds when she's blowing her tits off with a good fuck."

"Why do you care one way or the other?"

"Business. I'm a working girl. I don't think you're who you're saying you are around town. You just don't look like no lawyer. Me, I got to think you're some kind of a lawman. I figure you don't want nobody to know that, so I'm offering you a business deal."

"How much?"

"Only a hundred dollars."

"It would take you fifty cowboys to earn that much cash even if you humped up a storm on each one."

"So?"

"So what's the business deal?"

"You give me a hundred dollars and I won't tell my boss Tony Giardello that you're a Federal Marshal."

"I never pay blackmailers, they keep wanting more."

"Not this time. As soon as your sneaky, secret work is done here, I won't have anything to sell. Until then it should be worth a hundred."

"Be cheaper for me to strangle you and throw you into the alley."

"But a lawman wouldn't do that. And if you aren't a lawman, you wouldn't have any reason for killing me. So you won't." She unbuttoned her dress and flipped back both sides. Her breasts were brown tipped with small buds of nipples on softly brown aerolas. "Just to show you I ain't mad at nobody, I'll throw in an afternoon in bed to sweeten the pot, so as to speak."

Spur laughed and took out his leather billfold. From a secret compartment he took out a hundred dollar bill and tore it in half. He gave Lottie the smaller piece.

"You keep your mouth shut about whatever you think you know about me, which probably isn't right, and I'll leave the other half of that bill in an envelope for you. If you talk to anybody, I'll find out and I'll cut off your hair and shave your head. You won't make a dime whoring for three months. Fair enough?"

She used both hands and lifted her breasts toward him. "Hell yes. Now, you want to chew on these?"

Spur shook his head. "I'm saving myself for my wife. You wouldn't want me to lose my virginity here in a hotel would you?"

Lottie frowned. "You joshing me? You're serious?" Her grin exploded into a laugh. "Hell, you are joshing. Not a chance you're still a virgin. Stella saw damn well to that if by some miracle you lasted this long. You're a joker." She tucked the half a hundred dollar bill between her breasts and fastened the buttons on the top of her dress.

"You got an agreement. No talk, and that other half of the bill. How long?"

"A week should do it. Can't tell for sure. You'll know. I'll leave the envelope with your barkeep sealed up safe and sound, if you keep your part of the bargain."

She turned, then walked to the bed, leaned down and kissed both his man breasts where he still lay on the bed.

"Damn, but you would have been fun. Anytime you want a free ride, you stop by. Anytime!"

Lottie grinned and went out the door.

Spur lay there a minute longer. His logic was shattered. He had been working out his next few moves with Rush Sommers.

He gave up, went downstairs and had an excellent dinner, then found out where Tracy Belcher lived and walked up the hill past the houses that got better and better until he came to the street that held only the mansions of the mine owners. They planned it that way.

He wasn't sure why he was coming up here, although he had said he would last night at dinner. He was curious, he decided. Spur was a half hour early when he rang the bell outside the four story frame house with its three towers, a walkway between two of them, and a colorful variety of shrubs, trees and flowers planted around the formal garden inside a white picket fence.

A smiling Washoe Indian girl answered the door.

"Mistah McCoy," she said. "You expected. This way, please."

Spur nodded at the girl. She was definitely Indian with her black eyes and long black hair. The unusual part was that she was scrubbed so clean she would squeak. Her face was clear, her skin smooth. Her eyes sparkled. The girl wore a simple cotton dress drawn snugly around her waist. Her only bow to her heritage was a pair of white, doeskin moccasins.

She walked ahead of him and wobbled her little buttocks more than was needed for locomotion. Spur appreciated the show. They went down a beautifully decorated hallway to another wing of the big house, through a door into a garden room with a roof that had been lifted off to give a large variety of flowering plants some sun and night time humidity.

Through another door they came to a sitting room, with a small, low table in the middle and six large floor pillows scattered around.

The Indian girl dropped on one of the big pillows.

"I'm supposed to wait here. The door right over there is where you are to go." She smiled. "Have a good time," she said. Then she drew a book from under the pillow and began to study it. He looked as he walked by. It was a McGuffey Reader.

He knocked on the door, then gripped the ornate, gold plated knob and turned it.

Inside the room he was dazzled. There were fifteen lamps of various sizes and shapes burning brightly around the big area. It was a bedroom, more than twenty feet square, with a large round bed with no headboard or footboard in the center of the room.

Deep, thick carpet covered the floor. The ceiling was paneled with the exception of a section directly over the bed which was covered with large panels of expensive mirrors without a flaw or a waver in them.

"Like it?" The voice came from Tracy Belcher, who stepped from behind a screen that blended in so well with the far wall that he had not noticed it. She was dressed in a low cut gown, wore a diamond tiara worth hundreds of thousands of dollars, and a huge cut diamond nestled on a silver chain lodged in the cleavage between her breasts.

The gown was glimmering sheer silk with a dozen petticoats under it. She snapped her fingers and two Indian boys about ten came and stood one on each side of her. Both were naked, their little genitals absolutely flaccid and hairless. Both stared straight ahead. She reached out and one boy took each hand and led her forward toward the bed.

An ornate, silk covered stool sat near the bed. She motioned to it.

"Sit down and relax. You're early, so you get to watch the preliminaries, the foreplay." She laughed. "How do you like my bedroom?"

Spur almost blurted that it was a whore's dream, a cathouse paradise, but he caught himself. "It is amazing. I've never seen anything like it."

"The fuck you haven't! I patterned it after the best whorehouse I ever saw in New Orleans. The place was magnificent. Cost twenty dollars just to get in the door for the food and musical entertainment. The whores themselves were all overnighters at fifty dollars each! Those were the days!"

"The big spenders."

The two naked boys had led her to the bed, six feet away from Spur where they stopped as she sat down. The boys took over, knowing exactly what to do. It was a ritual.

First they carefully removed the tiara and put it in a velvet lined case. They unfastened the big diamond from around her neck and put it in a box. They removed the diamond rings and gold and silver bracelets from her wrists and ankles. When the jewels had all been placed in cases, the boys stowed them inside a concealed safe in the wall. They came back to her, kissed her cheek, and she fondled their small genitals.

When they did not get an erection, she smiled, kissed the small limp cocks and nodded.

The boys began to undress her. Spur sat on the stool, still surprised at the ritual, but reluctant to interfere. The boys unhooked, unsnapped and unbuttoned the flowing sheer gown, and put it on a hanger, then removed layer after layer of clothing until at last Tracy showed a thin, see-through silk chemise that came to her waist.

Below that she wore the traditional women's drawers, which extended like short pants down to each knee. But these were made of the finest dyed silks available, in a rainbow of colors. The boys unbuttoned them and slid them down slowly, giving Spur a delightfully paced strip tease show. When the drawers were removed from her pudgy figure, the boys took off her chemise revealing at last her best feature, surging, swaying breasts, pink nippled and with overly large pink aerolas.

The boys put each article of clothing away as it

was removed. She stood up and each boy kissed her breasts, then the pinkness of her crotch.

Once that was done they both laughed and giggled and she shushed them, indicated they should bow to Spur. Then they ran like two normal boys out of the room, each clutching a silver dollar that she had given them.

Not a word had been spoken in the room for ten minutes. Spur was aware that he had a surging hardon. He grinned. Never had he seen such a buildup, such a tease. He started to stand when she shook her head.

"We're not through yet," she said. A moment later the Indian girl who had met him at the door came in through the same door the boys had left. She too was naked now, her small, firm breasts hardly bouncing at all as she walked. Her legs were slender and graceful, her belly flat and her skin the shade of burnished gold. Her hair had been combed and brushed until it formed a black rain showering down to her waist.

She ignored the woman, walked directly to Spur and took his hand, motioning for him to stand. She led him to the other side of the bed where she indicated he should sit down.

Slowly, she undressed him, starting with his boots, then his vest and his soft brown shirt. When his shirt was off she nuzzled his man breasts, biting tenderly his small nipples, then brushing her lips over his mouth and gently moved her breasts in turn for his kiss and easy nursing.

Just as he was getting interested in the soft golden flesh, she pulled away and unbuckled his belt. When she had his brown dressup pants unbuttoned down the fly, she motioned for him to stand. He did and she slid down his outer pants but left his briefs on. His hardon tented out the fabric of the white underwear and she looked at it and stifled a giggle.

Lastly she removed his stockings, then looked at her mistress.

"Excellent, Canchuna, you may have the honor," Tracy said. She watched Spur McCoy, knowing this would be as interesting as making love with the big man the rest of the night.

Canchuna, the Indian girl, moved directly in front of Spur. He still stood by the bed. Gently she began to lower his short underwear. As she did she rimmed his waist with short, hot kisses from her reddened lips.

Spur gasped once, and looked down at the young girl. He had no idea how old she was, but she surely had been given explicit training in how to please a man.

The underwear slid lower, and again the trail of kisses, both in front and in back. Spur sucked in a breath, and she pushed his shorts down in back and her mouth attacked his buttocks, peppering them with sharp insistent kisses, then her tongue traced a delicate pattern over his twitching mounds until she came seductively close to his anus. He wanted to pull her around to the front but he resisted.

Now the fabric was at his penis and she came back to the front and stretched it out. Each inch she moved it outward to pull it over his stiff penis, she kissed his tool. He moaned the first time and his hardon began to jerk and twitch.

Ten kisses later the cloth slipped off the end of his enlarged cock and it swung upward. She caught it neatly with her lips and sucked four inches of him inside her mouth, starting an automatic back and forth motion that left Spur gasping and grabbing her head to stop the motion.

"Excellent, Canchuna! Wonderful. I couldn't have done any better myself. You have earned the right to stay and watch."

Quickly Canchuna stepped on the bed, put her arms around Spur's neck and kissed him hard on the lips. Then she jumped down and brought out a stack of large pillows, and lay down on them, resting her chin on her hands as she stared at the bed.

Spur walked around the bed and sat beside the slightly chubby woman with big breasts.

"I thought that was the main performance of the evening," Spur said.

She petted his still turgid penis and shook her head.

"Big cock man, that was just the appetizer! You have no idea what kind of pure delights I have in store for you before the night is over. Yes, the five of us will have a marvelous time, but I get to be first. Come down here."

She lay back on the bed and he lay beside her.

"Do you mind if the girl watches?"

"Why should I mind?"

"Good." She rolled on top of him, crushing him into the featherbed. She looked at him from a few inches away, her big breasts pressed against his body.

"Hey, Spur McCoy. You really know what a good woman is like? You been messing around with cunts for so long you expect it the first time you see some fancy tits prancing down the street. I know how it is with you men. I bet you've never been married. I know what good loving is, and it ain't always sex and sweat and panting. Yeah, I like to get fucked hard and fast sometimes, but I also like to get kissed when I'm not even thinking of kicking off my clothes. That's the kind of loving I'm missing. Hell, I can get a cock pushed into my hole any damn time I want to. All I have to do is crook a finger and the richest and best looking men in town run up the hill."

"Like I did."

"At least you put me off a day. I like that. Showed me you wasn't hard up for pussy." She rolled off him and caught his penis. "Yeah and seeing you all cock hard now makes me want you again, all low down and dirty fucking! But I can wait a while too. I've got more than the naked bitch side to me. Some women don't, you know that. You've popped enough whores in your time. Scratch a whore and mostly you'll find not much else but a cunt and tits."

She looked at him. "It bother you that I talk dirty?"

Spur smiled and shook his head.

"I need to talk this way once in a while. Never did till I got married. My old man would tease me into talking dirty. Helped him to get his juices moving." She sighed and sat up. Tears flooded from her eyes and she took a soft cotton towel the Indian girl handed her. "Christ, you must think I'm a dumb bitch, bawling this way. But thinking about my first and true love does that to me sometimes."

She wiped her eyes, smiled at him and rubbed her hands over his bare chest.

"Enough of the damn lecture, let's get on with the fun!" She looked at Canchuna and motioned. "Come over here, little princess. Show us how you masturbate."

Spur moved over and the slender Indian girl nestled between them, making sure her hips touched each of them. She reached up and petted Tracy's breasts, then with her other hand grabbed Spur's still hard cock.

Canchuna moaned in delight. She held Spur, but her other hand came back to her V of black pubic hair. Slowly she began to rub her belly, then the soft dark hair and as she did her legs spread slowly apart. She lifted them onto the legs of the figures beside her.

Faster and faster her magic fingers worked, massaging around her crotch, then working up one leg and down the other. She gave a little cry of joy as her fingers brushed her soft pink nether lips.

Spur watched, fascinated.

"Oh, yes, feels wonderful!" Canchuna said. Her hand began stroking Spur's erect phallus. He moved but she didn't notice. Her eyes rolled upward in their sockets until only the whites showed, and her breathing picked up.

109

Her slender fingers brushed her soft lips again, then found the hard node above them and touched it once.

"Marvelous!" Canchuna shouted.

Her finger twanged the node again and she shuddered. Again and again she strummed her clit and at each movement she grew more and more active. Her hips moved up and down, then side to side. Her breathing surged higher and faster until she was nearly panting. Her grip on Spur eased as she concentrated on her other hand. Then she pulled her hand away and with a little scream, pushed two fingers into her wet, streaming vagina.

"Oh, yes!" she shouted. "Yes, yes, yes!" she said again, as she pumped her fingers into her in time to the words. Canchuna sat up then, her legs spread wide, her eyes glazed, her hands both busy at her crotch.

Spur reached toward her and Tracy nodded. He touched one of her small breasts, cupped it and she gave a moan of pleasure. Spur fondled the mound, then massaged it and rolled her tiny nipple between his thumb and finger.

Canchuna screeched and her whole body shook as if she were being rattled by a big dog. She vibrated and trembled as wave after wave of sexual climaxes rifled through her. The spasms trailed off after a dozen separate and hard sets. She looked up at Spur and bent over, laying her face against his chest, putting her crotch against his hips. One long sigh came, then she nestled down and went to sleep.

When Spur looked at Tracy she finished wiping tears from her eyes.

"Wasn't that beautiful! The little darling may seem a bit wanton and sexy, but she is a guaranteed, bonafide virgin. Ain't no man ever knelt between her silky little thighs. You're the first man she's ever done that in front of, first man who has ever touched her when she's doing it. And that's all you're gonna do, so don't get no ideas. Far as I can figure the little sweetheart is fourteen. She's just a baby, and no bastard of a man's cock is gonna hurt her. Not for another three years, at least. By then she'll be a real beauty, a woman with good tits and narrow hips and she'll set the men wild.

"But you can bet your balls she's gonna be married before she gets cocked! And she's gonna come high. Damn high. Got to be at least a mine owner. None of them fuckers who work underground. My Canchuna is something special."

Tracy sat up. "Come on. I want you to carry her to bed. Try not to wake her up."

Canchuna never woke fully. Her eyes came open once as Spur carried her and she put her arms around his neck and kissed his cheek, then a tender smile came over her face, and she nestled down against his bare chest and slept again.

Spur laid her in her bed and Tracy spread the sheet and light blanket over her. Tracy bent and kissed her forehead and they took the lamp out of the room and closed the door.

When they got back into Tracy's big bedroom,

the two naked ten year old boys bounced on the bed. They giggled and laughed, but when they saw the naked adults they stopped.

"Boys help me around the house. Orphaned by a gunfight two years ago. Their mother had just died of the pox, so I took them in. You want to bugger them? They don't mind."

"How do you know?"

"They told me," Tracy said.

Spur scowled and his voice tensed with scorn. "Great, they told you so. If they objected you might throw them out in the streets and they'd have to beg or steal. Why so protective of Canchuna and so stupid with the two boys?"

"Because I hate all men, why the hell do you suppose?" She scowled. "Hell, you're right. No more of that for the small ones. Only happened once."

"Once too often," Spur growled.

She gave a curt gesture and both boys ran out of the room.

"I might bugger you," Spur said softly.

"Not the first time you won't. I want it long, and slow and sweet, like we was married or something and you came home from a hard day in the mine office and I was all shy and waiting . . . and hoping."

"I could seduce you."

"Be gentle," she said. "It's my first time." She exploded with laughter. "Yeah, my thousand and first time."

They sat on the bed and Spur reached in slowly

and kissed her cheek, then her nose, and at last her mouth. When their lips parted she nodded.

"Oh, yes, slow and gentle. I think I'm going to like this. And no dirty talk. Can I pretend we've only been married a couple of months?"

Spur smiled. "This can be our wedding night, if you like, and we're both only eighteen. This is your very first time in bed with a man. I've tried it a few times, but I'm still learning. How does that sound?"

Tracy looked up and blinked back tears. She rubbed them away with the back of her hand.

"Mr. McCoy, you touch my breasts again and I'll have to slap you."

"Mrs. McCoy, you gave me permission when we got married, remember? Now, just relax. I promise not to hurt you, and I won't do anything you don't want me to do. All right?" He kissed her lips tenderly.

"All right, Mr. McCoy. I guess the waiting is over. Show me what it's like to make love."

It was the most marvelous night Spur McCoy could remember.

TEN

A LITTLE AFTER six the following morning, Spur McCoy walked into the telegraph office on D Street. Canchuna had given him the closest and most comfortable shave he had experienced in months, then fed him breakfast and bubbled with questions about everything he did and everywhere he had been. She was especially interested in New York, Chicago and Boston.

"I want to go there as soon as I can," she had told Spur.

Now the agent looked at the telegrapher bent over his key. The man was receiving and would not be aware anyone was even in the building until the dots and dashes ceased on his keys. Spur read the notices on the public bulletin board, and saw an advertisement by the telegraph company giving the new rates for telegrams from San Francisco to New York. The first ten words cost four dollars, and each addition word fifty cents.

"Yep. Help you, young feller?"

Spur laughed and looked over at the telegrapher. He was apparently in his seventies: balding with fringes of white hair, snapping green eyes, wire rimmed eyeglasses and a tight, thin mouth that looked as if it would brook no foolishness.

"Spur McCoy. Are there any messages for me?"

"Know your name. Yep. One. Came in this morning, early." The man handed Spur a white sealed envelope. Inside Spur found a terse, hand written message:

"Exact day to launch company to come to you via San Francisco. Keep us informed." It was signed Halleck, who was General Wilton D. Halleck, his boss in Washington and the second man in the agency.

The doubletalk meant that San Francisco would telegraph Spur with the exact date for the mines to start the gold and silver bars on their way in the specially protected train toward San Francisco.

Until then Spur knew he could do little. He had already pinpointed two of the conspirators, and perhaps a third in Tony Giardello. He had no idea who the spy-robber was inside the sheriff's office. So he would have to work around the sheriff right now. He had to know the day of the shipment as quickly as the sheriff did.

Spur wanted to investigate the engineers who worked the trains, but he found that most of them were freight trains hauling the ore from the mines directly to the stamping plants in the valley at Carson City, twenty-one miles downgrade. That meant there were dozens of engineers around since trains maneuvered along the one line track almost constantly. During peak mining times as many as forty-five trains a day raced down the steep inclines on the track to Carson City.

Somehow, out of fifty or sixty engineers, he had to find the exact one who was going to run the special train. He decided to ask the sheriff if a man had been assigned. It may already have been done.

Spur folded the notice, took it outside and stood at the edge of the boardwalk and burned the piece of paper with the telegraph message on it, dropped the ash into the street and ground it into dust in the still dew-damp dirt.

Half a block up the street he spotted the barber opening up and slid into the shop for an overdue haircut. The barber made small talk, pointed to three moustache cups on the shelf for use by local businessmen, but could not interest Spur in parting with a dollar for a cup with his name hand painted on it.

Outside he sat in a chair leaned against the dry-goods store and watched Virginia City come alive. A wave of miners swept by toward the dank, hot holes in the ground. A few women ventured out to do some shopping. Children filtered past heading for the schoolhouse.

Down the street he saw a Negro woman come from one store, look into another and then walk rapidly toward him.

There were few blacks in the West. Texas had a great number, but few Negroes had wandered from the Southern states, especially into the far western states. The woman was slender, perhaps in her twenties, and Spur had trouble placing her in a category. Some western saloons advertised that they had Chinese and Negro whores, but this

116

woman did not seem to fit into that occupation. As she came closer he saw that she was nervous, frightened perhaps, but still he noticed that she was attractive. She kept looking behind her.

Five doors down from Spur she began to run forward. Spur saw three men burst out of a store and chase her. When she came up to him she glanced his way, then sighed and ran on past.

Spur moved from the chair in a swift, smooth surge and the big .45 Colt jumped into his hand covering the three men racing toward him.

"Hold it!" Spur roared in his best parade grounds army voice of command.

Two stopped at once. The third didn't notice him and continued another few steps before he saw McCoy and the gun pointed at him.

The closest man snarled.

"None of your affair, stranger. Put away the iron. I got no argument with you."

"But I have one with you. Why are you chasing the woman?"

"None of your fucking business!" the man screamed. He started to draw his gun.

Spur's .45 blasted one shot into the quiet morning air. The slug tore two holes in the bottom of the loudmouth's pantleg near his boot.

"I asked you a question," Spur said.

The other two men backed off, out of range, but stayed to watch.

"And I said none of your business. Now stand aside."

"You from Texas?" Spur asked.

"So what?"

"So leave the Negro girl alone. Lincoln freed the blacks, remember?"

"Damn shame he did."

"You turn around, drop that hogsleg on the ground and walk down to the corner, or the next round is going right through your kneecap. You hear good enough to understand that?"

"Yeah. And you better have your six-gun loose and ready next time we see each other." The gun landed in the dust, the Texan walked away.

Spur went back to the chair and leaned against the store. He kept his right hand free and the .45 available for a fast draw. But the three men did not return. A small boy picked up the Texan's six-gun and took it to its owner down the street.

The three men walked down a side street and Spur relaxed.

"Thank you," a voice said beside him. It had a slow and easy pace to the words, and the slightest trace of a southern accent. He caught a brief scent of perfume, then it was gone. He turned and saw the Negro girl standing beside him.

"Sir. I wanted to thank you. Those men have been bothering me since I got into town yesterday."

Spur stood and looked at the black girl who had rushed past before.

"Yes, miss."

"I really don't know how to thank you. I'm going to sing tonight in Miner's Hall, and I only stepped out of the International Hotel looking for some clothes to replace some I lost."

"Perhaps it would be better if I escorted you

back to the hotel, and tell the sheriff about your troubles. I'm sure he'll want to see that you have proper protection while you're in his town."

She smiled. Spur had noticed that she was lighter in color than many of the deep south Negroes, and now he realized that she was indeed an extremely pretty woman. Her figure was slender and she moved like a dancer as he walked beside her the three blocks to the hotel.

"I'm so thankful you were sitting there this morning. I'm afraid that wherever I go I find southern men who remember how they used to simply use Negro women, you know what I mean, whenever they pleased. Thank God for President Lincoln."

Spur nodded and opened the hotel door for her.

"I'm on the fifth floor. I like to be up high where I can get a long view. Would you see me to my door? I'll be extra careful after this. And I see no reason to trouble the sheriff."

They spoke little as they climbed the four sets of steps to the fifth floor. She stopped in front of room 505 and found her key. Spur took it and unlocked the door and gave the key back.

She watched him a moment. "I don't know . . ." she began. "Could I offer you a glass of wine as a thank you for rescuing me? It would have been just terrible if they caught me. I don't know if anyone would have raised a hand to help. They would have dragged me into an alley somewhere . . ."

"I'd be pleased to have some wine with you. My name is Spur McCoy."

She held out her hand like a man. "Hello, Spur

McCoy. I'm June Sue Lincoln. No kin to the President." They both laughed.

He shook her hand and walked into the room. It was much like his, but had a soft suitcase opened on the bed. A scattering of women's clothing was on top and a sheer nightgown of black lace laid out carefully.

She picked up a bottle of wine from the dresser and Spur noticed that it had already been opened. The beginnings of doubt filtered through this pleasant scene and bothered him. Was it too convenient for her to come past him on the sidewalk? Was it only happenstance that the "attackers" had been on hand and yelled at her? It could easily have been a set-up. But why?

June Sue went to the wash stand and found two glasses near the pitcher of water. But when she turned back, she aimed a small revolver at Spur and grimaced as she pulled the trigger.

His growing suspicion had kept Spur alert, and when June Sue turned to fire at him she shot at the place had had been when she saw him last. Spur had taken two quick, silent steps to the side. When he saw the gun, he jumped forward and swung his fist down hard against her wrist, knocking the six-gun to the floor before she could fire again.

The room rumbled with the sharp sound of the gun going off.

June Sue held her wrist, snarling at him in fury.

"You bastard! You almost broke my arm!"

"Fair enough, you tried to kill me. Why?"

The door to the small closet swung open and a

man with a sawed off 10-gauge shotgun leveled it at Spur.

"She don't have to say a word," the man said. "Drop your hardware on the bed careful like."

Spur had not seen the gunman before. He was black haired, with a drooping moustache, and a sun and wind burned face. An outdoorsman, not a miner.

The Secret Agent lifted his Colt from leather with his thumb and one finger and dropped the weapon on the bed.

"Tie him up," the gun wielder said.

The girl shook her head. "No, bad planning. How we going to get him downstairs and into the buggy if he's tied up without attracting a lot of attention? We take him down the back stairs, out the back door where the buggy is. When we get him out of town we tie him up, then I won't have any more trouble with him."

She put her hands on slender black hips and frowned. "Why the hell you hiding in my closet?"

"Because Mr . . . the boss man said to. Figured you might have problems with McCoy. Everyone else has."

She picked up her weapon from the floor, a make of .32 or .38 caliber pistol that Spur had not seen before. It was only about seven inches long overall. Deftly she took out the fired shell and put in a new round. She had five loads. She let the hammer down on the sixth empty chamber. She put on a jacket and stood next to Spur with the muzzle of the gun held against him. The way she draped the coat over her shoulder, no one could see the gun.

The shotgunner wore a pair of pistols on his hips. He put down the scattergun and took out a derringer. The hammer was cocked. He could fire the first barrel with minimum force on the trigger. The second trigger pull fired the second barrel on most derringers.

Spur knew this was the time to make his move, but he had few options. In the hall, as soon as they met someone, or maybe at the downstairs door, he had to try to break away. There had to be somebody around he could use to help escape from this pair.

The shotgunner was wearing a long black coat, the kind preachers sometimes wore, a style that many outlaws had adopted because they could conceal a shotgun or rifle so easily. This one did. The shotgun was under the coat and impossible to see.

The sunbrowned man walked on the other side of Spur and held his derringer against Spur's side.

"Don't even think about getting away, McCoy," the man said. "You make a fuss downstairs, and we blow your head off and run out the back door, free and clear. Don't think it won't work. Us two have done jobs like this together before. The only thing June Sue here is better at than being a gun for hire is in bed. She is fantastic at both. So don't make no dumb mistakes."

Spur heard them, but knew his chance was now. If he let them tie him up he was as good as dead from knife or bullet or just being thrown off a cliff. It had to be soon, damn soon!

They went out the door and Spur felt helpless. No one was in the hall. Down the first set of steps they met no one. On the second flight an elderly man and woman came up and Spur's shotgunner stepped forward ahead of Spur to let the old couple come up the steps. Spur kicked the kidnapper ahead of him, jamming his foot in his back and shoving the shotgunner, tumbling him down the steps.

In the same motion Spur spun swinging his fist hard as he turned. The blow caught the woman in the side, and she fell against the railing. Her pistol dropped to the steps and Spur rushed past her, up the steps moving ahead of the old couple. Neither of his attackers below could have a shot at Spur without hurting the elderly couple.

At the top of the steps Spur ran down the fifth floor hall. He darted in the first unlocked door that he found and locked in behind him. Then he checked the window. He as on the uphill side of the hotel, which meant it was only three stories from ground to fifth floor. A wide balcony extended from the fourth floor in back. It was only one floor down. Quickly Spur lifted the window, crawled out, hung by his fingers and then dropped the six feet to the balcony. He landed unhurt, and glanced up as June Sue looked out her window on the fifth.

As she tugged at the window, Spur climbed over the low railing, and wrapped his legs around the pole holding up the balcony, and slid to the porch below on the ground level.

He had just hit the floor and walked away when

he heard boots pounding the sidewalk coming up two levels from the front of the hotel. Spur ran into the store across the street, a drygoods establishment, and worked his way toward the back. There was no rear entrance to the store.

He went back near the front to watch the street. Before long, June Sue and the shotgunner were both at the back of the International Hotel talking. There was only one male customer in the store. He carried an old six-gun Spur wasn't sure could still fire. He ran to the man, said he was a lawman who needed help.

The man eyed him carefully, then nodded.

"Loan me your weapon and belt. Is it a .44?"

"Yep. Best pistol I ever had. Welcome to it. Name is Wellman. Bring it back here, you done with it."

Spur strapped on the gunbelt, and drew the weapon. It was old but had been well cared for.

As he watched, the shotgunner in his long coat went down the street, and June Sue came toward the drygoods store. Spur moved around to a section shielded from the rest by stacks of bolts of cloth and waited for the black woman. When she looked between the stacks of cloth she stared at the muzzle of his six-gun.

"Welcome, I've been waiting for you. Come in and show me both your hands."

She hesitated, then stepped forward. As she came within arm's distance, Spur slapped her hard on the side of the face. "That's for trying to kill me," Spur said.

She shrank back, but Spur held one of her hands.

"Where do you have the derringer hidden?"

"Suppose you find it."

"I will, and you make one sound and I'll strangle you right here. I still owe you!"

She tried to stop the concern from showing on her face but couldn't.

Spur checked her waist. She had on a one piece dress, and he felt no lumps around her waist big enough to be a weapon. He turned her around with one hand, keeping the pistol ready. He felt up from her waist to her breasts.

"Enjoying yourself?" she spat.

"No, just business. Her breasts were modest but had company. Between them he found a string and on the end of the string, taped to her right breast was the derringer. He opened the buttons on her dress, pulled out the weapon and cut the string, then let her button up the dress. No one had looked for cloth in that section.

"Now, where was that buggy you talked about? I want to have a talk with you where your buddy with the long black coat won't find us."

The rig was at the other side of the International Hotel. They walked to it without spotting her helper, got in and drove away.

Spur headed for the cemetery, down beyond the Consolidated California Mine and past the Ophir diggings. There were only a few houses beyond the Ophir and Spur drove down a track below the cemetery and tied the reins.

"Now, who hired you to kill me, and why?"

"Kill me, I won't tell you."

"I know a way. But first I need to check you for

weapons again, do a better job than I could in the store." He reached for her breasts, and she glared at him.

"If you're so excited that you want a quick fuck right here, just say so."

"I'm searching you, not getting sexy. Yes!" He found another lump, this time on her left breast. Opening her dress and pushing aside the chemise, he saw white tape that held a four inch knife against her breast.

"That's not a nice girl, June Sue. Not nice at all. And remember, when you make up your story about who you are supposed to be, get your facts straight. If you were in town to sing, it would be at Maguire's Opera House, not at the Union Hall." His hands now lowered, examining slowly up her legs under her skirt and she swore at him. But there he found nothing but firm, young flesh all the way to her crotch.

"Now, June Sue, hired gun and killer, who paid you to make me disappear in a grave out here in the Nevada wilderness?"

He turned to face her, looking past her back at town and the mine when he saw a puff of blue smoke from a clump of brush two hundred yards away. Almost at once something hit him in his back on the left side, spun him half around and almost out of the buggy. As he fell he heard the sharp crack of the rifle as the sound arrived after the bullet.

As he spun he dropped the borrowed pistol.

It was a frozen motion scene he saw taking place.

He fell and the six-gun clattered to the seat of the buggy. June Sue reached for it and Spur swung his right hand slapping at her arm. But she got the gun first and lifted it, her finger searching for the trigger. Spur hung on the side of the buggy, wondering why the rifleman had not fired again.

But he wouldn't have to. The black woman had the gun and lifted it, aiming it. He dove at her, his head hitting her breasts. She screamed in anger as his head hit her hands, throwing up the pistol as it fired over his head. Then both of them were in the air, tumbling, rolling out of the buggy, falling three feet to the dirt and rocks of the barren Nevada hillside. They landed behind the wagon and Spur's big frame pinned the black body to the ground.

For just a moment he wondered where the gun was. Then he remembered the derringer in his pocket. Both of his hands and arms still worked. But there was a roaring pain in his back, no, more like in his side. He could feel the blood wetting his shirt and pants now. He grabbed one of the girl's breasts and squeezed it until she looked at him.

"June Sue, I'd just as soon twist your tit right off, and I will unless you do exactly what I tell you. Is my message getting through to your brain?"

"You're a dead man, no matter what you do. Quint can drive nails with that rifle at this range."

Spur pushed the derringer under her chin, in the soft flesh between the bones and lifted it until she cried out in pain.

"I guess it will be more effective to blow your head off right here."

"No! No, I'm no good dead. What do you want me to do?"

"We're going to stand up in back of the buggy wheel."

"Won't work," she said. "That little house is a hundred yards away and Quint will cut you to pieces before you get there."

"But he won't shoot at you. You'll be along, June Sue. I wouldn't even think of leaving you here."

They stood slowly. She helped him. He kept the gun under her chin and grabbed her breast again as soon as they were behind the buggy wheel.

A rifle round whizzed past them and they heard the sound of the shot a moment later.

"A warning," she said.

"Let's call his bluff. We rush up to the house. I'll bend over so he can't see my head, but you stand tall so he can see you over the back of the nag. You stay tall or you lose one tit twisted off. Got it?"

She scowled at him, nodded without moving her head much so the derringer wouldn't hurt any more.

"Now!" Spur said and they took four steps and were behind the horse, their legs beside the gray's back legs. Spur bent over, but reached up and caught the reins.

"Next, we move," Spur said. He slapped the reins on the neck of the gray and said, "Giddiyap." The gray turned and stared at him a moment with one huge eye, then she stepped out at a walk.

They had gone ten yards when the rifleman put two rounds into the buggy's rear wheels.

"Trying to break the rig," he said.

Ten yards later the marksman changed his target.

Without warning the horse's head jolted toward Spur, the animal stopped walking, screamed with a voice so terrible and agonized that it could only be a death cry. The sound of the rifle shots echoed away into the hills. The gray shivered and slowly sank to her knees, then rolled away from them on her side and died.

Spur and the girl had jumped away from the horse. Instinctively the soldier in Spur looked for cover. He found a shallow water course, little more than two feet below the level of the gently sloping hill. He pulled the girl with him, and fell into the depression as a rifle bullet slammed through the air where they had stood.

Spur felt of his side. His hand came away wet with blood. He winced and she frowned.

"You hit bad?"

"It isn't good, but I don't know how bad. Sometimes a lot of blood . . . isn't all that bad."

"Sometimes," she said. The rifle spoke twice more, kicking dust and rocks on them.

"He doesn't care which one of us he kills," Spur said.

"That sonofabitch!"

"Who hired you?"

"That fucking Rush Sommers, big mine owner. He probably told Quint to use me to set you up, then kill both of us."

"Now you're thinking like a real bastard, the way Sommers thinks," Spur said. "You want to crawl down that way, the gully gets deeper. If your man Quint doesn't move for five minutes, we can get to the ravine and into the trees around the cemetery."

"I want to live. Let's go. Just so you don't twist my tits off."

Spur laughed. "Maybe later we can talk about that."

The girl winked and crawled away on her hands and knees, working downstream where the water course was deeper. Twenty yards down they climbed to their feet and ran bent over. Three minutes later they bolted from the edge of the ravine into the cemetery and a half dozen trees planted there ten years ago. They heard a shot but the slug did not come near either of them.

They sat behind a large marble headstone and caught their breath.

"So we're here," the girl said. "What the hell do we do next?"

ELEVEN

SPUR McCOY LOOKED at the pretty black girl sitting in the cemetery beside him.

"In my business the first job is to stay alive. It's what we call our first basic procedure. Without that it's damn hard to follow the rest of the rules."

"Would the fact that a sneaky little sonofabitch named Quint is running up the hill toward us have any bearing on our problem?"

Spur lifted over the top of the tombstone of one Orville Paddleford b. 1801, d. 1861. A man with a rifle ran hard up the slope.

McCoy dropped down and caught her face in one hand.

"Are we on the same side for the moment?"

"Until Quint is dead, that bastard!"

"We get him between us, within our short range. See that headstone over there, the little raised box affair?" She nodded. "Get behind it. And we'll try to get him in close so I can hit him with the derringer, or a knife."

"I need a weapon," she said.

"You get over there, I'll throw you my knife."

"Trusting."

"Staying alive."

"I can understand that." She bent over and ran across graves and weeds and the rocky unused plots to the larger grave marker. It was only twenty-five feet from Spur. When she reached it she waved and moved out of sight. Spur threw the knife, sticking it in a four-inch thick tree next to the grave. She looked at him, raised her brows in surprise, and pulled the six-inch knife from the tree.

Spur settled down, watching the killer's progress up the hill. Their small, feeble trap was situated almost on the near edge of the graveyard. If Quint came in at all, he might be in a position where Spur could get one shot.

Spur would rather Quint came close enough to tackle him and get the rifle. Right now the long gun commanded, dictated, the whole struggle.

Quint ran halfway up the slope and stopped. At once Spur knew the man had undergone no military training. That was an advantage for Spur. The smaller man rested below, looked at the few trees and plants and the grave markers above him, and started again.

He worked his way up a ravine, which afforded the most gradual route to the top. In doing so he was positioned so he would come out between the two waiting for him. He must feel safe with the rifle. Now he must also know that Spur had lost his pistol back at the buggy.

Quint paused again at the front edge of the cemetery. Spur figured the odds. Bolt action rifle. The man could get off only one shot if Spur was within twenty yards of him. One shot and in three seconds, Spur would be diving at his body.

If Quint came close enough.

If he didn't suspect a trap.

If he didn't kill Spur with the first shot.

Spur needed a distraction, a diversion. He found the largest rocks from the soil nearby, two about the size of baseballs. They might do the trick.

Quint stood, pointed the rifle ahead of him and walked with his finger on the trigger. If he stumbled he might lunge ahead, pull the trigger and accidentally kill a gravestone.

When Quint came into the cemetery he was closest to June Sue. Spur wished it had been the other way. The woman probably couldn't throw the knife. It would be a hand to hand weapon for her.

Quint moved slowly, checking to each side as he walked, watching behind gravestones, turning around now and then to look at his back trail.

He had just come to a point nearly between June Sue and Spur when he dropped to the ground and listened. Spur used the moment to throw one of the rocks. He lofted it over June Sue and it hit a grave marker making a cracking sound as the rock split apart.

Quint stood at once, ran a dozen steps that way, then turned and looked behind him.

That was when June Sue jumped from her cover and charged Quint. He must have heard her coming, because he started to turn back when she hit him. The rifle pointed toward the black woman when it fired. Her knife thrust into his body, but caught him high in the shoulder.

June Sue clung to him a moment, then fell away,

and Spur could see the gush of blood from her stomach.

In the few seconds after the shot, and before Quint could get his body into motion again, Spur raced from his hiding place. He had the derringer at arm's length, and pounded the twenty feet to where Quint was still staring at the silent form of June Sue.

He turned, but by then Spur was six feet from him, his finger pulling the derringer's trigger.

The little gun exploded as the .45 slug plowed out. Spur pulled the gun back on target after the recoil and fired the second round.

He saw the first round hit Quint high in the chest. The second round was buckshot. Fifteen small balls of steel slashed through the air and tore into Quint's face, destroying it. The shot disintegrated his nose, blinded both eyes and ripped half his cheek off. Four of the shots penetrated around his left eye ball and churned directly into his brain, killing Quint in a half a second.

Spur jumped over the dead man and knelt beside June Sue. He held her on his lap and her eyes flickered open.

"God it hurts!" she said softly. Then she screamed. The black woman sobbed for a few seconds then looked up at Spur.

"I'm dying, I know it. I've seen people shot in the belly before. Can't you make it faster? Two hours is a hell of a long time to wait to get to hell."

She coughed and spit up blood. Her face writhed from a sudden spasm of pain. She looked up at him. "Spur McCoy, do it for me. I know I'm already dead. Help me just a little and put a bullet through my brain."

Spur sighed. It's what he would want in her place.

"Look. It might not be that bad. I can get a doctor up here in half an hour. Some of these sawbones are good. They can take out the bullet, sew up the damage. I seen it lots of times."

"Not if the doc can't work on me for an hour. I'll bleed to death inside if you try to move me. Get one of Quint's guns. He dead?"

Spur nodded. "Good. Take one of his pistols. You don't even have to look. I thought I could do it myself, but I can't." She sobbed again. "Spur, I helped you get Quint. I could have warned him. You owe me, you handsome sonofabitch. Get his gun."

McCoy looked at her a long time, then went to Quint's body and pulled one of the pistols from his holster, checked the rounds, took out all but one and placed it in the black girl's hand.

"I won't hurt you, Spur McCoy. Truly I won't. But I can't do it myself. You must understand. Do it for me, but don't tell me when."

She gave the weapon back to Spur. At last he nodded. She kissed his cheek. "Thanks, Spur. In other days it might have been different between us. At least I did one good thing, right at the end."

Spur checked the weapon, moved it back out of sight. "You sure I can't change your mind about this."

"No way, Spur. I'll probably meet you later, in hell." She closed her eyes. "God but it hurts!" She

135

screamed. "Do it soon Spur! For God's sake do it soon!"

Spur lifted the weapon behind her and shot her in the side of the head. The round thundered through her head, slammed her away from him, and only a few spots of blood hit his pants. Spur laid the gun down beside her, stood and walked back toward town. Before he got there a deputy sheriff rode out to meet him. Spur motioned to the cemetery and said he would fill out a report for the sheriff later.

Spur stopped at the buggy with the dead horse and found the borrowed revolver. He took it back to the drygoods store. The owner said he would keep it for the man who had lent it. Spur held his hand over his bloody side as he went to his hotel. The bullet had cut through an inch of flesh in his side. Lots of blood, not much damage. He put on a bandage made from his handkerchief and taped it fast.

Rush Sommers had put out a kill order to him, Spur knew for sure now. He had to be careful around town. He needed a good base of operations. He would stay in his room until dark, then go to the Belcher mansion.

That night at eight, Spur went to the Belcher place.

"Tell Mrs. Belcher that the lawyer wants to see her," Spur told the maid at the door. A minute later Canchuna ran up to the door and unlocked it with her key. She hugged him and took his hand.

"So happy to see you!" she said, her small face blossoming in a grand smile.

"I'm happy to see you too, Canchuna. I have my bags. I want to rent a room for a few nights."

"The big bedroom?" she asked cautiously.

"No, just a bed where I can get some sleep."

"Good," Canchuna said. "Tracy is having a bubble bath. I'll tell her you're here."

Canchuna led him to a bedroom on the top floor that looked out over the whole little city. He could see gas lights burning on some of the street corners, more lights glowing in house windows. Virginia City was starting to grow up. But what could sustain it when the mines ran dry? And they would. Already the town had been through one bad depression from sixty-eight to seventy-two as one mine after another worked out of the lode.

Spur answered a knock on his door and found Canchuna with a tray that held a pot of coffee, three small cakes and three kinds of fruit.

"I thought you might want a snack," the girl said. She put the tray down and smiled, then slipped quickly out of the room.

A half hour later, the door swung open and Tracy walked in. She wore a floor length silk robe and her hair had been washed and dried and combed out.

"Welcome home," she said. "Hear you killed a couple of people today."

"Just one, actually."

"Seems like the word is out on you, Spur. A certain unnamed party has offered a thousand dollars for your head in a bucket."

"Figured it would come to that. The time must be coming down short."

"What time?"

"My business venture that certain folks don't want to go through."

"Oh. Then you're not really a lawyer?"

"Right, I'm a businessman."

"What's your business?"

"Death, violence and outlaws and criminals."

"Just had a feeling you were a law man. A U.S. Marshal, right?"

"Wrong. Sit down over here and tell me everything you know about Rush Sommers."

"That could take a long time."

"I've got all night. Oh, can I sack down in your bunkhouse for a few nights? The hotels are downright unhealthy."

She kissed his cheek. "Sweet Spur, you can bunk down at my place anytime you want to. As long as I get to be in the same bed."

Spur kissed her soft, waiting lips.

"Sounds like a marvelous arrangement." He put his arms around her and wrinkled his brow. "Now, give me a quick historical and current rundown on one tycoon named Rush Sommers."

It was a little after midnight when Spur left the big Belcher house on the hill and walked down to the sheriff's office. He had on a black hat pulled low, a borrowed blue miner's coat, and his spare Colt .45 tied down on his right thigh. No one should have any reason to recognize him. His side hurt, but not bad. Canchuna had rebandaged it.

He had sent a note to the sheriff three hours ago,

that he needed a secret meeting with him in the sheriff's office. The lawman was to tell no one of the conference, especially not any of his deputies.

They met in Sheriff Gilpin's private office that had a door to the street. No one saw Spur enter. The sheriff was staring at a report he had been writing. He looked up and scowled.

"I don't like the idea of some stranger coming in here and suggesting that I have a spy and a double dealer on my staff."

"Can happen to anybody, Sheriff. Don't take it personally. Right now I'm interested in the shipment of gold and silver due out of here sometime within the next week."

"What? You're not supposed to know about that! It's always a secret."

"Sure, Sheriff. Nobody knows except the mine owners, their security people, twenty-seven sheriff's deputies, the train crew, the switching crew, the men who will be called to transfer the boullion, and all the wives, sweethearts and whores who found out. A damn big secret."

"Well, at least we don't announce the shipment in the newspapers. You're here about the transfer."

"Yes. There could be some trouble. Who assigns the engineer to the special train?"

"The Virginia and Truckee Railway Company, with the approval of the mine owners. Far as I know it's already been done. We cleared three men and the mine owners pick one. Last three shipments been the same man, Guy Pritchard. He lives here in town. Usually runs the ore trains down to Carson City."

"Good, I'd like to go talk to him."

"Pritchard is a good man. Not a chance that he would give us any trouble. I'm in charge of the transfer from the miners' security men to the federal boys on the train. We go from one mine to another to get the bars. The gold and silver bars are sent from the reduction plants back to the individual mines for safekeeping, since the number produced in any one day is small. So security for the transfer of this big a shipment became a problem."

The sheriff shook his head. "Damn sure you're wrong about one of my own here being in on anything like this."

"Sheriff, anybody ever tried to bribe you? Now don't get riled. Every sheriff who ever pinned on his badge has been tested. What would you do if the bribe was for, say two million dollars, in gold bars?"

The sheriff stared at the federal law man. "You telling me somebody is offering one of my deputies two million dollars to help rob that gold train?"

Spur nodded.

"God Almighty!" The sheriff rubbed his forehead. "That much money would tempt Christ himself. No man I know could resist."

"That's why we have a problem, Sheriff. My boss says there could be as much as thirty million on that train. You can spread thirty million around to a lot of hired guns."

"I'm putting on a hundred extra deputies the day that silver and gold are moved."

"When will you know which day?"

"I get a coded telegram from San Francisco."

"I'll get one too, Sheriff. Let's hope they both give the same date. Now, tell me where this Pritchard lives. I want to pay him a friendly call."

A half hour later Spur McCoy knocked on a small frame house out of the downtown section of Virginia City. It had a white picket fence around it and one bed of carefully tended flowers in front. Water was such a scarce and expensive item in the desert mountains that gardening was a luxury.

A man opened the door.

"Yeah?"

"Guy Pritchard?"

"Yes. Afraid I don't know you."

"My name is Spur McCoy. I'm with the United States Secret Service Agency. I want to ask you a few questions."

"Me? Why me? It's almost one a.m. for Christ's sakes."

"That's what the questions are about. Can I come inside?"

"What? Oh, yes, come in." The man wore pants and no shirt.

The house was small, frame construction rather than the more expensive brick, and modest. The house had the look of a man living alone.

"Is your wife and family here?"

"No. I lost my wife three years ago. One boy went to live with his grandma back in Missouri."

141

"Sorry. I understand you're an engineer with the Virginia and Truckee."

"That's right. Best job in the world. Exciting."

"A feeling of power?"

"You bet! When them pistons slam home and the wheels spin it's a great, good, powerful feeling."

Prichard was tall and slender. Spur estimated he was 33 or 34. He had a large nose, deep set brown eyes, and dark hair. He wore faded pants that had been pulled on quickly after getting out of bed.

"That power go so far as to make you think you're above the law? That you don't have to go by the laws of the land?"

"No, sir. I've never thought that. I've been a good worker for the V & T. Been on the line since it was finished back in sixty-one. Started out as a brakeman when I was eighteen."

"Sheriff tells me you've never been in trouble with the law, at least here in Virginia City. That true?"

"Absolutely. No cause for me to hurt anybody. I drink a little now and then, but I'm the kind of guy who goes to sleep when I drink too much. I'm not a brawler."

"I hear that you've been picked in the past to be engineer on the gold trains that take the boullion from the mines to San Francisco."

"Right! We take it as far as Reno in a special train. Then it goes on the regular Central Pacific line on into Sacremento and San Francisco. Yes sir. That was a real thrill."

"Hear tell you've been picked to run the next one, too."

"That so? They don't tell us until the night before, so we can be sure to be here when the Special is made up. Be right proud to do it again. I get a bonus of a hundred dollars for the run."

"I heard you were getting a bonus of a million dollars."

Pritchard's head snapped up. His mouth came open and he let his eyes go wild for a minute before he recovered.

"What you mean?"

"I heard that if you run the train the way you're told, stopping it at the right place or slowing it down, you'll be paid a bonus of a million dollars."

"That's crazy. Who could pay a million dollars?"

"The men who rob the gold train. Out of thirty million, they could spare a million for you."

"Crazy, that's crazy."

"Yeah, right, Pritchard. That's what I told the man who suggested it. A million is way too much for a simple living man like you. You'd probably settle for five thousand."

Pritchard stood and walked the length of the room. He stared at Spur for a minute. Then his face worked into an angry scowl.

"I don't know who you are, or what you're trying to do. But I don't want you in my house. Get out. Get out! Right now! You come in here spouting lies, and I don't have to listen. I worked for this road for thirteen years! Hard work, and I don't got to listen to you call me a traitor!"

"Just passing on the rumor that I heard, Pritchard. An innocent man has nothing to worry about. You are innocent, aren't you?"

143

"I ain't done nothing illegal, nothing attal."

"What about conspiracy, Pritchard? That word mean anything to you? It means that two or more people get together and plan and take some kind of overt action to carry out a crime. Have you conspired to rob that train, Pritchard?"

"Out! Damnit! Get out of my house!"

Pritchard jumped at Spur but didn't swing. He wanted to. Spur saw that the man was furious. He was so angry and probably frightened that he ought to have done exactly what Spur wanted. Spur held up his hands and went to the door. He opened it and stared at Pritchard until the man looked away. Then Spur went out the door into the night.

Less than twenty minutes later McCoy watched Pritchard turn out the lights inside the small house and come out the front door. He moved uphill at once and Spur walked along in the shadows behind him a hundred feet. The man never looked back.

The route led past the mines and the stores, up to the residential sections and on to the top streets where the mine owners had built their large houses.

Pritchard went past the ornate fronts of three big houses, then paused at the fourth before walking quickly to the back door. Spur moved around so he could see the man knock and be admitted. McCoy went back to the front and studied the name plate on the fancy front door. The plate read: Rush Sommers, Esq.

Spur walked a block over to Tracy's big house and let himself in at the back gate with a key she had given him.

Tracy met him with a tray of food.

"Thought you could use a midnight snack," she said smiling. "That includes the food on the tray, or the hussy with her tits about to flop out of her gown."

Spur took a slice of watermelon and a chocolate cupcake.

"I'll be working most of the nights from now on, and getting some sleep during the day," he said. "I don't aim to let any hootenanny claim that outlaw reward on my hide."

TWELVE

TONY GIARDELLO KNEW people. He could tell a first time dance hall girl the minute he saw her, even before she opened her mouth. As a saloon, gambling hall and part time bordello owner he had to be able to pick them out.

He could tell the gamblers, too. The professionals were easy to spot, a bit over friendly, always with a story or a joke, but then deadly serious when the money was in the pot.

Usually he could tell when the slick boys were going to cheat. It was a gift he had. Sometimes he knew when an honest player was going to try to deal off the bottom. He had that feeling he could never describe and that almost always worked.

Part of his knowing people helped him to rise from a bank teller to the second to top man in a little under four years. He knew all the banking procedures by heart, and exactly where the firm was a little loose in its affairs. So one Friday night he made a highly illegal withdrawal of over thirty thousand dollars, jumped on the train and was well away from the Eastern seaboard by Monday noon when the bank president discovered the loss.

Soon there was a trail of Pinkerton men following him, but he changed his name and costume so often they had trouble staying up with him as he moved around freely. At last they lost him in Denver, where he had become a stocks and bonds salesman with a full beard and top hat. What had always amused him was how he almost sold one of the Pinkertons some gold mining stock one slow evening.

Now he had taken that ability to understand people and built it into a nice little bundle of money here in Virginia City. His saloon was doing well, and would flourish as long as the Comstock Lode held out. But the good pockets of ore were vanishing fast. The smart money, and the smart men were looking down the road for the next action, the next bonanza, or just another town that had some continuing reason for survival.

With his recent contacts and his skill in planning, Giardello had worked his way into the biggest deal of his life. If everything went as planned he could come out of this little operation with as much as fifteen million dollars! Tony knew Sommers would play it close to his vest, but if the mine owner did not pay off as they had agreed, the big man would have an extra .44 caliber navel. Fifteen million dollars!

Tony had picked his five riders the way he did everything, with a lot of thought, and as a last test, checking the men against his own gut feelings. He had found the five men he wanted over the course of a week from his own customers.

Many of the miners in town came from other occupations, a lot of them cowhands. Tony picked carefully, and told each one he tested and cleared that he would begin work tonight, a Tuesday.

They had come into the back door of the Golden Nugget at midnight and he sent them one by one to the Enright Livery stable, where Enright himself helped them find the best riding mounts, then picked out five sturdy pack horses or mules for each man. The animals were fitted with heavy load pack rigs that rode on the sides of the mounts.

As soon as each man was rigged out with his mount and pack train, he moved through the darkness to the first splash of green in Crooked Creek south of town. When the last one had been outfitted, Tony led them down the grade to the others. It had been two years since Tony had forked a horse, and how he remembered why he was never a cowboy. But the payoff would be well worth it.

He nodded to the others at the spot of green trees where the little creek bed lay. Crooked Creek had water in it only when a boiling thunderstorm dumped rain on the mountains, or a thick snowpack began to melt in the spring. Over the years the trees had lived from one rain to the next, so only the sturdiest with the deepest roots could survive. Tony nodded. He was one of the sturdy ones.

He looked at the five men gathered around him in the moonlight.

"First, your advance. Each of you gets fifty dollars right now."

The men cheered.

"This is the advance against the five hundred

dollars I promised you for the two weeks work. Now, as we mentioned before, for this kind of money you might have to do something you might not ordinarily do. I give the orders, you do the work, whatever it is. We all know from the start this is not going to be some kind of church picnic."

They all laughed nervously.

He handed out the greenbacks, and each man looked carefully at the cash in the light of the small fire they had built. The night already had a touch of a chill to it in mid-October.

"I'll lead the way down the trail. It isn't much of a track. At one time it was the southern horseback route into Virginia City from Carson City. It roughly follows the route of the train tracks. We'll move out slowly and should be there in an hour."

Someone moved in the brush behind him and Tony fumbled for his six-gun as he spun around.

"No shoot!" a woman's voice called. She ran into the clearing and Tony saw that she was a breed, half white, half Chinese. He knew her. She was just over eighteen. "No shoot!" she said again. She stood straight and tall and threw out her chest so her breasts strained at the cloth. She had inherited her mother's big breasts.

"My name is Lee," she said carefully. "My Tony bring me in from San Francisco to work for him. All time day or night I entertain you five gentlemen." She waggled her finger. "No more than one fuck a day for each man."

The riders whooped and hollered.

Tony lifted his hand for quiet.

"Hope you men appreciate this additional

benefit of working for a first class operation!" They shouted that they did, and quickly picked numbers one to five to see who would get China Lee tonight.

"Now, we should get moving on down the trail. Any volunteers to ride double with Lee?"

A large Irishman with a red beard from Wyoming won the right by grabbing her and throwing her over his back, then marching to his horse and string of pack animals.

They arrived at the base camp at a little after three a.m. The cowboys told Tony the time by checking the position of the big dipper as it worked its nightly circle around the north star.

"See the Big Dipper?" one of the men asked. "Spot them two stars on the outside of the cup. Call them the pointer stars. Follow a line straight up from them, or down, anyway a straight line and you'll find the North Star right up yonder."

Tony found it. "I'll be damned!"

"I can tell you the time near to fifteen minutes what it rightly is, just by looking up there."

They came to a heavy growth of trees, a few pines, some brush along the creek and a lot of willow and alder that screened it all from the railroad tracks three hundred yards above on the edge of the cliff.

"This is camp," Tony said. "Just tether the animals for tonight. Tomorrow I want you to make up a temporary corral from that extra quarter inch hemp rope we brought along. Might as well make a camp as comfortable as you can, cause you might be here for a week before you get to work."

"What we gonna be doing way out here?" one of the men asked.

"I'm gonna be screwing that little Chinese breed till I can't get it hard no more!" somebody shouted. They all laughed.

"What else you're doing, you'll find out when the time comes. It will be sudden and at night. That's all I can tell you. Now settle down for the night, and don't wear out my little Chink. I got to get back to town before daylight."

They waved goodbye to him and the man who held the magic number one, tied his horse and motioned in the moonlight to Lee.

"First we make pine boughs bed and put blanket over them and then fuck-fuck," she said.

His name was Teddy and he grabbed her and pulled her dress open and began eating her breasts.

"Wait, hell!" Teddy said between bites. He picked her up, carried her into the woods a ways and laid her down on a spot of grass.

"What's your fucking hurry?" she asked, her strange pidgin English gone.

"Never could stand to wait around for things," he said, pulling off the rest of her clothes.

"Don't you want a fire, so you can see me all naked?"

"Hell no. I just want to blow my nuts, and then get to sleep."

Lee shrugged. It was going to be one of those weeks.

A half mile back up the trail toward town, Tony

Giardello grinned when he remembered the expressions of the men when China Lee came up. They were so surprised he thought they had all shit their pants! She would keep them busy until it was time to get to work. China Lee would be one more of the crew who would not live to spend her bonus, but what the hell, it was a tough world.

He hated the horse he rode before he got back to the livery. Tony left the horse still saddled and tied to the rail at the stables and walked back to his saloon. He lived over the gambling hall and found Lottie snoring in his bed. He slapped her and she sat up, peeling out of her nightgown automatically.

"Not now," he snarled. "I'm too damn tired. You can massage my shoulders though. Damn, never gonna ride a horse again as long as I live!"

Lottie rolled him over and sat on his back, then leaned into him with her hands and punished his shoulder muscles with her massaging fingers until he wailed. She eased off at once and with soothing strokes on his shoulders and down his back, had him asleep in two minutes. She looked through his wallet, figured he would never remember how many small bills he had, and took fifteen dollars. She hid it in her shoe, then lay down beside him. When he woke up he would have a morning hardon and demand immediate service.

Sometimes Lottie thought it would be easier to be married and only have to worry about servicing one man. She shook her head. That would be boring, she'd go out of her mind in a week. Lottie grinned as she began to drift off to sleep. Tony had given her a twenty dollar bonus for telling him what she found out about Spur McCoy. That was the big reason they had put out the kill-reward on the Secret Service Agent. In this town McCoy wouldn't last more than two days. She went to sleep, still smiling.

Back at the mountain camp, Lee stood in the shadows and called softly. She had found only one more of the five waiting for her. The other three had been so tired they slept slumped on the ground wherever they wound up after hobbling their mounts and pack string. Leave it to a dedicated cowboy to tend to his horses before he thought about himself. She would never understand these men.

She fingered the pants pocket of the closest cowboy and removed his wallet. Silently she took out forty of the fifty dollars he had been paid. She went to four of the five and did the same thing, taking the wad of ten dollar bills and folding them tightly. She put the cash in a flat tobacco tin, closed the top, and looked for a good place to hide it. It would have to be a spot that would stay dry, not be obvious and be where she could find it again after this work was all over.

A hundred and sixty dollars! Think what she could do with that!

At last she found a place. The old lodgepole pine had been hit by lightning, and the top broken out fifty feet above the ground. A fire had evidently started because there was a blackened cavity burned in the base of the tree. Lee looked in it but could see nothing. The tree had been three feet thick at base, and the burned area was nearly half way through it. She felt upward as high as she could reach and found a narrow shelf where the fire had failed to burn. She pushed the tobacco tin up there. It fit well. It was back out of sight. A person would have to feel on top of the little shelf of the tree inside the burned area to find it.

The money would stay dry, it was safe and no one else would find it. And she could come directly to the scarred old snag later on and get the money.

Lee lay down on her blanket after slipping her dress on and nestled her head on her arms. After this week she would be a rich woman. Mr. Giardello had promised her two hundred dollars for the week's work with the five men. That with the hundred and sixty was a fortune!

Only for a moment did she think what the men would do when they woke up and found most of their money gone. She decided they would accuse each other. After all, she had no money, and certainly not theirs! A few seconds later China Lee slept.

The men all shivered in the morning when they woke up in the October chill of the six thousand feet elevation. They quickly found the good sized warming fire that China Lee had built. They looked in wonder at the cooking fire she had going, and at the kitchen gear that she had unpacked from one of the supply packs. Soon she had flapjacks with hot syrup and a pair of sunnyside up eggs and biscuits ready for each man. They ate quickly and with a good appetite. Then one of the men decided to look at the fifty dollars in his purse.

It was Teddy who unsnapped his long leather

purse and reached inside. When his hand came out with one bill, he exploded with rage.

"Which of you yellow bellies stole my money?" he roared.

"Nobody stole nothing," one man said.

"You probably gave it to China Lee for the pussy."

"Not a chance, she's paid for," Teddy said. "Who nipped into my purse while I slept?"

The other men began examining their wallets and snap purses, and there were more shouts of outrage.

"I'm short forty dollars!" one screeched.

"My whole poke is gone . . . no I got ten dollars left. Forty gone!"

All of them but one had had money stolen. The other four looked at him with anger. He quickly opened his billfold and spread out his cash. He had fifty three dollars and twelve cents.

"I always sleep with my cash looped over my underwear and lay on it," he said. "No bastard can lightfinger me that way."

Through the outbursts, China Lee had continued to cook flapjacks at the small fire surrounded by rocks pushed in enough so her heavy frying pan would fit over it. The men looked at her.

"China Lee has no money," she said quietly. "China Lee here to fuck-fuck, not steal money. Look in my blanket roll."

Teddy was not convinced by her protests. He went to her blanket roll and dumped it out. He found only another dress, a skirt, one blouse, and three hair ribbons.

"Please do not take the hair ribbons," she said.

Teddy jumped at her, grabbed her by a breast and pulled her toward the big fire.

"Whore, you tell the truth, or I'm gonna burn your hair off, you savvy? First burn it off your head, and if you still don't confess, then I'm gonna spread your legs over the fire and burn your pussy hair off."

The men laughed at the idea, but when Teddy began to push the back of her head toward the fire they pulled her away.

"What the hell you doing? This whore stole our money and hid it. What else could have happened?"

The men all yelled at once, then the big redhead pushed Teddy away from China Lee.

"Argue that later, Teddy. I tell you one thing for sure. You hurt this little lady, and you're the son-ofabitch who has to do the cooking for the next week. You want to do that?"

Teddy took a long breath. Shrugged. "Hell, guess good grub is worth the forty bucks. But the food better stay good, you damn sideways cut Chinese whore!"

For the next two days the food was the best any line rider ever had on the open prairie. That, and the service work China Lee did for each of them once a day, kept the five cowboys from tearing each other apart from boredom.

THIRTEEN

THE SAME NIGHT Tony Giardello positioned his five men with pack animals in the grove of trees a mile and a half from Virginia City on the downgrade toward Carson City, Deputy Sergeant Bert Anders left the sheriff's office at his usual time in his usual way. He always stopped by the open door to Sheriff Gilpin and chatted for a minute.

Anders knew he was a favorite of the sheriff. He had been promoted over older men in the department and men with more experience. But the sheriff liked Bert because he was more like the top man than the others. Bert had actually gone to two years of college back East, and was a thinker, more than a loud talking, guns first kind of deputy.

They talked about the upcoming election for a minute. There would be no real opposition running against Clete Gilpin, so he was a shoo-in for re-election. Anders mentioned how arrangements for the Johnson murder trial were coming along. It would be scheduled for the following week. Then he said goodnight and left, the same way he had been doing for three years.

Only this time he walked past the boarding house and went to the end of the street, then up to the back door of the big Rush Sommers mansion. A growling guard let him in. He knew Anders by this time.

Sommers was not pleased to be disturbed. It was a little after eight o'clock and he was contemplating which girl he would honor tonight in his bed. All three candidates sat in his den.

The closest to him was thin as a sapling, with almost no breasts or hips, but she often was Sommer's favorite. The things she could do with her limber body amazed him, and she had a way of surging him to new sexual thrills he had not even considered. She could even read. He had brought home some magazines from Denver and she was devouring them. She looked up and smiled, made a circle with her thumb and finger and pushed a finger from her other hand in and out of the hole.

Sommers laughed.

The second girl had everything the first lacked: a beautifully curved body with tits Sommers could get lost in, a wonderfully built girl with hips that could whack him as hard as he punched at them. She was amazing and loved to get her mouth around his hard cock. He sighed. Maybe her.

The third girl was younger than the other two. She said she was seventeen, but Sommers guessed she was about fourteen, but well developed. Her figure was smaller than the other one, but she had a delightful manner that captivated Sommers. She was so young, that was part of it, but someone had taught her how to make love to please a man in every way. Which one, which one?

Anders walked in.

Sommers shifted his attention with regret to the man. "Yes, Mr. Anders, Sergeant Anders. The most important man in our little operation. I hope you have good news."

"I hope so, Mr. Sommers." He glanced at the three women.

"They are with me. They have never seen you here, and remember nothing that you said since you weren't here. We go through this every time you come, damn it! What do you have?"

"The time is getting short. The sheriff hasn't had his telegram yet about the date, but today we got more instructions. The Federal people will put twenty men on the train. They will all be uniformed U.S. Army regular troops, and will come in from Carson City the day of the shipment. All will be confined to the car they come in and no one will see them."

"At least that's an improvement. Last time they sent them in and they ran around town getting drunk all day before they left on the train."

Anders stood and walked to the window, then came back. He looked at Sommers and rubbed sweat off his forehead.

"Mr. Sommers, I don't think I can keep on doing this. It just doesn't seem to be as good an idea as it did."

"What's the matter, you don't like money? A million dollars doesn't mean anything to you anymore?"

"A million? You said half a million before."

"So I just gave you a raise. I realize how important a man you are in this go around."

"Jeeze . . . a whole million. I still don't know. I've built myself a real life here, got promoted. I'm not running from anybody now, and that's a good feeling."

"Anders, you remember about that letter I have? The one from the police department back in St. Louis? The one that says they are still looking for the wild man who tore up a police station, and then attacked the Captain's wife and violated her and her two small daughters? Remember that letter, Anders?"

Anders sat down quickly in a chair.

"You promised me two years ago . . ." The words stuck in his throat.

"Of course I did. And I'm holding to it. All you have to do is tell me anything I want to know about the sheriff's office. What is happening, what is planned. This certainly comes under our agreement. And the million dollars. After things quiet down, you can quit your job and move to San Francisco where that bank account will be waiting for you. No pain, no problems."

"Damn, it all sounds so good."

"It will be good. Just like it's going to be good tonight. Stay here. I've got a spare bedroom for you. And someone to go with it to keep you warm. Have anyone you want," Sommers said pointing to the girls. "Hell, have two of them. You ever fucked two women at the same time, Anders? Pick out two."

"Oh, I couldn't do that."

Sommers laughed. "Yeah, I guess you couldn't. But I could." Sommers pointed at the two older

160

girls, and they grinned and moved forward. Cecil, the taller of the two with the big breasts opened the tight blouse she wore and let her soft, warm flesh tumble out. She held one nipple to Ander's mouth and he moaned and chewed on it.

"That's good, Sergeant. You're going to do just fine." Sommers waved them away still grinning.

Sergeant Anders walked in a daze with the two women. He was so excited that he climaxed in his pants before they got to the bedroom. Inside the room the girls sat on the bed with him between them, and quickly they undressed him, then slid out of their own clothes.

"I've died and gone to heaven," Anders said. The women laughed and rolled on top of him and started doing all sorts of strange and wonderful sexual activities that Anders had only heard of before.

In the den Sommers stared a moment at the big bear rug on the floor in front of the fireplace.

"Over here, Misty," he said, his voice thick and feeling strange as the desire pounded through him. She was so young, so soft, so unspoiled! Each time he convinced himself that she was twelve and a virgin and he told her to act the part. She cried and squealed in protest as he took off her clothes, and it made his desire mount higher.

Then when the issue was decided and she consented, she became a talented and marvelously efficient lover who knew exactly what to do so Rush Sommers could hold out for an hour of love-making before exploding in one tremendous climax that left him in his mini-death for an hour.

This time Sommers roused himself after half an hour. Misty had gone to her room and to bed he guessed. Slowly he dressed. He had one more task before the night was done.

Outside his driver had a closed buggy waiting. It was a little after midnight when he drove up to the Consolidated California Mine and went in the front door. He locked and unlocked two more doors as he moved through the office complex. Then he went down the steps to the company vault.

This was the place where the gold and silver boullion was held until it could be shipped to San Francisco. Even the gold and silver bars produced from ore sent to Carson City were brought back here for storage. It was a tremendous security problem.

On special shift at night, one workman had been altering the inside of the vault. The area was not a bank vault of iron and steel. Rather it was a room, a basement room, dug into solid rock, and protected by the whole office complex. There were three steel doors leading from the bottom of the stairway into the vault. It would take a thousand pounds of dynamite even to scratch the doors. Now all three stood open and inside the small quantity of gold and silver bars was covered by a tarp.

A man in his sixties stood beside the back wall.
"Evening Edgar."

"Got her done, Mr. Sommers! Not even you can tell where one wall starts and the next one stops!"

The hole dug in the solid rock had been framed in and a room built inside. That was several years ago. Now Sommers looked at the room and he had trouble telling the difference from the last time. He knocked on all four walls. They sounded the same.

"Double wall construction, same all around." Edgar the carpenter said.

"Looks good, Edgar. Where is the pressure lever?"

Edgar moved to a spot beside the door. There were two round black spots on the floor, circles the size of a dime. He stood putting his heels on the black spots.

"Stand here to trip the automatic locking lever, then press the top of the door frame, here. See how this top six inches is a pressure plate."

Edgar pushed the top of the door and a part of the wall at the back swung slowly forward. It was a three-foot wide section extending floor to ceiling.

"Close it," Sommers said, excitement building in his voice. "How do you close it?"

"When you want it shut, all you have to do is be sure not to stand on the spots on the floor and push the pressure plate." He did and the section slid back in place.

Sommers went to see where it closed. There were three vertical panels in each of the walls. The section closed along the vertical edge of one of the panels and was impossible to see that there was a movable part.

Sommers stood on the spots and pushed the top of the door frame. The secret door opened again. He left it open and walked inside. There was a three-foot wide alley between the new wall and the old one. It would be plenty large enough for what he had in mind. You could stack a lot of gold and silver bars in that small, narrow room.

He came out and Edgar grinned at him.

"Sure hope you like it Mr. Sommers! Just like you told me, nobody else knows nothing about this. Done it all at night. Just like you said to."

"That's fine, Edgar. Looks like I owe you some money."

"You said five hundred dollars, because it's so secret and all. And I said that was too much. But if you still think that's the right figure, I ain't gonna argue too much."

"I'll go back upstairs and meet you out in back by the tailings. Nobody will spot us there. Might as well keep this a secret all the way. I'll get some cash from the office. You go up and out the back door and then around. Be sure nobody spots you."

Edgar grinned, went out the door and up the stairs to the main office.

Sommers pressed the pressure plate that swung the weight that closed the door. He never asked how it worked, just so it did work.

He stared at the closed section of wall. Nobody would find it in here, nobody. Very soon now he would be rich, just tremendously rich!

Sommers went up the steps, closed the heavy steel doors and set the locks on them as usual, then slipped out the front door and went through shadows around the edge of the mining works to where the tailings were dumped.

Edgar came out of a shadow beside a small ore car that was pushed along the mine tunnels, then lifted to the surface on the elevator hoists.

"I sure thank you, Mr. Sommers. You just don't

know what this extra money is going to mean to me and the missus.''

He smiled, and Sommers hesitated. Men were so damn trusting. So stupid and naive. Sommers thrust a four-inch blade forward, ramming it up to the hilt in Edgar's belly and jerking it upward as he pulled it out.

Edgar's eyes flared in the soft moonlight, then he gagged and fell to the tailings. Sommers bent and slashed the old man's throat across one of the carotid arteries, and Edgar died in sixty seconds.

Sommers wiped the blade clean on the dead man's pants and walked back through the shadows toward the office. No one had seen him at the office tonight. No one had seen Edgar.

It was amazing how trusting some men became.

He hurried to his rig and the driver took him home. Once in his bedroom he looked down at the small figure that lay there naked and watching him.

Misty scowled in her little girl way.

''Daddy, you better spank me, 'cause I was a bad girl. When you was gone I finger fucked myself. Spank me, Daddy. Spank me until I get all good feeling again and sexy and you want me again!''

Sommers had not been able to explain the hardon he had as he came home in the buggy. Then he knew. The killing. He had enjoyed killing old Edgar, and it had given him a sexual stimulation.

Quickly he pulled off his clothes and lay on the bed, then spanked the child-woman beside him until tears touched her eyes, and she lifted herself over him and guided him deep inside her.

"Oh, yes! Daddy. I love that. On top is the most fun ever, don't you think, Daddy?"

As they made love he asked her who had taught her about sex, about intercourse.

"I thought you knew. It was my real daddy. I was ten when my mommy died and one night he came to my bedroom and said there were some things he wanted to teach me."

"My God, your own father?"

"Sure. Every night he came after that, and showed me his body, and touched me and told me about how I would feel as I grew older. I was already starting to get little titties and he played with them and we talked, and then he let me watch him jerk off. After a while I helped him, and slowly he showed me other things I could do for him. He went real slow. It wasn't until I was eleven that he actually pushed inside my cuntie. Ooooooh it hurt. But then gradually it didn't hurt so much."

"Misty, you aren't seventeen, are you?"

"No, but promise you won't send me away."

"I'll never send you away. Hold old are you?"

"Sixteen, couple of months ago."

"My God! Where is your father?"

"He's dead."

"How did it happen?"

"Oh, one day the preacher came to our house. He always walked in and made himself at home. He didn't hear him and he looked for us and found Daddy humping away at me. The preacher screamed and shot my daddy while he was still in me. Killed him. They didn't do nothing to the preacher when he told the sheriff what my daddy was doing. So I ran away."

Sommers started to push her away, then he swore, rolled over on top of her and slammed into her as hard as he could until he roared with rage as he climaxed. He wished he hadn't promised that he would not send her away.

She was only a child. But such a marvelous whore! He had no thought of turning her loose in a bordello. She would be a sensation but he sensed that she would die young. Somehow she would try to get between two men fighting over her lovely young body and she would be killed.

No, he couldn't let that happen. He would have to protect her, and nurture her . . . and love her!

FOURTEEN

THE NEXT MORNING Spur McCoy wore a black coat and soft black hat as he perched on the front of the fancy carriage and drove Tracy Belcher to her mine office. Pulled low, the hat covered most of McCoy's face, and nobody paid any attention to a buggy driver. He helped Mrs. Belcher down from the rig and to the front of the office, then returned to the carriage and drove away.

His first stop was a block from the courthouse. He went in the back way and soon caught the sheriff's eye. They walked back to the buggy.

"Anything happening yet?"

"No word from San Francisco," Sheriff Gilpin said. "They usually give us about six hours notice for a midnight departure. So there is lots of time left for today."

"Hear anything about a railroad engineer named Guy Pritchard?" Spur asked.

The sheriff rubbed his face with a big hand and looked strangely at McCoy.

"Why you ask about him?"

"I scared hell out of him last night. Told him who I was and what I thought he and some other people were planning to do. He threw me out of his house.

168

I waited to see where he would go. He ran straight to Rush Sommers' mansion and went inside. That was late last night."

"Interesting. You'll swear to that?"

"Of course, I just told you. Why?"

"This morning some swampers found Pritchard with three holes in his chest in the alley in back of a saloon. Been dead for five or six hours the doc says."

"Now the robbery team is without an engineer," McCoy said. "Pritchard has been their man. What will they do now?"

"Anyone of fifty men in town can run those engines," the sheriff said. "Company will simply assign another one."

"But the new man won't be in on the robbery conspiracy. It could be a point for our side. Remember, you still have a spy inside your outfit. Would the big miners know when the train is going? Guess they'll have to if they ship any gold or silver out. Is Sommers scheduled to make a shipment?"

The sheriff nodded. "Every mine in the area is shipping."

"Great way to keep a secret," Spur said. "I'll be in touch," Spur said then stopped. "Could you take a note down to the telegraph office for me? Send a brand new deputy and have him pick up any sealed messages for me?"

The sheriff said he would, and Spur pulled the hat down over his eyes and sat in the shade of the cool morning until the deputy came back. The only message was from his St. Louis office asking when he would be returning to town to clear off his desk.

He thanked the deputy and vanished down the block and around the corner. Spur drove back to the Belcher house. He parked the rig in back, unharnessed the horse and put her in a stall and hung up the leather. When he went in the house, Canchuna saw him.

"You have a visitor," she said. "Someone from the office with a message for you from Mrs. Belcher." Spur followed the sleek little Indian girl to the front sitting room where he saw Mary Beth Franklin. He remembered her. She was the slightly chunky young girl who had been handing out leaflets that first day Spur arrived in town.

"Miss Franklin," Spur said, bowing slightly.

"Oh, thank you, Mr. McCoy. Mrs. Belcher had me bring you a message. It's in this." She handed Spur a long white envelope that had been sealed.

"I'm working for Mrs. Belcher in the office now. She heard about my pamphlets and what happened on the street that day when you knocked down that awful man. She said my mother and I deserve the right to earn our living. I'm ever so grateful to you for what you did for us."

"It really wasn't that much."

"Oh, but it was!" her gray eyes snapped and her face became determined. She flipped her shoulder length hair out of her face and stared at him. "And now I have decided how I am going to show you my appreciation. Please don't deny me this one small pleasure." She took his hand and led him down the hall.

170

Canchuna had slipped away. Spur had no idea where Mary Beth was going. She stopped and opened a door, motioned him inside. She stepped in behind him then deftly turned the key locking the door.

Mary Beth leaned against the inside of the door, staring at him. For a moment fear stained her pretty face. She shook her head and smiled.

"I'm not good with words, Mr. McCoy. Would you come over here?"

Spur nodded and moved up to her. She put her arm around his neck and kissed his lips firmly. She came down off her tip toes and looked up at him.

"Was that all right? I'm not terribly experienced at kissing."

"That was fine, but I don't understand."

"That day in the street when the man took away my leaflets and you got them back. I . . . I . . ."

"Your smile was thanks enough."

"No. Because Mrs. Belcher heard about the trouble and she scolded Mr. O'Grady and then gave me a real job. Now we don't have to take handouts from the church people. So I really owe you a lot."

She found his hand and brought it up and pressed it against her breasts. "I thought you might want to . . . you know."

"Do you want me to?"

Mary Beth unbuttoned the white blouse she wore and let it fall to the floor. She took off the short chemise so her full breasts showed.

"I think I want to. I never have. I've heard women talk . . . kiss me again."

Spur kissed her lips, then picked up her blouse, but she pushed it away.

"No, it's been a long time I've been waiting, and wondering. Now I want you to show me how, right now. Nobody can come in, and there's a big couch right over here."

"Mary Beth . . ."

She took his hands, and pressed one to each of her breasts. "Please, Mr. McCoy. Please, right now. Say you will."

He smiled and nodded, and she reached up and kissed him again, then led him to the couch and sat down. He sat beside her.

"Mary Beth, I don't know what you've heard, but there is no big mystery about a man and a woman making love. Everyone can do it, and everyone is good at it. It's a marvelous, wonderful, natural thing to do."

He let her undress him. The blinds had been drawn in the room but still plenty of light came in. When Spur's clothes were all off, he bent and kissed her breasts and she trembled. He rubbed them softly and her eyes widened.

"That feels so . . . so warm and wonderful! I've never felt that way before!"

Spur kissed down her neck and then to her breasts. He trailed hot kisses around both of her breasts and at last working to the peaks and biting her erect nipples, then sucking on each one. Her hand worked down to his crotch and explored.

"So big!" she said looking at his erection. "Don't tell me that you're going to put that big thing inside me?"

"Wait and see," Spur said. They both were breathing faster now, the hot blood surging. He worked his hand down her leg and she snapped them together.

"Changing your mind?" he asked.

She scowled, bit her lip and shook her head. Slowly her legs came apart and his hand worked between them sliding slowly upward.

"I don't know what to do next," she whispered.

"Then just relax and find out what happens," Spur whispered back and they both laughed. His hand massaged around and around her crotch and at last she caught it and moved it over her swollen, moist nether lips.

Mary Beth moaned in surprise and delight.

"You never said it would feel this wonderful!"

She caught his face, held it with both hands and kissed him hard, her tongue darting inside his mouth, a low moaning sound coming from her all the time. When she let him go, she nodded.

"Please, Spur, push it in me right now! I can't wait a second longer. Right now, this very instant, please!"

Spur moved over her and when he thrust forward she shrieked in surprise and a little pain but mostly jubilation. She was so overcome with emotion she couldn't talk for a few moments. Then she hugged him to her.

"Wonderful, so wonderful! Nobody ever told me. Why didn't my mother tell me how fantastic making love is?"

Then she shivered and a sharp, quick climax shot through her as fast as a lightning bolt.

"Now I think I can die happy!" she said. As Spur began a slow rhythm, she climaxed again and again until she was sweating and limp.

Spur felt his own pressure building, and so did she and she revived to pound upward with each of his hard thrusts until he shot his load deep inside her and then collapsed.

"My God, but that was wonderful! I think I'll stay here all the rest of the day making love to you. Now I know why my mother told me making love was for married people. It's too good to let the secret get out!"

She chattered on for five minutes as Spur regained his strength, then he moved away from her and dressed quickly. He picked up her clothes and laid them beside her.

Then he found the envelope and tore it open. It was a note written by Tracy:

"Keep safe today, I have a surprise planned for you for our supper tonight. Don't let them collect that reward money!"

He read it, folded the note and put it in his pocket, then watched the slightly chunky girl putting on her clothes.

"I'm not at all self-conscious, dressing in front of you," she said in wonder. "Is that because we just made love?"

Spur nodded. "Isn't it a nice, warm feeling?"

"Yes it is, wonderful. And do you know what I'm going to do now? I'm going to take a close look at the three men who have been courting me and pick out the one I think has the best potential as a

174

husband, and then fall in love with him, and marry him!"

"And what about making love?"

"That, sir, is for a husband and wife! None of these men, or any others for that matter, will even touch my breasts, before I get married." She sighed and came over to him. "Since it is going to be a few months, would you touch me again, just for a minute?"

Spur smiled and put his hands under her chemise and fondled her breasts until she began to breathe fast again. Then he lifted her blouse and kissed each breast tenderly. She yelped and climaxed and Spur held her as she screeched as she rode through the spasms.

"Oh, good Lord! but that is marvelous!" She shook her head and smoothed down her clothes. "Well, that is that for a while. Spur McCoy, I want to thank you."

He silenced her with a sweet kiss on her lips.

"The pleasure was mine. Never underestimate yourself, Mary Beth. You are a wonderful woman, and you'll make any man you choose the best wife in the state."

She finished dressing and kissed his cheek.

"I hope the man I find is just half as marvelous as you are. But I know that can't be, so I'll take the best once I can catch." She smiled at him, turned and walked out of the room and toward the front door.

Spur McCoy went up to his room on the second floor and stared out the window. He saw Mary

Beth walking away. She turned once and watched the house for a moment, seemed to smile, and then walked quickly toward the Belcher mine.

The Secret Service Agent worked through his options. If he went on the street he would need some sort of disguise. He had nothing to check on today. The three leads he had were played out. He would sleep most of the day, and see what could stir up that evening. Right now darkness was his best friend.

Canchuna woke him just before six that afternoon. She kissed him softly on the lips and worked her hand down to his crotch. He came awake grabbing her hand, and when he saw who she was, he kissed her cheek and let her go.

"Miz Belcher says it's time to wake up a sleepy-head."

"You have an interesting way of doing it."

"It always works." She walked toward the door, then looked over her shoulder. "You coming?"

It was the first real dinner he had eaten at the mansion. They were in the big dining room. The table would seat twenty, but the three of them sat at one end. They had just started the first course when the front door guard brought a message. He gave it to Spur.

The agent opened it and read:

"Tonight is the night. We start picking up freight at ten p.m. All owners were notified." It was signed by Sheriff Gilpin.

"Important?" Tracy asked.

"Not at the moment. But I will be busy later tonight."

Spur finished the dinner, went up to his room and put on his sturdiest black pants, a long sleeved blue shirt and a jacket. He wore his half boots and the .45 tied low on his thigh.

Tracy stood in the door watching him.

"We ship tonight," she said.

"Sheriff said the same thing."

"You're here to keep them from stealing the gold and silver."

He nodded.

"I'll have almost a million dollars in boullion on that train."

"My job is to be sure you don't lose a dime's worth." Spur kissed her lips, then walked out the back door, heading for the sheriff's office. Next he would go to the Virginia & Truckee railroad passenger station next to the assay office and just down the tracks a hundred feet from the Consolidated California shaft house.

Spur McCoy had no idea how the gold and silver would be loaded, but he would find out and help supervise. There would be soldiers on the train, but he did not know how many.

A shiver darted up his back as he walked. Several men in town had waited almost six months for tonight to come. He was going to do his damnedest to disappoint them!

FIFTEEN

SPUR STOOD NEAR the office of the Consolidated California Mine and watched the loading procedure. He had walked up five minutes before and saw four men with shotguns standing near the building. One of them had come forward and challenged him.

"Who the hell are you, stranger, and what business you got here?"

"Who's asking?"

"Cartright, special Sheriff's deputy."

"My name is McCoy. I'm also a special deputy."

The man with the shotgun relaxed. "Yeah, heard of you. Gilpin said you might be around. They're about half done here. First loading."

Spur waved and moved on past toward the door.

The gold and silver bars were coming out of the company's vault, somewhere inside the office complex. The ten pound gold and silver slabs were brought out with each man carrying two. The men were checked at four points that Spur could see. A corridor of armed men, most with ten and twelve gauge shotguns, extended from the office door to the railroad tracks where a regular box car had its rolling door open.

Rush Sommers himself sat at a small table with two kerosene lamps on it at the front door of his office and marked on a paper the stamped number on each bar of gold or silver that came out. Two treasury agents sat at the table making similar marks and stamping number recordings.

Spur looked at the box car, and saw it was more than a standard freight car. Inside had been built a separate steel box. That box was of heavy sheet steel and had a complicated locking mechanism on it. Once it was closed and locked, it would take a lot of dynamite even to bend the structure.

Soon the last bar of silver was handed into the car. Sommers and the Treasury men came to the car, stepped inside to check the number of bars there against the count they had just made at the door of the office. A moment later they came down the slanted planks that led up to the rail car. The men nodded at each other, both shook Sommers' hand and they pushed the planks inside the car and the train prepared to move to the next mine.

The special deputies walked beside the train as it ground slowly from the Consolidated to the next stop. Spur made sure that Sommers did not see him. Now he wondered just what Sommers would do? Capture the train and blow it up half way between Virginia City and Carson City? Where would he take the gold? How would he transport it?

As he walked along beside the train, Spur heard someone coming up behind him. He turned and saw the tall, slender sheriff overtaking him.

"How many more to load, Sheriff?"

179

"Just starting. That was the first one."

"Any problems?"

"Not so far. They wouldn't hit us before we get all the stuff in one place. That is our dangerous time."

"Agreed. That means all the way from here to San Francisco."

"That's somebody else's problem once it gets over the county line," Sheriff Gilpin said.

The train wheezed to the next mine and Spur watched the procedures again. He roamed the area around the train and the mine, but could find nothing suspicious. It would take a fortified land battleship, and armor plated wagon to get away with any gold from here, let alone a force of a hundred to match the Sheriff's deputies. No. The attack would not take place here. It would be suicide.

The robbery try would come along the tracks somewhere, away from the town, away from all the guns, but where, that was the problem. Where would Sommers attack to steal the gold and silver?

A mile and a half down the rails from Virginia City, and over the bank to the small water course below, the five cowboys were getting restless. Night had closed in on them again and no word from the saloon owner.

The youngest of the crew came out of the darkness with Lee. Jimmy grinned and laughed as the man teased him about his time with Lee.

"Was she a good fuck for you, Jimmy?" one man asked.

"Best I've had," Jimmy said.

"Best of both times I bet!" someone jibed and they all laughed.

Lee had been going naked most of the time. The men liked it and it helped her keep them happy. She stood now, without clothes, backing up to the big fire they had going.

"Don't burn your pussy hair off!" One man crowed.

The big Irishman with the red beard called Red by the others, grabbed Lee by one of her large breasts and pulled her away from the fire.

"No more today," Lee said. "I did everybody. You Red was the first this morning."

"Once more," Red said.

She tried to pull away.

"Whore, you don't make the rules around here. We do. If we say you fuck all day and all night, ten times everyone of us, that's what you do."

Another man cheered.

Lee saw the mood of the men and shrugged. She was a survivor. She would be around long after most of these guys were dead.

"My blankets are over here."

"No, right here in the firelight," Red crowed. "I like to see you sweat."

He pushed her down in the dust near the fire, and the men gathered around.

"Want to see how an expert makes a half breed Chinese whore beg for a big cock?" Red asked.

The men cheered.

He lay half on top of her and began seducing her like she was a virgin, working slowly with his hands over her body until Lee began to react.

"Just do it!" she shouted at him.

"Hey, not until you're ready, not until you beg."

Red worked his hands over her again and again, moving his stiff phallus up to her face and then down, grazing it across her throbbing breasts.

"Come on you cunt, beg me to stick you," Red said. She refused and he teased her more and more. Then he tied her hands together and stretched them over her head and tied the long end to a tree. He spread-eagled her legs, tying each to a tree.

"Now you ready to beg for it?" he asked. The men saw that she had not protested when she was tied up. And now she writhed and panted on the ground looking at Red, watching him.

"Go ahead if you want to. You're just another dollar to me, you bastard!"

"You want me, you want it bad, Lee. Beg me for it, come on beg!"

She shook her head.

The next thing she saw was a slender knife that Red pulled from his boot. He lay the blade against her throat.

"You ready to die, whore?"

"I've been threatened before. Fuck me if you want to. Go ahead."

"Beg for it!"

"No."

He moved the knife to her breast and sliced an inch long line in the side bringing a ribbon of blood.

Lee screamed.

The intensity of the sound surprised all of them.

"No more!" she shouted.

"Then beg me for it inside you!"

"No."

The big redhead from Wyoming sliced again with his knife, making a bloodline appear on the girl's other breast.

She screamed and tried to claw at him but her hands were tied.

"You bastard! You fucking madman!" Her glances darted around the camp, looking for a friend. "Get this animal away from me, you guys! You're all in trouble if you don't stop him right now! I'll go to the sheriff. I don't have to put up with this. A little slapping around I can take, but no fucking knife! Get him away from me!"

The men looked at each other.

"Yeah, hell. Don't hurt her. You ain't got a right to ruin her for the rest of us."

Quickly the knife rested on the speaker's throat as the redhead glared at him.

"You still got any objections, asshole? Cause if you have you gonna be making them without being able to talk. Your throat is gonna be slashed open and you'll be drinking your own blood!"

"Hey, go easy there. It was just my idea."

The knife moved away and Red knelt over the girl. "Cunt, you must think you're the best whore in town. Christ, five guys to service for a week, maybe two. Only it ain't gonna work out that way. I don't stand for no woman to back talk me, especially a whore like you. Now, you apologize to me, and I just might let you go."

Lee tried to spit in his face. She missed. "You guys afraid of this crazy man? He's loco, can't you tell? Probably killed his wife. Cut me loose, or it's no more pussy for any of you!"

The redhead backhanded her on the face and her head bounced to one side and she screamed. Her voice echoed and re-echoed down the valley until it faded out among the lodgepole pines and mountain hemlock.

The knife rose again and drew a three inch deep slice on her upper left arm. It gushed with blood and Lee screamed again.

Red sat on his heels, stroking his erection.

"You want cock so bad you can taste it, whore. Tell me you want it."

Lee looked away. Red threw more wood on the fire so he could see her better.

He straddled her sitting on her crotch and watched her face.

"Give up the stubborn streak, whore. You lose, and you know it. Fuckers like you always lose, one way or another. You want me to cut one of your tits off?"

She glared at him a second, then turned away.

"Don't ignore me, bitch! My wife used to do that! I taught her a lesson. Am I gonna have to teach you one too?"

A grin came on his face and he moved between her legs and roughly drove into her vagina. He watched her as he pumped a dozen times.

"Oh, yes, the good stuff is coming. They opened the flood gates and it's coming, and when it gets

184

here, then I've got a big surprise for you, little whore. A big surprise!"

He laughed softly and settled down to pumping hard. As his breath began to come in short gasps he took the knife in his right hand.

Red's eyes closed and his face contorted, he drove into her brutally hard and at the same time slashed her throat with the knife.

As he watched the blood spurt from her throat, the woman under him writhed in her death throes and Red screamed to the greatest climax of his life.

"My God!" the nearest man said. "He killed Lee! Look at that!"

The other men gathered around the two bodies. Jimmy pulled his six-gun. "The bastard killed a woman!"

"She was just a whore."

"Yeah, but she was a woman. I don't hold with that." Jimmy stood in the firelight, his gun out.

Red came away from the dead whore slowly, his only concession to her had been to open his fly. Now his hand snaked down to his right hip in the shadows he drew his pistol.

The .44 roared twice in Red's hand and Jimmy, the youngest man around the fire, slammed backward as both rounds hit him in the chest and drove him into the darkness.

Red stood and looked down at Jimmy.

"The son of a bitch drew on me!" Red said.

They looked at Jimmy, and found he was still alive.

"No man got a right to draw on me!" Red bellowed in his own defense.

Jimmy could not talk. His eyes fluttered open, then closed. He lived for another fifteen minutes before he died.

They had just started to dig a grave for the two bodies when they heard a horse coming. All four men faded into the shadows until they saw the rider in the firelight.

"Yeah, what the hell you want?" Red called from the darkness.

"Got a message from Tony. He says get the camp closed down and cleaned up and be ready to move. There will be a train come along here sometime after midnight. You're to have the pack animals all ready."

"Easy to do that," Red said. "Tony tell you anything else?"

"Yeah," the messenger, a man in his twenties said. "He told me that you would pay me ten dollars for the ride."

Red laughed. "Yeah, he said you would be coming and that I should pay you off." Red's six-gun blasted twice and the rider jolted out of the saddle to the ground. He was dead by the time the men got to him. They stared at Red.

"Hell, I'm just doing what the boss said to do. He said to kill the messenger once he gave us the directions from Tony. I do what the fuck I'm told. Now, let's get these three bodies out of the way, get our gear together and be ready to ride at midnight."

* * *

Spur McCoy watched the last mine owner certify with the Treasury Department officials the number of gold and silver bars put on the train, and saw the three separate locking doors slide in place over the three-foot square opening in the vault-like interior of the box car. It would be a tough job for anyone to break into it.

"Won't be long now before I'm free and clear of this protection job," Sheriff Gilpin said. "I'll be glad when the train pulls out and the Federal officers take charge."

"That's when the real problems will come," Spur said. He stared at the train, trying to figure out the weak spots, the places where it was most vulnerable.

There were only four cars in the train, the engine and coal car, the gold vault car, the one passenger car with blacked out windows where Spur knew there were fifteen blue coated soldiers with loaded repeating rifles ready for a stiff fire fight if needed. The caboose brought up the rear.

The engine was the most vital part of the train. Stop the engine, you stop the train. Spur had cleared with the Federal men on board and the army people so he could come and go on the train. He told them he would be riding at least until the gold car reached Reno where it would be put on the main line.

Now he stepped into the passenger car and saw three army .45's lift to cover him as he entered the door.

"Evening," one of the army men said. "Glad it's you."

Spur waved at them and went to the end of the car. The door onto the little open platform where the passenger car coupled with the freight car was locked shut from both sides. McCoy went back to the caboose and climbed the metal ladder to the roof.

The train had not moved since the last gold and silver came on board. It was ten minutes until midnight.

Spur walked along the caboose top, jumped the short distance to the top of the passenger car and walked to the end. He jumped to the freight car that held the gold. There were no openings from the top into the car below. No explosives could be dropped down ventilator tubes, or any such openings. He moved on to the coal car and stared at it in the gloom of the half moon.

Nothing there but coal, a fireman to shovel it, and the engineer who drove the train.

Spur lay down on top of the box car, and felt the train lurch as the engine hissed steam and the string of units bounced and jerked as the train began to roll slowly down the track.

Yes, he would stay where he was. He had a good view of the whole train, could see any problems ahead and be ready for them. Nothing happened as the train rolled through Virginia City at ten miles an hour. It would not pick up any more speed until it left the city, and not much then because of the downgrade coming.

He saw a man move first out of the corner of his eye. They had just retraced their route past one of the mills, and a man dressed all in black jumped from a building near the tracks and ran hard, grabbed the rail along the coal car and boosted himself up to the coal pile.

The engineer had not seen the man move. The fireman was busy shoveling coal. Spur ran toward the edge of the freight car. The coal car was attached to the engine on this rig. He saw the man now, standing beside the engineer, a gun in his hand, as he yelled at the man who ran the train.

Spur watched with a frown. He could shoot the robber, but the man might live long enough to kill the engineer. There seemed no way to take the gunman alive.

Slowly the train picked up speed as it headed past the last few buildings and into the grade that would wind down over four thousand feet to the valley twenty-one miles away.

Spur lay at the edge of the jolting box car. He heard glass breaking behind him, then three thunderous explosions that rattled the train but did not blow it off the tracks. Spur ran back to the passenger car and saw smoke coming from the broken windows. He lay down and hung over the side so he could see inside the car. The section was shattered. A dynamite stick bomb thrown through the window? Probably. Then he noticed the soldiers. They were riddled with wounds, everyone he saw was dead or dying. He saw one sergeant still in his seat, the ends of two large nails sticking out of his head.

That was when Spur remembered the deadly shrapnel bombs he had seen made: nails taped to two or three sticks of dynamite. They created a grape shot effect and in a 360 degree zone. The soldiers could not help him defend the train!

Quickly he lifted back to the roof and ran along the top of the rocking train to the coal car. The man still had his gun trained on the engineer.

Spur took out his army .45 Colt and aimed carefully at the gunman. He must not let the jolting boxcar ruin his aim. In any case he had to aim as far from the engineer as possible. Spur waited for a relatively straight and even section of track, and he fired. The round tore through the shoulder of the gunman below. He slammed against the engine controls, then turned to fire to the rear. Spur's second round took him through the heart, and the engineer clawed at him to get him away from the controls. In doing so the engineer pushed the dead man out of the engine to the swiftly passing roadway.

McCoy jumped to the coal car, waved at the fireman who only then looked up, and moved toward the engineer.

"Somebody is trying to take over the train!" Spur shouted so the engineer could hear over the noisy steam engine.

The engineer nodded.

"Thanks for killing that bastard! He was bragging to me how easy it was to get on board."

"Don't stop the train for any reason before we get to Carson City," Spur said.

The engineer understood.

Spur looked up and saw a figure outlined against the sky standing on the coal car. He tossed something at Spur and then leaped back to the boxcar.

Spur McCoy looked down in the light from the fire box and saw a sputtering fuse of a dynamite bomb lying at his feet. The fuse burned rapidly, and he could see dozens of nails and staples taped around the two sticks of dynamite.

If it went off in the engine cab it would kill all three of them and the train would become a runaway!

Spur dove for the deadly dynamite and nails bomb.

SIXTEEN

THE DEATH DEALING nail bomb on the floor of Engine No. 20 of the Virginia & Truckee Railroad had a burning fuse not three inches long when Spur McCoy ended his dive on his elbows. He grabbed the horrendous device and tossed it out the big window opening of the engineer's cab.

Almost at once there was a shattering roar as the bomb went off before it hit the ground. It had dropped well below the height of the window and only three or four of the bent and twisted nails drove into the window and clattered harmlessly around the metal train cab.

"Close," Spur said as he stood. The engineer jumped back to the controls on the train, and slowed the line of cars as they started down the first grade on the twenty mile trip to Carson City.

Safe for the moment, Spur knew, but the man who threw the bomb was still on the train. Spur jumped on the coal and peered over the top of the treasure car. No one rode the top of the train. The killer could be between the cars or in the caboose or passenger car.

The Secret Agent moved cautiously, checking

every possible hiding place as he worked down the top of the gold car. No one lurked on the platform between the cars. He knew the door into the death car was locked from both sides so the man could not have entered that way.

A minute later Spur ran along the top of the passenger car and checked the platform between the passenger car and caboose.

No one there.

He eased down the ladder and looked inside the regular passenger unit that held the army guard.

For a moment it reminded him of the war. Blood and bodies were everywhere. One or two of the men might still be alive inside, but it was doubtful. He would check them as soon as he found the bomber. He went to the roof of the caboose. There was no entry through the front of the car. He had taken only two steps on the wooden roof when a rifle bullet plowed through the top of the caboose a dozen inches from his foot, then another, and another. He pulled back to the front of the Passenger car and waited.

It seemed the only solution. He waited for a slight upgrade, then went between the fast moving cars and worked to uncouple the cars. He had learned how in St. Louis from an old train man, and now the information came in handy. As the train slowed on the upgrade, he kicked the last release point and the cars came apart. The caboose slowed more and more and gradually the passenger car and the rest of the train pulled away from it. Someone appeared on the top of the caboose swearing. Spur dodged inside the passenger car as the rifleman fired six shots into the door of the train car, but missed Spur.

The agent looked at the death in the passenger car. Eight men had been killed outright by the three blasts of the small bombs. Two more must have lived for a few moments. One groaned where he lay in the aisle. Spur ran to look at him, stepping over bodies with no arms, and another with his head blown off.

The wounded man had no face, only a bloody mass of flesh. A massive wound in his chest bled a steady stream. Spur turned away. There was no way to save the man from death.

He ran out of the car, saw the caboose a quarter of a mile behind, and stopped on the tracks. Spur climbed to the top of the car and hurried forward to the coal car and engine.

"How far are we from Virginia City?" Spur asked.

The engineer looked outside.

"Maybe two miles, no more. Just starting."

As he said it a blast lit up the tracks a hundred yards in front of them. The massive explosion curled one of the tracks back like the stem of a wilting flower. Rocks and dust burst into the air with tremendous force, some of them raining down on the onrushing train.

"We're doing fifty miles an hour!" the trainman yelled. "No chance I can stop her. Jump on the uphill side!"

Spur looked on the downhill side and saw why. They were snaking along a sheer drop into darkness. He had no idea how far down it was to solid ground. He crawled to the right hand side door and motioned for the fireman to jump. Then Spur went off hoping for a soft landing.

The hard ground of the embankment where the track bed had been blasted out rushed up fast to meet Spur McCoy. He hit on his feet and tried to run, but the forward motion of his body jolted him ahead of his feet and he hit on his shoulder and rolled away from the deadly grinding wheels of the train.

He rolled, hit his head, rolled a dozen more times, then came to a stop against a huge boulder which had been blasted apart and shoved aside to make room for the tracks.

When he stopped rolling he could hear the wheels of the engine screaming as the engineer locked them and they shrilled steel against steel in a hundred foot skid.

But there was not time nor distance enough. The dynamiter had planned well. The blast came at precisely the moment when the engineer would not have time left to stop the train before it hit the blasted tracks.

In the faint moonlight Spur had seen the right of way filled with a continuing shower of sparks from the tracks and wheels, then he saw the sparks stop, the great hulk of the engine lifted as it tried to climb the twisted, upthrust tracks. It was an impossible task and the shattered track bed gave way on the outside of the cliff and the engine tilted, then slanted more to the side and rolled half over as it plunged off the tracks into the black void.

The treasure car and the passenger car followed the engine. They were locked tightly together, and Spur could only watch as the thirty million dollars in gold tipped over the side and vaulted into the black air space over the deep canyon.

Spur tried to sit up, but his scratching made noise, and he waited, counting the seconds until he could hear the crash below. It took too long! How deep was the gorge?

Then the sounds came, the crash of metal against rock, metal tearing, wood splintering, rocks crashing down from the small landslide, then the booming, blasting roar of the boiler exploding.

Spur waited but there was only silence. He was sure the engineer did not get out of the cab. He was on the wrong side, and he was locking the drive wheels until the end, hoping for time to stop his train.

At least the soldiers were all dead before they went over.

Spur sat up. He ached in every muscle in his body. His heavy jacket had protected his torso and arms, but his legs were scraped and scratched and his hands a mass of scraped off skin and raw flesh. He felt for his six-gun. It was still in place. The tie down had saved him, keeping the holster from flopping around.

The Secret Agent pushed on the rock and got to his feet. The caboose was out of sight a half mile down the tracks.

Spur walked unsteadily to the tracks and looked over the dropoff. It looked bottomless in the dark. Two hundred feet? Probably enough to crush the steel box inside the treasure car and pop it open like a cardboard box when you stepped on it.

He could not get down to the wreck from here. Staring through the gloom, Spur decided a quarter of a mile on down the tracks the cliff was not so sharp, and he figured he could climb down.

McCoy heard a groan and checked the right of way. Fifteen feet behind him he found the fireman. The man had a broken leg.

"Just stay right there, pardner. We'll get a work train or a handcar out here as soon as we can. Afraid thirty million in gold has to come before you do this time."

The fireman nodded. "Christ, but it hurts!"

Spur looked at the leg, straightened it out, causing the man to scream. Then Spur put some outward pressure on the foot and the fireman grinned.

"Yeah, that's better. I can stand it now. Thanks."

Spur patted his shoulder and limped on down the tracks. It was painful walking, as he made his way around the hole in the tracks and the fifty feet of roadbed that had been blasted into the gorge. It would take a major construction project before a train could run on the tracks again.

Spur's left knee collapsed and he almost fell. He caught himself and stood, tried the knee and found the heavy bruise on the side. He tested it and found that he could walk, if he took it easy. No hard running, no dramatic jumps.

It took Spur twenty minutes to work his way down the steep side of the canyon. He held on to scrub growth, worked along shelves of rock and at last got to the bottom. There was a dry watercourse but no wetness. As quickly as he could, he walked back toward the steaming mass of wreckage ahead of him.

There had been no fire. The furnace must have been smothered by the wreckage so there was nothing to burn. If the flames had worked into the brush and timber along the valley floor it could have been a serious forest fire.

He came to the dead engine first, crumpled and lying on its side looking like a beached whale, entirely out of its element and natural surroundings. The engine had hit the side of the cliff and rolled and tumbled. Two of the drive wheels had been knocked off, the smokestack had vanished, and as he got closer, Spur saw that the body of the engineer hung half out the window on Engine 20.

The two cars had broken apart and lay some distance from each other. He saw the treasure car next. It had hit boulders on the ravine floor and split open. The wood and metal box car had shattered, leaving the steel gold and silver vault, but it also had split. He heard voices as he worked closer.

Then the voice of Tony Giardello came through clearly.

"That's right. Pass out the gold bars first, put six of them in the canvas bags on each side of the pack horses, and move up the trail. The faster you work right now, the more money you'll make."

Spur wished he had a rifle. He couldn't see Giardello, but he could seal up the treasure vault until morning. Now he would need different tactics. He was sure all of the men up there were armed. He heard four or five other voices.

Without making a sound, Spur moved up and watched. If he started a fire fight, he could easily get pinned down and they would go on with their work. He had to wait and watch and find out what they were going to do with the gold. Where would it go? To a hidden cave somewhere?

He wondered how long it would take the train people to learn about the wreck? Did they have a hand car that checked the track every morning? He hoped so.

He worked ahead closer to the wreck, found a tree and stood behind it as he listened. The men were swearing at the weight of the heavy gold bars.

A short time later he heard Tony's voice again. "You're loaded. Just follow my directions and you won't have any trouble. As soon as you unload get back here. We've got to work fast to get it all before daylight."

Spur listened to the horses, figured they were moving upstream, back toward town! Why would they take the gold back to Virginia City?

Now he was as interested in finding out where the gold was to be taken as he was in stopping them. He had to do both.

Spur circled around the wreck. A few moments later he came to what had once been a camp. It could have been the point where the men waited for the train to come by. He was almost through the area when he saw a body at one side. He checked it and found two more corpses, one a naked woman.

In the dim light she looked part Chinese. He hurried on, walking carefully on his damaged knee. He should have no trouble keeping up with heavily laden pack animals. If they went all the way to town he would find out where they were going and get a horse for his return trip.

It took nearly a half hour for the pack horses to climb the trail toward town. They were still a half mile away when Spur sensed someone behind him. He moved in back of a boulder and waited. A few minutes later a second five horse pack string came along led by a tall man with red hair.

Spur drew his gun and stood up.

"Going somewhere, badass?" Spur asked. Red from Wyoming drew his .44 but Spur's Colt spoke first. The man grunted, tried to lift his gun again, then tipped off the horse and fell to the ground dead. Quickly Spur moved the string of pack animals off the trail into a spot of brush and tied them. He dragged the body out of the trail and hid it, then mounted the saddle horse and rode as quickly as he could up the trail toward town. He caught up with the pack string just as it wound through the near side of town and stopped at the back door of the office of the Consolidated California Mine.

Spur waited out of sight as he saw Rush Sommers in the light at the doorway. Then the unloading began as the pack horses came to the door and the gold was quickly transferred inside. Only Sommers and the pack train rider did the work. Unusual. But not unusual for secrecy, especially when Sommers was stealing his own gold and that of the rest of the mine owners.

McCoy led his horse out of hearing, mounted and rode for the sheriff's office.

Clete Gilpin was still up, waiting for any word of trouble.

Spur told about the wreck. ''Warn the railroad people not to let any trains move on the tracks,'' Spur said. ''Then send about twenty deputies down to the wreck as soon as it gets light. Not much we can do until then. We might even wind up shooting each other.''

He did not tell the sheriff about the pack trains. He wanted to take care of that little problem himself.

Now he rode for the crash. He was half way along the trail when he met the third string coming uphill.

Spur rode up to the man and pulled out his .45.

''You want to live more than twenty seconds, lift your hands and don't make a sound.''

The man did as told. Spur pulled the pistol from his belt, and ordered the man to untie the pack train and ride with him. Spur relaxed for a second, and the man drew and fired. He missed and Spur's reaction shot killed him. Then the agent led the pack train into the timbered section, just as the first pack train man came down the hill looking for a new load.

The outlaw came with his pistol out, and fired at Spur before McCoy was sure the man was there. Spur traded shots, then dropped off his horse and ran quickly from tree to tree, moving up on the gunman without letting him know his location. The rider was watching for the movement of another horse.

In two minutes Spur was within range. He stepped from behind a tree and leveled his pistol at the rider.

"Raise your hands and live," Spur barked.

The man dove off his saddle away from Spur, digging for his gun.

Spur had seen this done before. He waited until the man hit the ground on the other side of his horse. Spur shot under the horse, hitting the man in the shoulder where he lay on the ground. When McCoy saw the man lift his six-gun, the Secret Agent put two more slugs into the outlaw, ending his brief career.

Spur hid the body, moved the horses and pack animals over with the others, then rode quietly down the trail. Three pack trains were out of business. Were there any more?

He found out as he neared the wreck. Spur stopped, left his horse tied near the trail and waited behind a big ponderosa pine. He heard the clop of horses' hooves on the rocky trail long before he saw them.

The man leading them was on foot, the line around his left hand, a Winchester across his back and a pistol in his hand. Through the gloom of the half-moon night, Spur had not seen the man until he was within twenty feet.

"Hold it right there or I'll cut you in half!" Spur shouted. The man dove for the ground with the first word. Spur blasted three shots at the rolling figure. He stopped moving. When Spur came up to him and rolled him over with his toe, he saw that one of his rounds had taken the outlaw through the forehead.

Tony and anyone else at the wreck must have heard the shots. Now he had to move in and clean up. He had settled with four men, was there more than one more? Tony was out there.

Spur McCoy moved up slowly, every sense alert, his eyes probing the darkness as far as possible. He heard nothing as he stepped gingerly forward, not making a sound, not stepping on a dry twig. How many more men were around the wreck with Tony?

SEVENTEEN

McCOY STOPPED AND listened. He heard something not too far away. There was the flare of a match, then all darkness again ahead of him. In the total silence, saddle leather creaked, as if a man had just sat his horse.

Now the telltale sounds of hooves on hard rocks came through the quiet, slightly moist night air. Spur knew the sounds. They were made by another pack string and a rider leading them. He waited.

After a minute it was plain to Spur that the sounds had become fainter and now were gone all together. The rider had taken his pack train away from Virginia City, down the slope. Where was he going? It was more than twenty miles by trail to Carson City.

Spur ran lightly along the trail. When he came to the wreck site he paused to look at it. Twisted, tortured steel, splintered wood, and still a smell of hot metal and steam and water-soaked wood and fabric of the passenger car.

He picked up the trail and looked up at the stars. It was nearing two a.m. according to the Big Dipper in its nightly trip around the North Star. Lots of time to daylight.

He listened, but could hear nothing. The trail was still well defined even after five years of the railroad's installation. Few horses came over this trail anymore. It was faster and a lot easier to ride the rails.

McCoy did not think about his hurt knee as he jogged ahead. He was moving faster than the horses, and should catch up with them soon. A quarter of a mile downstream he came to a small offshoot canyon, not more than twenty yards wide, that angled back into the mountains. Tony and his helpers, if any, could be moving the rest of the gold to another spot.

Why? Stealing it from Sommers? Could be. Spur ran into the mouth of the small arroyo and saw fresh horse droppings. The five horse pack train had gone this way. He moved carefully now. There was no margin for error here. He wanted the advantage of surprise.

Tony Giardello had no thought that anyone was tracking him. He had put seventy bars of solid gold on the pack train, then hurried the mounts downstream to the first good hiding place he could find. He did not know the country.

This side valley looked possible. But now he was not so sure. He wanted to find a cave of some kind, or some big rocks where he could hide the gold bars between and then cover them with dirt and rocks. Each one of those ten pound bars of gold was worth three thousand, three hundred dollars!

He had seventy of the gold bars! . . . That was over two hundred and thirty thousand dollars! More than a quarter of a million! And he wasn't going to share this with Rush Sommers or anyone. He paused and looked into the darkness behind him. Had he heard something? He had been jittery all night.

Tony turned and moved his pack string deeper into the little valley. It petered out fifty yards ahead where the side ridges closed in and the ground climbed sharply into jagged, dry pinnacles. There had to be a spot here.

Then he saw it through the night gloom. It was an old white barked pine that had grown with two tops where they split off about forty feet off the ground. At the base was a jumble of boulders and rocks that had fallen from the desert dry upper slopes and been stopped by the sturdy trunk. He could rearrange the smaller rocks, clear out between the two larger ones, and have a perfect spot for the gold.

Tony had not done this much physical exercise in years, but the thought of that quarter of a million dollars on his horses spurred him on. He selected the spot and began throwing out the rocks. It was hard work and would take some time. He had to be finished shortly after dawn, because by then the place would be swarming with army and railroad men and deputy sheriffs.

Sommers should be happy with his share of the loot, even though they didn't get all of it. Tony still couldn't figure out why the pack train men didn't return after their first trip. Could they have tried a little *rob the robber* on their own? No, most of them were too stupid for that.

He wiped sweat from his forehead, then went back to pitching out rocks. Suddenly he stopped. One of the rocks he had thrown out came back into the pit. He reached for the pistol pushed in his pants belt.

"Don't move your hand any farther, Giardello or you'll turn into a corpse, a rich corpse, but dead as you can get."

"Who the hell . . . McCoy?"

"Good gamble, Giardello, nice guess. Looks like you're digging out your own grave."

Tony eased to a sitting position on the rocks, and kept his hands in front of him.

"Look, McCoy, let's talk business here. I'm a businessman. True I was once a banker, but that's a business. What do we have? We have a little over a quarter of a million dollars worth of gold. Raw, ten pound bars of solid gold."

"Which doesn't belong to you, Giardello."

"No, but half of it could. What I suggest is that we go partners, an even split right down the middle. You take thirty-five of the gold bars and I'll grab the other thirty-five. Nobody will ever be the wiser. And let Rush Sommers fry in hell wondering about it. He should have gotten his share by now."

"So Rush did set up the whole caper."

"Of course! That's the beauty of it! We steal from the master criminal, so it's really no theft at all. Isn't that ingenious?"

"From one point of view, Tony, it all makes good sense."

"Come closer so I can see you. I know we can work this out. You have the gun and I don't, so why don't we say you get sixty percent of the gold and I'll be happy with forty."

Spur shook his head as he came nearer. He watched Tony closely to be sure he wasn't up to any trickery.

"Now, that's better, I can see your face. Never like doing business with a man when I can't see his face. Oh, may I pick up a small stone from the pile here? Nervous habit, I like to have something in my hands. A tactile problem I guess. So, what do you think about the sixty-forty proposition?"

Spur stared at him.

"True, true, you could kill me where I sit and take the whole thing, but you're not that kind of a man. You would never shoot me down in cold blood, you'd need a reason. I want to give you a better reason, over a hundred and sixty thousand dollars! Think what you could do with that much money!"

Spur laughed. "Not a chance, Giardello. I'm going to enjoy too much turning you in and watching you hang for murder, conspiracy and robbery from a railroad train. I'll have a drink and watch you hang until you stop twitching."

"Too bad. You would have enjoyed the money, Spur. In that case no reason I should warn you about the rattlesnake coiled just below your feet. He's a big one well within striking distance."

For a second Spur McCoy felt the old revulsion billow up. Being an Eastern man born and educated, he had never been able to completely beat down his fear of the slimy killers. He shivered and laughed to cover his sudden anxiety.

"That's the oldest trick in the western book, Giardello. I'm surprised you would try something as dumb as that."

"All right, I warned you. Can I stand up?"

Giardello began to stand up as soon as he asked, Spur nodded and the tavern owner flipped the rock back on the pile. It hit and bounced down toward the ground, striking the rattlesnake which lay there, coiled two feet from Spur's boots.

The snake rattled.

Spur lunged forward, pulling down his pistol to fire at the snake.

Giardello jerked his own six-gun from his belt and snapped a quick shot at Spur. The round hit Spur in the outside of the thigh, and jolted him backward away from the snake.

Giardello scurried a dozen feet up the ravine, behind his pack horses. He fired once more at Spur who had escaped from the snake but was bleeding heavily from his thigh.

Spur had cover now behind one of the boulders Giardello intended to use for his private bank.

"No way out, Tony. That's almost a box canyon up there. I could pick you off in two shots if you tried to climb those cliffs."

Giardello did not reply. He had put the five horses in motion, moving them toward Spur. The saloon owner bent over, hiding behind the horses. Spur sighted in on the closest pack horse and shot it in the head. It went down with a scream of protest and died, stopping the other pack horses which were all tied together.

Giardello ran now with only his saddle horse as protection, trying to keep his own legs near the legs of the moving horse. Spur lifted up and fired twice. The second round hit Giardello just above the ankle and broke his lower leg bone. He went down in a bellowing rage as the frightened horse charged ahead into a gallop, dragging Tony for a few feet before he let go of the reins.

Tony laughed through his pain.

"Bastard McCoy, I've got you again. Now I'm downstream, and you have nowhere to go. You couldn't ride for help now if you wanted to. First you would have to catch my horse. You also need to get past me and I have twenty-four shots left for my pistol. How many you have?"

It would have been good to put Giardello on trial, especially if he would testify against Sommers. It wouldn't work out that way. Spur reloaded his six-gun, pushing out the used rounds, filling all six chambers. Then he stood up, spotted Giardello twenty yards away and fired all six rounds. Three of them struck Giardello. The gambler, saloon owner, ex-banker, and current robber, died there in the Nevada dust and rocks with his quarter of a million dollars. One of his dreams had always been to die rich.

Spur McCoy tore up his shirt and tied strips of cloth together to make a bandage. He put a thick compress over the bullet wound and then wrapped it so tightly he could hardly walk. He struggled to the nearest pack horse, cut the traces from it with his knife and hoisted himself on the animal's back only after he walked the bay to a large rock.

It was almost four a.m. when he had the pack horse back at he wreck. He tied up the mount near his other horse, and investigated the wreck of the passenger car. It lay on its roof. All fifteen army troopers inside were dead.

Spur came out shaking his head. He had used a tightly wrapped handful of dry weeds to make a torch to check out the troopers. Now he made one more, lit it and looked inside the steel box where the gold and silver had been stored.

The box was crushed, the locking devices of no value since the whole end of the box where they had been placed, had sprung open, popping one side of the box outward. There was still over half of the gold and silver left in the vault.

He would have to wait for the sheriff to arrive. McCoy did not know for sure if he could ride back up the trail. He felt lightheaded and wanted some water. The bullet in his leg had not come out, but he had stopped the bleeding. He found a stick to use as a crutch and walked back to the camp the robbers had set up.He found two canteens and a ten gallon can of fresh water. Eagerly he drank, filled a canteen and took it with him.

He would try to get up the hill.

Spur remembered getting to his horse, mounting from a wheel of the engine, and then riding up the trail. Somewhere along the line the horse stopped because the man was not guiding her. The sorrel lowered her head to chomp on some grass and Spur McCoy fell off over her neck and lay without moving in the trail.

Sheriff Gilpin had left Virginia City an hour before dawn, and ridden as fast as he thought practical. He had forty men and twenty pack animals. The only way that gold and silver could be protected was to bring it out by horse or mule to the nearest mine and store it there under maximum security guard until it could be shipped again by train.

He had sent one man ahead as a scout, to ride three hundred yards forward to look for any signs of life, any trouble and especially for Spur McCoy. The scout came racing up the trail when they had gone what Gilpin figured was a mile and a half.

"Found a big man in the trail, Sheriff. He's got reddish brown hair, a moustache and mutton chops. Sounds like he's Spur McCoy."

Three of them rode forward quickly and Sheriff Gilpin got there first. He dismounted and checked Spur.

"Shot, not too bad. Must have lost a lot of blood." The sheriff used his own canteen to wash off Spur's face and then splashed cool water on Spur's hot brow. Five minutes later Spur came back to reality and shook his head.

"What the hell happened?"

Sheriff Gilpin laughed.

"Glad to see you're still alive. You want to ride back down to the wreck with us?"

Spur nodded and two deputies helped him on his horse. Once astride he seemed to gather strength. The sheriff handed him a small flask.

"Got some special help," he said.

Spur smelled the flask, tipped it and took three big swallows and shook his head.

"That should either cure me or kill me. Let's go."

He showed the sheriff where the three loaded pack trains were, and the sheriff took charge. He held them for one trip up the hill.

McCoy sat by a small fire where coffee boiled, and watched the sheriff operate. The bodies of the soldiers were brought out of the car and laid out in a row. The rest of the gold and silver in the wrecked treasure car was brought out, counted and loaded on pack horses.

With dawn, Spur felt better. He had downed two cups of coffee and eaten three chocolate bars the sheriff had brought along as emergency energy food.

He told the sheriff about Tony Giardello, and led a team in to bring back the body, the pack horses and the extra gold from the dead mount. Giardello was tied over a pack horse and brought back to the base camp.

The sheriff found the former camp and the three bodies, but Spur had no idea how the deaths had happened, except that one was by knife, two by pistol.

Sgt. Anders was assigned to lead the pack train up the hill with the bodies. There were twelve soldiers, the engineer, Giardello and three from the robbers' camp. Belatedly Spur told the sheriff

213

about the four men who had led the pack horses, and their bodies were found and sent up the trail.

By ten o'clock that morning the sheriff's flask was empty, the coffee was gone, and they had the last of the silver bars loaded on board the pack horses. Spur weaved slightly as he sat his horse, and the sheriff assigned a man to ride beside Spur and hold him on the mount if necessary.

It took an hour to wind up the trail to Virginia City. Half the town turned out to watch and a hundred special volunteer deputies were on hand holding every shotgun in town, lining the route the last quarter of a mile to the Julia mine. They had decided that the vault at the Julia was large enough, and that it would take a week to get the trains running again.

Around the clock guards would be provided, five men for each mine, each with a shotgun.

Spur had been taken directly to Tracy Belcher's house. She was there to meet him and Doc Burkhalter arrived shortly afterward to dig the slug out of Spur's thigh.

Spur bit the piece of soft pine, spit it out and swore for two minutes until he passed out. Then Doc worked the bullet free and stitched the wound closed before McCoy came back to consciousness.

Just as the doctor finished the surgery and Spur was taken away to his bedroom, the sheriff came in. He spoke softly with Mrs. Belcher.

"There is no mistake, the Treasury men are still in town and we have counted the gold and silver bars six times. The total is accurate. We are missing fifty bars, that's one full pack train of those five horses that the robbers had outfitted. As you know, that much gold is worth a hundred and sixty-five thousand dollars. We need to find out what Mr. McCoy knows about it as soon as possible.''

EIGHTEEN

SPUR McCOY CAME back to consciousness just before supper time, and Tracy Belcher stood by his bed waiting. She cooled his forehead with a damp cloth as she had been doing for two hours. He watched her a moment, smiled and cleared his throat.

"Sweet man, you're back with us. We were all worried."

"I was a little worried myself." He shivered as a tremor of pain scouted through his nervous system.

"Hungry?" she asked.

"I could eat half the tailings in Gold Hill!"

"You must be feeling better. Drink this." She put a tray near the bed. On it were three glasses: one filled with iced tea, another with milk and the third with sweet grape juice which she had shipped from San Francisco in cans. "The doctor said you needed lots of fluid. You lost a great deal of blood."

"Sawbones!"

"At least he got the bullet out. I wasn't going to try."

"When I went into a raging, screaming fit you would have done it."

"Shut up and drink," she said with a soft smile.

An hour later Spur had downed the iced tea and the milk. He sipped at the grape juice and it reminded him of the San Francisco country. The meal Tracy brought was recuperation food, as she called it, mashed potatoes and gravy, a slab of roast beef two inches thick and dripping red juices, three kinds of vegetables which Tracy had sent in by special freight on the train each week, thick slabs of wheat bread and marmalade, and scalding hot coffee.

She kept the sheriff out of the room for another half hour, then she brought in the lawman.

"Sheriff, you should be missing some gold," Spur said. "If he had a full load I'd say it's about fifty bars. Gold or silver, I'm not sure which, but don't worry. I know exactly where it is, and I know who stole it and I'll take you there, but I need a day to get back on my feet."

Sheriff Gilpin chuckled. "Tracy tell you what I wanted to talk to you about?"

"Nope. But I wanted to talk to you. If I hadn't been dumb enough to get shot we'd have it all settled by now."

"Why not just tell me and let my men clean it up?"

"This gets a little more personal, Sheriff. It's one arrest I want to make myself. Tell the Treasury boys all is safe."

"They probably will be asking you themselves."

Spur shook his head. "Not after that meal. I'm going to be sleeping the clock around first. Just leave any important messages with my pretty nurse over there."

217

Tracy smiled, took the sheriff's hand and led him out the door.

Spur watched them go, his head drifted back to the pillow and before he knew it he was asleep.

He slept until noon the next day when dreams woke him. In the dream a deputy sheriff chased him, screaming that he was guilty, and should be punished. When Spur came fully awake he realized he had two men to confront, Rush Sommers and the traitorous deputy, whoever he might be.

Spur sat up in bed and for a moment his head spun, then steadied. He looked at his leg. It was red and swollen under the bandage, but the cutting to find the bullet had not touched any major muscle bundles. Slowly he flexed his leg, bending his knee, then extending his foot. Yes, everything worked. He should be able to walk.

Where in hell were his pants?

He stood on the soft carpet just as the door came open and Tracy peered in.

"What are you doing?" she asked, alarmed.

"Looking for my pants. I've got a date with the sheriff."

For five minutes Tracy argued. He was still too sick, he should be in bed for another three or four days. At last he convinced her that he needed to get some work done, then he would rest. She brought him clean clothes from his suitcase and he dressed. She watched, enjoying the reverse strip tease.

"I'll satisfy your special needs later," Spur said.

"Damn well better. You don't know what it did to me having you in bed and not able to take advantage of you."

"Try me tonight," Spur said.

It was hard to get the pants on. His leg hurt more as he moved, but he gritted his teeth and dressed. When he walked to the door he stumbled and she caught his shoulder before he fell.

"Just need a little practice," he said.

By the time he got to the front door he could walk almost normally, but each step sent a dagger of pain up from his leg. Tracy's small rig sat at the front door, a horse in the traces, and the lines wrapped.

"You want a driver?" she asked.

He shook his head, touched her shoulder in thanks and walked to the buggy, blinking wetness back from his eyes, as his damn leg really started to hurt.

When he stopped in front of the courthouse, he stopped a deputy and asked him to see if the sheriff could come out and talk. The tall, thin lawman was out the door quickly.

"Climb on board, Sheriff," Spur said. "We'll go for a short ride."

The sheriff sat beside Spur as they drove to the Consolidated California Mine.

Spur tied the reins, left the rig directly in front of the fancy wooden building, and with only one small gasp of pain, walked into the office.

Rush Sommers must have been watching out a window. He met them at the door.

"Find the rest of our gold, Sheriff?"

"Not so you could notice," Gilpin said.

"But we know where it is," Spur said.

Sommers looked at him sharply. "If you know

where it is, why don't we have it?"

"Soon will," Spur said.

"Good. I can't afford to lose even a share of that missing gold."

"We'd like to take a look at where you stored your gold before the shipment," Spur said. "Just a routine survey."

Sommers couldn't hide his surprise, but he did well. He shrugged. "Sure, of course. Anything to help the law catch those murdering robbers. I can't figure out who would try something like that."

They walked through the office and down a flight to the basement, then into the area where the locked steel doors stood. Sommers spun dials and soon had the big vault-like door open. They stepped inside the area dug out of solid rock, but walled in to look like any room.

"This is the spot. All we have in here now are two silver bars. If you check the boullion number you'll see they were not part of the shipment we made the other night."

"This vault looks a lot like the others," Spur said. He watched Sommers and the man seemed to relax a little.

"Sheriff, maybe each of the mines should take back their part of the gold and silver bars for safe-keeping," Sommers said.

"Can't do that, Mr. Sommers. It's all under the control and protection of the Federal Government. It's the Treasury Department's responsibility."

Something was different about the vault. Then Spur had it figured. It was a "new" lumber smell.

Sawdust. There had been some new construction done in the vault recently. Why? And where? He looked critically at the walls. All were of the same construction, with vertical paneling over a stud wall, he figured. Single wall construction. The paneling had been painted and all four walls looked about the same.

He concentrated on the three non-entry walls. Any of them could have been altered, moved, added on to. Spur studied the floor. It was of heavy pine planks, two-inch, he guessed. It had been varnished to preserve it. At the right hand edge of the floor he saw scratches.

"Well, have you seen enough? Two bars of silver won't help much." As he said it, Sommers headed for the vault door.

"Wait here, Sommers!" Spur said sharply.

"Oh, what for?"

"Something is wrong here, Sheriff. There have been recent changes made in this room, and I want to find out what they are."

"This is a vault!" Sommers said. "What changes can you make in a vault, rearrange the silver bars?"

"Maybe you'd like to tell us, Mr. Sommers," the sheriff said.

"The only changes were made when we took out a half million dollars of silver bars and entrusted them to you and the Treasury people."

Spur went to the three walls and pounded each with his fist. All had the same sound, all solid stud wall construction. He groaned as he went down on his knees at the wall and examined the floor. Sweat popped out on his forehead as Spur crawled around the three sides of the wall looking critically at the foor.

At last he nodded, stood and shook his head. "Very neat, Sommers, and it almost worked. If we didn't know you were behind the robbery try in the first place, we would have missed this entirely."

"What do you mean, behind the robbery attempt? I had nothing to do with that terrible attack."

"We will argue that in court, Sommers," Spur said. "Because right here we're going to find the evidence that will convict you, and set your feet to twitching and jiggling at the end of a rope."

Sommers tried to laugh, but it came out hollow. "Sheriff, what is this, some kind of a bad joke? I've shown you the vault, now I have a business to run, can we go back up?"

"Not until Mr. McCoy is satisfied. Mr. Sommers, do you have a weapon?"

"Of course, should I go get it?"

"No, I just wondered if you had one on your person?"

"No, Sheriff. I don't carry a gun in my own office."

Spur leaned against the wall near one end. He pushed, but it did not give. He thumped it again with his fist, and about three feet in from one end it took on a more hollow and less solid sound. McCoy grinned and went back to his knees. He gave a short cry of pain, then looked at the floor. He traced a pattern for a moment, then stood.

"Sheriff, I need a crowbar and a sledge, an eight-pounder will do."

"You have no right to destroy any of my private property."

"You're right, Sommers, so you can sue me for any damage."

The sheriff went to the stairs and called to a deputy he had posted there. He gave orders and returned.

"What do you have, McCoy?" the sheriff asked.

"Scratches, Gilpin. The wall is not nearly as solid right at this end." Spur took out his knife and slid the thin blade into a narrow crack between two of the vertical boards that made part of the paneling.

"And see here. There's a crack from the floor to the ceiling. Then down here on the floor, look at this scratch. It describes a perfect arc from this point near the wall, to a point two feet into the room. What do you suppose made a scratch like that, so geometrically perfect?"

The sheriff shrugged.

"One thing it could have been was a nail or a small rock lodged in the bottom of a door that opened outward. This three foot section of the wall is a concealed door of some kind. My money is bet on our finding a secret room in back of this wall, and in that room we'll find the missing fifty gold bars."

"Interesting," the sheriff said. "What do you have to say about that, Mr. Sommers?"

Spur and the sheriff turned to look at the mine owner. They stared at a matched pair of derringers, both with large, ugly bores, and both double barreled.

"I always carry buckshot in these, gentlemen. With four shots I can hardly miss. Both of you lay down your weapons on the floor. One at a time, and slowly. I'd hate to get blood all over my vault."

"Let's talk about this, Rush," the sheriff said.

"Talking time is over, Clete. Put down your weapon, right now."

One six-gun lay on the varnished floor.

"If you think you're going to shoot us, Sommers," Spur said, "remember that deputy is coming back soon."

"Two or three bodies more, it doesn't make that much difference."

"Then you did steal the gold? It is behind this wall?" The sheriff stared hard at Sommers.

"I'm going to put my weapon down," Spur said. "Don't get frisky with those triggers." Spur bent, his thigh giving him problems. He groaned as he got down. He was farthest from Sommers, partly shielded by the sheriff. As he lifted from the bent position slowly, he pulled a four-inch knife from his boot sheath and held it along his leg.

"Sheriff, I don't answer silly questions. Both of you move over there in the far corner."

They walked slowly. The deputy called just then from the top of the steps. Sommers glanced upward. As he looked away, Spur raised the knife and threw it. The blade turned once and jammed hard into Sommers' right shoulder. He dropped the derringer he held in that hand and when it hit the floor it discharged. The inside of the vault was rocked by the explosion of the big round and birdshot bounced around the inside of the vault.

Sommers screamed in pain, looked at the two lawmen, then ran up the steps, the derringer in his left hand waving at the deputy.

Spur grabbed his .45 off the floor and ran up the steps. The deputy lay on the office floor, his knees drawn up, his hands cradling his genitals as he vomited to one side.

A male clerk stared in disbelief at the scene.

"Where did Sommers go?" Spur demanded. The clerk could not talk, he just pointed through a door that led toward the back of the office. Spur raced in that direction. He felt a rush of power, of new energy, as if a great energizer had been released directly into his nervous system. He no longer felt the wound in his leg. He raced through the door into a supply room and then onto a porch.

Across thirty yards of a dirt road, Spur saw Sommers whipping a saddle horse away from a hitching rack and around a hoist building. He vanished before there was time for a shot.

Spur ran to the hitching rail, leaped on a gray that looked deep of chest and spurred the big mount around the same building. Sommers raced down the alley to the next street, then continued south, out of town.

Sommers was not much of a horseman. He pushed the black at a furious gallop. Spur reined down to a trot, and watched the mine owner whipping the black for more speed. There was no place to hide in the desert-like, bleak hills of the six thousand foot level of Virginia City. No trees, no brush, only rocks and sand, a little soil and few houses spotted along the road.

A quarter of a mile ahead the black faltered and slowed. Spur could see the mine owner lashing the black, spurring it with his heels, but the big horse slowed to a walk, then stopped, and turned its head in wonder at the rider.

Spur picked up his speed now to a canter and closed the gap with the black. Sommers urged the horse into a walk, and then a gentle canter, then the horse wobbled from side to side, and suddenly stumbled and fell.

Sommers leaped clear, rolled in the dust and lay there, not sure what had happened. He sat up shaking his head. Spur put a .45 slug into the dirt at his right side, then one to his left. He rode up and stared down at the man.

"Time to go back to town, Sommers."

The mine owner shook his head. "Not going. I couldn't stand a trial and all the people staring at me and knowing what happened. I couldn't stand that."

"You don't have much choice. Stand up and start walking."

Sommers remained in the dust. "I have a choice. You have three shots left in that pistol." He raised a derringer from where it had been in his hand at his side. "I have two shots. Now the choice is yours, McCoy. Either eat birdshot for breakfast for the next ten years, or shoot me. If you don't do the job right, I still have those two shots to make sure. I'm going to try to kill you when I count three. So you see, Federal Secret Service man, the choice is yours."

Sommers lifted the deadly derringer. It might not kill him at the fifteen foot range, but it would put a lot of holes in Spur's hide. He lifted his gun, aiming for the mine owner.

"One . . . you still have time, McCoy. Gun me down."

Spur shook his head.

"Two . . . one last chance, McCoy. You'll be a hero. Damn smart you finding that scratch mark. I sure as hell never saw it. Get ready to hurt like hell, McCoy."

Spur watched the man, stared at his trigger finger. He saw it start to tighten.

McCoy had trained himself in split second decisions. Now he made one. He would fire after Sommers did.

The little derringer spoke sharply. Spur had seen the hammer falling and squeezed the .45's hair trigger. The agent tensed for the rain of buckshot but it never came. He saw the derringer pointing in the air and the first shot from his .45 tearing through Sommers' left eye.

The mine owner slammed backwards, his life snuffed out in a hundredth of a second as the lead plowed into his brain tissue, mashing vital nerve centers.

Spur stepped off the horse, and slid his six-gun into his holster. He picked up Sommers and laid him over the saddle. Spur checked the black. It had died from being ridden to death. Slowly Spur walked his gray back toward town.

Each step now sent a jagged chorus of pain signals to his brain. A quarter of a mile had never seemed longer.

Three horses raced toward him from town. Sheriff Gilpin led the men. Spur stopped and waited, leaning against the black.

Ten minutes later Spur rode back to the Consolidated California Mine. Sommers' body was laid out on the board porch of the mine office, and already a dozen curious gawkers gathered around.

"Did you look?" Spur asked.

"Nope. Figured that was your right to see it first."

They went down to the vault. A sledge and prybar lay on the floor. The sheriff looked at the scratch mark again.

Spur held the prybar pointed end on the small crack between the boards and a deputy gave the other end two whacks. The bar penetrated two inches and Spur pried to the side putting all of his weight behind the three foot bar.

A screeching of wood against wood came, then the door popped open and swung wide.

Spur looked into a three foot space in back of the wall. He saw a jumble of gold bars on the floor and the old wall.

Spur leaned out and waved. "There is your missing gold, Sheriff, all safe and sound."

Spur sat on the steps and rested. The sheriff sat

down beside him and offered a flask from his hip pocket.

"A little medicinal spirits?"

Spur sniffed the whisky, nodded and tipped the flask. He wiped his lips and winced as the leg thundered its discomfort.

"One more problem. You've got a traitor in your outfit. Know who he is?"

The sheriff shook his head.

"Let's get down to your office. I've got an idea that might smoke out the son of a bitch."

NINETEEN

TWELVE DEPUTY SHERIFFS on the night shift from six p.m. to six a.m. sat in chairs in the small meeting room at the jail and listened to Spur McCoy. They had been told who he was and why he came to town. This was what the sheriff told them was a "wrapping up of the Great Train Robbery Case." Spur took over.

"Men, the Sheriff said we had wrapped up this case. With Rush Sommers and Tony Giardello dead, and the other participants in the actual takeover of the train all dead, he's right in one sense. But then we come back to the conspiracy . . . to the idea and plots and plans to do the deed. I'm sure that as law officers you know this too is a felony and punishable by a stiff jail term. What we're now starting to investigate are those others in town who we feel were participants in the robbery as conspirators."

He looked around the room. Nobody blanched or jittered nervously on a chair.

"Some of you men may be involved in carrying out this investigation. We'll have ten or fifteen leads to track down, and a lot of questions to ask.

But what we thought would be a massive job is suddenly much easier." Spur took from the small table beside him a weathered and worn notebook with removable pages. He held it up.

"This came into our hands late today. It looks like a total and complete record of all of the fringe participants in the conspiracy from the very first. One thing you can say for Rush Sommers, he kept accurate records. He has everything down in black and white, listing dates, everyone present, all those spoken to about the idea, those who were shut out, and of course everyone who participated.

"This notebook could be very bad news for a few citizens of Virginia City."

He paused and took a drink. Two or three of the men stirred in their chairs. It could be just the long speech he was giving.

"I don't want to keep you away from your duties, and I've used up more than my alloted time now, so let me say that you'll be hearing from us again about this book, and we may ask some of you to help us track down some clues.

"In about half an hour the sheriff and I are going to take some big pads of writing paper and start making lists of every name mentioned in this log book. Incidentally, it continues, day by day right up to late this afternoon. That Rush Sommers was a stickler for putting down facts, and especially who he paid.

"We have a record that he gave Guy Pritchard three hundred dollars just two days ago. That was the day before Pritchard was found shot to death in an alley, and we have a witness who saw Pritchard go into Sommers' house about two a.m. the day he was found dead.

"Well, thanks for your time, and you'll be hearing from us."

Spur left the room and the men filed out. He went into the sheriff's office and they talked in low tones for a few minutes. Then they left his door open and began going through the pages of the old book.

"This better work, McCoy. If it produces nothing in the first three hours, our bluff comes up a cropper."

Spur shifted his hurting leg to relieve the pain. "It's got to work because before midnight I'm going to get some laudanum and conk off for about three days."

Spur turned the blank pages of the old notebook. It was tattered and worn, one that the sheriff had used in Texas more than twenty years before. They wrote names on a list, any names they could think of.

Sgt. Anders came in, and Spur picked up the book so that Anders was unable to see that the pages were blank.

"We've got a disturbance in the Golden Nugget saloon, Sheriff. Do you want to be down there?"

"No time right now, Anders. Take care of it the best you can."

The sergeant looked at the list of names, nodded and went out. He walked to the last cell in the jail. It was empty as were the other three cells. He stared at it for a long time, then went back to his desk just inside the front door. For a moment he thought about his ancient .44 hanging on his hip.

Then he sat down at his desk and began to write on a piece of paper with a pencil.

"To Sheriff Gilpin and All Others Concerned:

"This being the 22nd day of October, in the year of our Lord 1874, I take pencil in hand to do hereby detail, write, and affirm that the following statement is true.

"My real name is Albert Anderson. While in Virginia City I have been using the name of Bert Anders. I am from the city of St. Louis, Missouri where for six years I was on the police force. I did leave that city after committing an illegal act, and have since then changed my name, and my life. For the past seven years I have served as a deputy sheriff in this county in an honorable, truthful and upright manner.

"Six months ago I was approached by certain parties who suggested that I might be able to help them with information from the sheriff's office. They made it known that they knew of my past, and if I did not cooperate they would telegraph St. Louis with my whereabouts, and notify Sheriff Gilpin to hold me for transport to Missouri as a captured fugitive.

"I was forced to cooperate with them in every way. The main purpose of this cooperation was to reveal to them any and all facts that might affect the proposed robbery of the Treasury Department train of gold and silver bars leaving next in October of 1874.

"I have told them everything they wanted to

know about the plans, the safeguards and the protection designed by this office.

"This therefore is my confession for violating the public trust, for violating my oath of office, and for being a traitor to the sheriff's office and my good friend, Clete Gilpin.

"May God have mercy on my soul."

He signed the paper, folded it and put it in his pocket, then walked back to the last jail cell and closed the door. He sat on the floor in the corner of the cell, took his .44 and blew a hole through the side of his head.

Spur and Sheriff Gilpin heard the blast of the gun and went racing from the room.

"In the jail!" somebody shouted. Six men ran that way. Two stood, stunned as they stared in the last cell.

Spur beat the sheriff to the scene.

"Open the door!" he said.

One of the deputies unlocked it and Spur ran in, with the sheriff right behind him.

Spur touched the vein at the side of the sergeant's throat.

"He's dead," Spur said.

The sheriff saw the folded paper extending from the sergeant's pocket. He opened it and read the first page.

"Everyone back to work," the sheriff said. "Johnson, you take over the sergeant's desk. One man go get the undertaker."

He stood and went back to his office.

"It was Anders. Sommers or Giardello was

blackmailing him for some early crime in the East.''

"Now it is wrapped up," Spur said. "Sometimes a bluff works better than a month of digging up the facts.''

"Especially when you have twenty-six suspects. I did not consider Anders to be a suspect. But it's reasonable that Sommers would want somebody in the upper management team of the department.''

Spur moved his leg and winced.

"I'd guess you need a ride back to Tracy Belcher's mansion,'' the sheriff said.

"If you have a spare rig.''

A half hour after Spur got back to the Belcher place, the doctor arrived at Tracy's insistence to check his patient. He stitched up one part that had broken open, doused the wound with alcohol, and wrapped it with a clean bandage.

"We're not sure why alcohol does such a good job, but the idea now is that there are millions of little bugs that hurt us and make us sick, and cause infection. The alcohol can kill off a lot of them on the outside of the body, and prevent them from getting into the tissue or the bloodstream.

"You'll be good as new in a week. In the meantime keep off that leg. Make Tracy serve you night and day, and no strenuous exercise.''

Tracy ushered the sawbones out the door, and Spur called for a whisky and two tablespoons of Laudanum. He knew the drug, used mostly to kill pain, was a tincture of opium and that continual use could make a person as totally dependent on it as many Chinese who became saddled with the opium habit.

Tracy came back. "You haven't eaten a thing today, have you? I know you didn't have any breakfast and no dinner, and now you've missed supper. Don't move, I'll be right back."

Before she got away Spur grabbed her arm and pulled her over to the bed. He kissed her lips and she sighed and snuggled closer. His hand closed around one of her breasts and Tracy squealed with pleasure.

"Wait, love. First you have supper, then for dessert you can just eat any part of me your little mouth desires!"

She slipped away and came back in twenty minutes with a bottle of whiskey and a small bottle of laudanum. She spooned one measure into his mouth and let him chase it with whisky.

"Can you rest easy for half an hour? Your supper will be ready then."

Spur said he could.

"Did you hear the news? The Mine Owner's Alliance has determined that there should be a reward for the breakup of the robbery attempt on the shipment. They have decided it should go to you."

"I'm a Federal employee. I can't accept a reward for doing my job. Not a chance. I'd be fired in a week."

Tracy opened her blouse and let her big breasts billow out. She sat beside Spur on the bed.

"Maybe you should wait until you find out how much the reward is."

"Doesn't matter."

"It's twenty thousand dollars! We decided it was worth it to offer a reward."

"That's most charitable of you. I have a better suggestion. Why not put that twenty thousand dollars in a fund? The family of every miner who gets killed in a mine accident gets a grant from the Virginia City Miner's Benevolent Fund of a thousand dollars. You could start with Mary Beth Franklin's mother."

"Oh." Tracy thought about it. "Yes, I like the idea. I'll talk with the Alliance. It could mean a lot of money if we have a bad accident."

"But it would be worth it for the peace of mind of the miners."

By the time they had the idea talked through, Canchuna came in with the dinner on a rolling cart.

Spur looked at the food. "I'm so hungry I could eat it all!" Spur said.

"Good, I like my men with a little meat on them," Tracy said.

Spur blinked once, feeling the effects of the laudanum. The pain had eased, and he ate the fried chicken and the fresh fish that had been brought in by train from San Francisco and kept iced all the way. He had four kinds of fresh cooked vegetables and two desserts, then a bottle of wine. He sighed and leaned back against the pillows.

"You going to go to sleep on me?" Tracy asked.

"You don't know what laudanum does to me, do you?"

"You should have told me that first. You are going to bob off on me, aren't you, Spur McCoy?"

She looked at him. His eyes were closed, his breath came light and evenly.

"McCoy, you sneaky big bastard! When you wake up you are going to have to make this up to me."

But she was smiling as she cleared away the tray and rolled it into the hallway. She slipped out of her clothes and settled into the big bed beside Spur.

It had been years since she had snuggled up against a sleeping hunk of a man—and just gone to sleep. One night wouldn't hurt a bit.

By noon the next day Spur had his affairs in order. He had fired off three telegrams. Two to his office in St. Louis, reminding Fleurette Leon that he was intending on coming through there before his next case. He gave her some specific instructions. The last wire went to his boss in Washington D.C.

"To: William Wood, Capital Investigations, Washington D.C. Gold all safe, robbery went awry. Perpetrators all died in attempt. One suicide. Tracks being repaired as quickly as possible. Serious wound in leg will require a week's medical leave here. Will return to St. Louis as soon as rail link is repaired. Signed/Spur McCoy."

He showed the wire to Tracy.

"A week? Only a week? After I rescued you, saved your life, became your nurse, your housekeeper and your cook, and you're only going to stay for a week?"

Spur looked surprised and she stood beside him where he sat in a soft chair that had a view of the mountains out the window.

Tracy slipped out of her robe and shook her naked, pudgy figure at him, bending so her big breasts threatened to suffocate him.

"Hey, I was just joking. I know you're a damned fiddle-foot." She pushed one of the large brown nipples into his open mouth. "I also know a hell of a good man when I sleep with one, and I'm going to keep you warming my bed just as long as I can, and with every bump and grind and tit and pussy that I can use. My old ma didn't get no fools!"

Spur pulled her down on his lap, favoring his sore leg. He kissed her lips tenderly, barely touching them.

"Oh, damn! Where were you ten years ago when I really needed you?"

"Probably raising hell with some sexy little red-head!"

"Be serious, you ass!" She kissed him back, just as tenderly. "I just wish that we had met ten years ago. Back before I knew Belcher. Damn! What a team we could have made!"

"You're turning me down? You mean I'm too late?"

"Be serious. Look, I've heard men say that sometimes their juices get to running and they just want to grab some willing woman and have a hot, fast fuck. No strings, no talk, just sex, quick and wonderful. I've felt that way sometimes too. But not now. Right now I want to walk you over to the bed and have a soft, gentle, much talk and loving session that I can remember for twenty years as the best lovemaking of my life. Do you understand? Do you think you could work with me on a project like that?"

239

Spur kissed her eyes, then lifted her off his lap and stood up. He hobbled to the bed and stretched out. She lay down beside him but not touching him.

Spur McCoy turned toward her. "About that long, slow, marvelously loving time. I sure want to try. We've got a week to see if we can get it all done, just exactly, precisely right."

"It may take a lot of practice."

"I always have been good in rehearsal. Let's give it a try."

They did.

It worked out beautifully.

Spur McCoy missed the first train for Reno a week later.

He was three days late reporting back to work.

He lost twenty-seven dollars in pay for the three days.

When he wired the story to Tracy, she fired back a wire.

"Only nine dollars a day? Wish to buy nine hundred dollars worth. Please rush the product to me by return rail transportation."

Spur laughed at the letter, but deep down in his heart, he wondered what a hundred days with Tracy Belcher would be like, say in a luxury hotel in San Francisco, with a window that overlooked the bay.

Slowly Spur McCoy looked back at his desk piled high with notices, telegrams and instructions from Washington D.C.

He grinned, said a little thank you to Tracy, and dug into the stacks of paper.

WYOMING WILDCAT

Chapter One

June 14, 1873. Laramie, Wyoming. Altitude: 7,163 feet.

The redheaded man leaned toward the fire toasting his hands. He and his partner had just finished supper and cleaned up their camp. The sun wouldn't be down for two hours. On the other side of the fire the blond man lowered his coffee cup and grinned.

"We made good progress today, buddy, but it's a long way yet to the northern Wyoming border."

A rifle shot cracked close by and the redhead jolted forward, back-shot, his body slamming toward the small fire. He fell directly on it, smothering the flames. The rifle round had shattered his spine, killing him instantly.

Before the blond man could move, another long gun spoke and the bullet tore through his side, pounding him backwards away from the fire, dumping him in the dirt and grass. He knew he was

wounded seriously but he wasn't dead yet. He
clawed at the six-gun in his holster, but the rifle
fired again and the screaming hot lead hit the side
of the wounded man's head, pitching him flat to the
ground.

The two shooters watched the scene silently for
ten minutes, and when neither victim moved, they
walked cautiously up to the small campsite where
the bodies lay. The smell of burning cloth came
plainly to them. They hoisted the body out of the
fire and poured coffee from a nearby pot over the
smoldering shirt.

"Dumb asses," Charlie Breen said. "Get our
horses." It was an order. Turk Gallager looked
at his boss, then trotted back 50 yards where they
had hidden their mounts, and rode up leading the
second quarter horse.

"Get down and help, stupid, we got work to do,"
Breen snapped.

"Could burn most of it," Turk suggested.

"Hell, no, we do as I planned. Now get busy."

Both men took shovels off the horses and began
digging in the soft soil. They dug a trench three
feet deep, two feet wide, and six feet long. They
dumped into the hole all of the dead men's camping
gear, blankets, and food and the equipment from the
packhorse. Then they shoveled in the dirt, tromping
it firmly as they went, so there would be less of a
sinkhole after the next rain.

They collected two rifles and the two revolvers,
then dragged the dead men down to the Laramie
River and pushed them in. They watched to be sure
the current picked up the floating bodies and moved
them downstream, which was to the north.

When the bodies vanished around a bend, the two
men finished the burial of the gear, and spread leaves

and twigs and small branches over the spaded-up area to make it look natural again. Then they tied lead lines to the dead men's three horses, mounted up, and rode away to the south.

"At least we won't have to worry about them two bastards and another damn railroad they were going to bring in here to the valley," Charlie Breen said. "Won't have to worry about that at all."

The Laramie River, running full and hard with the snow melt from high in the Medicine Bow Mountains, and encouraged by a drenching thunderstorm which blanketed the whole area that morning, carried the bodies along for a quarter of a mile before the first sank. The second had floated face skyward most of the way, rolling over now and then. Suddenly the eyes of the man shot twice snapped open, and a strangled cry of agony ripped the silent Wyoming landscape.

The man thrashed at the water, trying to keep his head above it. His motions were desperate, frantic, not swimming but more a terrible flailing of the water to deny it the right to claim his life. His battle went on time and time again as the current carried him swiftly down the rain-swollen river. For more than an hour the man fought the surging dark flow.

Once more his head sank, but bobbed back up, and he flattened out on the surface. One of his arms came out and his feet kicked, churning the water. He slanted toward the shore with a definite but weak swimming stroke.

Three repetitions later his strength was gone, his arms wouldn't move, and his head sank again. The man desperately rolled over on his back, trying to float in the choppy current.

At this point the Laramie River made a sweeping curve to the left, but the man's last bit of swimming momentum carried him straight for the shore. There a constantly changing bar of sand and rocks extended into the stream. His shoulders hit first, and he turned over and clawed up on the sand spit, gasping for air.

With the cleansing water gone, blood oozed out of the wound on the side of his head, then ran down his cheek and at last clotted. He made some weak moves to crawl up farther on the sandbar, but had no strength left.

No logical thoughts came to the man. His actions had been purely those of survival, animal instincts, what any animal might do to try to save its life. He stared at the blue sky but didn't recognize it. His side continued to bleed where he lay half in and half out of the water. He had no thoughts. He was more dead than alive.

His eyes dropped shut but some survival instinct made him snap them open. A moment later they closed again and he fell into the oblivion of unconsciousness.

A half mile downstream on the river that flowed to the north, Wade Johnson made one last swing on his gray looking for stray cattle. He knew he was half a mile inside the land claimed by the big Circle B Ranch to the south of them, but he had already found four strays with the Bar-O brand on them. He had left them a mile back with his partner. Now he cantered along the river looking in creeks and draws that fed into the river from the broad Laramie Valley.

He had little hope of finding any more steers or calves. The ones that had strayed this far into the other ranch lands had probably been swept up by the

Circle B's roundup and re-branded by now. Damn, that made him mad, but it was a case of a mouse fighting with an elephant.

Wade was a medium-sized man, five-eight, 150 pounds with brown hair and brown eyes. He was a good cowhand, had been pushing around steers since he was 16, eight years ago. He was the working foreman of the four hands at the Bar-O Ranch.

He completed his swing, came to the big bend, and started to head back, but decided this was an easy spot to get down to the water to give his gray a good drink. Wade walked her down toward the river and saw the sandbar. He wondered if there would be any gold in there if he panned the gravel.

Something had been pushed up on the sandbar by the high water in the Laramie. A log probably. It was merging toward dusk as he rode closer and on to the river. Then he saw that the object half in the water was a body. He dropped the reins and swung down and ran to the man.

"Lordy!" Wade said out loud. The guy had been shot in the side of the head. Most of his head and neck were bloody. Another red splotch showed through his shirt on his side. He must be dead. Wade bent over him and the man groaned.

Wade jumped back a foot realizing the man was still alive. He caught him under the arms and dragged him up the grassy bank. The victim still had a gunbelt on, but no weapon. His face was wind- and sunburned like he was an outdoorsman. His hands were calloused and work-worn, but didn't show any rope burns, so he probably wasn't a cowhand.

Wade pulled a second kerchief out of his saddle-bags and made a pad of it, and used the kerchief around his neck to tie the pad in place over the wound on the side of the man's head.

Then he found his extra shirt in his saddlebags and tore it into strips. With part of it he made a heavy pad and tied it fast to the man's side. That might stop the bleeding.

How to get him back to the ranch? If he laid him head down over the saddle he'd bleed to death for sure. It took Wade five minutes to boost the man up into the saddle. Wade held him in place and then tried to mount behind him. After three tries he made it.

Holding the barely breathing man with both arms in front of him, Wade began walking his mount back to where he'd left the strays.

"What the hell you got there, Wade?" Lew called as Wade rode up. Lew was the other hand from the Bar-O dragging for strays.

"Found him half in the river. Somebody shot him twice but he ain't dead. You get them critters back to our side of the range any way you can, Lew. I got to get this guy to the ranch."

Wade tried to trot, but he couldn't hold onto the dead weight of the man's body. At last he walked the gray. He figured he was eight miles and two hours from the ranch.

It was well after dark when he rode in with his burden. He went right up to the ranch house back door and bellowed for Vincent. He came out quickly.

"Wade?" Vincent asked peering into the night. "Good Lord, you have Lew in front of you on the saddle? What happened to him?"

"Ain't Lew, Vincent. Some stranger. Found him halfway in the Laramie River. He's been shot twice and is near dead. Hold him steady and I'll get down."

Together they carried the wounded man into the

parlor, where they spread two blankets on the couch and put him there.

Melody came running in as soon as she heard the men. She was slender and tall, willowy and pretty with soft brown hair and green eyes. "Goodness, what happened? Who is he? Is he one of our new men? Where was he? Oh, Lord, he's been shot!"

Vincent eased the bandages off and looked at the side wound. "At least the lead went in and right on out. His side is not a big problem. Doubt if the slug hit anything vital.

"Melody, you better find something to tear into bandages. We're gonna need a lot of them, and some of that salve we use on cuts and hurts."

She nodded and hurried into the bedroom.

Vincent shook his head. He was tall with long rangy arms and legs and a flat belly. At 28 he was lean and fit and learning the ranch business here on his widowed sister's spread.

"This man has a nasty head wound. I saw some like this during the war. Not a good sign. If the bullet had gone inside where it hit, it would have killed him. This one bounced off his skull, tore out some of it. Just how much is the question. Rattled his brain around something fierce.

"I saw some men with head wounds less serious than this who lost their sight, some of them couldn't speak. Lots of them couldn't walk anymore. Hard telling what kind of damage it will do."

"Want me to ride to Laramie and bring out Doc Daisley?" the foreman asked.

Vincent shook his head. "No, the damage has been done. Another half a day won't make any difference. But you best head out early in the morning and bring him back. All we can do now is get our guest as comfortable as we can. We'll re-bandage him and clean him up and get him into some dry clothes. My things should just about fit him."

Wade motioned to the wounded man's hands. "He's not a cowboy, that's for sure. His hands are calloused, but no rope burns. Can't figure out what he was doing way out there without a horse."

Melody came back with long strips of sheets and some heavier pads. She brought a pan of water and two towels and a washcloth. She frowned as she watched the man lying there so still.

"Tomorrow morning he's going to wake up and be much better. I just know he will. He'll tell us how he came to be here and who shot him and then we can tell the sheriff. Now. Let's get him into some dry clothes. Wade, there's supper for you and Lew in the kitchen. You go and help yourself. The rest of us have eaten."

An hour later they had the man cleaned up and in a nightshirt and tucked in snugly on the sofa. He still hadn't said a word, or shown any signs of regaining consciousness.

Vincent looked in a small leather purse the man carried. He had two twenty-dollar gold pieces and a letter from someone in Kansas, but it was so blurred and wet that they couldn't read any of the names.

"So, looks like we don't know who he is or even have a name to call him by," Vincent said. "Doc Daisley might know of somebody who's been missing. If we don't hear in a day or two, I'll go in and talk to Sheriff Vail."

"We'll know before then," Melody said. "Anything more we can do for him right now?"

Vincent shook his head. "This is the hard part. Reminds me of my days in the army. We just have to do what we can for him and wait and see what happens."

Melody pulled the rocking chair over and sat down. She picked up a book and rocked a little. "I'll watch over him a while," she said. "He might wake up and wonder where he is."

As she rocked, she watched the man. He looked young, maybe not any more than her own 24 years. She didn't know the color of his eyes, but his hair was light, almost blond, and he had cut it fairly short, probably to take care of it more easily. Calloused hands, so he was a working man, not a merchant. Clean shaven. He wasn't a large man, maybe five-eight and 150 pounds. She was guessing at most of it, but it seemed the thing to do.

Melody rocked and tried to read the book, but mostly she kept looking at the half of his face not covered by the bandage. She remembered the ugly wound on the side of his head just above his left ear and shivered. The human body was so fragile and broke so easily, especially the head.

She sighed. She had seen one man she loved die. She refused even to think about any feelings for this man. He was simply a stranger who needed help.

Vincent came in and checked him. Vincent had worked during the war in a small hospital that moved around near the front on the Union side. He had seen hundreds of wounded men.

"Best if we just let him be until morning," Vincent said. He touched her shoulders and she stood.

"I'm glad you're here, big brother. You know just what to do for him. Thanks. Now I think I'll get some sleep."

She went into her bedroom, looked at the picture of her late husband on the dresser, and blinked back tears. Stanley had been hurt before he died. Trampled in a stampede that never should have happened. She had held his hand for three months.

Then one beautiful afternoon when they carried him outside to see the sunset, he had just slipped away from her. It had helped to make her strong.

She undressed and slid into bed. She would not be overly concerned with this new man. He'd come to her ranch from nowhere, and he would recover and return where he belonged. Anyway, he probably was married.

She absolutely would not concern herself with this tragically wounded man. But Melody couldn't get him out of her mind, and it took her an hour to get to sleep.

Chapter Two

When Melody came downstairs the next morning after the stranger arrived, she went to the couch and found that he was awake and his color looked a little better.

"Hello, I'm Melody Orville and this is my ranch. Some of my men found you half in the river and brought you here. It seems that you've been shot, twice."

She paused and watched him. His eyes moved, looking at her but his face showed no emotion.

"We sent to town for Dr. Daisley to come out. He should be here by noon and he can patch you back together. You gave us quite a scare."

Again she waited. He nodded slowly as if he understood.

"What's your name?"

He frowned, looked from one side of the room to the other, and at last shrugged. "I don't know," he

15

said in a whisper that she barely heard. Melody built creases in her forehead.

"You mean you don't know what your name is?"

Slowly he nodded.

Melody's frown was full blown now. "Oh, dear."

"Water, please," he said softly, but with more voice this time. It seemed about half normal.

"Yes, of course. I'll bring some right in." As she left the parlor, she realized she had not even combed her hair this morning. She had thrown on the same dress she'd worn yesterday. Now she touched her hair, went to the pitcher, and poured a glass of water. Then she dumped it out and walked to the well just outside the kitchen door, primed the pump with a cup of water, and pumped a fresh pitcher full for the breakfast table.

When she took a glass of water to him, he nodded his thanks and drank only a little, setting the glass to one side on the small table they had pulled up beside the couch.

"Do you know what you were doing on the Laramie River maybe ten or twelve miles from town?"

He pinched his eyes and looked at her.

"Why were you out on the Laramie River with no horse, no food, no gear?"

"Sorry, I don't know."

Vincent came in and heard the last response. He grinned at the man on the bed.

"Damn, thought we were going to lose you there for a while. You look a hundred times better this morning. You got shot up a little. At least you didn't drown. Did you just tell Melody you don't know what you were doing out there?"

"Afraid so. Sorry."

"And you have no idea what your name is or where you live?" Melody asked.

"No idea at all."

"The important thing is what do you want for breakfast. Eggs and bacon, hotcakes and syrup, or some scrambled eggs and country-fried potatoes?"

"Hotcakes," he said almost smiling. "Coffee?"

"You bet, coming up." Vincent tugged at Melody's arm and she went to the kitchen with him.

"I've seen this before. Remember I said during the war some of the men with head wounds forgot how to walk, how to talk? Some of them also forgot everything that happened to them before they were shot. That's this man's problem. With some patience and care, we can get his body well. If we're lucky, he'll start remembering a little at a time."

"Oh, my. Sounds like a long process."

"I can ask Doc Daisley if he can take him in at his little clinic beside his office."

"No. We found him. We'll stand by him as long as he needs us. Just so he doesn't die."

Vincent touched his sister's arm. "Hey, not much chance of that now. He's past the critical point."

"Then it's settled. We'll see what Doc Daisley says. Now, I better get our guest some breakfast. Oh, some for you too, big brother?"

Later she watched her guest eat. He was hungry and she figured that was a good sign. She chatted with him as he ate, telling him about the Bar-O Ranch, how many hands they had, and her plans for the future. At last she looked at him and met his glance.

"What are we going to call you? We need a name. What's your favorite man's name?"

"Merle."

"All right, then we'll call you Merle. Does the name have any importance to you?"

He started to shake his head, then stopped. "No, no

special significance. It might have been my father's name. Looks like I didn't forget everything."

"Are you a cowboy?"

"No, but I'm good at riding and roping."

"Well, you remembered that. Where do you live?" He sighed. "Sorry."

When the doctor came he complimented Vincent on his bandaging, and snipped off some dead skin, put on some salve and medication, and bound the side wound.

"This one should heal up quickly. No real damage to anything vital."

"Doctor, I'm afraid I've lost my memory," Merle said.

The medic nodded. "Yes, a hard blow like that rifle bullet gave you could do it. But with most of the cases like these I've heard about, it's only a matter of time before the memory returns. I'm afraid that wound on the side of your head is going to leave a scar. But with any luck your hair should cover it." He added some medication and salve and then a bandage.

At the well house, Vincent talked with the doctor.

"Do some asking around, Doc, could you? Ask in town if anybody is missing. This man might be somebody folks in town know."

"I'll do that, Vincent. I know most of the folks and he's a stranger to me. But I'll ask around. You be sure to keep him bandaged and see that he gets lots of rest in bed for a week at least. He's had quite a shock to his system. Oh, you might try to get him to talk as much as he can. That might stir some memories and get him started back to a full return of his memory."

It was just after midday when Wade Johnson rode

in with his horse lathered. The foreman's face was red and he was angry.

"Get me a rifle and come along. We got some trouble in the south range."

"What kind of trouble?" Melody asked.

"Three men I swear are Circle B riders are yahooing about ten head of our cows and calves to the south. Rustling our stock."

Vincent tossed Wade a rifle and mounted up, and the two men rode out south at a canter to check out the situation.

"Sure it's Circle B men?" Vincent asked.

"Damn sure. Tall, thin guy with a black hat and rides a white stallion. Know that horse anywhere."

"Then let's ride a little faster. They can't move them cows any quicker than a walk. How far to get to the boundary between our spreads?"

"They had another three miles when I left them," Wade said. "Getting damn bold if you ask me."

"Too bold. A few rifle shots over their heads should convince them to ride for home without our animals."

"By rights we should hang the bastards," Wade said. "Mr. Orville would have considered it long and hard."

They rode faster then, and came on the rustlers more than a mile inside the property line. They rode hard then to cut off the three riders and 10 cows and calves.

When they had the angle on the trio, Wade put a rifle shot over their heads. The three men stopped and talked with each other. Then they turned, left the cows and galloped at full speed south and away from the beef.

Wade put two more shots after them, not really trying to hit them. When they were out of rifle range, they stopped and made angry gestures, then continued on toward the Circle B Ranch.

Vincent watched them. "We're going to have trouble with that outfit," he said. "Real trouble. I don't see any way to stop it. They keep pushing us, taking little bunches of our stock here and there. It mounts up. They could run us out of business. We've got to stop them."

"Put a couple of rifle slugs through one of their men and that will stop them in a rush," Wade said. "Most cowboys don't sign on for gun work."

"Except you, Wade." Vincent nodded. "Let's get these animals bunched up and driven back closer to the ranch buildings."

"You know that we're starting to overgraze part of that range."

"Yes, right, damn it. We'll have to move most of them north in a week or two. Let's get these up a ways from the boundary line. At least they won't be so tempting."

Two hours later, the men rode back into the ranch buildings. Wade went to the corral to finish the work he had started. Vincent put his horse into the near pasture, and threw his saddle on a pole in the barn.

The cattle business was all new to him. He'd come out when Stanley, his brother-in-law, had gotten trampled a year ago. His little sister had needed help with the ranch. He'd never married, and when he got the telegram, he'd left his job in a big store in Chicago and traveled west.

He was supposed to go back, but he'd hung on. At least he realized he was needed here to help run the ranch. When Melody's husband died, he'd dug in and decided to stay. Melody had agreed with him and made him a full partner.

But sometimes a situation came up that he just didn't know how to handle. Maybe he should have tried to shoot those three men. They were criminals, felons. Maybe he should have. Rustling cattle was a hanging offense in Wyoming.

He went into the house, had a long drink of cool water, and looked up as Melody joined him.

"How is our visitor?"

"We decided to call him Merle. He suggested it. We think it might be his father's name or maybe that of a brother or friend."

"Merle it is."

"He's feeling better. He's eating well, which is a good sign. It's going to take time for him to heal."

Vincent told her about the try at stealing their cattle.

"I'm going to take a buggy tomorrow and drive over there and give that terrible man a piece of my mind," Melody said. "We can't let him get away with this."

Vincent shook his head. "You try that and he's gonna shoot your horse and you'll be walking back home. Best leave it alone for now."

"But he makes me so angry."

"We just bide our time. He'll step out of line one of these days and we'll trip him up. You wait and see."

At supper, Merle felt well enough to sit up halfway and eat off a tray. Melody took her supper off a tray near him so they could talk.

"Merle, what kind of work do you do?" she asked. "Is it work with your hands?"

"Oh, I'm a . . ." He stopped. "For a minute I thought I knew, then it slipped away."

"Let's talk about what we know about you, Merle," Melody said. "This morning we decided to write down what we figured out, remember? So far we decided that you're right-handed, that you know how to read and write, and that you probably had an eighth-grade education."

She watched him a moment. "Now we can add that you have good table manners, are soft-spoken. The men noticed that you have calluses on your hands, but no rope burns. They told me this means you do some sort of physical labor, but you aren't a cowboy."

He looked up. "Oh, I remember I can ride a horse. Last week I fell off when my horse almost stepped on a snake and reared up." ·

Melody smiled. "Good, that's wonderful. You remembered something from last week. Where were you riding? Who was with you?"

He put down his fork and touched a napkin to his lips. "I just can't remember."

She smiled. "Now, don't you worry about it. We'll figure out sooner or later and get in touch with your family. Did you have one brother or two?"

"Two," he said, and then smiled. "Yes, two. One of them was Merle and the other one . . . Charlie!"

"That's fine, Merle, just fine. Oh, shall we still call you Merle?" He nodded.

When the supper was over she took away the dishes, cleaned up the kitchen, and came back in with a deck of playing cards.

"Let's play some gin rummy," she said, sitting down near his table and spreading out the cards.

He nodded. She dealt out nine cards to each of them and then one extra to him. They completed the first hand and he won. Melody smiled. "Now, look at this, you know how to play gin rummy and you beat me. I'm writing everything down on this pad of paper. I'll leave it with you and you can read it over and add anything as you remember it."

He took the cards and shuffled them. "Poker," he said. "Five-card draw, jacks or better, and no wild cards, no special house rules, two matches ante."

Melody laughed with delight. They were progressing quickly. She watched Merle as he dealt. He had stubble on his face now. He hadn't asked about shaving and she hadn't mentioned it. He was a good-looking young man. She had guessed he was about 24. Her Stanley had been 25, just a year older. She shook her head. That was no way to be thinking.

This man was wounded grievously. When he was well he would ride back where he belonged and the ranch life would forge ahead. Merle had nothing to do whatsoever with her dear late husband Stanley. She put the whole idea out of her head and settled down to playing poker with the kitchen matches she had counted out for each of them.

In about an hour, Melody won all of Merle's matches. She picked up the tablet again.

"Knows how to play poker, but is not very good at it," she said as she wrote. She laughed as she looked up at him. A little smile curled around the half of his face she could see.

"Afraid so," Merle said; then he looked away. "Damn, I wish I could remember who I am."

Chapter Three

Spur McCoy came out of the sheriff's office in Laramie with a large frown and a bigger problem. The United States Federal Secret Service agent had figured this assignment would be a cinch. Interior Secretary Columbus Delano had raised a rumpus about two of his key surveyors in Wyoming Territory who had been missing for three weeks.

Surveying was not the safest of jobs, especially in country where a survey line might have to run directly through an Indian tribe's sacred lands, or into rugged mountains, or even through the middle of contested lands in a range war.

None of those problems seemed to apply here. He'd heard of some surveyors who'd stopped their work for two months and panned for gold on a particularly tempting mountain stream. Others had given up in the middle of a big job like this for all sorts of reasons from a woman to a card game to a sheriff who recognized the surveyor from an early picture on a wanted poster.

General Wilton D. Halleck, McCoy's boss in Washington D.C. and the second man in the Secret Service, had laid out his assignment plainly in a telegram:

TO SPUR MCCOY IN DENVER HOUSE DENVER COLORADO *STOP* PROCEED TO LARAMIE WYOMING *STOP* INVESTIGATE TWO MISSING DEPARTMENT OF INTERIOR SURVEYORS *STOP* THEY WERE WORKING NORTH SOUTH DIVISION LINE OFF BASE LINE OUT OF LARAMIE *STOP* INVESTIGATE SOONEST *STOP* REPORT PARTICULARS WITHIN ONE WEEK *STOP* GENERAL HALLECK WASHINGTON DC SENDING *STOP* ACKNOWLEDGE *STOP*

He had arrived in Laramie last night on the train out of Denver up to Cheyenne and then on the main line to here. He'd found a hotel room, and this morning had tried to get some idea what he needed to do. He had no idea how far the pair of surveyors had gotten out of Laramie heading north. Missing. That could mean anything.

The sheriff had almost nothing. He had a telegram inquiry from the Department of the Interior about the two men. His wire back to them had said he knew nothing of their movements. Next had come a wire informing him an agent would be on hand to investigate.

McCoy had the names of the two missing men, Red Arbeck and Jas Buckman. Both had registered at the Northern Hotel there in Laramie 18 days ago. There was no trace of them since.

McCoy was a big man, six-two and 200 pounds and without more than half an ounce of fat on him. He kept in trim, and spent at least half of his time outdoors, so he was tanned and slightly windburned by the elements. His dark brown hair was full around his ears, and matched the color of the thick stubble that covered his face. He peered at the world from alert green eyes. His low-crowned brown hat had a ring of Spanish silver coins around it.

He stopped in at the local surveyor to get his bearings. The old surveyor peered up from a drawing board where he was plotting out a surveyed property. He put down his ink pen and sighed.

"Yep, sure they stopped by. Professional courtesy. Besides, they wanted to know where the railway survey bench mark was. Told them. A ground-level concrete monument just north of the tracks off C Street. I'm glad they got here. They're working on the north-south division line off the base line."

McCoy didn't say anything. The old surveyor sighed again. "You don't know what I'm talking about, do you, son? All right. Before we could be a territory our boundaries had to be surveyed. That meant we needed a starting place, a *surveyed* starting spot that connected up with another *surveyed* starting spot, so we had an absolute positioning. You can't go by a river or an old oak tree the way they did years ago. Them things move and change.

"This ain't just a metes and bounds job here. We're talking baseline and division line, and over somewhere near Rawlings there'll be a center line. From these lines the whole damn territory is surveyed from and described. Every legal description will refer to it as something like range twenty-four west, township ten north, and then the rest of the legal boundaries.

"Hell, we've all been waiting for it to come in so we could justify and in some cases correct the legal descriptions."

"So you were glad they were here?"

"Absolutely. I bought them both supper and we had some drinks afterwards. Must have been two, three weeks ago now."

"So they worked due north from the bench mark?"

"Right as rain, young feller."

McCoy thanked him, walked to the livery stable, and rented a horse. He picked out a prancing claybank that had good eyes and a deep chest. Some folks called a horse with this color a dun. It was a pale canvas color with the tail, skin, and hoofs a soft shade of black. She had a softer shade of pale yellow hair down her back.

He stopped at the general store and bought a minimum of cooking gear, and enough food to last him three days on the trail. If he didn't find something by then, he'd be back in town anyway.

He took off north from the bench mark using a hand-held compass. The route followed up the middle of C Street and quickly out of town. He rode for an hour and saw no one and no houses, farms, or ranches.

Then a half hour later he spotted a small ranch just off the Laramie River, which had angled off west of the due north course. He figured he was maybe five miles from town.

A young man in his late twenties bobbed his head.

"Morning. My name's Dornbecker, and this is my spread. Step down and come in for a cup of coffee and some cinnamon rolls."

There was a drink of cold water from the well, then the coolness of the kitchen. McCoy told the rancher his quest.

"Sure, I remember them coming through. Two gents with a bunch of equipment. Set up this thing they called a transit that had a little telescope on it and lines and charts and things. Said now I could get a firm legal description of my ranch."

"How long were they here?" McCoy asked.

"Just passed through. The wife gave them a cup of coffee and some apple pie. Then they filled their canteens and kept 'chaining' as they called it. They had a whole batch of steel stakes and plumb bobs and everything."

"Come past close?"

"Just out there maybe a hundred yards. Got here near suppertime so I rode out and asked them to come back and eat; then they slept in the haymow. They were up and gone before breakfast. Seems like they were supposed to get so many miles done in a day."

"How far to the next ranch north?" McCoy asked.

"Oh, from here, my place goes about three miles north, then the Circle B takes over and it goes to hell and gone up there. Least he claims it as his range. Probably don't own more than one or two homesteads up that direction."

"Big outfit?"

"Biggest around here. He makes it a hobby to gobble up smaller ranches. Tried with me, but a couple of rounds from my shotgun discouraged him."

"What's the man's name?"

"Charlie Breen, not one of my favorite gents."

"How's that?"

"First off, he's rich, got more cattle than he knows what to do with. He's stingy, and mean, and I'd just as soon have a new neighbor."

"Afraid I can't help there." They talked about the weather, and the price of steers at the railhead, and McCoy finished the big cinnamon roll and his coffee. "Thank your wife for the roll and coffee and thank you for your time."

He moved out across the wide valley of the Laramie. It stretched for 20 miles one direction and probably 35 or more the other. The river drained a huge area. Ideal for cattle. From what the surveyor had said back in Laramie, the team would be putting down permanent markers every 15 to 20 miles.

When they could, they would use an outcropping of rock and bury a steel stake in it topped by a copper cap designating the bench-mark position with data on it.

He had found one half a mile back, and now checked the direction with his compass, picked out a point due north, and rode toward where the small creek slanted on west toward the larger Laramie River.

A half hour later, McCoy had just come into the edge of the brush when he heard somebody singing. A woman. He edged his claybank forward into the trees. On the other side of the creek he saw a wagon rigged up like a stagecoach. A team of mules had been unhitched and grazed nearby.

In the edge of the creek sat a young woman playing in the water. She was naked and cooling off from the warm summer day. The girl was brown as a baked apple, slender with big breasts. She scooped up the water and dropped it on her breasts, and crooned and sang as she did.

She had strong shoulders and her brown hair framed her pretty face. She scooped more water on her breasts and rubbed them, then tweaked her nipples and rose from the water on her knees, showing her brown muff of crotch hair as the cool water ran off it.

As he watched, another young woman came out the door of the wagon and headed for a small cooking fire. She was dressed. From the looks of the camp they had been there some time.

Squatters, or just some folks pausing on their way west? Almost nobody drove a covered wagon west anymore. Not when it was so much simpler to ride the train all the way to Sacramento and Oakland if you wanted to.

Pleasant as the sight of the nude young woman was, McCoy turned his claybank to go around the brush 100 yards higher on the creek and avoid them both. As he swung his horse around, he stared into the twin muzzles of a sawed-off shotgun held by a man with a full beard, angry eyes, and the dirtiest clothes McCoy had seen in a long time. The man was ten yards away and on foot.

"Spying on us, was ya, stranger? Enough of that. Now you lift them mitts into the air and slide down on this side of that nag slow and easy like. I surely don't mind blowing you in half, but damned well hate to wound that good-looking horse. Get down easy now."

McCoy did as he was told. The way the man was dressed struck a responsive note and he scowled. He'd seen a man like this before.

"Look, I don't mean any harm. I was just moving downstream and going around your camp here. Why don't you put down the weapon and nobody gets hurt and I'll be on my way. There is no cause to be holding that shotgun."

"Yeah, you'd like that, wouldn't ya now?" The man stepped closer and McCoy could see that he was in his forties, and looked like he hadn't had a bath in a year. His hair was long and matted. His eight-inch-long beard was also matted and stained by tobacco juice. The man spit to one side and grinned. More tobacco juice ran down his beard.

"Damnation if the girls ain't gonna thank me. I'll be a hero around here. Leave the horse and walk forward, arsehole. I'll bring this right nice horseflesh."

McCoy tried to stall. "I'm sorry about looking at your daughters. My mistake. I'm on my way somewhere and if I don't arrive they'll come looking for me, ten, maybe fifteen of them, and they always ride armed."

"Hell, I'll tend to them when they find us. If they find us." The man giggled like a schoolgirl. "Damn if I ain't gonna do my girls up proud." He sobered. "Now, you lift that hog-leg out of leather by one finger and your thumb and bend down and slide it to the ground easy-like. Be obliged if you'd do that right now."

McCoy had a rule never to give up his gun. He started to lift it, stared into the shotgun muzzles from ten feet away, and knew he was dead if he tried to fast-draw this man. Nobody alive could beat a trigger pull on an already aimed shotgun. Besides, this ugly excuse for a man was a rawhider. He took what he wanted, and killed anyone in the way with no more regret than McCoy would killing a pestering fly.

McCoy bent down and put the weapon on the ground.

"Walk ahead, feller, walk on ahead a dozen steps and stop." When he stopped, McCoy looked behind him. The man picked up the Colt .45 and admired it, shoved it in his belt, and motioned with the scattergun.

" 'Bout time you meet my two girls. I call them Silly and Punkin. They' gonna love you."

The man fired a round from the shotgun into the trees and brush, and the girls jumped up and stared his way. The naked one stood there not self-conscious at all.

"You there, Pa?" the one at the stream called.

"Hell, yes, girls, I'm here. Come see what I ketched for you to play with."

Both girls ran toward him. The naked one moved as naturally as if she had on a full set of clothes. The other one wore a long skirt and a dirty blouse that was torn down from one sleeve showing the side of her breast.

When McCoy stepped from the fringe of brush into the open, both girls squealed in delight and ran toward him.

"I get him first," the naked girl shrilled. "You said it was my turn next, Pa, you promised."

"Oh, Pa, you brought us a present!" the clothed one shouted as she ran up.

"Pa, I hope we can keep him for a while to play with. You promised us it was our turn. Remember?" The dressed one came up closest and stared at McCoy.

"He's a big one, Pa," the naked girl said. "Bet he's hung like an old stud horse. Can I look right now? Can I look at his crotch, Pa?"

McCoy figured it was his last chance. He dove toward the one with clothes, grabbed her around the waist, and held her in front of him. The shotgun lifted to cover them both.

"Don't shoot, Pa!" the girl screamed. Before McCoy could do more than start to turn toward the naked girl she was on him, her strong right arm around his neck from behind, choking him. She knew what she was doing. He let go of the girl in front of him and rammed one elbow backwards to try to hit the girl's stomach. She avoid his repeated thrusts with his elbows and tightened her choke hold.

He tried to kick behind him, and then bent forward to flip her over his back. That would have worked, but just at the time he needed to throw her forward, her arm tightened again and the lack of oxygen staggered him and he fell forward. Before he hit the grass and dirt under the trees, he started to pass out and the naked girl let off her choke hold.

He had time only to hear the ring of laughter from the girl's father and the roar of the shotgun as McCoy faded toward total blackness. Just as the darkness closed around him he wondered if he was merely fainting or if the damn rawhider had blown him in half.

Then he didn't think anymore and everything was one huge wall poster of black on black.

Chapter Four

Charlie Breen stretched, sat up, and then lifted out of bed. He slept in his red long johns winter and summer. He scratched his crotch, then wandered out into the hall and looked out the east window. Weather always came from the east. He was hoping for a good day.

A woman giggled.

Charlie Breen wheeled around and saw the female two doors down in the entryway to Kevin's room. She wore a half petticoat and nothing on top, her breasts swinging as she pointed at him with one hand and laughed.

"I do declare, Mr. Charlie Breen, you are standing there in your unmentionables," the woman said. Kevin Breen popped out of his room and covered up the woman. He had on only the bottoms of his red underwear.

"Kevin!" Charlie roared. "What the *hell is that*

34

whore doing in my house? I won't tolerate a fallen woman in the house where your mama lived and died. God rest her soul."

Kevin Breen was certainly a branch off the Breen tree. He was almost six feet tall, built wide and solid like an oak, with a short neck, a bull of a head, and a fleshy face that crowded in on his small black eyes. His black hair was tousled and tangled from sleep.

"Oh, damn, Pa. Don't be so persnickety. Flossy and me got married last night, so she ain't a whore no more."

"You what?" the enraged elder Breen bellowed. "Impossible. No Breen would ever marry a whore. Get her out of here this minute."

"See, Kevin, told you it wouldn't work. Old Charlie Breen ain't that dumb." Flossy walked toward Charlie, her hips swinging, her naked full breasts bouncing and jiggling enough to grab Charlie's full attention.

"Hey, Old Charlie, how about a quick trip to heaven this morning between my lily white thighs? I aim to please, Charlie. Your aim will help. Ask Kevin. I pleased him seven times last night."

Charlie stood there a minute watching her come, then jumped toward her as if with a bayonet in his hand. "Out! Out! Out of my house! Kevin, you ever bring a fucking whore in here again, I'll send you to a line camp so far up north you'll have frozen fingers for breakfast. Get her dressed and put a big hat on her and drive her back to town. Do it now!"

"Hey, Pa, it was just a joke. Flossy and me got drunk last night and we decided to surprise you this morning. No harm done. I swear, I never seen you look so outraged in your whole life."

"Get that bitch out of here now, Kevin!"

"Come on, Pa. Flossy told me you've diddled her a few times in the past."

"Out!" the elder Breen roared, and stepped back into his room. He had a good ranch here, and a son who should be taking over more and more of the responsibilities. He wasn't. Kevin worked the ranch, and did his share, but all the management was up to Charlie. Who was going to take over when Charlie got caught in a draw one of these days with a crazy wild range bull who kept charging?

Charlie kicked into denim pants and shirt, pulled on a heavy plaid shirt as a jacket against the morning chill, and stomped down to the kitchen.

Carmelita, the cook, had just piled a second helping of hotcakes and eggs on Charlie's plate when Kevin came in.

"Ain't you gone yet?" Charlie snapped.

"Lady is dressing, and I figured I'd take her up some breakfast."

"No damn breakfast for a whore in my house. Christ, Kevin, it's like you're stomping on your mother's grave."

"Don't mean no harm, Pa. We was just having a little fun."

"You get her into town and get your arse back out here. We got to cut out the rest of them steers from the spring roundup and get them ready to drive to the railhead. You can have some food when you get back."

Charlie stared his son down until Kevin turned and went out the kitchen door and climbed the big staircase to the second floor.

Fifteen minutes later Charlie had finished his breakfast and stood in the parlor watching the buggy roll out from the shed and move down the lane toward the river road that led into Laramie.

At least that much was settled. Kids just didn't have any respect for their elders or their parents these days.

Charlie was a large man, like his son. Nearly six feet tall and thick at the shoulders, and now at the waist as well. He weighed more than 210 pounds and was slowing down at 52, and he admitted it. He couldn't stay out until two in the morning drinking and whoring and be up at six with the sun ready to put in a full day's work.

He had spent 15 years on this land building it into one of the biggest and best ranches in Wyoming. He didn't want to pass it on to some boozing and whoring kid who would ruin it and lose it in ten years.

Sure, he had squatted on this land before it could be had any other way, and now he ran squatters off if they even thought about staying anywhere within 20 miles. It was his land, no matter what the damn land office said, and his men and his guns would keep it that way.

He saw his foreman coming and walked out to meet him. They had a tough day's work on those steers. A lightning storm had scattered them two days ago and they still hadn't got them bunched together yet. As soon as they were ready they would drive them down to Laramie, all of ten or twelve miles to the stock pens at the rail yard.

He would make certain the usual two lookouts were posted well out from the ranch buildings, so they didn't get any surprise visitors. He'd had enough of those the last few weeks. They had a ranch to run, not a country inn for social gatherings.

As he walked, he was trying to figure out which of the small ranches surrounding him he wanted the most—the Bar-O to the north of him, or the smaller but better situated MW just to the south. He was favoring the Bar-O. The fact that a widow was trying to run the place swayed his decision. Her husband had been trampled in a sudden stampede about a year ago.

Yes, he figured the Bar-O Ranch would be the best to take on. He could offer to buy her out. No, that would cost too much. It would be cheaper and more entertaining to scare her and run her out of the territory. Yes. He would do some planning on that.

Something cool and soothing stroked his forehead. It came again along with some low, soft voices, women's voices. The coolness touched his forehead, and it eased the throbbing headache he now realized he had.

Spur McCoy lay without moving. He was trying to become totally awake, to remember. . . . Then he did remember, the strong arm around his throat, the darkness, and the shotgun blast.

He wasn't dead. McCoy knew this because he hurt too much to be dead. His throat ached, his head boomed like a bass drum, and even his wrists hurt. Wrists? He must be tied somehow. He fluttered his eyes, then opened them.

"Well, well, the sleeping beauty wakes up."

He blinked again. Then his eyes focused and he saw sitting beside him the naked woman who had choked him into unconsciousness. She wrung out a cloth in a pan of water and put the coolness back on his forehead.

"I didn't mean to hurt you, but you were about to get away and we couldn't let you go. You just got here," the naked woman said.

Up close he saw that she now looked more like the man of the trio. Her long hair was dirty, unwashed and uncombed. But she evidently had been washing her body. It glistened with good health, and glowed brown from the sun in an all-over tan, including her thrusting, full breasts.

Even her areolas had tanned a little, a pinkish tan.

He tried to lift one arm, but found it held by a wire that had been wrapped around his wrist.

"Yes, you're tied down. Oh, you can move around, you just can't go far. Can't let you do that. Pa promised us we could play with you."

For the first time he looked down and saw that he was naked. All of his clothes were in a jumbled pile, along with his gunbelt and boots.

"What's your name? Mine is Silly. Not my real name, but what Pa calls me. What's yours?"

"Spur."

"Oh, good. I like that. You've got a fine-looking spur right down there." She moved over him and her breasts hung down toward his face.

"Spur, you want to take a bite? Want to chew a little? I'm here for you. You can play with me just anyway that you want to."

He felt her hands at his crotch and he realized that his legs were spread and tied down as well to stakes in the ground. Her hands caught him and fondled and toyed with him, and he started to become aroused.

His mouth opened, and she laughed softly and lowered one breast into it.

"Yes, oh, yes, that's a good boy, Spur. I think you and I are going to do just fine." She changed breasts in his mouth and stroked him, and suddenly Spur realized that he was fully erect.

"My, what a good boy! He's so ready." She moved upward then and caught his hand and pushed it between her legs. "You find anything you want to play with in there you just go right ahead. I want you to enjoy this too. Then maybe we can get two or three times before my turn is over."

"Silly, you really know how to get a guy excited, don't you? What if I don't want to play?"

She laughed, and her hand pumped his erection three times. "Oh, you want to play. You just might be a little mad at first, but you'll love it. I bet you never tried it this way before."

She giggled. "Oh, yeah, Spur, that's the way. You have magic fingers after all. Ooooooooooooh . . . yeah, that's nice fingering down here. Hey, I think we're both about ready."

She moved so she squatted with one foot on each side of his hips and held his manhood up straight, then adjusted her hips and found the slot and slowly sank down on him.

"Oh, Mary, Margaret, and Aunt Julia, but that is fine!" Silly shouted as he lanced upward inside her. She settled until they were at maximum penetration and then she ground around a little with her hips.

"Delicious." She lifted up and went all the way down, and then again and again. At last she reached her bare feet backward so they extended down beside his legs and she leaned forward.

"Spur, old cock, I'm going to ride you like a two-bit pony in the carnival. This is one ride you're never going to forget."

Silly crooned and sang to herself as she humped and slanted forward and back and set up a rhythm that set her on fire. She lasted for two minutes. Then she brayed and vibrated and screeched in passion and trembled and shook like she was coming apart.

"Damn you, Spur, you lasted longer than I did." She ground her hips against him and squeezed with her inside muscles and Spur felt himself building to a peak. He grunted and humped upward, firing his salvo again and again until he was dry, and then let her fall on him for a rest.

Five minutes later she roused and lifted away from him and sat there watching him. She turned and looked on a little rise nearby where the man and the other young woman sat watching.

"Let's keep him at least a month," Silly said. "He's good, he's damn good. I want him to stay."

"Hell, girl, you know we got to move. We sell what we can in Laramie and then head into Colorado fast as we can."

"We could chop off one of his feet and keep him as a pet," Silly said.

The man with the matted beard spit tobacco juice at a grasshopper and missed. "Can't do that. Have to keep him tied up all the time. Just won't work. Nope. You two can play all you want today. Tomorrow we move on into Laramie."

Spur McCoy lay there trying not to believe what he had heard. They were going to use him like a stud horse and then shoot him in the morning. He tried to pull up on one leg. He couldn't budge it a fraction of an inch. The stake must be solid in the ground. As he pulled, the wire bit into his ankle. The same thing happened with his wrists.

There was no way he could get free. These raw-hiders had done this before. They were excellent at what they did. What did that leave him? He couldn't get to his gun.

Somehow he had to get control of one of the girls. How? He put his mind to it. If he didn't he wouldn't see another sunrise.

The other girl, Punkin, had been watching him. She walked over and stared down at him.

"It sure as hell looks like a little worm right now," she said. She laughed. "Hell, I can make him hard again when I want to. All I have to do is try."

She went back to the fire and evidently finished cooking something. The three of them ate. Silly didn't put on any clothes. Evidently she liked going naked, McCoy decided. By stretching one way he could touch the stake. It was a round piece of wood, and the wire was evidently wrapped around it and then driven in so the wire was underground. He tried working the stake, and at last got it moving.

If he had enough time he could get that one free. He worked at it and then saw the trio break up. Punkin came down and stared at him. She still had her clothes on, an old skirt and a dirty blouse with the torn sleeve. He could see flashes of one breast through the side of the sleeve.

Punkin sat down beside him and looked at him. "You like it, don't you, this fucking?"

"Most people enjoy making love, especially with a partner who they admire or love or have a tremendous attraction for. With Silly it was more like a pair of dogs going at it."

Punkin laughed. "I don't like to take my clothes off."

"I've noticed," Spur said.

"That bother you?"

"Does it matter? You plan on killing me anyway, don't you?"

"Not me. I don't do the killin'. Silly don't mind. But usual Pa does that himself."

"It won't bother you when your pa shoots me?"

"Depends how good you are at fucking."

"I'm plenty good. If I had my hands free I'd seduce you so slick you wouldn't even know what was happening."

"Bet you could. But it can't happen that way." She paused. "You can still do it if I don't get undressed the way Silly did."

"Sure, I can do it anyway you want. I could even get you if you lay on your back on top of me this way."

"Couldn't either. No chance you could get inside me."

"Sure I can. You want them to watch?" he asked, pointing at the pair on the little rise.

"Sometimes I tell them to go away until I'm done."

"Do that now and I'll be able to fuck you a lot better. You'll enjoy it more that way, Punkin."

She watched him, then nodded. "I'm a private person. I'd like it better that way." She turned and looked up the slope.

"Hey, Pa, you, Silly. Get your asses out of here. I want to do my man-fuckin' without a bunch of wise-ass comments and onlookers. Get over the hill, or go in the wagon."

They growled and swore, but a minute later they were out of sight and McCoy felt the first glimmer of hope. She watched up the hill to be sure they were gone, and that gave Spur a few more seconds to work on the stake holding his right wrist by the wire. He had to get it free in the next minute or two or he was going to be shot dead by that damn rawhider!

Chapter Five

Punkin kneeled beside where he lay and her long skirt hiked up on her legs. She brushed it down with a touch of modesty. She stared down at him. Spur McCoy had seldom seen a woman as dirty and unwashed as she was. He couldn't think about that. She had to be his savior. He had to at least pretend to be excited by her. She looked at him.

"I usual need a little warming up before I can get real sexy. Then I love it." She lay down beside him so his left hand could reach her breasts. "Touch me and feel me right there. Don't try to hurt them. A man did once and I tore his throat out. He wasn't a nice man at all."

She lifted her dirty, torn blouse and settled down so his hand could touch her breasts. They were larger than Silly's, he guessed. Spur rubbed them, tweaked her nipples, and fondled them, and soon he could feel them heating up.

"Yes, yes, I like that," she said. He saw that her eyes were closed. Spur worked at the stake holding his right hand. He could move it half an inch each way, but it wouldn't lift out yet. He kept rubbing her breasts.

A moment later her hand on that side reached out and found his crotch. She came up his leg and caught his scrotum and toyed with it, gently squeezing his testicles. Then she moved her hand higher and caught his soft penis.

"Don't worry, I'll get him hard. I'm good at that. Yes, yes, your hand knows what to do. I'm going to move higher so your hand can go lower."

She moved, and he kept his right hand still as she did so, but she never opened her eyes. His hand brushed her skirt and she flipped it upward so his hand came between her bare legs.

"Slowly, slowly," she said. He could hear her breathing hard now. Spur worked the stake more. Now he could push and pull it an inch each way. He had to be able to pull it up soon.

He moved his hand up and down her bare legs, just brushing her crotch hairs, then sliding it back down. She was panting now.

"I'm almost ready," she said, her eyes still closed. "Touch my little cunnie, rub me down there."

Spur was doing two things at once, and now and then he got mixed up, but his fingers found her nether lips, moist and hot, and he could feel new juices flowing.

"Oh, yes!" she said softly. "I'm ready, and you're hard as a steel stake." She opened her eyes and looked at his eyes.

"Can you really do me from the back lying down that way? Bet you can't. I'll flip up my skirt and sit on your hips and you go ahead and try."

She hovered over him, then eased down on her back, her soft buttocks on his crotch.

"I don't see how you can get in me that way."

He gave a hard pull with his right hand and the stake eased upward, and then it was out of the ground. His right arm was free. He grabbed the stake and lifted his hand toward his side. One look at the slope showed neither of the other rawhiders was watching them.

In one swift motion he wrapped the wire around Punkin's throat and pulled it tight.

"Punkin, don't make a sound or I'll strangle you, you understand?"

She nodded.

"What you must do if you want to stay alive is pull out the stake holding my left hand. Do you understand?"

She nodded again. Tears slipped down her face and fell on his chest.

"Do it now. Work the stake back and forth until you can pull it out. Not a sound."

She worked on the stake, and he could see it was almost out.

"Hey, you two fuckers down there," Silly called from the wagon. "You making any progress? I know you're slow, Punkin, but damn, I want another turn or two 'fore it gets dark."

"Answer her that you're doing fine," Spur whispered. He loosened the wire around her throat.

"You just shut up your face, Silly. I'll do fuckin' my own way in my own time."

"Christ, what a ninny!" Silly shot back, but she didn't come outside to check on them. Spur tightened the wire.

"Get it out of there, come on!" Spur whispered. She tugged again and this time it came out. All the time he had been pulling and pushing with his legs on the bottom stakes. The wire had rubbed raw spots on his ankles, but he'd made progress.

"Now, Punkin. Both of us are going to sit up and you pull the stake out on my right leg, and I'll do the one on my left leg, understand? Then we lay right back down with you on top."

This was the risky part. If the old man looked out at them, or if Silly decided she wanted to watch . . .

They sat up, and he saw that the stakes had been loosened a lot by his motions. She pulled one out and he got the other one out. They lay back down.

"Now, you unwind the wire from my right wrist, then from the left. Don't make a sound."

Punkin was shivering. At last she looked at him. "I'm glad you're getting away. I'll come with you. I can wash and dress good. Let me come with you."

"You help me get away and you can come. First I need to get dressed. You lay right here while I get some clothes and my boots on. Is my six-gun with my clothes?"

She nodded.

"I'll let go of the wire if you promise not to scream or yell. You give me away I'll strangle you. Understand?"

Her eyes—brown, he noticed now—watched him. Then she nodded.

He got to his clothes, pulled on his pants and a shirt, then his boots without socks. He left his hat and neckerchief. He buckled his six-gun on his hips and jumped up and ran into the woods and brush. A minute later Punkin saw him gone and rushed out following him.

"Jeeeze, you gonna take all night, Punkin? You just supposed to get poked once, you know." The voice came from the wagon. "Damn, she must be panting so bad she can't answer."

Spur was 20 feet into the brush when he realized he didn't know where his horse was. He saw Punkin charging after him, and he waited.

"Where's my horse?"

She pointed upstream. They moved through the brush and up along the small creek. Another 20 yards and he saw through the cover where his clay-bank and the two mules had been picketed in fresh grass. The animal was still saddled, but the Spencer carbine no longer rested in the boot.

He motioned for the girl to stay where she was, and he walked into the open, lifted the reins from the ground tie to a bush, and walked the claybank into the brush and out of sight.

"What the hell!" The rawhider's voice bellowed into the afternoon sunshine from behind the rise of land. "Bastard's getting away!" the man shouted. Spur stepped into the saddle and Punkin stood there, not looking so big now.

"Take me with you. He'll kill me for sure now that I helped you."

"He your pa?"

"Lord, no. He saved me from a raid he made on a ranch. I used to be married."

Spur put down his hand and removed his foot from the stirrup. She stepped into the stirrup and he pulled her up and on board behind him. Then they charged upstream, using the brush as cover. That way they had a chance.

He heard a pistol shot behind them, but figured that was mostly in anger. Then the shotgun boomed and he knew that was a hopeful shot. The rawhider hadn't seen them yet.

Spur kicked the claybank and urged her ahead faster under her double load. They crossed a small open space and Spur McCoy took a look behind. He could see the small rise where the wagon had been hidden behind, and at the same time he saw a puff of blue smoke. He ducked and kicked the animal.

"He's seen us and is shooting. Bend down."

He heard three more shots then and realized the rawhider was using the Spencer. One of the rounds sizzled overhead. The second one seemed to come closer, and then he heard a cry from behind him.

"I'm shot!" Punkin whispered. He darted the mare back into the brush with her burden. Spur heard three more shots, but the marksman had no target now. He was just hoping.

Spur tried to turn in the saddle. "Punkin, is it bad? Where are you hit?"

"In the back. Not sure I can move."

He slowed the claybank, held the woman, and looked at her. Blood ran down her back, staining the dirty blouse. He held her and kicked his leg over the saddle and dropped off the mount, then caught Punkin as she fell toward him.

He checked his six-gun. Yes, still loaded. He looked at Punkin. She whispered something, then shook her head. A soft wail came from her and, in the flutter of a hummingbird's wing, the woman died. He lay her head down softly on the grass and tied his mount. Then he took a fresh box of .45 rounds from his saddlebags and pushed them in his pants pocket.

An eye for an eye.

Not a chance he was going to leave it this way. No telling how many innocents this rawhider had killed. He was no better than a rattlesnake. Worse. He was a wolverine. He killed for the sheer pleasure of the hunt.

Spur crawled up to the edge of the cover looking downstream. He saw a way he could get past the bald spot without showing himself. The stream cut a fair channel here with the spring run-off. He could bend over and slip along the 40 feet of open space to the brush on the far side.

He figured that the rawhider wouldn't chase him. He might have seen his round hit Punkin. He would be hitching up and be on the move. He and the girl would try to defend themselves if Spur came back. The killer was counting on the idea that once he got away from being so close to death, any normal man would just keep on running.

Spur bent low and ran along the edge of the water with the three-foot bank covering him. He was not an ordinary man. He hated rawhiders more than any other criminal in the West. They were killers by surprise, totally amoral. They would come on a small ranch and ask for a drink of water and directions. Then when they were sure how many people were there, they would kill everyone without warning.

Next they would loot the house for anything of value they could sell, steal any horses available, burn down the house and barn, and move on to the next target.

This was one rawhider who had done his last killing.

By the time Spur had crept silently through the brush along the stream and come to where he could see the open spot where the mules had been, they were gone.

He had expected that. He then ran across the opening to the small rise where he looked down at where the wagon had parked. It also was gone.

There had been a chance he could beat them. They had won the first round. Spur jogged all the way back to where he had tied his horse. He watched the silent form on the ground for a moment, then told her spirit he would be back. He mounted the claybank and rode to where the wagon had stood, and then began tracking it.

There is no way to hide the movement of a heavy freight wagon, which is what he figured this one must be. The steel-rimmed wheels sank three inches into the packed dirt, and in softer areas cut in six inches.

Spur checked the sun. There were three, maybe four hours until dusk. He would catch them long before that. He did not know precisely what he would do when he caught them. The man he especially wanted, the tobacco-chewing killer. That man would die.

The trail headed toward Laramie. Spur was not sure how far from the town they were, six or eight miles perhaps. He tracked them from the back of his horse. The mules were working hard, moving much faster than they wanted to. The rawhider must be rushing to some defensive position. He had at least one rifle, maybe more. In the right spot he could hold off one man with only a pistol until darkness.

Then he could move out into the night and no one without a lot of torches or a lantern could track him.

An hour later, the wagon turned south on a road of sorts that ran along the river. Now it would be harder to track the big rig. A buggy cut into the trail, and then a farm wagon for a time, but it turned off.

Another half hour went by, and the sun was moving closer to the western mountains. He caught the turnoff. It was as if the rawhider wanted him to see it. The tracks slanted directly at a heavy stand of trees and brush near the river. Was this his fort?

The trees were about a half mile away, downstream at a 45-degree angle. Did the killer think that Spur would ride innocently toward the trees, watching the wagon tracks?

A half mile was a little less than 800 yards, and the Spencer was no good at that distance, but many other rifles were. Spur dug his heels into the flanks of the claybank and she surged ahead, not at the woods, but at right angles to the woods section, which was downstream.

He charged for the cover of the brush and trees along the Laramie River. There were no fences or ranches or farmers in this area, so nothing stopped him from reaching the river. Not even the booming shot of a Big Fifty buffalo gun spoke from the woods.

He hit the cover, dodged into it, and rode south. Twice he had to show himself to get across thin patches of brush, but again there was no response from the heavy woods. That had to be where the rawhider had holed up. There was no better spot, and he couldn't make it into town and safety before he was caught.

It was what Spur McCoy would have done in the same situation. What else? Put yourself in your target's shoes. What would you do in this case? He had two shooters. Spur was sure that the naked girl, Silly, could shoot a rifle as well as he could. Where to place her? Why not up front? They had plenty of warning that he had not fallen for the direct-approach trap.

Instead he was coming up through the woods. Why not send naked Silly about 50 yards upstream in a good ambush spot and wait for Spur to blunder into her sights?

It was what Spur would do.

He slowed when he was 100 yards away from where he expected the wagon to be. He got off the claybank, rubbed her down a moment, tied her to some brush, and then lifted his six-gun and began to move like a ghost through the trees and brush along the Laramie river.

He had been trained in silent movement by an Indian friend, and could move at a steady walk, yet not break a stick, not let a branch swish back, not give away by any sound that he was coming.

Somewhere ahead were two gunmen waiting for him. One naked and furious, the other deadly and devious. With any luck he would have to kill only one of them.

Chapter Six

Spur McCoy stalked the pair so silently not even the birds stopped their singing. When he was 50 yards from where he figured they might be, he stopped and watched. He lay behind a cottonwood tree near the chattering Laramie River and waited.

Five minutes later he heard someone clear a throat to the left and ahead. Another five minutes and he saw a woman's naked leg stretch out from behind a tree not 20 yards from him, then vanish behind it again.

He checked both sides of the big cottonwood. It was bare to the grass. There was no place at ground level where she could be watching for him downriver. About three feet up the trunk, a small branch sprouted with a flurry of bright green leaves. A face could be in there somewhere, but he doubted it. She was waiting for him to come past her. Then she would shoot.

His guess was that she had the shotgun. Since the old man probably considered himself the best shot, he'd use the Spencer and a brace of revolvers.

After neither of them had moved for another five minutes, he began working soundlessly forward toward the girl's tree. He moved like an Apache crossing a naked plain—so slowly that the movement itself would not attract a watching eye.

He limited his breathing to short, silent breaths, so she wouldn't be able to hear that. He didn't have to figure out a strategy. He knew instinctively what to do. She would be facing away from the river toward the largest slice of the woods. He would come around the tree the other way, hoping to find her back.

A minute later he completed the short trip and stood near the tree. He holstered his six-gun, then lunged around the tree from the right side. Her bare back was to him. He made just enough noise so she sensed someone behind her and started to spin around.

His arms captured her. One arm snaked around her naked waist and yanked her a foot backward toward him. The other hand came down across her mouth and nose, clamping both shut and pulling her backward. Then he reversed his pressure and rammed her forward so she fell face down in the grass and leaves.

Four seconds after he made his first lunge the girl was flat on the ground under him, his hand still holding her nose and mouth, and his other hand still around her waist.

He whispered to her softly. "I'll let open your nose so you can breathe, but I don't want you to move or make a sound, agreed?"

She made no sound.

"If you agree nod your head."

Still she made no sound except a swallowing so she could re-use the air in her bursting lungs. He twisted her face to the left so he could see it. She'd been without air long enough. He eased up on his fingers, letting her nose free so she could breathe.

Long, full breaths strummed into her lungs. He gave her 30 seconds to catch up on her lack of oxygen.

"Where is the crazy man?" Spur whispered.

She mumbled into his hand.

"If I let go of your mouth you've got to promise not to scream."

She nodded.

He let his hand off her mouth.

Silly, screamed. "He's over here!"

Spur hit her.

His right fist connected with her jaw from ten inches away and it jolted her head sideways, knocking her out. Spur watched the brush ahead of him and to the left. He heard something. Then all was quiet.

He used his neckerchief to tie her hands together after pulling them around a three-inch-thick cottonwood sapling that was 30 feet tall. That would hold her. He picked up a .44 revolver she had been carrying and pushed it in his belt. Then he moved soundlessly forward.

Brush wiggled to his left 25 feet away. He froze, .45 up and cocked. The brush quieted. Then the rawhider lifted to his feet, the rifle at the ready.

Spur fired twice. He couldn't tell if he'd hit the rawhider, but he saw the tobacco-stained beard going down behind some leaves and brush. Nothing moved. He waited what seemed like three or four minutes, then charged upright through the brush toward the spot where the man had dropped.

He wasn't there.

Spur looked at the brush. It left a highway of tracking signs. The rawhider had gone through the brush silently but left a trail. Spur checked the apparent trail ahead as far as he could see, then followed it to the next sign. The trail veered back to the side of the stream. Across it he could see a horse standing untied, munching on grass.

Spur figured the odds. The rawhider had abandoned the girl, and was on his way back to wherever he had left his wagon and all his worldly goods. The horse was available and safe.

The special agent checked the Laramie River, picked a shallow spot, and waded across, getting wet only to his chest. He walked up slowly to the untethered mount, caught the reins, and lifted into the saddle. He could see the signs of the other mount, and quickly picked up a trail and rode out of the brush.

He had ridden only 50 feet when a rifle shot slammed into the crisp mountain air and a slug whistled past him. Spur bent low behind the neck of the horse and charged straight ahead. The sound came from upstream in the edge of the brush. Now he could see smoke drifting up. Spur shifted to the right side of the horse and slid half out of the saddle as he had seen the Apaches do, but he didn't do it as well.

The second shot from his own Spencer carbine hit the horse in the side and she hesitated in her gallop. Then a moment later her front legs folded and Spur pitched over the neck of his dying mount toward the brush. He hit on his hands and then shoulders and rolled into the heavier brush as one, then two, then three rifle shots drilled through the brush, lead searching for flesh. They missed.

He lay still, watching the blue smoke rise. The rawhider was off his horse lying in the brush, making a small target. Range, 30 yards. Too far for a Colt .45 revolver.

He wormed his way through the bottom of the low brush toward the heavier growth. Once there he could lift up and walk forward bent over. Not a twig snapped. He heard a horse call out. Then the sound of creaking leather.

Saddle. He was mounting.

Spur came up on a run, slamming through the brush, dodging trees, aiming for the clearing another ten yards ahead. He came out of the last of the cover just as the man swung his leg into the far stirrup.

The agent's first round hit the rawhider in the shoulder and slammed him out of the saddle on the far side of the mount. His next drilled under the belly of the horse slashing into the rawhider's thigh and dumping him on the ground.

The man didn't move.

Spur wasn't sure how much time he had. He figured Silly could chew through the cloth in ten minutes. He'd been gone that long already. He darted for a big cottonwood ten yards away so he could see around the horse.

Twin shots blasted from where the rawhider lay, but Spur got to the tree with only a grazed left side.

"Give it up and you'll get a fair trial!" Spur shouted.

"Hell, yes, twelve reasons to hang me. Seen it happen before. Blame every killing on me within a hundred miles."

"And only half of them were yours. Tough. Give up or you're a dead man. At least you'll have a fighting chance."

"Where's the girl? You kill her?"

"No. I tied her up. This is your last chance to live."

Spur stood up behind the cottonwood. It concealed him. He risked a look around the left side of the trunk. He could see where the killer lay, half behind a fallen log. He dodged back. A moment later Spur leaned around the right side of the tree and fired twice at the largest part of the man he could see, his chest.

One of the rounds caught him high and he screamed.

"Throw out your six-gun and the Spencer and any other weapon you have and I'll see if I can tie up those holes in you."

"Damned decent of you," the rawhider said, then fired. The round hit Spur in the left arm and spun him around. He slid behind the tree and grabbed the hole in his upper arm.

The agent had been shot before. He never got used to it. It hurt like a hot branding iron. He gritted his teeth at the pain. He let go of his arm and looked around the tree at where the rawhider had been.

He wasn't there.

Spur checked the surrounding area. He watched each section carefully, then moved to the next. On the third square of brush and trees that Spur checked inch by inch, he spotted the rawhider. He was in the open concealed by only a few leaves and small shrubs.

Spur McCoy lifted his six-gun, pushed out the fired rounds, and put in enough so there were six chambers full. Then he aimed and fired four times. The form stopped moving.

A string of profanity spouted from the brush and Spur grinned. The tough old killer was hit again but still alive. Spur rushed forward a dozen yards and flattened behind a log. When he looked over the top the form had not moved. One arm extended to the side. The wrist and hand were bloody. A revolver lay six inches beyond the fingers. One down.

He lifted up and ran another ten feet at right angles to his location and dove behind two small trees. When he looked around them, he saw the rawhider's other hand on his chest trying to stop the flow of blood.

Spur McCoy came to his feet and walked up on the rawhider.

"Not much fun being shot, is it?" Spur asked.

The bearded man stared up at McCoy, a snarl on his face. "You should know, you're leaking red yourself."

The rawhider coughed and spouted a gout of blood. He gagged, spit out more blood, then lifted up so he could breathe.

"Never thought I'd go out this way, bested by some damn kid with a six-gun."

"You got too greedy, old-timer."

"Ain't that old. No more'n thirty-five."

"Nobody can get that dirty in only thirty-five years."

"I done it. No regrets. You take care of that Silly. There is a big chunk of good woman. She was a whore before I stole her. Get her back to a house, where she belongs."

"Where's your wagon?"

"In the brush back where we tried to trap you. You sure as hell didn't look so damned smart." He coughed again, then screeched in pain and tried to sit up. He couldn't make it. He fell on his side.

"Oh, damn, but that hurts!" He screamed again. Then he did manage to sit up, but when he did, he gave one last bellow of terrible agony and fell over, as the last breath gushed from his lungs.

Spur took the Spencer and the six-gun and then rolled the body deeper into the brush. He'd bury him if there was time. Now he ran back to the Laramie River, waded across, and then jogged back the way he had come toward where he had left the girl.

She wasn't there. Only the chewed-in half neck-erchief. He ran for the wagon. It was about where the dying man had said. Only now it was moving. The team of mules were tugging slowly on a slight upgrade through soft footing back toward the river road. They had just come out of the brush where the rig had been hidden. Spur put a round from the Spencer across the front of the mules.

Someone inside the covered section of the wagon pulled back on the reins and the mules stopped.

"The man is dead," Spur called. "He shot Punkin and she's dead. You don't have to be the third one, Silly. Just come out and let's talk."

He waited a few seconds, hoping she didn't have another rifle inside the big canvas rig.

"I've got no fight with you, Silly. I have no charges to place against you. You're free to go, but first we need to talk."

He waited.

She appeared at the front of the covered wagon.

"What we gonna talk about?"

"What you're going to do next. I know that most everything in that wagon is stolen property. Not a chance to get it back to the ones it belongs to. You

figure you could get a job at one of the fancy houses
in Laramie?"

"I figure I could." She vanished for a minute, and
when she came back she had on a dress. She buttoned it down the front and jumped down from the
wagon and moved toward him.

"You saying I can just walk away from all this?"

"You kill anybody back there along the way?"

"No, sir. I done raped a few men but they liked
it."

"And you figure you can hire on at one of the local
houses of true pleasure?"

"Usually I can get a job whoring."

"We've got a spare horse and two mules and a
whole wagon load of gear. The old man keep any
money hid out?"

"Sure. I've got it, near two hundred dollars."

"Good. Here's the deal. You take off that dress
and find some soap and wash your lovely body and
wash your hair three times, and then comb it out
and braid it. Then get a dress on and find all the
clothes that will fit you and put them in a bag. Then
you can take this horse and ride into Laramie free
and clear."

"Honest?"

"Seems fair to me."

"Even after I staked you down and sexed you
good?"

"Still seems fair to me. You didn't hear me screaming in pain or protest did you?"

Silly grinned. She ran back to the wagon, threw
out some clothes and a carpetbag, then a cake of
soap and two big fluffy white towels.

She took the soap and towels and headed for the
river. "Hey, man. You gonna help me take my bath?"
Silly stripped out of the dress and stood there in a

shaft of sunlight coming through the trees. She was built lean and ready, a luscious, marvelous naked body with big breasts and a tiny waist.

"Love to, Silly, but I've got to get this wagon into Laramie before dark. First I'll go get my horse, then Punkin. I figure she deserves a decent burial. I'll be back in time to rinse you off. Now get to washing."

It took Spur McCoy to just before dark to get Punkin's body into the wagon and trade horses, then tie his mount on the back and get ready to move.

Silly had finished her bath and washed her hair and dried it enough to braid it in one large braid down her back. She sat the saddle astride and rode alongside as they moved toward Laramie. A mile out she looked up at him.

"I better ride on ahead. Won't do me any good seen with you. You take care and come see me sometime." She grinned and rode off for the town ahead.

He got there fifteen minutes later. Spur turned the body over to Sheriff Vail and explained the circumstances.

"What does this have to do with your finding them two surveyors you came here to hunt, McCoy?" the sheriff asked.

"Not a thing except I was following the survey line north when I happened on this trio. Just as soon I hadn't." The sheriff grunted and had him sign a statement about the circumstances of the woman's death and that of the rawhider.

"What happens to the wagon and the mules?"

"I saw a Baptist church on my way into town. I figure the best thing to do is donate the whole thing to the church. They can sell the mules, then have a lay-out sale on the parsonage front lawn and sell everything they can for the benefit of the church."

"Sounds fair. Damn rawhiders. Lucky you got away with your life. They don't hold much with fair play."

McCoy nodded. "I got one bullet hole to attest to that, Sheriff. Where is the town's doctor?"

By the time Doctor Daisley had his arm checked, medicated, and bandaged, it was too late to move north. Spur took a room in the Northern Hotel. He was almost asleep before he realized that the rawhiders had stolen all of his camp gear and food. He'd have to buy some more in the morning.

Chapter Seven

Once again, Spur bought some provisions and headed out on the trail of the surveyors. He passed the first ranch, and then where the rawhiders had stopped him. He found another concrete post with a bench mark on it, and knew he was on the right track.

He rode due north and worked along, finding indications of some brush slashed for better visual line, and then he found a second mark, this one a steel pipe in the ground with a copper plate on it.

He crossed several miles and figured he must be on the next ranch by that time. He came out of a screen of willow and spotted some cattle and a man who turned his horse and rode toward him, shouting. Spur stopped and waited for the cowboy.

"What the hell you doing here?" the cowhand demanded.

Spur was at once alert and angry at the question.

"I'm riding through, that going to hurt anything?"

"Damn well might hurt you if our foreman catches you. We got instructions not to let *anybody* ride across Circle B range."

"Doesn't sound friendly," Spur said, his hand easing down beside his six-gun.

"Ain't my doing, it's what old Charlie Breen says, and his word is law around here. Best if you head back the way you come and nobody gets hurt and I don't even have to tell the foreman I caught you here."

Spur made sure he could recognize the spot again. "In that case, I guess I can move north by some other route." He turned and walked his claybank back into the brush. When Spur was out of sight he sat his horse and watched the cowboy. The hand sat where he was, his right leg crooked on his saddle as he rolled a smoke. Then he walked his animal toward the brush.

Spur figured it was better if he didn't confront the man. He turned and rode out to the south, not looking back. He knew the cowboy was watching him.

There was another way. He knew the surveyors had been at the first ranch. He would leapfrog ahead and talk to the people on the third ranch due north of Laramie. If the surveyors had been there he'd ignore the Circle B Ranch and keep following the surveyors. If the two men hadn't shown up at the third ranch, then there would be some serious questions to ask the man who ran the Circle B. Charlie Breen, the cowhand had called him.

Spur swung to the east planning to go around the Circle B Ranch. About three miles over, he came to the edge of the Laramie River. There was a wagon road there. Certainly no man owned a county road even if it went across his property. Spur moved out north faster, urging the claybank to six miles an hour, and it was just after noon when he saw a ranch ahead that must be well north of the buildings for the Circle B outfit.

He found a lane leading from the road over to the buildings near the river, and rode that way. It was a small spread, two barns, a good log ranch house, and two smaller buildings. There were three corrals and two cowhands who looked like they had just come in from a long ride.

One of them rode over to him.

"Afternoon," Wade Johnson said. "This is the Bar-O spread. I'm foreman Wade Johnson."

"Spur McCoy. Howdy. Much better welcome than I got on the place to the south."

Wade snorted. "Yeah, the Circle B down there ain't the best place to try and get friendly. They're known to chase strangers off with a few rifle shots."

"Looks like I just missed that kind of welcome."

"You want to step down? I'm sure that Mrs. Orville would be pleased to say hello. She runs this place."

Spur got down, tied his mount to a hitching rail near the well house, and went up to the side door with the foreman.

Wade stepped inside and called, and a minute later a young woman in her twenties came out. She wiped her hands on her apron.

"Goodness, company. I was just fixing to make a cherry pie. I'm Melody Orville. Welcome to the Bar-O Ranch."

"Thank you, ma'am. I'm Spur McCoy and I'd appreciate it if I could talk to you for a minute."

"Of course. Come in and I'll get you some lemonade or some coffee, whichever you prefer."

He settled for some cold lemonade and sat at the kitchen table.

"I'm looking for a friend of mine who is supposed to be surveying the division line north right through this part of the county. I can't find him anywhere. Has there been a two-man survey team through your place lately, last two or three weeks or so?"

"I don't remember any of the men talking about such a team. Let me ask Wade." She came back a moment later. "Wade says none of his men have reported a survey team."

"It was supposed to come out of Laramie on a course due north, which would put it only two or three miles east of here. Are you sure that nobody saw two men and a packhorse working along sixty-six feet at a time with a surveying chain?"

"We still have two men out. I'll have Wade ask them when they get in. That won't be until about five. Would you stay and have supper with us? We don't get many visitors."

"I'd be pleased to stay, if it won't put you out any."

"No, oh, no, not a problem at all. While you wait would a piece of apple cobbler taste good? I can also offer you some cream for the top."

Spur laughed. "Here I've fallen into heaven and I wasn't even looking for it."

Melody blushed prettily. "Well, not heaven. Wait until you taste the cobbler before you decide." She felt the blush, knew it was showing. She didn't care. He was quite the most handsome man she had seen in . . . well, years. His dark brown hair was longer than most men wore it and his stubble interesting. What excited her the most were his green eyes.

She glanced at the supple, relaxed way he sat in the chair and the way his thick thighs stretched the legs of his pants. Now she blushed again. She shouldn't be thinking such things. But she reversed herself at once. It had been almost a year and a half since Stanley got hurt. She hadn't known a man since then. It was only natural to think wild things like that when such a sexy man sat in your kitchen.

She served him the cobbler, refilled his lemonade glass, and excused herself.

"We have a sick man I need to check on. I'll be right back."

She walked to the parlor and smiled at Merle. "Do you want some more lemonade?" she asked.

Merle looked up and shook his head gently. Anything else would let loose bells ringing for five minutes in his head. "No, this is fine. Did someone come?"

"Yes, a man hunting a pair of surveyors. I don't think anyone has seen them. Looks like you're running out of reading material. Next time somebody goes to town I'll see if we can find a book or some magazines and two or three newspapers for you."

"I'm sorry I'm such a burden to you."

"Nonsense, Merle. Only Christian thing to do. Besides, I enjoy talking with you. I'm guessing that you come from someplace well east of here, maybe all the way to Chicago."

He frowned, and felt it pull at the bandage on his head. "No, Chicago doesn't sound right."

"We'll work again on it. I better get back to the visitor. If you want anything, you call."

When she went back to the kitchen she paused and looked at the strong profile of the man in the chair and the way his shirt strained at his chest and arms. He was a tall man and so nicely proportioned. She felt heat rise in her chest and she shook her head and walked out to the stove.

"That's the best apple cobbler I've had in years," Spur said. "It has just the right amount of cinnamon in it, the way Mom used to do it."

"Thanks, I'm flattered. It's an old family recipe. Are you from around here?"

"No, just passing through and figured I'd see my friend."

"What's his name, maybe I heard it in town."

"Larry, Larry Stirling. We always called him Silver, and it made him mad."

She laughed. "Tell me about yourself. What do you do for a living?"

"I'm in land sales. I'm always looking for good property that might interest some of the Eastern land speculators. So far it's worked out rather well."

"Just don't try to sell any of the Laramie River. It's all spoken for, for more than forty miles along here. You know this is one of the few rivers in this part of the country that actually runs north."

"That did surprise me. Must be just the way the land lays here."

She was a friendly lady and Spur enjoyed talking with her. Twice more he noticed her blush. It wasn't from anything he had said. She was an attractive person. Maybe 24 or 25, with long brown hair, soft green eyes, and a slender figure at five inches over five feet. That made her taller than the average woman. She had a nipped-in waist that made her bosom seem larger. Once he caught sight of a trim ankle as she turned and her skirt flared out. He could see little else of her. The dress she wore buttoned to the chin and down to her wrists.

Later, Spur took a walk around the ranch. It was a small but growing one. He figured in another ten years it could be a power in the area. He talked to the foreman a moment.

"Sorry our last two men aren't in yet. But I doubt if they have seen that survey crew. That would be unusual out here, and we are always talking about anything unusual."

"I better wait and see. Oh, is there a Mr. Orville?"

"No, sir, not for more than a year now. He got caught in a stampede after a lightning storm and just never got well. Her brother, Vincent Canning, is here, though, and he's helping her run the ranch."

Spur grinned. "But he isn't a rancher, so mostly it's you who is keeping this spread together."

"Now, Mr. McCoy, I didn't say that." He shrugged. "I guess it's partly true. But I'm happy here."

The two riders came in and confirmed that they hadn't seen anything of a survey team. Spur was suddenly restless. He went back to the kitchen and met Vincent Canning.

"Good to meet you, McCoy. Wish we'd had better news for you about your friend. Maybe you got here ahead of him."

"Possible."

Vincent excused himself to go wash up and they were alone in the kitchen.

"Mrs. Orville, I better not stay to supper. I want to get back to town in time to ask around a bit."

He had moved toward her where she stood at the stove and she turned suddenly, almost touching him.

He put out his hand to steady her and caught her shoulder. She swayed forward and her breasts touched his chest. For a moment they were so close he could have kissed her. He smiled and her expression was one of sudden desire. Then it faded and she eased back from him.

"Excuse me, I'm a bit clumsy at times."

"No, my fault." He smiled. "That was interesting, though, and very nice."

This time she blushed hotly and he touched her shoulder. "I didn't mean to embarrass you. But the fact is you're a most beautiful and intriguing lady. Now, I really should be riding. Thanks for the cobbler and the lemonade. Maybe I'll be through here again hunting my friend."

"Yes, I hope you come back." More color came to her face. "I enjoyed our talk this afternoon." She reached out her hand and he shook it.

"I enjoyed it too. Thanks again." He turned and walked toward the door and she looked at her hand where he had touched it and smiled.

"Good-bye, Spur McCoy. You'll have to come back when you can stay for supper. I'm really a good cook."

He grinned as he went out the door, anxious now to get back to town. When he talked to the local surveyor before, he hadn't asked him if the men had hired a local helper to pound stakes and run errands for them. He knew some survey teams did that.

He rode at a quick pace and got to the surveyor's shop just before he closed. Spur went inside and the older man looked up.

"Yes. The man interested in the survey team."

"You have a good memory for faces. Did the team hire anyone from town as a helper?"

The surveyor nodded. "Yep. You didn't ask me about that before. Young man named Arnie Land-houser worked with them a couple of days. I recommended him. Works with me at times."

"Where could I find him?"

"If he ain't home, which is doubtful, he'd be at the Pink Pelican Saloon. You ever seen a pelican? Don't think I have. Them are sea birds. The Laramie River is a long way from an ocean."

Spur waved a good-bye and walked down Main Street until he found the Pink Pelican. It was a saloon for drinking and cardplaying, no whores. He found Arnie Landhouser deep in a game of dime-limit poker. If a man tried hard he could lose five dollars in an evening. Of course Spur knew that five dollars was also a week's pay for most of the working men.

He watched a while, then asked Arnie to drop out for a couple of hands.

"I need to talk to you, Arnie," he said.

Arnie scowled, then shrugged and folded his cards and stepped back. Spur bought him a cold beer at the bar and went right to the point.

"You worked with a team of surveyors two or three weeks ago. Can you tell me which direction they went and how far they got?"

"Sure. I pounded stakes, took sightings, and held plumb bobs for them same as I do for any journey-man surveyor. Earned a dollar a day. We worked for two days. Late afternoon the third day they sent me back to town for more wooden stakes and steel stakes. They hadn't brought enough along.

"I got them and headed back, but when I got where I had left them, they were gone."

"Where was that?"

"Out about, what, seven miles north, I guess. We made a small camp in some woods just up from the river, even though that was about two miles from the line we were surveying. That way we had water for the horses and for us, and more wood for our fire."

"Is that on the first rancher's land or into the Circle B property."

"Oh, we was well into the Circle B by then. You know what happened to the two men?"

"No, that's what I'm trying to find out. Could you take me back to that same spot where you left them?"

"Sure, I'm a surveyor, I remember landmarks. Never have forgot one. Take me someplace and I can find it again damned near blindfolded."

"Even if it's on the Circle B land?"

"Yeah. We was on it for more than a day. I figured they must have had special permission. I've heard how Crazy Charlie Breen shoots at people who come on his place. Course we wasn't nowhere near the ranch buildings."

"Somebody out there damn near shot at me today. But now it's dark and they can't see us. You have a horse?"

"Sure."

"I'll pay you five dollars to lead me to that same spot on the Circle B where you left the two surveyors."

"Damn! Five dollars! I'm ready, let's go right now. We can't get to Circle B land soon enough."

Chapter Eight

The claybank stared at Spur as he led her out of the stall at the livery stable.

"One more ride, then you can take a rest," Spur told her as he put on thé blanket and the saddle.

The two men rode onto Circle B land just after dark and found no guards or lookouts in that area. The young surveyor checked the land, and they slanted west to the Laramie River.

"We worked on the Circle B for maybe a short day, then I took off for town. But we'd already laid out our camp, so I know exactly where it is."

It took them two hours to find it after one detour and another short ride back along the river.

At last the youth nodded. "Right up there by those willows and the two cottonwoods. We camped right there."

They rode into the area, and in the moonlight it looked like no white man had ever set foot in the place.

"You said you made a fire ring?"

"Right, a little one, with dry rocks, about two feet across. It should be here with ashes and maybe a discarded tin can or two."

They ground-tied their horses and covered the area on foot.

"Goddamn, I know it's here somewhere. Has to be. Them two cottonwoods. Right over here." He walked one way, then another, and dropped to his knees. He brushed back leaves and some small branches.

"Soft dirt, McCoy. Shouldn't be any soft dirt out here." McCoy went to the spot and lit a stinker match, and when it flared up they both dug. On the second clawing handful, Arnie came up with a handful of ashes.

"Knew this was the place," Arnie crowed.

McCoy looked around. "If they had a campsite here, somebody went to a lot of trouble to cover it up. Did you usually clean up a campsite this well?"

"Hell, no. We made sure the fire was out, and picked up our cans and trash and buried them. These guys have a lot of respect for the land. But, hell, we never tried to hide the fact that we'd been there. Somebody did here. Buried the fire, smoothed it out, then put leaves and some brush over the site."

Spur sat back on his haunches Indian style and studied the area. "We'll have to come back in the daylight if we want to find anything else. That could get involved."

"So what else are we looking for?"

"Two graves, plus another soft spot where all of the camping equipment and the survey materials were buried. This was a neat job. It has to be to cover up a double murder."

"My God! If I hadn't gone to town, I'd be underground here somewhere with Jas and Red?"

"Good chance."

"Who did it?"

"That's what I'm trying to find out. You've been a good help. Next time I come up here I figure I'll bring the sheriff along and a search warrant."

"Bring me along too. No charge. I owe it to Red and Jas. They were both all right guys."

Spur hunkered down there looking at the area, trying to feel it out.

"How do you find if a grave is here?"

"I'll get a steel rod and sharpen one end and then jam it into the ground every two feet in a pattern around this area. If there's any fresh digging, the probe will go in fast and easy."

"I can do that. Yeah, I want to come along."

"Arnie, we don't know who did this. It still might not be murder, but we can't be sure. I don't want you telling a living soul about this little exercise tonight or about the chance that the men were killed. The same murderers might add a third name to the list, yours."

Arnie gulped.

They rode back to town, but McCoy wasn't ready to sleep yet. It still bothered him that the men had vanished so completely. An unmarked double grave had to be the answer.

He decided to try the gambling halls, and at the third one, the Lonesome Eagle, a familiar face leaned over his table.

"Hi, cowboy, want to tickle my fancy?"

"Well, I just might. Sit down at my table. What's your name?"

"Sandy, everyone calls me Sandy."

He grinned. From Silly the rawhider woman who had spread-eagled him and then sexed him to Sandy. She had made an easy transition. Her hair had been cut so it came just below her shoulders. She was clean, and even smelled good as she leaned over the table toward him.

"You're looking much better than the last time I saw you."

"I worked at it. I know what this business takes."

"You'll do fine. I'd say it's a good step up, but not the last one you can take."

"I've got to go," she said. "Business calls. I wanted to say hello. One of these days I'll see you again." She waved and walked away, her round bottom twitching delightfully inside the tight skirt.

Spur found a poker game with a dime limit, lost three dollars in an hour, and went back to the Northern Hotel and dropped into his bed. He'd struggled with it all evening and still wasn't sure what he should do tomorrow. Finding one hidden fire in the dark, with the help of a young man who might or might not be that reliable, simply wasn't enough evidence to go to Sheriff Vail and ask him for a search warrant. Just not enough. Damn.

That same night, Charlie Breen and three men moved out from his ranch buildings, north heading for Bar-O range. He was launching his all-out assault on the Widow Orville to drive her off her range. Shouldn't be hard. A foreman who could be bought, a brother who knew nothing about cattle, and what, four more hands. Should be a cinch.

He started that night by riding into the Bar-O range as far as he needed to find 25 head.

"Twenty-five or thirty of them critters," he called softly to his foreman. "We just want enough so they know where the stock went if they try to track them. Yes, damn it. I *want them to know* where the steers and cows went. That's the whole idea."

They rounded up 35 critters and bunched them, then drove them slowly back toward the Circle B range.

It was a simple job for the five men, and they soon had the animals over the boundary line and then deep into the Circle B lands.

"Let's take them south of the ranch buildings," Breen said. "We'll get out the gear tomorrow and re-brand all of them so there won't be any hassle at the chutes when we start selling them."

Kevin rode up spitting dust. "Pa, why the hell we driving this bunch straight into our land? Won't they know where the critters went and who took them?"

Charlie Breen swore softly. "Damn, I explained it to you this afternoon. We *want them* to know we took the stock. It's the start of our campaign to force them out of business. Shouldn't be hard. Just do what you're told and don't try to think so much. I'll do the thinking for all of us."

Kevin scowled and rode away after a young heifer who had turned back toward the other ranch. He headed her and turned her and brought her back to the small herd.

In the morning Charlie Breen would send a crew to over-brand the Bar-O into the Bar-B. They had done it several times before with small lots. Then they put a diagonal line over the old brand as a vent. That told the inspector that the cattle had once been Bar-B but had been sold and now had the regular Circle B on the hip nearby.

Breen got to bed about one in the morning, but was up by six and heading another crew out to the Laramie. The flood tide of the past three days had dropped off remarkably and the river was almost back to normal. Now he'd finish the work he'd been doing for a month on the dam. He'd driven posts into the riverbed at a narrow spot and dropped in logs in front of them, and then piled on enough dirt and rocks to make it watertight. He'd left an opening ten feet wide for the flood tide to wash past.

Now he'd drop in the big gate he'd made after floating it into place. He rode out with the crew and surveyed the dam. The high water had washed out part of the dam, but after a morning's work they had that part repaired.

He supervised floating the gate, made of sturdy pine logs and sawed into four-by-twelve bridge planks. He floated it into place, and then two of his heaviest men got on it and tipped the bottom end of it down into the current.

The force of the water caught the ten-foot-wide heavy gate and pushed the bottom of it underwater until it was almost standing straight up. At the same time the current carried the gate downstream and slammed it against the retaining posts. The pressure of the water held it in place. Men quickly nailed planks on both sides to tie the gate into position.

Breen stepped from the water to look at the flow beyond his dam. It had drained down to a trickle, maybe three feet wide. Down from a river 20 feet wide and three feet deep!

The Bar-O would be screaming for water in two days. He went to the overflow channel they had dug to the left side. It soon began sending out water from the buildup behind the dam. The water flowed into a sinkhole of ten acres that had once been a lake thousands of years ago. It would hold the flow of the river for two weeks at least. Then the overflow from the lake would make its way back to the river.

By then he would blow the gate out of position with a dozen sticks of dynamite. But long before that he would have driven the Bar-O widow off her range.

Breen sat there on his horse and grinned. Damn but it was interesting how you could work people around and get them to do exactly what you wanted them to do.

That morning he had sent out his two best marksmen with rifles and plenty of rounds. He'd told them to ride in as far as they could to Bar-O range, then find a good defensive position and wait for some cowboys to show themselves. When the Bar-O cowboys arrived on the scene, the sharpshooters were supposed to kill the men's horses and put them on foot and running back for the ranch.

He'd get a report when the men got back after dark.

"Now, what the hell else did we have planned for the Widow Orville?" Breen asked his foreman.

"We talked about burning down a barn, dropping a stick of dynamite into the well, and stampeding the horses out of the two corrals."

"But for all of that we have to get up close. Somebody could get shot."

"Bound to happen in a war. We also wanted to grab about five hundred head of their stock. That would take ten men to get it done at night."

"We have rifles enough for all ten of those men?" Breen asked.

"Yes, I picked up three more last time I was in town. We're ready whenever you are, Mr. Breen."

They walked toward the ranch house.

After the midnight ride, Kevin Breen had slept in that morning. Now he looked out his bedroom window on the second floor and swore. He ran back to his bed and dropped on top of the naked woman who lay there.

"We got to rush now, Carmelita. You remember, don't tell anybody about this or I'll cut a tit off. Understand? Pa is riding back into the yard."

Their Mexican cook did not understand English well but she nodded. She was small with long black hair and brown eyes, a tiny waist, and the biggest breasts Kevin had ever seen on so small a woman. Kevin bent and sucked on her breasts, then bit her nipples until she whimpered. He came away and went between her brown thighs and slammed into her.

"Oh, my, yes, now that is good poon! Damned nice even if you are a Mex." He pumped hard for a minute, then rolled over both of them and put her on top.

Carmelita giggled and began bouncing up and down on him and then moving forward and back like she was on a stallion. He rolled her back over and settled down to some serious copulation. He knew his father would be coming to the house soon looking for some dinner.

Carmelita would have to fake that somehow. One thing he loved to do was make love. He'd popped Carmelita only once before and she'd told him no more. But with no one else in the house that morning, he had seduced her on the kitchen floor. Then she'd gotten excited too, and they'd run upstairs for the comfort of his bed for the second time. It had been a slow one, gentle and soft and satisfying.

Now he was blasting away like his life depended on it. "Damn, I know I can make it three times. Always have before." He pumped again, then lifted Carmelita's bare legs to his shoulders, almost standing her on her head, and drove into her like there was no time left until the world ended.

"Yes, yes, now we're making it!" he whispered. He heard the door slam downstairs and gunned against the small Mexican woman until he blasted the last of his juices. It had been glorious! He had exploded into a million pieces and only now came back together again. He lay on top of her panting until he thought his lungs would never get enough air.

Then he reached down and kissed her cheek before he rolled off the woman.

"That was great, Carmelita. We'll have to fuck again sometime. Now get your sweet little ass and big tits into the closet quick. My pa's coming upstairs. He'll chop off both your tits if he finds you here."

The woman jumped off the bed, big breasts bounding as she hurried into a closet and closed the door.

Kevin pulled on his long johns and then his pants, and was stuffing his shirt inside when his father called from the hallway.

Kevin went to the door and walked out. "Hey, you're back. I just couldn't get moving this morning after that rustling job last night, Pa. How did the damn dam go?"

"Not funny, son. It happened. The Laramie is shut down for at least two weeks. Mrs. Widow Bar-O is gonna be hurting in a day or two."

"Great. What's next on our campaign to drive her out of business?"

"Not sure. Probably a midnight run into their west pasture beyond the river and bring back about five hundred head."

"Yeah, Pa! I like the way you're thinking. I was afraid you might go up there and burn down the ranch house or something. Remember, you promised that I got to run that operation up there when we get our hands on it."

"I won't forget. But it's about time you take more responsibility around here."

"I will, Pa. Promise I will. When do we go to get those Bar-O critters. Tonight soon as it gets dark?"

"Can't do it any sooner. All we have to do is wait for dark and get our ten men and ride."

"I'm with you, Pa."

Chapter Nine

Rustling cattle was so easy that Charlie Breen wondered why he bothered to let his cattle breed and wait three years for the steers to get big enough to sell.

He and nine men swept the west range beyond the Laramie River and about halfway into the 20-mile-long Bar-O range. They found fewer cattle than they expected, but pushed all the critters they could find—calves, range bulls, cows, and steers—ahead of them. By the time they got down to the boundary between the two ranches, Breen figured they had about 400 head.

Good enough for a start. They would drive them all the way down to the south range on the Circle B and put picket sentries out to watch for any retaliation.

By the time his men had pushed the bawling, protesting cattle the 15 miles south, Charlie Breen had worked enough. He peeled off and went to the ranch house while the men drove the cattle another five miles south.

In the morning another crew would go out and get busy with the branding. Four hundred head, at an average of $50 a head, meant he had taken in $20,000 tonight. Not bad for a night's work.

He saw by the clock that it was nearly four in the morning. He was about due for a run into town. Twice the past week he had seen Carmelita in the kitchen and almost talked to her about the rest of her duties—in his bed. But he didn't. Good cooks were too hard to find to fuck around with one. And Carmelita was a good cook. He'd go to town next week for sure and get his ashes hauled properly.

Breen fell on the bed, grinning as he went to sleep.

Riders on the Bar-O discovered the missing cattle and the plain trail that led south the next morning about ten o'clock. First they found the tracks of the large group, then of a smaller herd.

"Yes, ma'am, they're gone," Wade Johnson reported to Melody. "They was rounded up and driven straight down to the Circle B. Old Charlie Breen is telling us we're in a real war. I'd guess were missing close to five hundred head."

"We've got to do something about it," Vincent shouted. "We can't just sit here and let him rustle out stock. We'll be broke in two months and with no steers to sell."

"He's got more men and more guns than we have," Melody said. "We can't make an all-out attack on him. That's obvious."

One of the hands rode in, found out where Wade was, and walked over to the front screened porch and motioned to the foreman.

Wade talked to him and came back a minute later.

"Looks like we've got more trouble. Fred just came back from across the river. He says the Laramie has dried up to a trickle, not more than two feet across."

Melody looked at Vincent. "Oh, dear. What could have caused that?"

"Either the whole country dried up, or somebody upstream has put a dam across the river, creating a lake behind it or diverting the water into a low place to insure plenty of water for the rest of the summer."

"It's fitting a pattern," Vincent said. "Breen stole our cattle, he puts a dam in to cut off our water, and yesterday one of our cowboys lost his horse when he was scouting down on our south range looking for cattle. Breen is staging an all-out attack on us."

"What are we going to do about it?" Melody asked.

"Strike back, ma'am," Wade said. "That's my suggestion, fight fire with fire."

"How exactly?" she asked.

Wade looked south from the ranch house. "We've got company. A single rider coming."

"Looks like that tall gent who was here the other day looking for those survey guys," Vincent said.

"Yep, same hombre, same horse," Wade agreed.

The three of them waited until Spur rode up. It was just past noon.

"Afternoon, folks. Am I interrupting a conference or something?"

"Yes," Vincent said. "We just found out our neighbor to the south has declared war on us."

"Is that right?"

Vincent filled him in on the three violations.

"Sounds downright unfriendly," Spur said. "Charlie Breen is being a problem for me as well. Maybe we could team up our forces."

"What do you mean?" Melody asked, smiling at the tall man.

"I need to look at a campsite that has been covered up down on the Circle B range near the river. It could have been the last camp of the two surveyors I'm looking for. It's closer to this side of the boundary line of the Circle B than the other side. They seem to patrol that other part more as well."

"We been talking about riding down that way and see if we can bring back our cattle," Vincent said. "Course we might not get started until toward dark."

"A kind of midnight cattle sale?" Spur asked.

"Sort of," Melody said. "We've been talking about fighting fire with fire here. I don't see any other way. If we let him rustle our cattle we'll be out of business. I was hoping that you'd ride along with us. We only have four hands and the three of us makes seven. I'm going, and with you that would make eight."

"We're talking about rustling cattle here, Mrs. Orville?"

"Not in the least, Mr. McCoy. We're looking for cattle with our brands on them that might have strayed down across the line. Happens all the time."

"Oh, well, in that case, count me in. I'm not partial to outfits that shoot at strangers who just ride on their range. When do we leave?"

Wade grinned. "Good to have another hand along. I figure we should pull out about five, which will put us at the property line at dusk."

"Have you had any dinner yet, Mr. McCoy?" Melody asked, her smile broader now.

"Fact is, I haven't. Wasn't any cafe between here and town for me to stop at."

"Come inside and let me make you a sandwich, and I think there's some fried chicken left over, and plenty of coffee."

Vincent headed toward the barn. "I'm going to check out our mounts and tell the men what's happening. We need to get two riders back from the north range as well."

They waved, and Melody and Spur walked toward the back door of the ranch house. He led his claybank, tied her to the hitching rail, and held the door open for Melody.

In the kitchen she looked at him and he saw the hint of a flush at her neck.

"I'm glad you came back," Melody said. She made no move to get any food ready. She stared at him with a small smile. Spur recognized the look. He walked over to her and picked up her hand.

She sucked in a quick little breath as he touched her hand.

"Melody, I came back mostly to see you again. I hope that doesn't offend you."

"No . . . no not at all . . . I'm . . . I'm glad you came."

They stood closely together. "Would you be shocked if I asked if I could kiss you?"

Her smile brightened and she let out a soft sigh and shook her head. She leaned toward him ever so slightly. He reached out and held her head with both hands and kissed her lips softly, then came away.

"Oh!" she sighed. "Oh my," Her eyes opened and she watched him. "Spur McCoy, could I ask you a question?"

"Of course."

"Could you do that again?"

He put his arms around her and drew her tightly to his chest and kissed her softly, then harder, came

away and nibbled at her lips. Then when they parted
a bit, he kissed her again and brushed her lips with
his tongue.

"Spur McCoy, I haven't been kissed that way in
more than a year. It's a dangerous game."

"I hoped it was." He kissed her again, her breasts
pushing hard against his chest, and now her hips
thrust forward to press at his hips. This time her lips
parted and his tongue explored, then retreated, and
he let her try. When at last their lips parted, Melody
was breathing heavily.

"I think . . . I think we better go upstairs before
someone comes in here and surprises us." She held
his hand and hurried to the near end of the living
room and then up the steps to the second floor. They
went down to the end of the hall to the big master
bedroom. She let go of his hand and closed the door
and turned a key in the lock.

"The men will be busy until suppertime." She
sighed and smiled. "Oh, it's been such a long
time."

Spur said nothing. He bent and kissed her neck,
and then her ear and her nose and again her eager
lips. She clung to him. He eased her down on the
edge of the bed.

"Yes, Spur, oh, please, yes!"

He kissed her and pressed her gently down on the
bed on her back, and one hand covered her breasts.
He petted one, caressing it softly. Then as the kiss
lasted, he worked through the buttons and under
her chemise.

Melody gasped and her eyes went wide as his
hand closed around her bare breast.

"Oh, yes! Yes, my darling Spur. Yes!"

He raised up and unbuttoned the fasteners down
to her waist, spread the cloth back, and lifted her
chemise to her neck. Her breasts had flattened as

she lay, but were throbbing with hot blood as her areolas became pinker and her nipples lifted as they filled with hot blood.

"Kiss them," she whispered.

He did and she writhed a minute, then smiled and put her hands on the back of his head holding him there.

"That feels so *good*. It's been so long. Not once since Stanley was hurt. Not *once*!"

She moved his head away and sat up. Quickly she pulled the dress off over her head and then the chemise. He bent and put one breast into his mouth as if it were a hanging grape.

"Sweet, so sweet," she said. "Yes, wonderful." Her hands played with the hair on the back of his head, and he left the globe and she unbuttoned his shirt and vest and spread them. She made a soft noise as she played with the hair on his broad chest.

"Oh, my!" she whispered.

Spur pulled off his boots, kicked out of his pants, and then pulled down his short underwear. He was hard and ready, and Melody sat there a moment simply staring at his erection. Then she bent and kissed the purpled head and held him gently in her hand.

"Glory, oh, glory. I want him deep inside me!" She pulled down the soft white drawers she wore and kicked them off, sitting beside him with no hidden secrets.

They both stretched out side by side on the big bed and he kissed her again. Then she found him and held his erection. She took one of his hands and pushed it down to her crotch where her legs parted slowly.

"Such a long time," she breathed. She yelped when his fingers strummed her tiny node, and four times later she rumbled into a climax that shook her like a tabby cat with a mouse. She tapered off, then charged into another series of vibrations and spasms that made her mew and cry softly.

When it passed she wiped a tear from each eye and looked up at him.

"Please, Spur. Would you pleasure me now, please? I couldn't be more ready."

He kissed her again. "Are you sure?"

"Yes, absolutely sure."

He moved between her spread white thighs and eased down.

"Yes, yes, right there, oh, yes. Ohhhhhhhhhhhhhh yessssssss."

He slid all the way in and she hugged him to her so he couldn't get away.

"Beautiful!" she crooned. "Wonderful." Her lips lifted toward him making the penetration even deeper. "Darling Spur, poke me now."

He worked with her gently. Then as her hips responded, they beat a rhythm faster and faster. She climaxed twice more as they stroked, and then he couldn't stop and pounded hard at her, lifting higher, brought his knees up more, and emptied himself into her, and she caught him and held him tightly as he went through his little death until recovery.

They lay locked together.

"Yes, yes, that's the way it used to be with Stanley. You are only the second man I've ever slept with. Did you know that? Only the second. My husband was my first and only. But now I realize there must be another man in my life soon. I need one. I need to be loved. Not every night but often. I need the release, the reassurance."

It was nearly a half hour that they lay there talking, kissing gently. She made no attempt to arouse him again. "Once is enough right now. Maybe later, tomorrow, or the next day. Right now I have my memories."

She looked at the alarm clock on the dresser and smiled. "I better get up and start some supper. I cook for the whole crew and I don't want them all yelling at me."

Melody stood and stretched without being self-conscious. She smiled at him as she dressed. He waited until she was done. Then he dressed quickly and they went downstairs. Her flush was gone now, and she led him into the parlor.

"Someone I want you to meet. We call him Merle even though we're sure that's not his name. He lost his memory and we're trying to help him regain it. He's been here, about three weeks now I guess, and we're making progress."

In the parlor a man sat in a big chair. His head was still bandaged, and he was dressed in clothes slightly too big for him. He looked up from a magazine as they came in.

"Merle, I want you to meet Spur McCoy. He's going to be with us for a while. We're going on a scouting expedition tonight to try to get back some of our stock that strayed."

He looked at Spur and held out his right hand. "Pleased to meet you,. Mr. McCoy. That's Irish, I remember that."

"And you're right-handed and had a good upbringing," Spur added.

"Besides that, Merle is good at gin rummy, not too sharp at poker, and claims he's not a cowboy, but we think he grew up on a ranch. Just where we haven't figured out."

Spur dropped into a chair across from Merle. "You ever play baseball? It's getting to be quite a popular sport."

"I did play. I was shortstop and batted eighth. That means I wasn't a great hitter." Merle looked at Melody with a surprised expression. "Well, I never thought about that before. I played baseball. A school team or a town team, I don't know. I'm sure I wasn't on one of the professional teams."

Melody headed for the door. "I've got a supper to get ready. I'll leave you two together." She looked at Spur and her eyes twinkled and she gave a soft sigh, turned, and went to the kitchen.

Chapter Ten

They had an early supper at four o'clock, and then all eight of them rode out, Spur included. Only Merle was left at the ranch. Melody went with them. She wore pants and a shirt and boots and a hat but carried no gun. Everyone else had a rifle and a pistol just in case of trouble.

They rode for an hour, and were almost off their land. A short time later they stopped where three posts had been driven into the ground.

"This is our property line marker," Wade said. "We put the posts in every two hundred yards two years back so we know for sure where the line is. On the other side of these stakes is the Circle B."

"How far are we riding in before we start driving animals back to the north?" Spur asked.

Melody looked at Wade. "You know the most about these sort of things, Wade."

"My suggestion is that we go to the other side of

the range, the east side, and sweep in about five miles, at least until we see a lot of stock. Then we'll start pushing them north and gathering them into a long line. They'll drive best that way."

It was slow going then. Wade insisted on riding a quarter of a mile ahead to watch for guards or some kind of defenders. He found none.

Spur rode near Melody and grinned at her in the moonlight. "Oh, I forgot to ask. How will we be able to see the brands in the faint light?"

"That we'll just guess at, and figure it out tomorrow morning when it gets light." She laughed. "You really don't believe that, do you?"

"I have to believe it. I'll tell you why later. I had a good talk with Merle. He's an honest, fine man. I'm betting that he'll get his memory back before long. He told me this afternoon he remembered his mother's name was Mary. He wrote it down on that memory pad of his."

Melody sobered. "Yes, he is nice. I've been a bit smitten with him since the day he arrived here almost dead. I haven't let myself feel anything for him. I was so afraid I'd love someone and they would be snatched away from me again."

"I'm sorry about your husband, but this is different. He's in no danger now."

"What about us, Spur McCoy?"

"Not much of a future, I'm afraid. You must have figured out that I'm some kind of a detective, and that I won't be staying around once I've found out what happened to the two surveyors."

"Yes, I thought of that. But this afternoon was so . . . so wonderful."

"For me too. But that can't change things. In a week or two I'll be gone. Now Merle, or whatever his name really is, will find his memory and then discover, I'll bet a bundle, that he's fallen in love with you."

Before she could say anything, Wade came galloping back.

"Right ahead more than four or five hundred head, and fairly well bunched. All we have to do is get behind them and drive them north."

He started assigning duties, and the men spread out. He put Melody at the point to head back toward the ranch. He and Spur took drag to roust any cows or calves or steers that slowed down or tried to turn off.

There was one man on each side of the herd near the front and one more on the side toward the back. Three of them rode drag.

Most of the animals had been bedded down for the night. The men rode through the herd slapping the cows with ropes and prodding them with sticks, getting them on their feet and moving north.

It took an hour to get the critters all up and awake and moving. They bunched them, then spread them out as they drove them north so they were about ten cows wide and half a mile long.

So far there had been no sign of anyone from the Circle B Ranch. Spur liked it that way. He had convinced himself that he was not committing a felony here, that he was surveying the land for a ride back tomorrow in the daylight to check the Breens. He hadn't figured out just how to do it yet, but he definitely wasn't rustling cattle tonight. He knew that for sure.

An hour later they had the lead animals close to the edge of the property line. They kept moving them along, cracking them with ropes, waving hats at the laggards, prodding them with a long stick as a last resort.

They moved them another hour, and figured they had crossed the line with all of the animals.

"We'll bed them down right near the ranch house. Then we can watch them," Wade suggested. Vincent nodded, and swung the animals to the left toward the ranch buildings.

By midnight they had the cows, calves, and steers bedded down less than a half mile from the ranch buildings.

They left Wade and another man to ride around the cattle for three hours as night herders. Two new men would be roused at three A.M. to take over the duty.

"Everybody sleeps with his boots on tonight," Vincent said. "I don't want them Circle B hands to surprise us. I'm going to do some patrol work a half mile to the south watching for anybody just to play it safe."

Spur had been invited to stay the rest of the night. Melody had a glint in her eye as she asked it, but Spur said he appreciated it and he'd find an empty cot in the bunkhouse. He watched Melody telling Merle how the round up went.

She was bright and pleasant with him, and as Spur watched he could see how Merle was hanging on her words. The man was so much in love that he must remember how that felt.

Melody looked up at Spur. "Let me get you a cup of coffee before you go out there. You'll need it. Those guys snore all the time."

In the kitchen, she made sure they were alone, then rushed to him and kissed him and pressed hard against him. When her feverish lips left his she put his hand on her breasts.

"Once more. In my bedroom. You can go out the side door but then come back in quietly. I'll be waiting for you." She moved a hand down to his crotch and rubbed him gently. "You come back to me once more or I'll hate you forever."

"What about Merle?"

"I plan on marrying Merle, but not until he gets well. And I don't want to scare him by suggesting he take me to bed before we're married." She grinned. "With you, it's different. I know you're hung like a stud horse and I've seen you in action, and I want one more ride before you fly away from me forever. Promise me you'll come?"

She kissed him again before he could reply. Her mouth was open and so was his, and they washed each other's tongues for a moment and her hand rubbed his growing erection.

When she eased away he laughed softly. "You make a great argument. I'll be back in when things quiet down. Now give me that coffee, or was that just a sneaky female trick to get me out here?"

The coffeepot on the wood stove was still warm. He sipped at the brew and then let the back screen door slam but stayed inside. He settled down in a kitchen chair as she took the lamp and said good night to Merle, who had returned to the couch in the parlor. She climbed the stairs, and then all was quiet in the house.

When Spur heard Merle snoring contentedly, he climbed the stairs, staying close to the wall so the boards wouldn't creak, and went down to the big bedroom at the end of the hall. It looked safe enough.

Melody sat at the window in a soft cotton nightgown waiting for him.

"Good, I don't have to stick a knife in your ribs," she said. She lifted off the nightgown and caught his hand and tugged him toward the bed.

"It's going to be better this time, I know, because

I'm going to blow out the lamp and have you all to myself in the glorious dark. Just you and me and love wonderful love and the darkness."

She blew out the lamp, and undressed him in the faint moonlight coming in the window. When they lay close to one another on top of the sheets in the cool Wyoming night air, she whispered to him.

"Tonight I want to make love the wildest, craziest way that you have ever imagined. I get to choose first, and then it will be your turn."

Their romp was delicious and quiet and exhausting. The second time around, he proved to her that a couple *could* make love standing up, and then they collapsed on the bed for a quick rest.

It was over two hours after he came upstairs that Melody brought out bread and cheese and a bottle of whiskey she had brought up to her room that afternoon before they left. She took out apples and some fresh-picked black cherries and they had a snack.

As they ate, McCoy pulled on his clothes over her protests and then sat beside her, her breast in his hands, her lips on his.

"Hey, I need to get a little sleep. I have a tough day tomorrow."

"You can sleep anytime—alone. When else can you sleep with me?"

"Probably never again, which will be my loss." He kissed her on the forehead and stood. "I really do need to find the bunkhouse and a blanket. If I wake up, I'll see you at breakfast."

The next morning, Spur missed breakfast. Four men were out in the range re-branding by dawn. They **turned the Circle B into the Circle O, then put a** vent line through it and burned in their own brand, the Bar-O.

Spur missed out on the branding. He had a cup of coffee in the kitchen from Melody, who was friendly but cool. When Vincent left for the branding she sat down beside him and whispered, "What if I got pregnant yesterday or last night?"

"Has been known to happen," Spur said. "Might be a good idea to seduce your sick friend in there. He looks hale and hearty to me, well enough for one good roll on the couch. Then if anything does happen, you'll have a ready-made wedding, even if a bit late."

"I've been thinking the same thing. But then I didn't get pregnant after three years with Stanley, so maybe I won't this time. Maybe I can't."

Spur kissed her good-bye on the check, said he'd be back, and rode out south toward the Circle B Ranch. He was going to get a look at that campsite today one way or the other.

He was halfway there when a rifle shot slammed over his head and he ducked and dropped off his horse on the off side to protect himself from the gunfire.

"Stranger, you got a minute to get back on that nag and ride the other way."

"I've come to see Charlie Breen on important business."

"Strange way to come to our ranch."

"I'm new in this country and I'm afraid I got lost trying to find your spread."

A man rode up on a sorrel with a rifle trained on Spur. "What kind of business you got with Mr. Breen? He don't stand for unannounced guests."

"It's personal business with Mr. Breen only and it doesn't concern you."

The rider stopped 20 feet away. He rubbed his jaw. "Damn, he said keep everybody out of here."

"He's gonna be damn mad and chew your ass when I don't deliver what I got to deliver. What's your name, cowboy? I'll need to tell him who to blame."

"Christ!"

"That one of the new Remington rifles you're holding?" Spur asked.

The man looked down at it and shook his head. "Naw, an old Spencer, one of the . . ." When he looked back at Spur the hammer on his Colt .45 had just clicked back into place and the muzzle was aimed directly at the rider's heart.

"Toss the rifle to me, and that side arm, and we'll ride in and see your boss. I promise you won't get in any trouble. You can count on that."

"Damn, I'm in trouble already."

"At least you're alive and not shot up. Unless you think that rifle can beat a six-gun at close range."

The man shrugged, tossed Spur the rifle, and then eased his six-gun out of leather and handed it to Spur.

"You lead the way, sport. You know the direction we're going."

It took them almost an hour to ride on to the ranch. Spur wasn't sure what he was going to say to the ranch owner. When they came within sight of the ranch house, Spur closed the gap so he rode a foot from the other man, and drew his Colt and leveled it at the guide.

"This is just in case some trigger-happy rifleman wants to pick me off before we get to the boss."

A rifle shot slammed over Spur's head and he grabbed the rider beside him and jammed the six-gun hard into the cowboy's ribs.

"The next shot that comes anywhere near me means this man is dead!" he bellowed. "Now put down the damn rifle, I just want to talk to Charlie Breen!"

Chapter Eleven

Spur McCoy held the gun against the lookout's side as the two horses walked side by side up to the back door of the ranch house. He could see at least two rifles trained on him. He ignored them. Surely Breen wouldn't shoot him down and sacrifice one of his own men.

They stopped the horses at the back door and Spur bellowed in his best parade-ground voice, "Get Charlie Breen out here, right now!"

A tall, widely built man in his early fifties came out the back door with a scowl on his face.

"I'm Breen. What the hell you want?"

"Tell your riflemen to put down their pieces and then we'll have a talk."

Breen shook his head. "Hell, all right. Put them away, boys. This one looks harmless. Get back to work."

When Spur saw the two rifles vanish he looked at

Breen. "Now tell the other two men to put their long guns away, no halfway measures."

Breen laughed. "Not the chowderhead most salesmen are. Mace, Jody, I've got it covered. You two get back to work too."

When Spur heard two men move, he poked the guard again. "We get down together, between the two animals. Slow and easy and there won't be any trouble."

The guard nodded. The two men slid off their mounts together so they were between the horses. They walked out with Spur's gun still in the guard's ribs.

"Inside, Breen, and then we'll talk."

"You don't take no chance, do you, cowboy?"

"I'm still alive." Once inside the back door, Spur nodded at the guard and he scooted outside. Spur held the six-gun as he watched Breen. The man wore iron. Slowly Spur put the weapon in his holster.

"It wouldn't be a good idea to try to outdraw me. You don't know if I'm faster than you are. Besides, there's no need. All I want to do is talk to you. Twice your guards turned me back. I don't take kindly to that. It makes you look like you have something to hide."

Breen let out a held-in breath and snorted. "Hell, just trying to get some work done. I run a ranch here."

"Do you have something to hide, Breen? I'm tracking a pair of surveyors out of Laramie. They went through the ranch south of you heading your way. I found bench marks just outside your property line. The same two men never surveyed anything on the other side of your property in the Bar-O Ranch. What happened to them?"

"How the hell should I know? I'm not paid to keep

track of surveyors. I had my place surveyed when I bought it five years ago."

"That's not what I'm talking about. These men were putting in reference points for a north-south division line in the territory for land parcel description."

"I ain't seen the men. None of my men mentioned anything about seeing them. That's the end of the discussion. Good-bye, whoever you are."

"Not quite that easy, Breen. I have a witness who saw the men working more than three miles into your property from the south. You or some of your men must have seen them."

"No. Nobody saw any damn surveyors. The men would have told me. We don't let strangers wander around on the Circle B."

"Breen, if you're lying you'll wind up in prison. Do you know that? These men are missing, may have met with foul play. You're dealing here with the United States Government. Those men were U.S. Department of the Interior government surveyors. If you're stupid enough to have me shot on my ride out, there will be a dozen U.S. marshals and detectives in here in two weeks and they'll come with warrants and take your whole damn ranch apart until they find the answer.

"You deal with me, or you deal with a whole platoon of investigators who can throw you in the local jail until you rot. Now which is it going to be?"

"I'll ask my men if they've seen any government surveyors on the place in how long, three months?"

"No, in the last three weeks."

"You sit and wait and I'll have my foreman go ask everybody in the yard. I've got some men out riding."

"I'll settle for that."

Spur sat and waited for ten minutes. Then Breen came back in shaking his head.

"Told you. Nobody has seen any strangers who weren't asked to leave, and none of them were surveyors."

"I'll have to accept that for now. When your other men come in, you check each one of them. If any of them have seen the surveying team, you get a rider in to notify the sheriff pronto."

"I can do that," Breen said, anger clouding his steady gaze. "Now get the hell off my ranch."

"Of course, and I'll put in a good word for you with the governor." Spur stared at the man for five long seconds, turned his back on him, and walked out the door. His horse was where he had left it ground-tied in the yard. He stepped in the leather and at once felt the gunsights on him.

Not even Breen would be that dumb, he told himself, and realized there must be countless men in their graves who'd said the same thing in similar situations about other stupid men.

In the living room window, Charlie Breen watched Spur McCoy riding at a walk down the lane to the River Road. He grabbed his Big Fifty rifle and sighted in on the man's broad back.

Not a man on his place would say a word if he blasted the damn detective off his horse with a round in the back. Not a man would talk. A flush glowed on Breen's face and he heard someone come in the back door.

"Goddamn, almost done it," he said as he lowered the rifle.

"Who was that, Pa?" Kevin asked.

"Just a visitor asking a bunch of questions," Breen said. The bastards could look all day for a year. They didn't have the bodies, and they couldn't do much

without them. Evidence. They had to prove there
had been someone killed. The Laramie River was
well known at flood tide for not giving up bodies.
Often a body was forced under brush or into a deep
hole and covered up with silt so quickly they never
floated. Let them look, they can't prove a thing.

"You sound mad."

"Yeah, happens sometimes. Any truth to that
report about some missing cattle?"

"I just got back. We figure about five hundred
head, more or less. They got rousted out of their
bedding-down spot last night sometime and driven
straight north into Bar-O range. We followed them
in about a mile, then came back. My guess is they
took more from us last night than we got from them
the other night."

"Goddamn! That ties it. Get back out there and
pick out the ten best gunhands we have. We're going
to pay a visit to the Bar-O tonight. If they want a
war, they sure as hell gonna have one."

"Before dark or after?"

"After. Never go on a raid in the daylight unless
you know they don't have anybody who can shoot a
rifle. We'd lose half our hands that way. At night we
can hit hard, and get away without a scratch. Make
sure the men have thirty rifle rounds each and forty
cartridges for revolvers.

"Still can't believe it. Didn't think that woman or
her Eastern-bred brother would have balls enough
to come down here and steal any of our cattle. Don't
matter. After tonight they won't have a hell of a
lot left."

"Pa, we won't burn down the ranch house, will
we? You promised me I'd get that place when we
take it over. I don't want a burned-out house."

"Yeah, I remember. We'll get the barns. Get out

there and pick the men. Get blooded ones if you can, and any who were in the war."

They rode out from the Circle B buildings promptly at 6:30 P.M., and headed north hugging the river road that would angle them toward the ranch downstream.

Twelve men rode, all armed, all well aware that they were on a war-type raid that might well result in gunfire and being wounded or dying. But with the darkness to hide them the odds were good they all would ride home tall in their saddles instead of being tied over their saddles.

"The river road route is a mile longer than going cross-country toward the Bar-O," Breen said. "They probably won't have out any guards along the road. If we find a guard we try to kill him silently. If we meet no guards, we ride in quietly, walk up the last two hundred yards."

Breen looked at his son. "You brought along the dynamite?"

"You bet, Pa. A three-stick bundle with a foot-long fuse."

"You know how to use it?"

"Can't just drop it in, the water would put out the fuse. I figure to light it with a minute fuse, put it in the bucket, and let the bucket down the well until it hits water and floats."

"Should work," Charlie Breen said. "Well's our first target. I want two men to take the dynamite. Two more men will be setting fire to the smallest barn, and four more will be silently attacking the corral, stampeding the horses out of them. I think they have two corrals there now.

"The whole secret here is not to make any noise at all until the dynamite goes off in the well. Then we get our work done and pull back and lay down a barrage of fire at anyone we see who moves. If they try to put out the fire in the barn, they will make themselves excellent targets."

Everyone was assigned a job, and they continued riding. It was past nine o'clock when they pulled up 200 yards from the ranch buildings. They had circled around from the road to the rear of the barns and the corral.

Kevin Breen and hand called Lucky took the dynamite, left their horses, and began moving up on the well. If they met anyone they were to mumble a greeting and walk right past them. If they were stopped they had to disable their questioner without a sound.

Kevin and Lucky walked toward the well by going past the big barn and straight to it. The well was about 30 yards from the ranch house and away from the barn and corrals, which were on the downslope to protect the ground water.

They were within 20 yards of the well when they spotted a man lifting a bucket of water off the windlass. He nodded at them, then frowned in the faint moonlight.

He dropped the bucket of water, his hand darting for his holster. "Who the hell are you guys?" he called. His six-gun came up and he could see the other two drawing their weapons. Wade fired from the hip, hitting the smaller of the two men, who slammed backwards into the dirt. The second man carried something and lunged toward the well.

Wade fired at him, missed.

"We got trouble out here!" Wade bellowed. He fired again at the shadow running for the well. His round went low, and snarled through Kevin Breen's right thigh. He screeched in pain, dropped the unlighted dynamite, and tried to fire behind him. He then evidently changed his mind, and turned and raced into the darkness.

Wade put two rounds into the black night after him.

Four men stormed out of the bunkhouse armed with rifles and pistols.

"Check the corrals, two of you," Wade bellowed.

Two men ran out of the ranch house kitchen door.

"What's happening?" Vincent called.

"Raiders, trying for the well," Wade shouted. "Probably more of them around. You other two men, check the barns."

Vincent and Spur McCoy ran up to the well. Spur touched the man he saw slumped there. He was dead. He picked up the six-gun that lay beside him and ran for the barn. They smelled the smoke before they got there. Smoke and flames gushed from the rear of the barn where a six-foot stack of leftover hay had been piled against the barn.

The hay burned brightly and the flames ate into the wood. Vincent ran into the light of the fire and two rifles cracked. He screamed and staggered back out of the firelight as the rifles fired again from the darkness.

"Stay back from the barn," Spur brayed. "It can't be saved. Don't give them a target."

A shot from a pistol cracked and three men ran toward the corrals. Two shadows inside had been herding the cow ponies out the open gate. One of the Bar-O hands sent there waited for an opening, then fired twice at the shadow, and saw him stagger and fall, then get up and vanish into the dark.

Wade and another hand ran up and slammed the gate shut. At least half of the horses were gone.

"Check the back of the other barn," Wade screeched. "Don't let the bastards get it started on fire. Two more of you go back to the ranch house. Protect that too."

By that time the light from the burning barn had lit up the whole ranch yard. Now and then a rifle spat from the darkness, and one round tore though the upstairs window that had a light in it.

Wade ran toward the house, his six-gun ready.

Spur checked the big barn adjacent to the second corral. They ran inside and found no fire, then went outside and lay in the darkness just out of the light from the fire and watched the darkness ahead. No one tried to get to the big barn.

Another spate of firing came from the darkness. McCoy took a Spencer rifle from one of the cowboys. The next time he saw a winking light of a rifle firing, he put four quick rounds into the area, and then rolled away six feet and lay behind a log left over from building the barn. Two rounds came at his former position.

Spur sent four more hot lead slugs at those shots and ducked behind the log. That was the end of the rifle fire.

Spur left the two men to protect the back of the barn, and ran to where he had seen Vincent limping away from the burning barn. He found him behind the small well house. Vincent held a folded-up neckerchief pad over a wound in his leg.

"How is it?" Spur asked.

"Not too bad. Slug went all the way through. Damn but that hurts. First time I've been shot."

Spur took off his kerchief and tied the other one tightly in place over the exit hole of the wound, then stood and helped Vincent hobble back to the dark kitchen door.

Spur knocked on the door. "Friends coming inside," he said. Someone pushed open the door.

There had been no firing outside for five minutes.

"Sounds like they have pulled back," Vincent said in the darkness.

"Melody, are you here?" Spur asked the black inside of the kitchen.

"Yes."

"Is there a room without windows?"

"I've hung a blanket over the kitchen window. This room is black to the outside unless the door opens."

"Good. Light a lamp. Vincent got winged in the leg out there."

"Oh, Vincent!"

"It's not that bad," Vincent said. "I'll live."

"I'm going back outside and check with Wade," Spur said.

"We lost the small barn?" Melody asked.

"I'm afraid so," Vincent told her. "Be lucky if that's all we lost."

Spur slid out the black kitchen doorway to get a report from Wade just how bad the damage really was.

Chapter Twelve

Spur found Wade watching the burning barn. The last wall of the building fell down into the flames, sending up a huge shower of sparks and sailing embers.

"Looks like you got off cheap," Spur said.

Wade nodded. "I killed one of them. What are we supposed to do with him?"

"Dump him just over the property line and let them find him," Spur said. "You check all of your men?"

"Yes, all accounted for. Vincent was the only one to get shot. How bad is he?"

"Slug went on through. He'll be hurting for a week, but no major damage."

Wade face showed angry in the firelight. "I figure half of our riding mounts are scattered over the prairie. They burned down a barn, and shot one man. That guy I shot in the leg was carrying something to the well. Let's find out what it was."

They found the dynamite with the help of some torches.

"The question is now how we answer this," Wade said. "I don't know what the owners want to do, but I'll have some suggestions if they ask. Could do it all in one trip. You know that the river almost dried up? Those sons of bitches upstream on the Circle B must have put in a dam. That's a job that needs to be taken care of damn quick before our cattle start dying."

Spur tossed the dynamite in the air and a few inches and caught it. "You have any more dynamite?"

"Couple of cases in the other barn. Let's go see the boss. First I want to set a guard. They could come back later."

Twenty minutes later Wade had made his case to Melody and a wincing Vincent. As they began talking, Merle came out from the living room.

"I'd like to sit in on the talk," he said. Melody nodded. When Wade finished, Melody's forehead crinkled into a frown.

"I don't know, this is almost at the point of getting out of hand," Melody said. She sipped at a cup of coffee in the still blacked-out kitchen and watched Vincent and Spur. "Mr. McCoy, what do you think of Wade's plans?"

"Time I made a confession," he said. Quickly he told them who he was, who he worked for, and why he was in the area.

"So I'm a lawman. I can help you defend your ranch from a wanton attack. I can fire in self-defense. I even stretched my position a little and helped you regain your rustled stock. But I can't go along on a battle in this range war.

"My advice is that if I were trying to save this ranch I'd do just about what Wade suggests. If you don't strike back, you might as well fold up and sign over the ranch to Charlie Breen."

Melody looked at Vincent.

"I agree with McCoy. But how can I suggest we ride up there when I can't even ride? It's a trip that has to be taken, and done tonight when they won't expect it."

"One thing I can do," Spur said. "If that dam is on the Circle B range, it's an illegal dam on a federal waterway and there I do have jurisdiction. If you folks are riding north anyway, I might tag along and look for that dam."

An hour later, Vincent waved at them from the back porch. He had a chair there, a mug of coffee, six cookies, and two rifles, one a Spencer loaded and ready to spit out eight rounds without reloading.

"I'll be on lookout," Vincent said. "Anybody coming this way will get a belly full of lead."

Melody rode with them. She didn't want to go, but she knew she had to as long as she was the principal owner of the ranch. She had given Vincent 49 percent, so she was still boss.

They took the rest of the hands. That made five men for the assault force on the Circle B Ranch, and Spur to track down the dam. In his saddlebags he carried four dynamite bombs made of six sticks each and each fitted with a two-foot-long fuse and a blasting cap.

Just before they left, one of the hands rode up with a saddled horse.

"I found him just beyond the barn. His reins were caught on some brush. It's not one of ours, must be from the Circle B."

They held a lantern up and found the brand identifying the horse as from the spread to the south.

"Tie the body on over the saddle," Spur said. "You can deliver him back to his home ranch. Just leave the horse tied to a tree down there somewhere near-by. They'll find him."

Soon they were ready and rode to the edge of the ranch, where Spur wished them good health and turned over to the river. Since they had no idea where the dam was situated, he would have to follow the waterway until he found it.

He was amazed at how much of the water the dam had stopped. The trickle in the bottom of the streambed wasn't enough to keep two steers alive on one hot, thirsty day. He wondered what kind of luck Wade and his men would have at the Breen ranch. He wished them well and hoped that none of them got shot. Things could get wild over there before it was over.

He kept riding in the moonlight along the stream-bed. After what he figured was five miles, he saw the moon glinting off water ahead. It was a lake on the other side of the river. A big lake.

As he rode up, he could see the spot where the dam had been put up. It was in a narrow place in the river, and a spillway had been cut out of the far bank.

It took him twenty minutes to figure out where to put the four bombs so the fuses wouldn't get wet. He had the bombs wedged in between the posts sunk deep in the riverbed and the side of the big gate-like device that must have been levered into place somehow in the middle of the span.

He lit the fuse on the far side, walked across the three inches of water to the near side, and lit the other fuses, then ran back 50 yards to wait for the explosion. The two-foot fuses took about two minutes to burn, then one went off slightly before the others.

A loud cracking roar like an exploding artillery shell shattered the stillness, and the flash of the explosion turned the night into noontime for a half a second. In the flash, he saw the far side of the gate blasted to the side. Then the water gushed through the hole.

The second explosion a half second later powered the heavy gate into the dry riverbed 20 feet downstream, where it was quickly engulfed with the swirling, roaring surge of water from the pent-up Laramie River.

He stood on the bank and watched. It took only ten minutes for the backed-up water to churn through the wide, deep gate in the dam and flow downstream.

Spur rode to the east, watching for the Circle B Ranch buildings. Soon he heard some distant sounds of rifle fire. Then it eased off and soon all was quiet.

Three miles later he could see a soft glow of a fire to the east and he rode north and slightly east toward the spot. When he was within a quarter of a mile, he knew it was the Circle B Ranch buildings.

The long two-story ranch house was little more than a smoking mass of hot coals and burning timbers. He skirted the place and rode faster to the north then. When he got to the Bar-O buildings, he came in quietly so no one would shoot him.

Lights burned in the kitchen. The blanket was off the window.

He found three of the hands as well as Wade and Vincent, Merle and Melody all sitting around the table.

When Spur came in the door, they looked at him

but nobody said a word. The three ranch hands shook their heads and went out the door.

"My fault," Wade said. "If I hadn't suggested we raid the Circle B, Greg would still be alive."

"It was my fault for agreeing to the raid," Melody said.

"It was nobody's fault," Spur said. "No matter what happened. Tell me what did happen."

The others looked at Wade.

He took a deep breath.

"We got up there and me and Greg went in to light a fire under the ranch house. We had some kerosene and it burned well, but just as we got out from under the place, three guys ran at us with rifles. We split up and charged into the darkness, but Greg caught a round and he's gone."

"Any other damage to the place?" Spur asked.

"Yeah. We dumped their corral and all the horses got out. We tried to set a barn on fire, but it wouldn't burn. Then they were all over the place, shooting and screaming, and we pulled back and watched the ranch house burn.

"I found Greg's body and we brought him back. I'll quit and move on tomorrow if you want me to. Let me know in the morning. Now I think I better stand guard until daylight."

"It wasn't your fault," Spur said as Wade walked out into the night.

The rain came, not a drizzle, but a hard rain pushed by a steady east wind. Spur ducked into the kitchen and saw Vincent and Melody in a quiet talk. He went in by the fireplace. Merle had started a fire when it grew chilly, and now with the rain slamming down it was welcome.

"A bad night all the way around," Merle said.

"Turned out that way. But there's a chance the

bold front these people put up just might have saved the ranch. Charlie Breen is not the kind of man who likes to be confronted. He'd rather roll over someone without any opposition. He might think hard before he makes another attack."

"I don't know much about attacks," Merle said. "I was too young for the war. Only sixteen when it ended." He looked up and a smile broke out on his face. The bandage had been reduced now, and his smile was a wide one.

"I remembered something else! Great! No war, and I *was raised on a cattle ranch*." Merle laughed. "I'm remembering more. The ranch was in Kansas . . . just outside of . . . of . . . Damn, that I can't recall."

"You're making good progress, Merle. Anything about your name yet?"

Merle shook his head. "Not a glimmer. But I'm feeling better. My side doesn't hurt at all anymore, and my head is feeling better. I can even bend over and straighten up without losing my balance."

"Merle, that's wonderful!" Melody said. She had walked up as he was talking. "First thing I know you'll want to get out of the house and ride around the ranch."

"That's what I want next," Merle said, smiling. "Maybe next week."

"I hope so," Melody said, then turned to Spur. "Mr. McCoy, I hope you plan on staying the night. With this rain and all, no sense you trying to ride anywhere."

"If it would be no trouble."

"No trouble at all. Let me show you where the guest room is. I'm about ready to collapse myself."

"I can fix my own bed on the sofa," Merle said.

They said good night, and Melody carried a lamp and led Spur up the stairs to the bedroom next to hers. She opened the door and lit a lamp that sat on a dresser.

She turned and stepped close to him and kissed him hard on the lips, her breasts pressed against his chest. Then she eased away from him.

"I want you to come to my room tonight after the house settles down, but I decided not to ask you. I . . . I must start to consider my future. You understand?"

She took his hand and put it over her breast, and he caressed her softly through the cloth.

"You do understand, don't you?" she whispered. "I can't fall in love with you, so I won't make love with you again. Oh, how I would love to love you the rest of the night!" She kissed him again, then pushed away and rushed out the door. She came back and picked up a lamp and went next door to her room.

When she closed it, Spur listened from his door, and he heard the bolt slide firmly in place.

Spur smiled and closed his own door and threw the bolt and sat down on the bed, more tired than he had been in some time.

By morning the sky had cleared, and Spur ate breakfast with Merle and Melody. She talked with Merle almost all the time, urging him to remember things.

"How big was your ranch?" she asked.

"We had two homesteads owned and another five or six thousand acres we controlled. It was a small operation, but it kept us alive. I wanted to get away and go to school. Yes! I remember, I went to Kansas City, Missouri, to study drafting!"

"Not much call for draftsmen in Laramie, Wyoming," Spur said. "Why did you come to Laramie?"

Merle's brow furrowed and he squinted his eyes, but at last he sighed and shook his head. "No idea."

"Just when did Merle first arrive at the house?" Spur asked Melody. "What day was it that Wade found him half in the river?"

"About three weeks ago. Yes, it was on my mother's birthday. She would have been forty-four years old, I remember. So that makes it on June 14th. Today is July 5th. Looks like we missed the parade in Laramie on the Fourth of July."

"The 14th," said Spur. "No wonder you look so good, Merle. You're almost a new man."

"Except for a lot of my memory. I'll keep hoping."

"Living on the ranch, did you get into town to high school?" Spur asked.

"Nope, Pa said I was needed there on the ranch, so I only got my eighth-grade diploma." Merle grinned. "Damn, one more item for my book."

After breakfast, Spur saddled the claybank and rode up to say good-bye to Melody.

She stood close to the horse and touched his hand. "Tall man in the saddle, I'll always remember that afternoon we had."

"I'll remember it too. You work on Merle and get his memory back. You working on that plan to take care of any pregnant emergency?"

"I'm working on it. Soon perhaps. It has to work. At least I'll know he's going to stay around."

"Hope so. Now, I have a man to see about a pair of murders. I hope I'm making some progress." He waved at Melody, then at Vincent, who sat on the back porch, and rode south toward the river road into town.

He wasn't going all the way. Once he passed the Circle B Ranch, he found some brush along the river road and settled down to wait. The rainstorm last night had been heavier than he had guessed. There were some new furrows cut in the dirt road and along the stream where gushers of water had stormed down the slopes toward the Laramie. This country could use all the rain it could wring out of the clouds.

It was just before noon when Spur saw a man riding out from the Circle B Ranch. Spur had been prepared to wait all day if needed. The man came down the river road heading for town on some errand or shopping mission.

Spur lifted his six-gun from his holster and mounted the claybank. He held her muzzle closed so she couldn't do any horse talk with the other animal and give him away.

When the rider came into the stretch of brush and was out of sight of the ranch, Spur charged out of cover directly at him. He was no more than ten yards away.

His Colt aimed at the man's chest.

"Hold it right there, cowboy, and you won't get killed. Hands up high. You and me are going to have a long talk."

Chapter Thirteen

When Spur McCoy rode off, Melody turned and went back into the ranch house with only one purpose, to help Merle to seduce her. It was quite simple really. She had slowly and powerfully fallen in love with the soft-spoken man who had been a patient in her house for the past three weeks.

She had been with him every day, had feared for his life, and then ever so slowly she had known that she wanted to be with him for the rest of her life.

When Spur McCoy had darted into the picture, it had been a wild, crazy, lustful adventure, and she didn't regret it. But in that emotional loving, she could have become pregnant. It was about the right time of the month.

So now, logically, realistically, she had to lay the foundation for a marriage if the pregnancy had happened. That was what brought her back to Merle. He was solid and true. He was a man who would do the right thing if she were with child. But she wanted him to believe it was his if it happened.

There was little she could do that morning. The hands were out gathering up their horses. Some of them had wandered off five or six miles after they had been turned loose by the Circle B hands. They might never find them all. Vincent sat in the kitchen groaning from time to time as he moved. She would put him into bed this afternoon to get a good nap. That would be the time to go see Merle.

Before that she got the kitchen cleaned up, readied a light dinner for whoever showed up, and talked with Merle.

"Have you ever played anagrams?" Merle asked.

"Take a word and see how many other words you can make from the letters? Yes, now and then."

"I do it a different way," Merle said. "I use a long word like 'differentiate,' and then make up words going all ways from that word. Like straight down from the D we could put dilapidated. Whenever one word crosses another word already there, all the letters must match and still make a real word."

"That sounds interesting. Where did you learn to do that?"

"While I was in Kansas City. This young lady taught me. Her name was Pauline." Merle grinned and let out a whoop. "Hey, another bit of my past. Pauline was the daughter of a friend there in Kansas City. Another clue."

They played the game, getting a tangle of words and giving up trying to cross some, but crossing others and even filling in some of the squares he drew so they could keep the words straight both up and down and horizontal.

She put her hand over his. "Merle, I'm so proud of you. You're making such good progress in remembering. By the time your head is all healed up, I'm sure you'll know everything that you did before you were shot."

His hand trembled under hers. She held his hand tightly. "I don't mean to embarrass you, Merle. I guess you know by now that I'm becoming ever so fond of you."

She looked up and he lifted his brows.

"I thought I was dreaming, making up things. You've been so kind and attentive. I fell in love with you the very first day I opened my eyes and saw this angel looking back at me."

"Oh, my!" Melody said. "That's such a good thing to hear! I had no idea!"

They were sitting close together at the table. She leaned toward him gently, and he leaned in and a moment later their lips met in a soft, gentle kiss. She pulled away and sighed.

"That was nice, Merle, so very nice."

"But . . . but I keep thinking that I'm not even sure if I'm free to think about a beautiful lady like you."

"You don't wear a wedding band," she said. "There's no sign that there ever has been one on your wedding ring finger."

"Yes, I thought of that. But I must know for sure who I am before I can even tell you know strongly I feel about you."

"But *I* can tell *you*, Merle. You know I've been married. Three years, but we had no children. I don't know why. It might be me. You should know that, Merle."

She reached out and kissed his cheek, then pulled back. Yes, a good start. She spotted a word she could fill in putting an O between two adjacent words with an F on one side and an R and M to fill in the word FORM.

"Hey, that's a good one," Merle said. His smile was fuller now, as he showed more of his feelings.

"I better finish getting dinner. You work on that puzzle."

After the crew had dinner in the kitchen at the long table, and the dishes were cleared and washed, Melody suggested that a good nap would help Vincent's leg heal. She rousted her brother up the stairs to his bedroom, then came down.

Merle was in the parlor near the couch. Melody went in and they began working on the puzzle again, trying to fill in empty spaces. They sat closely together and she moved casually, letting her leg touch his. She moved it away at once.

"I really meant what I said this morning about being terribly fond of you, Merle."

"I'm glad. Would it . . . would you mind if I kissed you?"

"I'd like that."

He leaned in and kissed her lips, and slowly her arms came around him and the kiss lasted a long time.

When their lips parted she sighed. "Oh, Merle, that is just wonderful. Would you kiss me again?"

He did, and at last their lips parted. A moment later she stood quickly and went to the parlor door, closed it, and slid in the lock. The drapes were still drawn from the previous night when the parlor had become a bedroom.

She walked back and sat beside him, kissing his cheek, then his lips.

"Oh, please kiss me again, Merle. Again and again." After another kiss she eased backward on the couch and he followed her. She smiled at him and took one of his hands and pushed it over one of her breasts.

"Please touch me, Merle. It's been so long."

He watched her sternly for a moment. "Darling Melody. Are you sure?"

"Yes, oh, yes. I've never been so sure of anything in all my life."

He petted her, and a minute later she undid the buttons on her dress front and his hand went in under her chemise onto her bare breasts.

"Oh, yes. Oh, darling Merle, yes!"

She reached for his crotch and found the hardness and rubbed it, fumbling at the buttons.

"Darling, I'll be careful of your side," Melody said softly.

They sat up and he helped her off with the dress, then her chemise. He gasped at the beauty of her bare breasts, and fondled them, then kissed them.

Then he was in a hurry. She pulled down her drawers without taking off her petticoats, and he opened his fly and went between her spread thighs.

He thrust into her opening and at once he climaxed, thundering into her a dozen times, and then he lay there panting and gasping for breath.

She stroked his hair and kissed his cheek and told him how delighted she was that she could help him and glad that they had this time together. But she held him inside her as she felt him shrinking.

When she let him leave her she said that that was his time, and now it was her turn. She helped him to take his clothes off and then make love to her slowly, and with the right build-up she climaxed four times, and then four times again before he did his second time, and they both were smiling and panting when it was over.

She dressed and told him she was fine.

He sat up and stared at her. "Good Lord, what if . . . what if you become pregnant?"

"Such things have been known to happen. If anything like that does occur, I'm sure that you'll do the right thing. I don't care if I get pregnant or not. I'm just thrilled that you love me, Merle, and that we're going to find out for sure who you are.

"It doesn't matter what happens now. I want to marry you no matter what. We'll find out your real name and that you're not married, I'm sure. Why would you be married and way out here away from your wife? No, I'm sure you were adventuring in some way."

She kissed his lips, then eased away from him, her smile genuinely pleasant. He was a tender lover, and she had no doubts that he would be a fine husband.

"Now, young man, I do have some other duties here beside serving you. You are ordered to take a nap to help in your recuperation. I'll come back in later to see how you're doing."

He motioned to her. "Melody, will you marry me?"

She watched him a minute, then nodded. "Oh, yes, Merle! I'll be delighted to be your wife. Just as soon as we know for sure about your right name and when you get well." She kissed his lips, a firm, passionate kiss, then eased him down on the couch and pulled up a comforter over him.

"You rest now, husband-to-be. We won't tell the others about it yet. See if they can guess. Is that all right?"

He nodded. She smiled at him and hurried out of the room.

Melody leaned against the door a moment in reflection. Well, she'd done it. She'd seduced the poor man and he'd thought he had made the first advances. Now she was covered just in case her bleeding stopped next month.

As she walked to the kitchen she admitted to herself that she had gone to bed several nights wondering if this handsome young man who'd dropped into her ranch out of nowhere might end up in her bed as a lover. She hadn't thought much about a husband, but now it was the best solution to all of her problems here on the ranch. Merle knew ranching. She smiled.

Spur McCoy rode up to the Circle B cowhand. He was not more than 25, probably the last man hired on the spread.

"Look, son, I got no fight with you. There's just a few questions I need to ask you. You tell me easy-like and you'll be on your way into town in five minutes, you understand?"

"Yes, sir, but then why the six-gun?"

"That's in case you don't understand. Just so there won't be no trouble, take out your hog-leg and pass it over to me gentle-like holding tight on to the barrel. Understand?"

"Yes, sir." The young cowpoke did as ordered.

"Now ease out of the saddle on this side and hit the ground."

Again the young man did so. Spur stepped out of the saddle and ground-tied the two mounts, and motioned for the boy to go into the woods a few paces.

"We'll start off easy. What's your name?"

"Logan, Brady Logan."

"You ride for the Circle B?"

"Yes, sir."

"You been there more than six months?"

"Just about."

"Then you worked there three weeks ago?"

"Yes."

"See how easy this is? Now, about three weeks ago, did you hear about two men who came on the place and wouldn't leave?"

The lad hesitated, than at last nodded. "Yes, sir."

"Were those two men surveyors?"

"I heard they were."

"What happened to them, Brady?"

"I . . . I don't know."

"Did someone ride out to settle matters with them?"

"I don't know."

"Were the two of them killed out there, Brady?"

"I just don't know."

"Three times you told me that, Brady. I can run you into town, swear out a warrant for you, and charge you with murdering those two men. You know that, don't you?"

"Yes, sir."

"So I'll ask you again. What happened to those two surveyors who we know were on Circle B property?"

"I don't know."

"Hate to do this, son, but I can also arrest, try, and then hang any man I think is an outlaw. I have special license to kill from the President of the United States. Get on your horse, son, but don't touch the reins."

Logan stepped into the saddle.

"Now, turn around and sit on the rump of the horse facing backwards."

When the young man had done that, Spur tied his hands behind his back. He took a lariat from his saddle and cinched up the noose, then slid it over Logan's head and tightened it around his neck.

"Yes, I know, Logan. No hangman's knot so it won't break your neck clean and quick. Look at it this way, you'll have three minutes longer to live before you strangle to death. This way I write in my report that you were convicted and hung for the deaths of the two surveyors."

Logan was no longer grinning. He'd seen hangings or heard about them.

"Look, I'd rather go to town to jail."

"Not a chance now, it's gone too far." Spur picked up the loose reins and led the kid's horse to a cotton-wood tree with a low thick branch. It took Spur three throws to get the light roping line over the branch and the end of it hanging back down. He took the rest of the line over to the tree trunk and tied it off.

He rode back to the kid and stared at him.

"Now, you want to change your story? What happened to the two surveyors on the Circle B range?"

"I don't know."

"Too late now, kid." Spur whacked Logan's horse with the palm of his hand and the startled animal surged ahead. The rope dragged the screaming Brady Logan off the back of the horse and held for just a minute. Then the tail of the rope pulled free of the slip knot Spur had tied and Logan fell into the dirt and leaves, the rope still tight around his neck.

Spur got off his horse and pulled the knot to loosen it. Then he shrugged.

Logan had stopped screaming. He glared at Spur.

"What the hell, the rope came untied. The branch broke. It was too little for your weight. I'll do it right this time."

"Wait . . . wait a minute. I ain't dying for them. Look, I'm not sure what happened, but I'll tell you what I know."

"That's all I'm asking."

"Okay, can you untie my hands?"

Spur did so.

"What happened three weeks ago?"

"We knew they were there. They traded shots with one of our men and he came back scared as hell and told the boss. He and our foreman, Turk Gallager, took off both mad as wet roosters. They both had rifles and a box of shells. The boss was screaming at Turk about something.

"The guy the surveyors traded shots with was my buddy, and said the men were surveyors, all right. Two horses and a packhorse and a lot of gear.

"The boss and Turk came back about three hours later, almost at dusk. They brought in three extra horses, two with saddles and one pack animal. Nobody said nothing to us about what happened."

"Were the three horses branded the next day?"

"Yeah, Turk did it first thing. Vented one brand and put on the Circle B."

Spur lifted the noose off the cowboy's neck.

"Logan, I want you to swear to me that you won't say a word about this to anybody, especially no one at the ranch. Will you promise me that?"

"Yeah, I guess."

"You might also have to swear to the same things you told me in court, if it gets that far. If it does, Breen won't be able to hurt you."

"Yeah, okay. You figured the two men were murdered out there?"

"Sure could have happened. Now, get back on your horse and go into town or wherever you were headed. Hope that rope didn't burn your neck too bad."

Spur watched the hand ride off toward town. McCoy had some time to kill. He was going back to that campsite and see what he could find. He was more convinced than ever that there must be two graves, or one double grave, around there close. He still didn't have any hard evidence to get a search warrant. One more trip into the breach.

He rode toward town for two miles to be sure he was well below the Circle B property, then cut over to the river. It was about noon. He dismounted and ground-tied his horse in some spring grass and lay down in a patch of sunshine for a quick nap. Nothing much he could do until it got dark.

Chapter Fourteen

A fly woke up Spur two hours before dark. With the troubles at the Circle B lately, he figured they might not be patrolling this section of their range quite as well as they had before. He found the last bench mark on this side of the Circle B property line and headed due north. It was barely five o'clock and he figured he had at least three hours of daylight left this far north in the summer.

He kept a sharp lookout and rode for an hour without spotting any Circle B riders. He came over a small rise in the land and saw two riders ahead driving six cows and calves back north. He paused and let them get out of sight, then continued.

Twenty minutes later, he saw the two cottonwood trees and the spot where he and Arnie had uncovered the hidden fire. He dug a little more at the fire and found a spoon. He wiped it off and put it in his pocket. Then he began looking over the area. The run-off from the rainstorm had carved out new furrows through the gently sloping land where it headed down to the river.

In one place the furrow had dug in deeply and washed away a two-foot-wide section. He went there and checked it. Dead brush and leaves half covered the area. He kicked it aside and saw the dim outline of a rectangle that had sunken in three inches.

A grave!

Then he noticed where the water had washed away the dirt near one end. It looked like a bundle of sticks showing in the ground. Why would someone bury a batch of sticks? He pulled one out and grinned. Not sticks, stakes. Survey stakes!

He dug with his hands into the loose dirt, and soon found the pointed ends of what looked like tripod legs. The kind a surveyor could use on a transit! Just below the end of the legs he found the double circle of a surveyor's chain. It was a thin, half-inch-wide continuous steel tape that some surveyors were using now, exactly 66 feet long and used to measure the land.

He pulled it out and wiped off the dirt. Just then he saw two cowboys riding toward him not 200 yards away. One of them shouted. Spur grabbed the chain and the stake and pushed dirt back in the hole covering the tripod legs. Then he ran for his horse.

The riders came from the south. The only route he had out was to the north. He sent the claybank across the river and to the west, then swung north and kept riding hard. He heard a pair of rifle shots but no lead came near enough to hear.

Damn, he wished he'd had more time to dig. Throw the bodies in the bottom of the grave and put the survey equipment on top to hold them down. Then cover up the whole damn thing.

Yeah, now he had the evidence he needed for a search warrant. The warrant and then the bodies. Now that he was free of the chasers, he swung to the south angling back to the river. Instead of going to the Bar-O why not go to the sheriff? He had plenty of evidence now to convince him to ride out to the Circle B and inspect that grave.

With the bodies and the gear, they would have enough evidence to bring Charlie Breen and his foreman to trial. The testimony of Logan and the surveyor's helper should be enough to convict them.

It took him two more hours of serious riding to come into Laramie. By that time it was dark and the sheriff wasn't anxious to take a nighttime grave-robbing expedition.

"It could be moved by tomorrow," Spur argued.

"Yeah, and we could get our heads shot off going in there in the dark," Sheriff Vail said. "Discussion is closed. We'll leave at daylight and ride directly to the so-called grave. Now get some sleep, McCoy. You might need it tomorrow."

He went to his little-used hotel room and slept. Nobody tried to kill or seduce him. It was a little disappointing.

When morning arrived, Spur McCoy was mounted and waiting at the sheriff's office at daylight. Sheriff Vail yawned his way up about twenty minutes later.

"Just you and me, McCoy. This better be good."

They rode out the river road to the spot McCoy figured they could turn off and angle up to the wooded spot and the gravesite. It was a three-hour ride, but there seemed to be no cowboy activity in the area.

Spur breathed a sigh of relief when they got there and saw that the ground was exactly as he had left it.

Both men took shovels off the backs of their saddles and began to dig. They pulled out the surveying stakes first, and then the long tripod that would hold the transit.

They found the transit unharmed in its leather case. They found another chain, a leather satchel that contained all of the record books and reports of the surveyors. In two cloth sacks they recovered the remains of a food supply. There was camping gear and one small tent, poles, and stakes.

Quickly they came to the bottom and hard dirt below.

"Where the hell are the bodies, McCoy?" Sheriff Vail thundered.

"I don't know. But that transit tells the story. A surveyor won't give up his transit to a thief. He'll fight for it. It's like a cowboy giving up his gun. He'd rather be dead."

"Looks like the men are dead, McCoy. I don't argue that. But where the hell are the bodies?"

"I don't know." He looked around. "They must have buried them somewhere else." He took his spade and began jamming it into the ground every two feet as he worked across the 50-foot-wide cleared spot near the campfire hunting a second spot. He went across and moved down four feet and worked back.

Nothing.

"Two men rode out here with rifles, Sheriff. Those same two men went back to the ranch three hours later with two extra horses and saddles and a pack-horse. I've got testimony that the two surveyors were at this spot about three weeks ago. They had surveying equipment and two saddle horses and a pack-horse. What's your conclusion?"

"That they got killed. But I still need bodies to charge anybody with murder."

"Sheriff, say you're the killer. What would you do with the bodies?"

"Get rid of them. Takes a lot of digging to bury a body. These gents must have been tired by the time they buried all of the camp gear and surveying equipment. Hell, I'd probably have thrown them in the river. It was a lot higher then, near flood stage about three weeks ago. We had a drunk who drowned trying to walk across the Laramie where he always used to."

"The river!" Spur shouted. "Yes, so there wouldn't be a grave here. What would the river do with a body, float it north?"

"A man's body sinks right away, then after the gas builds up inside it when the body rots, it rises and floats some more. Reckon it could go all the way to New Orleans: up the Laramie to the North Platte, down to the Missouri, and then down the Mississippi. Course, the Laramie is known to be unkind to bodies. Sinks them and covers them up so deep with mud and silt that they can't rise, or might tangle one underwater in roots and heaps of brush and logs in the river."

"So we might never find two bodies dropped into the river," Spur said. He laughed. "Might not unless one of them *wasn't actually dead when he was pitched in*."

"What's that mean?"

"Sheriff, you've seen a man hit in the head by a rifle or pistol bullet and live, haven't you?"

"Sure, happened in the big war all the time."

"Head wounds bleed like wild. Man might look dead and gone and not be all that bad hurt."

"Slanting wound by a rifle bullet," the sheriff said. "Yeah, knock out the victim so he looks dead. Blood all over the place. Feels dead. Throw him in the river and he floats. Could happen."

Spur told the sheriff about Merle out at the Bar-O Ranch.

Sheriff Vail pushed his big hat back on his head and stared at the water.

"Yeah, could have happened. A man could revive when dunked in a cold river like the Laramie. Came to and tried to swim, passed out, went under. Came to again and tried to swim or at least float. Yeah, a man could work downstream five or six miles that way. Which is what it would take to get him from here to near the Bar-O ranch lands."

"I know for fact that Merle was dragged out of the river on June 14th. Now I have to find out when Arnie Landhouser left the surveyors to ride into town. He's a sharp kid, he'll remember."

"Too damn bad that guy lost his memory," the sheriff said. "But if he got rifle-shot, chances are he never saw the men who tried to kill him anyway."

"He might not, but even if he didn't, the men who shot him won't know that. How would you react if you came face-to-face with a man you thought you had killed, shot dead, and buried in the river?"

"Scared out of my britches."

"That's what I'm hoping. Now my next job is to bury this stuff again. Except for the transit, which I want you to take back to town, and the bag of records. I'll take that to the Bar-O and try to jog Merle's memory."

"We gonna bury the rest of this again?" the sheriff asked.

"Right, so we don't tip our hand. We bury it and scatter leaves and brush over it so they won't suspect a thing just in case one of the hands comes past this way."

It took them two hours to get the job done. Then

the sheriff rode south and Spur turned across the river and swept west away from it to angle around the Circle B Ranch buildings.

He saw no outriders, and arrived at the Bar-O about two in the afternoon. He said hello to the hands, and went up to the kitchen carrying the scuffed leather satchel. Melody met him at the door.

"You seem to turn up here unexpected a lot lately," she said, smiling. "You're still the most handsome man I've ever seen." She said the last line softly, then opened the door and let him into the kitchen.

"How's Merle?"

"Fine. He went on a ride this morning. Said cantering hurt his head, but a steady walk is just fine. He remembered some more things about his past."

"Where is he now?"

"In the parlor resting."

"Have him come out, I want to show him some things."

Melody frowned her curiosity but went for him, and they came back in hand in hand.

"Afternoon, Mr. McCoy," Merle said.

"Hi, Merle. Hear you're riding a little now."

"Yeah, I'm trying."

"Good. Now I want you to look at this satchel. Ever seen it before?"

"Don't think so."

Spur opened it and took out a leather-lined record book. He handed it to Merle, who examined it with interest. He began to read some of the entries.

"Seem to be some kind of a record book, dates and places and chains taken and distances."

"What kind of a book is that, Merle?"

"Record book."

Spur took out a sheaf of papers that were written orders for a survey team to work specific areas. Merle looked at them with interest.

"Merle, what's a transit?"

"Oh, that's a repeating theodolite."

"What's that?"

"An instrument with a sighting tube in the form of a telescope and horizontal and vertical scales so set up that horizontal and vertical angles of the object looked at in the telescope can be read from the scales."

"Who would use an instrument like that?"

"Why, a surveyor, of course, Mr. McCoy."

"Have you ever been a surveyor?"

Merle looked confused for a moment. He reached and held Melody's hand. "I . . . I'm not sure. I know a lot about the equipment. I remember doing some survey work, with my grandfather as I remember. Yes! I did chaining work for him. He was a surveyor back home in Kansas."

Spur showed him two names written on the survey orders. "Do either of these names seem familiar?"

Merle looked at them a long time, then shook his head.

"Would you write each name for me on a piece of paper?"

Melody went to a small drawer in the counter and brought back a pad and a lead pencil.

Merle sat down and wrote the first name, Roger Red Arbeck. He did it slowly, looking at each word in sequence. Then he looked at the next name and wrote it quickly, surely, never looking back.

"Jas Buckman," Spur said. "Merle, you wrote that name like you'd been doing it for years. Do it again."

He wrote it on the paper directly under the place he did it the first time. The signatures were identical.

"Merle, I think your name is really Jas Buckman. Jas!" Spur said the name sharply as in a call for help. The man's head snapped around quickly in response.

Melody was wiping tears from her eyes. She put her arms around Jas's neck and kissed his cheek.

"How does the name sound, Jas?"

"Familiar, vaguely familiar. But am I just *wanting* it to sound that way?"

Spur told them both what he and the sheriff had found on the bank of the river on Circle B land.

"The sheriff and I think that two men from the Circle B shot both you and Red from long distance, figured you both were dead, and threw you into the river. You revived and managed to swim and float, probably going in and out of consciousness, for nearly five miles down the river until you grounded on that sandbar that Wade told us about.

"Right now I'd bet a hundred dollars that you're Jas Buckman, surveyor for the United States Government working a divisional line from the Wyoming base line north to the border."

Merle sat with his head down, thinking. At last he looked up. "Have you been through everything in the bag?"

When Spur shook his head, Merle began taking everything out and looking at it.

"I seem to remember some pictures, a tintype that costs me a dollar . . ."

They searched through the bag, and in the bottom found an old cigar box with a string around it. Inside rested some personal letters and a three-inch-long tintype. Two men sat in a formal pose for the camera. Spur had never seen the other man. The shorter one was the man they knew as Merle.

Jas Buckman held the picture tightly and let his head down on the table and cried.

"My name is Jas Buckman. I'm a surveyor. My name is Jas Buckman and I'm a government surveyor!"

Chapter Fifteen

Melody put her arms around Jas Buckman and hugged him as he lifted up from the table.

"I am Jas Buckman and I'm a surveyor!" he said again, tears of joy seeping down his cheeks.

"At last we know!" Melody said. "I'm so thrilled for you!"

"Letters—weren't there some letters in that box?" Jas said.

Spur handed him the box and he began to sort through it. He found six letters to him from the same address in Minifee, Kansas. He glanced up at Melody.

"I think that I better go through these alone. I need to learn as much about my past as possible. Just knowing my name doesn't help that much with what I've forgotten."

"We understand," Melody said. She and Spur went into the living room and told Vincent about their discovery. He nodded.

"Damn glad. Merle . . . Jas is too fine a man to have to be wondering all the time about his past."

"Jas has asked me to marry him, Vincent," Melody said. "We decided to wait until we can learn as much about his past as possible. Now I just pray that he isn't already married back there in Minifee, Kansas."

"My guess is that he isn't married," Spur said. "Most surveyors are the adventurous type—at least for a while. Chances are good he isn't married."

They talked for 15 minutes. Then Melody looked in the kitchen. Jas was still reading letters. Vincent wandered out to the corral to see what the hands were doing. Spur waited until he was well outside.

"Melody, do you have any protection in that other matter?" he asked.

She smiled. "You don't need to be so delicate," she said softly, watching the kitchen. "Yesterday Jas and I had a wonderful lovemaking session and settled our future together. Just as soon as he finds out all he needs to about his background, we'll be married. He should be discovering most of that right now."

Jas came into the living room, hurried to Melody, and caught her up and whirled her around.

"I'm not married!" he said. "I just kept reading letters from my mama in Minifee until she mentioned the fact and urged me to get married and give her some grandchildren."

Spur held out his hand to Jas. "Congratulations. I'm glad you have that settled. From the looks of things your memory will be coming back more and more. But right now I have something that can't wait for your memory."

"What's that, Mr. McCoy?" Jas asked.

"The sheriff and I figure you were shot from long range with a rifle, so you never saw your assailant.

Not even your perfect memory would help us there. We are certain who did the shooting, but we can't prove it. What we want to do is set up a little drama with you in the main role and try to scare the truth out of one of these guys."

"Sounds good. I show up and confront one of them, and he thinks he's seeing a ghost."

"That's about it. You feel strong enough to ride into town?"

"Absolutely, especially if it'll help nail the bas— the guys who shot me and Red."

"Melody, I hope you still have the clothes that Jas wore the day Wade pulled him off that sandbar."

Melody frowned. "I put them in the woodshed to wash, but I forgot about them. Yes, I'm sure they're out there. Let me go look."

"I figured we could ride into town tonight, and make some arrangements with the sheriff," Spur said. "Tomorrow we'll try to surprise the foreman of the Circle B, Turk Gallager."

"Do I get to do some playacting? I used to do some back in Kansas with a little theater group we had."

"I'm counting on it. Together with some catsup and some flour paste to make you look a lot deader than you are now."

"This is one performance I'm really going to enjoy."

Melody found the clothes, and they stopped her before she could wash them. They told her what they would do.

"I hope it works."

When they got ready to ride to town, Melody gave Jas a solid kiss that embarrassed him.

"I'll get used to it," he told her.

They got to town a little after suppertime and

ate at the Wyoming Cafe. Then they talked to the sheriff.

"So, you're the ghost we've been hunting for the last week or so," Sheriff Vail said. "Glad you made it. Shot that bad, you had a mighty strong will to live." He paused a minute. "Oh, just out of curiosity, can you swim?"

"Love to swim, spent most of every summer swimming when I was a kid in Minifee, Kansas."

"Figured as much," the sheriff said.

Spur had the plan worked out. The sheriff wrote a letter as Spur suggested. It read:

Turk Gallager
Foreman: Circle B Ranch.
Mr. Gallager. Legal documents have arrived here for you in care of my office since the sender did not know your current address or place of employment. These documents are sealed, and are from a law firm in Chicago. An accompanying letter instructs me to find you and have you pick them up in person.

The law firm letter said that a will is involved and a good sum of money which will be available to you through their office once you see the documents, sign, and return them to the firm in Chicago.

The date on the law firm letter is nearly a month ago. I don't know if there's a time element here, but I would suggest that you come to my office as soon as possible to sign for the documents and relieve me of their responsibility. I am sending this letter to you by a special rider, since I have no way of knowing when you might be in town. Sign the enclosed receipt for the letter so I can prove it was delivered to you this date.

Sincerely: J. Vail, Sheriff Albany County, Wyoming.

Dated this 7th day of July, 1873.

They went over the letter and both were satisfied with it.

"Yes, I do receive things from time to time and have to act as a finder of lost persons. This isn't unusual. All we want to do is get him to town where we can have our little seance with Jas here." The sheriff signed the letter, sealed it in an envelope, and went to find somebody who wanted to earn two dollars that evening by riding out to the Circle B. The sheriff advised him it might be safer if he arrived there well before dark.

Spur arranged for a hotel room for Jas at the Northern Hotel. They had ridden directly to the sheriff's office when they left the cafe. Now Spur hustled Jas into the hotel and up the stairs. He didn't want anyone to see him who might remember him. Word could get back to the Circle B. He and Jas played gin rummy that night in the hotel room and shared four bottles of cold beer from the saloon across the street.

Jas remembered more about his childhood, and his family.

Spur watched the man putting his whole memory back together again with a faint smile. It was like seeing a man reborn. Jas remembered that he did help his grandfather with surveying, then lived with him one summer and studied and learned the trade from him. His grandfather then set him up in a surveying business. After two years he went to work with the government as a surveyor, and had been halfway to Oregon and back.

When it was dark, the two took a walk down one side of Laramie's main street and back the other side, then stopped by at the sheriff's office and learned that the messenger had brought back a signed receipt from Gallager that he had received the letter from the sheriff.

"I figure he'll be here before noon tomorrow," the sheriff said.

"We'll be here all set up and ready by nine o'clock and wait for him," Spur said. They walked back to the hotel and had a good night's sleep.

The next morning Spur bought a pound of flour at the general store and a bottle of catsup, then went with Jas to the building right behind the county courthouse and started experimenting.

First Jas put on the dirty, torn clothes he had worn that day he was shot. The shirt was still blood-stained, and the catsup made the side wound and the blood look more realistic. They would put more on it just before his time to "perform."

Spur mixed small bits of the flour with water and tried smearing it on Jas's hands and arms to make them more "dead"-looking. At last he found the right mix and painted Jas's hands and arms, then touched them with streaks of blood from the catsup bottle.

He did the same thing to Jas's head where the wound was, spreading the white on first, using some charcoal out of the fire to blacken around Jas's eyes. Then he lathered the catsup "blood" on the actual head wound and to cover the small bandage that was still there. The new "blood" covered the side of his head, most of his forehead, and half of his face and neck. The result was the best "dead" man who ever walked the streets of Laramie.

Jas sat in the empty building reading the Chicago

newspaper he had bought in the general store. Spur went up front to the sheriff's office to wait for the killer.

They had the routine worked out. When Gallager came in, Spur would go out through the jail and bring in Jas. They waited until 9:30, when the sheriff motioned to Spur.

"That's our man just dismounting out in front. Go get your dead person."

Spur hurried to the back and motioned to Jas, who put on his act, walking forward with arms stiff, knees stiff, and an angry glare on his face. They slipped into the jail and moved toward the sheriff's office. Spur let Jas go first. They could hear the two talking.

"Yeah, I got the letter," the sheriff said. "How do I know that you're this Turk Gallager? We're not acquainted. You have somebody who can swear to your identity?"

"Sheriff, I worked at the Circle B for two years. I get my mail out there—"

Gallager looked up at Jas, who stepped into the room. He walked with frozen joints and headed for Gallager.

"What the hell?"

"Why did you kill me, Gallager?" Jas said in a monotone laced with anger.

"What?"

"On the river. I was a surveyor." Jas took another step.

"Sheriff, stop him!" Gallager shouted.

"Gallager, what's the matter with you. Who are you talking to? Stop who? You loco?"

"Him!" Gallager pointed to Jas, who took another stiff step toward him. "That ghost, that walking dead man. Can't you see him?"

"Just you and me in here, son," Sheriff Vail said. "You gonna get me some identification—"

Gallager reached for his six-gun. "Christ, I'll kill you again. I have a right to defend myself."

"You are crazy, Gallager. Just you and me here. You draw that weapon I'm throwing you in a cell."

Gallager looked at the Sheriff, then back at Jas, who was only four feet from him now. Jas reached out with his whitish-bloody hands stretching toward Gallager's throat.

"No, no. We killed you once. Damn you, stay dead!" Gallager drew his weapon, but the sheriff knocked it out of his hand. Jas grabbed Gallager by the throat and the man crumpled. He was wailing and screaming.

"No! No! Don't kill me. He made me do it. He made me. He shot you. I shot the other one. Breen hit you in the side first, but didn't kill you, then he hit you in the head."

Jas dropped to his knees and put his hands around Gallager's throat. The cowboy seemed paralyzed with fear.

"No, don't kill me! Breen made me shoot. Then we threw you both in the river. Never find the bodies. We buried all the stuff and took the horses back to the corral."

Jas looked at the sheriff. "That's enough for me," Sheriff Vail said.

Jas doubled up his fist and pounded six hard blows into Gallager's unprotected face before Sheriff Vail pulled him free.

Spur stepped around the corner and grinned.

"Well, Gallager, looks like you rode the range for the last time. The sheriff's got two ropes just waiting to be stretched."

Gallager sat up. He stared at Jas for a minute,

then rubbed his hand on his face and saw the whiteness come off.

"God, I've been suckered. You ain't dead at all. No ghost can hit that hard."

"No thanks to you. You tried your damnedest. Now I'm going to try to make you dead—legally, of course. You're a dead man right now. You just don't realize it yet."

Spur grinned at Gallager. "What an asshole. You just confessed to murder and attempted murder. That letter about some big inheritance really got you excited, I guess. I figure with the trial and everything, you've got about three weeks to live."

"You can't prove a thing," Gallager said, sitting up against the wall.

"We've got your confession made to three reliable witnesses, including the one who you tried to kill," Sheriff Vail said. "A jury in this town will believe that."

"So, Gallager, you going to hang for both killings all alone? Why not have some company up on those gallows? All you have to do is write out that confession you gave us and sign it, and then we can go out and pick up your former boss, Charlie Breen."

"He didn't—"

Spur roared at Gallager, cutting off his words. "The hell he didn't! We have witnesses who will say he rode out on the afternoon of the 14th of June with you and you two came back about three hours later leading two extra saddle horses and a packhorse. A little hunting will turn up the new brands on the horses, and Jas here will be able to identify them.

"No reason for you to hang alone. It was Breen's idea to kill them. Why take all the blame for it yourself?"

Gallager scowled, then snorted and stood up. "Yeah, hell, you're right. That bastard has never done anything for me. I'm not dying for him. He can hang for his own dirty deeds. Where's some paper and pencil? I'll give you the whole damn story."

Gallager frowned. "How . . . how did you make this surveyor look like he was dead?"

"A little charcoal, and flour and water and catsup, of course, and a lot of fear on your part," Spur said. "You *knew* he was dead, you saw him shot, saw him thrown into the river. So you saw here today only what you knew had to be true."

"How . . . how did you stay alive?" Gallager asked Jas.

"The shot on my head was only a glancing blow, but it bled like crazy and knocked me out. You figured I was dead and pitched me into the river. From what they say I swam and floated and sank and came up and swam again for five miles down stream. Floated mostly, I'd guess, until I washed up on a sandbar down there and Wade, the foreman of the Bar-O, found me when it was almost dark."

"Enough of that," the sheriff said. "Gallager, you start writing your confession. I want to know everything you did that day from the time you left the ranch yard until you came back and re-branded the horses."

Chapter Sixteen

It was 10:30 when they left Laramie for the ride to the Circle B Ranch. The sheriff said they would be gone over dinner and he hated to miss a meal. So they had soup and sandwiches at the Wyoming Cafe because the roast beef wasn't done yet.

Jas Buckman had washed off the flour, water, catsup, and charcoal and looked human again.

"Won't need the fancy decorations with Breen," Sheriff Vail said. "He don't have to say a damn thing. We'll just arrest him and bring him back to town to stand trial."

"I hope it's that easy," Spur said.

"That's why I've got you and Turk here along," the sheriff said. "We all will help persuade him to come back."

Turk rode his own horse, was not tied in any way, and had a rifle in the boot of his saddle and a six-gun showing in his holster. However, there was no cylinder in the six-gun and the rifle had no rounds in it.

"You do as we say and it might help you at the trial," the sheriff told Turk. "You mess things up out there and you're liable to get yourself killed in a shoot-out. You don't want that, do you, Turk?"

They rode at a walk to ease any pressure on Jas. He would ride toward the back when they confronted Breen, then be brought up if he was needed. They had told him in detail what Charles Breen looked like if he needed to pretend to identify him.

They came down the lane toward the Circle B Ranch about one o'clock. Turk rode ahead with the sheriff as he normally would do. He talked to a guard at the one-mile point and they went on past. At the bunkhouse, he called out and two men emerged.

"Where's Mr. Breen?" Turk demanded.

"Inside, Turk," the cowhand said. "He's—he's had a drink or two."

"Ask him to come out. Tell him the sheriff is here to see him."

The hand vanished inside. The four men remained mounted. Spur kept his gun hand ready. They had come past the remains of the ranch house. It was nothing but a few log beams and a stone fireplace's tall chimney now naked against the sky.

Breen came out a minute later, rubbing his eyes. He looked as if he had just tried to dress. His shirttail was half in and half out. He wore a six-gun on his hip. His eyes were red.

"Yeah? Sheriff? What the hell you want?"

"Like to ask you if you know anything about two government surveyors who came through your place about three weeks ago—June 14th, to be exact."

"Hell, no. Now I got business. Good-bye."

"Not that easy, Breen," the sheriff snapped. Breen looked up, anger clouding his eyes.

"You ain't the first person to come here jawing about them damn surveyors." Breen looked up. "Yeah, you . . . the big guy on the claybank. You was here few days back. Told you then . . ."

Spur had motioned for Jas to come up toward the man on his mount.

"Charlie Breen, don't you recognize me?" Jas asked. He still wore the bloody tattered shirt and had a small bandage on his head.

Breen looked up. Squinted. He shook his head. "Who the hell are you?"

"I'm one of the surveyors who was working through your ranch. Remember? You didn't kill me with your first shot? You had to shoot me again, in the head."

Breen swore and grabbed at his six-gun. He had just gotten it out of leather when Spur drew and fired in one swift point-your-hand shot. The lead smashed into the weapon just as it came out of leather and ripped it out of Charlie Breen's hand.

"Bastards!" he bellowed. He darted inside the bunkhouse and was gone.

"Check the windows," Spur shouted. "Turk, you move an inch and you're dead." Spur slid off his mount and ran alongside one of the sides of the bunkhouse. There were no windows. When he came to the far end he realized it had a door there too. It swung open.

He saw Breen with a rifle and a six-gun vanishing around the near side of the small barn.

"He's in the small barn," Spur bellowed. Jas kicked his horse into motion toward the barn. The sheriff had run inside the bunkhouse.

Spur charged on foot toward the barn 30 yards away. A shot dug up dirt at his feet as he ran. He zigzagged, and another shot missed. Jas got to the barn before he did and slid off the horse. He wore a six-gun he had brought from the ranch, and now lifted it with the hammer cocked.

Spur dodged twice more and made it to the barn. He panted as he leaned against the raw wood.

"Stay here and keep that horse ready," Spur told him. "I don't want you getting shot again."

Spur charged through a small door at an angle and dove as he hit the floor. A shot barked in the darkness ahead and whined off the floor into the wall.

Spur rolled behind a horse stall and lifted to look over the manager. A shot crashed from inside the barn and wood splintered just to his left.

"You've got no place to run, Breen, might as well give it up."

There was no-reply. A moment later he heard the creak of leather. Breen was saddling a horse! Spur lifted up to look in the direction he had heard the sound. All he saw was a blur as a gray pounded the dirt floor and burst out a side door.

Spur ran back out the door he had come in by and grabbed the horse Jas had brought. "Tell the sheriff Breen's mounted and riding south," Spur shouted. Then he was riding as well.

As he came around the barn, Spur heard a rifle go off. Breen had calmly sat on the gray 50 yards away. waiting for him. The lead came so close Spur felt its heat. Then he flattened out along the animal's neck and charged straight at Breen. The man had tried only one shot. Then he turned and spurred the gray due west toward the cover of the Laramie River's brush line half a mile away.

The gray was a strong horse and fast. She gradually gained as they both galloped for the brush. Spur eased off on his bay and watched the big gray flying. When Breen entered the woods, he turned and looked behind him, then slanted south into the brush.

Spur angled toward the river so he would come in well behind Breen. There was too much cover and brush and ideal spots for ambushes in there. He got to the brush about two minutes after Breen vanished. There was no one else coming from the ranch.

Spur moved through the willow and across the water at a shallow spot, but did not see the ranch owner on the far side. He rode there for a quarter of a mile, then stopped and listened.

Somewhere ahead he could hear a horse crashing through brush. Spur rode hard, galloping in the open space just beyond the brush line across the river. This way he should be able to overtake the runner, even get ahead of him. It was easier riding through the open than through brush as heavy as this.

When Spur stopped the next time, he heard nothing. He waited a minute, and then caught the sound of brush and hooves again. It was slightly behind him. He waded across the Laramie and worked as silently as possible into the heavy brush and trees. Willow and cottonwood made up most of the growth here.

He eased off the bay and ran soundlessly to a large cottonwood about in the middle of the 15-yard-wide swatch of brush and trees on the east side of the Laramie.

For a moment he heard nothing. Then the sound of a horse walking came clearly. Each hoof seemed to find more dry sticks to break and brush to crush down.

He waited. The sounds stopped. Spur dropped to the ground behind the big cottonwood and peered out through the grass and weeds. He could see the shape of a horse and rider through the willows. They were motionless, the other man listening for his pursuer.

Evidently satisfied, the rider moved the animal forward. Spur cocked the Colt .45 in his hand and waited. The horse and rider came closer. When Breen was 30 feet away, Spur stepped out and aimed at the man's chest.

"Hold it right there, Breen," Spur barked.

Breen kicked the horse in the flanks and it spurted ahead. Spur fired. A willow shoot no larger than a man's finger took the full force of the bullet five feet in front of the target, slanting the lead two feet to the side so it missed the rider.

Breen surged away from Spur toward the heavier brush and protection. Spur fired again, but the growth was too thick. Spur ran and jumped on his horse and plowed through the thicket after Breen.

The ranch owner had a good lead again by the time Spur got mounted and chased him. Breen charged through the heavier willows and back toward the river. It was not deep here, about two feet, and Breen ran his mount into the water. The horse took three steps on this near side of the stream and stopped. She tried to pull her hooves out of the bottom but couldn't.

"Move!" Breen yelled at the animal. But she couldn't. He jumped off, and had started to take the reins to lead the animal across the stream when he realized that he couldn't take a step forward. He dropped the reins and leaned out, stretching for the dry land only six feet away. He couldn't reach it.

Breen screamed as he felt his feet slipping deeper into the suction-like hold the river sand had on him. Already the horse was up to her belly in the water.

"Quicksand!" Breen bellowed. He drew his revolver, wishing he had the rifle still on his horse. He'd taken the revolver from where he kept one hidden in the barn.

"This way! I'm over here!" Breen bellowed. He slipped lower, and now tried to flatten out on the water that covered the quicksand. It slowed his progress for a moment. Then the sucking sand caught at his chest and began to seep around it, letting him sink into the slippery particles of sand that would not support even their own weight.

"This way, over here, hurry!"

Spur heard the words, and rode up so he could see but still be out of pistol range. What he saw sent a shiver up his spine. He'd been involved with quicksand only once and it was not a good memory. He grabbed the rifle from the boot and rode up to 30 feet.

"Throw the pistol on the shore and I'll help you," Spur called.

Breen laughed and fired, but the round missed. Spur had drawn his own iron and he returned fire, the bullet hitting Breen in the shoulder and spilling the iron from his hand. He tried to grab it but it sank quickly just out of his grasp.

Spur ran down to the very edge of the hard soil and held out the barrel of the rifle to the sinking man. It was too short.

"Get a branch or a tree, hurry!" Breen pleaded.

Spur found a dead tree three inches thick that had fallen. He tore it loose from the roots and ran with it back to Breen. He laid it on the shore and

stretched it out six feet to where the man struggled.

Now Breen was up to his shoulders in the murk.

"Don't thrash around, that makes you sink faster,"
Spur said. "Grab the tree trunk and try to pull yourself forward."

Already the far end of the dead treetop had vanished in the soupy, watery sand. Breen tried. His
hands grasped the tree and Spur stood on the end
of it, but Breen worked no more than two or three
inches toward the shore.

The quicksand closed over his shoulders, and now
only his neck and face and arms showed.

"Finish me, McCoy. Put a bullet through my
head."

"I can't do that."

"Then give me your iron with one round and let
me do the job."

Spur fought with himself a minute. It was what he
would want if he was in the same situation. He took
out all but one live round, and tossed the weapon to
Breen across the six feet of deadly quicksand.

Then Spur turned and walked away.

Almost at once the revolver fired. Spur spun
around and dropped to the ground, a bullet in his
right thigh.

Breen wailed in laughter. "Christ but you're stupid, McCoy," Breen screamed. "Double damn stupid."

"You're the first dying man I've trusted who has
tried that," Spur said. "Most men get a little religion
when they know they're dying."

The quicksand worked up to his chin. Breen still
had his right hand above the mass. He clawed at
the unstable sand. He dropped the revolver in the
quicksand and tried to swim his way to the shore.

His other hand came out of the goo for a moment. Then he screamed as the sand and water flowed over his mouth and he reared back his head.

"Noooooooooooooooooo," he wailed.

His hands and arms vanished.

The quicksand bubbled as it covered his mouth and then his nose. He stretched as high as he could, but a moment later the surging flow of the quicksand oozed over his eyes and then the top of his head and he was gone.

The horse had fared better. She had evidently hit just the side of the sink. Two legs were on solid ground. She was up to her belly in the murk but sinking no lower. There was a good chance Spur could save her.

He looked at his shot thigh. The slug had gone in but not out. Damn! He took off his neckerchief and tied up his leg right around his pants leg. Then he got a lariat off his the saddle and roped the gray's neck and snugged down the rope around the saddle horn and began backing up his horse.

The bay in the sand screamed in anger and frustration. Then she seemed to tighten up and give the rope a firm unit to pull. Slowly she eased to the side and away from the sink.

Five minutes later Spur had her pulled from the edge of the quicksand. He sat there ten minutes resting both mounts, looking at the grave of the killer and wondering what his last thoughts were as he suffocated under the water and quicksand.

Better he didn't know.

Chapter Seventeen

Supper at the Bar-O Ranch that night was a celebration feast. They had a bottle of whiskey that Melody had been saving for a special occasion.

"We are announcing our engagement," Melody said, holding Jas's hand. "We're in no rush, but probably sometime in late July."

"A toast to the bride!" Jas said, lifting his shot glass. The others toasted.

"So much has happened so quickly, it's going to take me a few days to just settle down," Jas said. "I'm remembering more and more. Riding out to the Circle B Ranch I remembered how Red and our helper and I chained our way up there to the Circle B, and how we fired over the head of a cowboy who came to run us off.

"I even remember the fire and that last cup of coffee after our supper. The shooting and the river I don't remember at all, and for that I'm thankful."

"And now the law will take over and punish that Turk person," Melody said. "I'm sure he'll be convicted and sent to prison for twenty years."

"Tomorrow I want to go back to that grove and dig up the rest of our equipment. I'll write a letter to my supervisor and tell him what happened, and where the equipment is. I'm through surveying. Fact of the matter is, I'm back to my roots, back on a ranch. And if I play my cards right I might get to live here in the ranch house."

Spur concentrated on the fried chicken and giblet gravy and the mashed potatoes. It was ten times better than store-bought cooking.

"Oh, Kevin Breen rode over late this afternoon from the Circle B," Vincent said. "He and I had a long talk. His father's death has really brought him up suddenly. He admitted that he'd been drinking too much and running around and gambling. Now he says he has a ranch to run, and he's going to do it the best he can.

"He said there won't be any more stealing cattle and re-branding them. He told us to figure out about how many head we've been missing over the last two years and he'll drive over that many to us.

"He said from now on we have a joint roundup and separate the cattle by brand so there won't be any misunderstandings."

"Glory be, I never ever thought we'd see that day," Melody said.

Vincent cleared his throat and they all looked at him. "I guess this is as good a time as any. Melody, you know I came out here on a temporary basis a year ago. I stayed on and tried to help. But now, I figure that it's time for me to be moving back to where I belong.

"Not even Wade can make a cowboy out of me, and certainly not a ranch manager. Melody's got herself a good man now, who knows ranching, and can even put up with her, so I figure it's time I get back to the store."

"Oh, Vincent, are you sure?" Melody asked. "It's been so good having family here."

"I'm sure. I'll be leaving right after the wedding."

Wade spoke up. "When Kevin Breen came over to talk, he also brought those three horses, the ones Jas and Red used on the survey party. He said Jas should have them."

"Good," Jas said. "Tomorrow we go out and bring back the surveying equipment. I'm interested to see that place again and I want to follow the river down to where Wade found me. Just curious."

After the fine supper, Spur said he had to go in and see the sheriff. They said good-bye. Melody hurried out as he was about to ride off and caught his hand.

"Spur McCoy, I owe you a special thanks. I never would have been able to approach Jas if it hadn't been for that marvelous lovemaking we did. So you know our door is always open here whenever you pass near us."

"Make it a point to check up on you," Spur said. He gave her hand a squeeze and rode down the lane on his claybank.

He caught the sheriff just before he went home at about eight o'clock.

"Sheriff, you did a good day's work," Spur said, slumping in the chair beside the lawman's desk.

"Didn't do such a bad piece of labor yourself, Spur McCoy. Glad I didn't find you out there before Breen went under that soup. Damn I hate that stuff. Got caught in it once in Texas. Took three men to pull me out. I'm gonna ride out there and have the Circle B fence that place off so we don't lose anybody else, or any cattle in there."

"I'll be past tomorrow to write you a deposition on Turk giving all of my experience with the problem. That can't hurt your case any when it comes up."

"Reckon they'll send out a new team of surveyors?"

"Bound to. The division lines need to be drawn and the whole territory needs to get the re-survey done. Oh, how late is the telegraph office open?"

"Until along about now. You might catch him."

Spur got there in time. The operator waited as Spur wrote out the telegram. The operator was young, eager. He looked at the address and whistled.

"Wow! I've never sent a telegram to Washington, D.C., before. What's this Capital Investigations, some kind of a detective outfit?"

"Right, mostly just boring things."

He sent the wire that said:

TO W HALLECK CAPITAL INVESTIGATIONS WASHINGTON DC *STOP* FROM McCOY IN LARAMIE WYOMING *STOP* SURVEYOR PROBLEM SOLVED *STOP* FULL REPORT FOLLOWS *STOP* AVAILABLE *STOP* ADVISE *STOP*

Spur watched as the message was sent, then headed for his hotel. A nice long sleep and he'd be ready tomorrow morning to write his report and send it by mail on the train to Washington. His boss should have it in two days. He loved this fast train service.

His thigh sent a darting pain through his body that made him gasp and grab the side of the telegraph office. He'd forgotten about the slug in his thigh. He limped down to the doctor's office and saw a light was still on.

It took the medic ten minutes to find the slug and drag it out. Spur sweat gallons and bit a piece of white pine almost in half to keep from screaming. At last the lead bullet was out and the doctor offered Spur a shot of whiskey. He bandaged the leg, took the two dollars, and sent Spur on his way.

In his hotel, McCoy nodded to the clerk, asked for the key for the Room 22, and started to go up. He had been thinking about having a good bath. He turned back to the clerk and asked for a tub and five buckets of hot water to be sent up to 22. He tipped the clerk 50 cents and paid another 50 cents for the tub and water. It was splurging, but money well spent.

Twenty minutes later the tub had arrived, one of the four-foot-long ones made of lightweight metal of some kind so it could be carried. The water was near boiling and the man who brought it also left him three fluffy white towels.

Spur had just started to undress when a knock came on his door. He frowned, but slipped into his shirt and went to the door. When he opened it a rather tall woman with long brown hair and a hat covering most of her face bolted past him into the room. She laughed at his surprise and threw off her hat.

"Spur McCoy, you don't even recognize me, and after all the good times we had together."

He frowned, then laughed. "So, Silly who is now Sandy, I figured you'd be working."

"Was, but this is special. Gave the room clerk two dollars to send someone to tell me the minute you got into your hotel room. He did like a good boy. You don't even look glad to see me."

"Oh, I am. How is the work going?"

"As usual. Hey, looks like you were fixin' to have a bath. Let me help. Been a bunch of years since I've given a man a bath. Course, I don't want to get my clothes wet."

She slipped out of her blouse, and had on nothing else under it. Her big breasts swung out and danced a minute. He watched them and she giggled.

"Damn, good to see that you still appreciate the best set of tits in the territory. No biting until you're bare-assed in the tub. Come on, strip, big stud, I want to see your lean, muscular body and your whanger all nice and soft."

She helped Spur to undress and he poured the water into the tub. They had brought an extra bucket of cold and he needed it. It was barely cool enough to sit down in, but he managed it.

"Yes, a good-looking body is hard to find on a man these days. Most of them are too damn short and fat. Why do men get fat?"

"Same reason women get fat, from eating too much and not exercising enough. You almost never see a fat Indian. Hey, you wouldn't get fat either if you had to work as hard as those Indian women do."

"I work hard enough at what I do," Sandy said. She slid out of her skirt and was naked. Spur looked up at her.

"Wish I had a picture of you naked that way," he said. "Make a damn pretty photograph."

"A photographer came past yesterday wanting to trade his work for ours. One of the girls did and got two nice tintypes. She had her clothes on, though. Wanted to send one to her mother in Virginia."

Sandy knelt down beside the tub and began to wash Spur's back.

"Okay, Sandy, what do you want, or what do you need? You didn't come over here on a charity mission for the sake of making me feel better."

She stopped washing and dropped the cloth, then moved around where she could see him.

"Yeah, true. And usually I don't do backs. I . . . I got a mite of trouble. Somebody saw Punkin here in town the day she was buried. Somebody here knew her and said they had seen me with Punkin back down the trail somewhere.

"The madam came and talked with me. She said I better have a good story about how Punkin got shot in the back with a rifle bullet 'cause she didn't want a whole lot of legal-type trouble."

"Did you tell her what happened?"

"No, couldn't do that. Didn't want to involve you none. I swore up and down that I never had seen Punkin and the other woman had bats in her attic."

"The madam didn't believe you."

"Said I had two days to remember, and that was yesterday. I was hoping that maybe you could go to with me and back up my story."

"Might be arranged," Spur said. He grinned and handed her the cloth. "Depends how well I get my back scrubbed, and the rest of the evening."

"Why, Spur McCoy, are you trying to bribe me asking for sexual favors in exchange for something?"

"No, ma'am, not at all. Just that I am sitting in a bathtub buck naked and you're there with some soap and I figure since I can't even reach my back . . ."

Sandy moved around him and pushed one of her breasts into his mouth. He chewed a minute and grinned. Then he came away and chuckled.

"By George," Spur said. "I really do think she has it figured out."

Sandy giggled, and took the cloth and scrubbed furiously on his back.

"Tomorrow we'll go see the madam, and I'll verify that you had nothing to do with the demise of Punkin. I'll tell her the whole thing, about how you helped me escape from the rawhider who was planning on shooting me dead the next morning."

"Think she'll believe you?"

"Sure. Why would I lie? Now, enough of that washing my back. They said this tub is big enough for two. So climb in. I've been looking forward to washing your back, and your front. But I'm starting with your front."

Spur grabbed the soap and helped her step in and sit cross-legged in the tub in front of him.

"Now there is a marvelous sight," he said, looking into the water between her crossed legs.

"Spur McCoy, shut up and wash. It's going to be a long night before you get any sleep."

 **DIRK FLETCHER**

A double blast of hard cases and hussies for one low price!
A $7.98 value for only $4.99!

Bodie Beauties. Fighting alone against a vicious band of crooks, Spur receives unexpected help from a lovely lady of the evening. If Jessica doesn't wear Spur out, he'll put the crooks away forever.
And in the same pistol-hot edition...
Frisco Foxes. While taking the die for a gold coin to the San Francisco mint, McCoy has to fight off thieving bastards who want to get their greedy hands on the dies, and bodacious beauties who want Spur's loving hands all over them.
__3486-7 BODIE BEAUTIES/FRISCO FOXES (two books in one) only $4.99

Kansas City Chorine. While trying to catch a vicious killer, Spur tangles with a pompous preacher who is fleecing his innocent flock and a blonde chorus girl who is determined to skin him alive.
And in the same exciting volume...
Plains Paramour. Spur is assigned to hunt down a murderous hangman in Quintoch, Kansas. But a sexy suffragette with some liberated ideas keeps him so tied up in the bedroom he has little strength left to wrap up the case.
__3544-8 KANSAS CITY CHORINE/PLAINS PARAMOUR (two books in one) only $4.99

Dorchester Publishing Co., Inc.
65 Commerce Road
Stamford, CT 06902

Please add $1.75 for shipping and handling for the first book and $.50 for each book thereafter. NY, NYC, PA and CT residents, please add appropriate sales tax. No cash, stamps, or C.O.D.s. All orders shipped within 6 weeks via postal service book rate. Canadian orders require $2.00 extra postage and must be paid in U.S. dollars through a U.S. banking facility.

Name _____
Address _____
City _____ State _____ Zip _____
I have enclosed $_____ in payment for the checked book(s).
Payment <u>must</u> accompany all orders. □ Please send a free catalog.